COLD
HEARTED

COLD
HEARTED

Toni Anderson

ALSO BY TONI ANDERSON

For John Wilson Anderson.
Whose life story would make a great book.

Content Advisory: like all my books this story contains references to situations that might make some readers uncomfortable (i.e. sexual assault, murder).
For more information:
https://www.toniandersonauthor.com/content-advisory

CHAPTER ONE

H E SPOTTED HER across the street, blonde hair shining like polished gold in the sunlight, her lithe body tormenting every Y-chromosome in a hundred yard radius. He pulled out his cell and took a snapshot to immortalize the moment. He'd thought she said she was returning later in the week. Obviously he'd been mistaken. He dialed her number and watched her pull out her phone. He waited for the matching smile to form on her lips, for her eyes to light up. Instead, she checked caller ID, grimaced, and let the call go to voicemail.

Horror rushed through him as she re-pocketed the phone and turned back to her companion. *What the fuck?* He killed the connection and collapsed to a nearby bench, hidden from sight by a mass of tangled bushes.

He'd thought she loved him. That she wanted to *be* with him…

God! He'd given her everything she needed, laid it out like a feast on a platter with a fucking apple stuffed in its mouth. *She played you, dumbass.*

Fury flayed his skin. Rage so hot and pure that the blood coursing his body burned his bones. She thought she could dismiss him? Like he was nothing? Like he hadn't risked everything for her? His hand strangled his phone as he imagined it squeezing her alabaster neck.

A noise brought him back to himself, and he drew in a long breath.

A laugh.

A giggle.

His head jerked up. Students milled around. They were relaxed and happy after winter break. The monster had been caught. They were safe. Life could go back to normal.

Sheep.

How could they think they were *safe* when the person they were having coffee with might be a predator dreaming about ripping into their soft, white underbelly? Why were they so willing to swallow bullshit as long as it was confidently labeled "truth"?

The system was broken. Bad guys walked free every single day. Good guys rotted. Innocents died.

Idiots.

A cute freshman smiled shyly at him from the bench opposite. He stretched his mouth into an answering curve that revealed nothing of the shock and disappointment that still rippled through him. Women liked him. So why the fuck did she think it was okay to ignore him?

A plan formed in his brain—a plan that buzzed along his nerves with the blistering speed of electricity.

Should he do it?

It might mess up things, and he didn't want to go to prison, but it would certainly get her attention. His brain raced over the possibilities. He knew how to do this. He knew how not to get caught. And it might keep things interesting. Life had been pretty fucking boring lately and, as he'd found out last year, there was nothing quite as satisfying as revenge.

The student hiked her bag on her shoulder and got up to

leave. He eyed the flirty plaid skirt she wore over opaque black tights and tall black boots, then jogged to catch up with her. Made a joke. Made her blush.

It was almost too easy.

He laughed and realized he was enjoying himself again. The excitement resurrected something inside him that was both heady and familiar. Something that scared him enough to keep it tightly leashed and under control. Something he'd denied himself for ten long months.

He reined in the thrill that fizzed through his bloodstream. He needed to be careful. The memory of the disgraced former quarterback reminded him he couldn't afford to get cocky. No way in hell did he intend to share the asshole's shame and degradation. But he knew the system. Knew the flaws. She was going to regret not taking that goddamned phone call for the rest of her life.

———————

CASSIE BRESSINGER SMOOTHED out the single sheet of paper and read Drew's small, cramped handwriting for the seventh time that day.

> *Cass,*
>
> *I was trying to figure out something interesting to tell you, but after only a month I'm already running out of material. I mean, there are only so many adjectives I can invent to describe the three shades of gray that make up the decor here—snot, Minnesota, and dead rabbit are my newest favorites. I probably wouldn't win any prizes in English class, but as I got kicked out I*

guess it doesn't matter.

Three shades of gray—hmm, there might be a book in there somewhere…

Fifty Shades this place is not. Not to say there isn't plenty of banging going on from the grunts and groans I hear at night. Someone somewhere is enjoying the fuck out of somebody else.

I think it's consensual…

An ironic concern for a convicted rapist but, hey, who wants to be predictable?

Honestly, Babe, I'm at the stage where protecting my own ass has become my #1 priority. Luckily, I'm a big motherfucker and spent years on the gridiron, staring down people desperate to drill me into the ground. I could do with my offensive line in here though…

Crap.

I didn't mean to talk about this shit and I'm running out of writing paper so I don't want to start over. Plus, my fingers are getting cramps from holding a pen. Yeah, me, former star athlete whose hands were supposed to be his golden meal ticket. Getting cramps from writing a freaking letter! More irony ☺

Enough about me. How are you? What's happening with your courses this semester? You said you were going to try and get into law school. Please don't do that because of me!!! The last thing I want is for you to be stuck in a stuffy courtroom listening to god-awful testimony and watching people's lives disintegrate. Run away and join the circus. Take a year off and travel the world.

Seriously.

And make sure you write and tell me all about your adventures, okay? I'm living vicariously. And if you want to have sex with other girls—that's okay. Feel free to write and tell me all about that, too. Kidding! Well…kind of kidding and now kind of horny, which is a pain in the ass. Obviously the DA was right to classify me as a dangerous sex fiend.

Fucker.

Okay, gotta go. Time for me to go line up for sloppy mashed potatoes and sausages that look like severed fingers… Ugh, okay, just grossed myself out.

Don't worry about me—I got this.

Love you. Miss you.

Drew. X

Someone knocked on the door and Cassie jumped. Tanya Whitehouse sauntered in before Cassie had a chance to hide the letter.

"That from Drew?" Tanya was wearing skinny jeans, her favorite strappy black top, and sparkly earrings. Her lips glowed in glittering magenta. Going out. Doing normal things like a normal person.

Cassie popped a shoulder and nodded.

"He okay?" asked Tanya.

"He's incarcerated with rapists and murderers for crimes he didn't commit," she bit out. "What do you think?"

Tanya placed her perfectly manicured hand along Cassie's forearm. "You know what I meant."

Always patient. Always reasonable.

Cassie swallowed the anger. She wasn't patient, and she wasn't reasonable. But Tanya was only trying to help. All her friends had been nothing but supportive throughout this entire nightmare.

"He says he's okay." Cassie swallowed the knotted lump of grief that had taken up residence in her throat and tried to find her rationality. "I think he just says that to make me feel better."

"You going to visit him?" Tanya asked gently.

Cassie nodded. "I'm driving over with his dad at the end of the month. Drew doesn't want me to come, but I—"

"Maybe he's right."

Cassie sat up on the messy bed. She knew where this was going. "Please don't tell me I'm wasting my life. Drew *is* my life."

Tanya grabbed Cassie's hand and squeezed hard enough to hurt. "I just don't want you to be sad for the next thirty years."

Her vision blurred, but they both pretended Cassie wasn't crying. Even she was sick of the incessant tears. "I won't be." She was lying. "Anyway, he can still appeal."

There was an awkward silence when Tanya didn't say anything. Cassie's gaze shifted to the image on the front of a magazine. Easier to look at some movie star complaining about her messed up childhood than dealing with the sort of truth that dug holes in your soul.

"Hey," Tanya said brightly, "there's a party over at Riddell Hall. Wanna come with?"

Cassie shook her head.

"Come on. It'll be fun," her friend urged.

Going to a party would remind her of all the times she and Drew had hung out. She didn't want to acknowledge the aching void of his absence—especially not in public.

"I have an assignment due tomorrow. I really need to finish it." She crawled over to her bedside table in search of a tissue.

Tanya lightly flicked the magazine, mockingly. "Well, you better get on with it then."

Cassie slumped back to the bed, ashamed of how piteous she'd become. "I can't face seeing people," she admitted. "Not yet. Maybe coming back to school was a mistake."

"You did great. Take it slowly. You'll get there, and we'll all be waiting for you on the other side of this."

Cassie nodded. The problem was there was no 'other side.' Drew's loss was like a rip in her chest that got bigger every day. "The world thinks he's a monster."

Tanya wrapped her arms around Cassie in a quick hug. "We love him. We know he's a good guy and would never touch those lying bitches."

"I don't know how this could have happened."

"You can't lock yourself away forever, Cass."

But she wanted to.

She didn't know why she'd come back this term, but hanging around her parents' house with nothing to do was worse. Christmas had sucked balls. Now she needed to figure out a way to move on without giving up on the man she loved.

She gripped her friend. "I love you, Tan. I'm sorry I'm such a bitch."

"I love you, too, baby."

She forced herself to pull away and wiped her eyes. "I really do have an assignment to finish."

"Then get to it, slacker." Tanya gave her arm a noogie.

Cassie forced a smile. She'd blown off cheerleading practice earlier today, and if she did it again, the coach would throw her off the squad. She didn't care, except it would screw with her scholarship, and her parents weren't wealthy. She couldn't afford to get thrown out of the program, and she needed a good GPA to have a hope of getting into law school. But every time the football players ran onto the field in their black and gold jerseys, it was like someone was pouring acid in her eyes. Knowing everyone's life went on while Drew sat locked up in a cell. Her throat constricted. Some days it felt like the pain would consume her whole.

She stood and pushed her friend toward the door. "Go. Have fun. Kiss some hot guys for me."

"If I can find someone worthy enough, I intend to do a lot more than kiss him. So don't worry if I don't come home tonight. I'll text you." Tanya grinned. "Mandy's studying in her room. Alicia is still at the library but said she'd be back just after ten as per usual. She might come to the party later, so if you change your mind…"

"Maybe," Cassie lied. "You be careful out there. Guard your drink," she warned. Because if those women had been raped, there was still a dangerous criminal on the loose, and no one knew it.

"I will, honey. Jillian's going to be here any minute to give me a ride."

"Go. Have fun."

Tanya turned and smiled at her sadly, touching her arm. Cassie felt the punch of it near her heart. "You'll get through this, Cass. You don't have to forget Drew, but you need to keep living your life. He'd want you to do that."

Cassie's lip wobbled as she remembered what he'd said in his letter. She crossed her arms over her chest as she watched her friend jog down the stairs, grab her coat, and race out the front door. She had to believe a miracle was going to happen and that Drew would be freed, but it seemed futile. The judicial process was so slow it took months to even schedule a court hearing. In the meantime Drew was forced to live amongst killers and thieves. Getting raped in the showers wasn't something anyone should have to worry about. Who could live like that?

That bitch Donovan had a lot to answer for. The blonde detective probably thought this was over.

It wasn't. It would never be over.

Anger grounded her. Without it she'd be so damn lost.

Across the hall, Mandy turned her music on full blast. Cassie slipped on her noise-canceling headphones and stared at her computer and thought about the paper she needed to finish. Instead she pulled out a pen and notepad and started to write back to the man she loved, stopping only once to wipe away the tears that insisted on falling.

CHAPTER TWO

Detective Erin Donovan got into her Ford F-150 truck, slammed the door, and turned the key in the ignition. The five-liter V8 engine roared to life. Today was her first day back after a Hawaiian vacation, and she was reeling from the ferocious drop in temperature combined with jet-lag that battered her senses.

She blasted the heater, giving it time to defrost the thin skim of ice that coated the interior of the windshield. She should check job vacancies on the islands—they needed cops in Hawaii, too, right? Living in Upstate New York was like living in a frickin' refrigerator.

The town of Forbes Pines in St. Lawrence County was less than fifty miles from the border. They were so close to Canada they could practically smell the polar bears. She snorted at her own joke. Forbes Pines was a highbrow college town of about fifteen-thousand people and, up until about seven months ago, the natives had been friendly. The southern outskirts of town bordered the Adirondacks, and the whole area was spectacular, especially in fall when the trees changed color.

No matter how beautiful, it still didn't feel like home. After the sensational trial that had ripped the town apart last December, she doubted it ever would.

She jammed the edges of her down parka together and

rubbed her chapped hands. As a police officer, she prioritized access to her sidearm over comfort, but there was a fine line between safety and stupidity. Tonight she was seriously questioning which was more likely to kill her first—the cold or a perp. The mercury was in the low teens and sidewalks were piled with dirty ice and slush. It hadn't snowed since Christmas Eve nearly two weeks ago. Not that she'd cared—she'd been too busy soaking up the sun on the white sand beach.

It had been her first vacation in years, and she hadn't wanted to come back. She frowned, trying to remember the vacation before that. Her stomach lurched like a drunk on the subway when she did. Her honeymoon. God. The reminder was like a blow to the kidneys that robbed breath and made her insides bleed. She closed her eyes and was immediately assaulted by the image of Graham putting his off duty SIG Sauer P239 to his head. Her limbs twitched in a never-ending battle, torn between running toward him and running away.

She jerked her eyes open, heart pounding, sweat clammy on her skin. Her breath formed a cloud of vapor. Damn. She'd thought she was over the flashbacks. A tap on the glass had her heart exploding in her chest. She swiveled in her seat. *Shit.*

Ully Mason, a patrol officer from the Forbes Pines Police Department, stood on the tarmac, stamping his size twelve boots on the unyielding ground. Trying to get her breathing under control, she moved her hand away from her sidearm and buzzed down the window.

"Got a call about a possible intruder at Cassie Bressinger's place." He eyed her steadily from under thick dark brows.

"Again? I thought things had calmed down over there?" Erin's head hurt. Dispatch had been getting almost nightly calls for months now. She'd thought the fun and games had ended with the trial. Obviously not.

A small smile curved Ully's mouth. He was a good-looking guy, and he knew it. "Guess they heard you were back."

"Jesus, Mary, and Joseph." The college kids had a better grapevine than Crimestoppers. Officially she was off duty, but if these bogus calls didn't stop, the chief was going to have a coronary. "I'll meet you there. If we don't find any evidence of an intruder this time, we'll arrest the caller for wasting police resources." She checked her watch. Ten p.m. "Let's see if we can figure out a way to put an end to this bullshit."

"I need to gas up on the way over." Ully wrapped his fingers over the top of her window. "Don't go in without me. I can just see the head of the cheer squad swearing under oath that she shot you in self-defense."

"She'd enjoy it, too," Erin agreed.

Ully let go of the glass and walked away to his black and white cruiser. Erin buzzed her window back up. As far as Cassie Bressinger was concerned, Erin was the devil incarnate. Maybe she'd give Cassie something to bitch about this time.

The frost finally cleared and warmth filled the cab. The Forbes Pines PD shared the large rambling red brick monstrosity of City Hall with the courthouse, DA's office, and city offices. Politicians and lawyers liked to grandstand on the marble front steps. Cops and criminals skulked in the back entrance.

Erin pulled out of the police station and took Roosevelt Road, then turned right along Main Street past the beautiful park that gave the town a natural elegance. Tall elms and wrought-iron benches lined the central walkway. On the other side of the park, the old sandstone edifice of Blackcombe College gave Forbes Pines a dignified, moneyed air. The college dominated every aspect of the town with at least half the population being students, or former students who couldn't bring themselves to move on. Faculty and staff made up a large proportion of the rest of the town, and most of the local businesses depended on the university for survival.

She often kidded with the other cops that they were more like campus cops than real police officers. That was before the trial made international headlines and cemented her position as Most Hated Woman in the county. Erin drove onwards, intending to do a big loop around the southern perimeter of university grounds to where the sorority and frat houses were located on the far eastern edge. She wanted to get a feel for the mood of the place in the wake of Drew Hawke's conviction. It would take Ully at least ten minutes to fill up, so she had time. Term had started today and, despite the hour, there were plenty of students milling around in small groups. They eyed her truck suspiciously as she drove slowly by. Outside one of the large frat houses she locked gazes with Jason Brady, wide receiver for the Blackcombe Ravens. Wearing track pants and a Raven's long-sleeved tee, he stood on the curb next to his jeep with his hands on his hips. He spat on the ground and mouthed the word *cunt* as she drove past.

Good times.

She carried on, past the gym complex, the faculty of science. Another half mile, and she cruised up and down the streets either side of Cassie Bressinger's house. No sign of anyone lurking. She stopped the truck a few houses down from the small clapboard building. Many of the houses in this neighborhood were rented to students. A few belonged to low income families—research assistants, sessional instructors. Cassie Bressinger's neighbor had a small plastic swing-set on a postage stamp-sized front lawn.

Last time Erin had visited this address, she'd arrested Cassie's boyfriend. No wonder the girl was about as friendly as an injured boar. There was a light on deep inside the belly of the house but nothing outside or downstairs. She tried Ully on his cell but couldn't raise him. There were several reception dead zones, and the gas station was in one of them. She didn't have a police radio in her truck tonight.

She sat for a moment with the engine running, then felt ridiculous. She'd spent five years as an NYPD beat cop, and one year as an NYPD detective. She wasn't some rookie who needed her hand held. Unlike most TV shows depicted, detectives didn't normally work in pairs. Especially not in small rural departments. They worked alone, and they got the job done without a trusty sidekick.

Cassie and her friends were probably sitting in the dark watching her and laughing their asses off, planning to repeat the routine, *ad infinitum*. Erin turned off the engine and killed the lights. She grabbed her flashlight from under the seat and got out of the truck.

Last year had been the most grueling of her professional career, but it had ended with a conviction of the serial rapist who'd terrified campus. She should feel safer, they all should, but this was a football town, and the players ranked right up there with Holy Trinity. By arresting the star quarterback she'd brought herself nothing but trouble, and right now, she was about as popular as Pilate after the crucifixion.

A siren went off in the distance, the sound echoing for miles across the stark winter landscape. A dog barked a few houses down, but the street itself was deserted, everyone tucked up warm and cozy in their homes—like she should be.

Dammit.

She crossed the road, then climbed the three steps of the sagging front porch. There was a moth-eaten couch to the right. Standing to the left of the door she knocked and waited. An eerie silence greeted her.

"Forbes Pines PD." She knocked harder. "Cassie Bressinger, you reported an intruder. Open up, please." No one wanted cops in their neighborhood so she'd make sure the locals knew exactly who was responsible for this late night visit. She knocked again.

Where the hell was Ully?

If she'd really thought there was an intruder inside the house she'd kick down the door, but she doubted the chief of police wanted that sort of heavy-handed police work. He wanted the incidents to die down naturally without escalating the drama.

A plan that currently wasn't working.

There was a narrow path between the fenced yards of this house and the next. She made her way through, the edges of her coat brushing the wood on either side. At the back of the property she stood on tiptoe and swung the flashlight over the top board. She shone her beam into the shadowy recesses, revealing overflowing trashcans and several boxes of empty bottles stacked outside the back door. No sign of a break-in.

Something launched itself against the fence beside her, and the whole thing shook violently. Her heart ricocheted between her ribs and her spine. A frenzy of barking told her it was just a dog—*Jesus H. Christ*. The damn thing was lucky she hadn't shot it.

The jolt of adrenaline ramped up the tension and dialed her mood up to pissed. She strode back to the front of the house, intending to hammer on the door, but saw one of Cassie's roommates walking toward her along the sidewalk.

"What are you doing here?" Alicia Drummond demanded loudly. She carried a pile of books, and a hostile attitude. The feeling was mutual.

"Police received a call about an intruder from this address," Erin told her with a smile that could rip flesh from bone.

"Sure they weren't talking about you?" Alicia scoffed. She was a snotty law student on the fast-track to becoming a snotty defense attorney.

Erin kept her retort to herself. Her mother always said, "If you can't say something nice, don't say anything at all." Of course, her mother was one of the few members of the family who wasn't a cop. Her father's response was always, "You have the right to remain silent. Use it." Erin lived by his maxim.

Alicia balanced the heavy books under one arm while she dug for her keys. "We don't want you here. You need to leave before I make a complaint."

"Nice try, Alicia." Erin leaned against the siding. After only a few hours' sleep and a five-hour time difference, she had zero tolerance for bullshit. She just wanted to go home to bed. "I need to talk to Cassie, because she's the one who reported the intruder. I'm going to need her to come down to the police station and make a full report. Anyone else in the house at the time of the call also needs to come in." The more inconvenient she made the consequences of this prank, the sooner they'd get the message that this was not okay. Cops had better things to do with their time.

Alicia threw her a look of utter loathing. Then she went inside and flicked on the hall light. She went to slam the door in Erin's face, but Erin stuck her boot in the gap.

"Alicia," she warned with enough of an edge that the girl met her gaze. "Cassie needs to stop making false reports before she gets herself into serious trouble."

Alicia's gaze narrowed. "Fine. I'll tell her to stop being so resentful just because the cops locked up her boyfriend for thirty years. I mean, what's thirty years?"

"Tell it to the judge and jury. I'm not the one who convicted him." Erin removed her foot, and Alicia slammed the door shut in her face. Erin dragged a hand through her hair. These young women were so full of righteous indignation she actually admired them. Pity the guy they believed in was a violent scumbag.

She headed back to her truck, wondering where Ully was and whether she should wait for him to turn up or just call him on her drive home. A scream rent the air and raised every hair on her body. She turned and ran back toward the house and collided with Alicia on the garden path. The woman who hated her guts threw herself into Erin's arms and sobbed loudly. "Oh, my God. Oh, my God!"

"What is it?" asked Erin.

"They're dead!"

Erin's heart raced even as she braced herself for some dumb practical joke. "Who? Who's dead?" She took a step away from the hysterical girl and made Alicia sit on the curbstone. "Who is dead?" she repeated sharply, trying to penetrate the fog of hysteria that encased the usually unflappable law student.

"C-Cassie and M-Mandy." Alicia's skin was gray, her expression shell-shocked.

If this was a joke, Erin was going to make them all go

before the judge. A black and white cruiser pulled up in the street behind them. Ully. Finally.

He joined her. "Sorry, someone ran a red, and I pulled them over."

"We have a report of two fatalities inside the house," she told him.

Ully's eyes widened as he radioed for backup. They'd both assumed this was another false alarm. Her pulse thumped heavily in her veins. Had she screwed up? Had she been outside feeling sorry for herself as someone slaughtered two girls inside?

She pulled her Glock from its holster and climbed the steps. Ully did the same, and they entered the front door fast, clearing the downstairs room by room—the living room and kitchen, downstairs bathroom. A door off the kitchen had probably once been a dining room but had been converted into another bedroom. Alicia's books and bag were strewn carelessly on the bed.

It was quiet inside, the ominous feeling of dread moving sullenly through the air.

Erin jerked her chin toward the stairs and up they went. The door to the first room on the left was wide open. A girl lay on the bed staring unseeingly up at the ceiling. Erin recognized her from the trial last year, but didn't know her name. There was bruising on her neck, and the whites of her eyes were spotted red.

Erin ignored the way her heart jerked in her chest and moved to the center of the room as she and Ully finished searching the space. Once they were sure no one was hiding in the closet or under the bed, she pressed her fingers to the girl's carotid.

The skin was warm, but there was no pulse.

Erin caught Ully's gaze and shook her head, and they moved to the next room, checking under the bed, behind the door, and in the attached bath. Empty.

Horror spiked as they entered the last bedroom. Signs of a scuffle were obvious. Papers and bedding lay strewn across the floor. Jagged shards of a broken mug were scattered on the carpet. Cassandra Bressinger lay naked, spread-eagle, wrists and ankles bound to the four corners of the bed. The same MO Drew Hawke had reportedly used to rape his victims, except she was face up, and battered until she was almost unrecognizable.

Erin and Ully exchanged a glance. Had they been wrong? About Drew? About Cassie's crank call? Shock and horror and an awful sense of culpability ripped through Erin. If she'd broken down the door earlier, would she have saved the lives of these two young women?

To ground herself, Erin focused on the ritual of the job. Secure the scene. Assess the victim. She and Ully cleared the room, made sure there was no threat to life before Erin pressed her fingers to the side of this girl's throat. No pulse. She hadn't been dead long, but long enough for her lips to turn blue and eyes to glaze over.

Careful of where they stepped and what they touched, she and Ully cleared the rest of the house. Sirens screamed as more uniforms started to arrive.

"Secure the perimeter," she told the senior patrolman. She didn't want every cop in the town trudging through the crime scene or seeing the bodies. "I'll make the calls." Crime scene techs, the coroner, their boss. "And get someone to take Alicia Drummond to the police station to get a statement before she talks to anyone else."

Ully nodded and was already speaking into his radio.

The first call Erin made was to Harry Compton.

"What the hell do you want?" he answered groggily. There were only two detectives on the small Forbes Pines PD, and only one of them had recently taken a Hawaiian vacation.

"Double homicide on Fairfax Road."

"Fuck," Harry said and hung up.

A man of few words.

Then she called Chief Strassen and told him the case they thought they'd won last month was far from over. And the town that hated her guts was about to crucify her.

———————————

A BITTER NORTH-WIND funneled down the street, an omen for the hostility Darsh Singh was bound to encounter in the next few minutes. It was still dark out. Snow lay in dirty patches on the barren ground. He'd thrown on the clothes he'd been wearing earlier that day, grabbed his belongings, and hightailed it to the airport. Now a thin navy windbreaker with "FBI" stenciled across the back in acid yellow was all that stood between him and a polar vortex determined to suck New England into the cold depths of hell.

He'd been on a job in Boston when he'd gotten an urgent call from Acting Supervisory Special Agent Jed Brennan. On medical leave since before Christmas when Brennan had taken a bullet during an assassination attempt on the president, the agent had stepped in as temporary head of BAU-4 after ASAC Lincoln Frazer snapped his Achilles tendon during a criminal apprehension on the Outer Banks the day before yesterday.

Considering Frazer had bagged a serial killer who'd been active for nearly twenty years, Darsh figured it was a small price to pay.

Darsh's own desk was overflowing with active case files. A series of rapes in Portland. A cluster of homicides in DC, not to mention the white slave ring he'd been working in Boston. But within twelve hours of coming back to work, Jed Brennan had received an anxious phone call from the Department of Justice about a potential goat-rope—a double homicide at Blackcombe College, Forbes Pines, Upstate New York.

Blackcombe was renowned both as an undergraduate teaching institution and a world-class research facility, but that wasn't the reason for its more recent brush with fame. The media spotlight had been focused sharply on the town following the high-profile trial and conviction of the star quarterback for a series of rapes last year. The trial had ripped the town apart with opposing camps coming to blows on the courthouse steps and a near riot occurring when the verdict was read.

Brennan had pulled Darsh off his other cases and told him to make *this* his priority.

It was a delicate situation. Darsh had been tasked with not only examining the latest murders, but profiling the other crimes as well. To figure out if these new killings were a coincidence, a copycat, someone deliberately trying to make the Hawke conviction look shaky, or if the local PD had messed up and doomed an innocent man to prison. And he had to do it without pissing off the locals when they knew they were gonna be put under the microscope.

Darsh pushed through the crowd of spectators who lingered despite the lateness of the hour and the sub-zero temps.

He hoped someone here had the smarts to photograph the onlookers in addition to the crime scene. Killers often came back to observe the chaos they wrought. It was all part of the thrill. Unlike most fictional killers and rapists, the real life versions were generally as smart as a thumbtack. He flashed his creds at the police officer manning the outer perimeter and ducked under the tape. "Agent Singh. FBI. I need to speak to whoever's in charge."

"*You're* FBI?"

He ignored the skepticism. "That's what they told me when I graduated the academy." He pocketed his gold shield as the officer shouted to one of her colleagues before leading him to the two-story clapboard house surrounded by yellow crime scene tape.

"Sorry." The rookie was flustered. A dark blush worked its way into her cheeks and matched her cold-looking nose. "I wasn't expecting a fed to show up."

Darsh signed his name on the log, put paper covers over his boots, latex gloves on his hands, and walked into the house. It was just as cold inside—front and back doors were wide open. At least it would slow decomposition.

The rookie button-hooked a right and walked up to a blonde who wore a gray pantsuit beneath a black parka with a fur-lined hood. The blonde had her head down but seemed vaguely familiar.

She looked up, and a pair of smoky blue eyes collided with his. Every neuron in his body sparked to life as recognition slammed into his gut. Her pupils dilated, but apart from that, she betrayed no visible reaction.

Fuck.

There was no smile. No "Hey, how're ya doin'?" But then

their last encounter had been conducted under very different circumstances. Horizontal. Naked. Panting.

She'd turned him inside out in a way no one else ever had, and that was *before* he'd found out she was married.

He glanced at her left hand. Bare.

His pulse sped up, as if he hadn't learned his lesson the first time. She tucked her fingers up her sleeve, perhaps sensing his gaze.

The rookie spoke into the blonde's ear, and the woman narrowed her eyes, clearly weighing the professional implications of his presence rather than the personal ones. Darsh stared right back. Under his jacket, he wore black tactical pants, a black T-shirt, ATAC boots—much the same as he'd been the first time he'd bumped into her in a bar after spending an intense, sweaty day training with the FBI's HRT. She'd been at Quantico doing a training course for law enforcement. He'd been about to go undercover and was supposed to be keeping a low profile. He hadn't told her he was part of the FBI's BAU—but his omission didn't come close to hers. And it still burned that he'd slept with a married woman.

Her mouth turned down at the edges, and he tried to forget the fact he'd spent hours kissing those lips—and every other inch of her body. As if reading the direction of his thoughts she glared at him and turned to the evidence tech she'd been talking to, dismissing Darsh like he was a nobody.

He shoved down a grin. If it hadn't been the scene of a double homicide he'd have laughed. He was used to working with women who busted balls for breakfast. He actually enjoyed the challenge of them. He stood waiting patiently until she deigned to speak to him. Forty-six seconds later, she walked across the room to where he'd planted himself beside the door.

"You're FBI?" She held out her hand for his creds. Took them and examined them carefully. "Not a Marine then?" she muttered under her breath, proving she definitely remembered their night together three years ago.

"Once a Marine always a Marine," he told her truthfully.

"*Semper Fi,*" she muttered sarcastically.

Always faithful.

"Well, that's *my* motto." He plucked his creds out of her grip, and she flinched.

Up close, those unusual eyes stood out against creamy skin and thick dark lashes like a wash of color in an otherwise pale complexion. There were shadows beneath them, bruises of fatigue dappling tender skin, speaking of a double shift dealing with brutal reality. He told himself it didn't matter. All that mattered was helping catch this killer and making sure the local cops weren't incompetent hicks.

"This isn't a federal case." Irritation frosted her tone.

Hell, snowmen were warmer than this woman appeared on the surface—except he knew that beneath the icy exterior was a core of molten fire. "No, ma'am."

"Detective," she corrected, those sharp eyes of hers apparently tracking his thoughts. "Detective Erin Donovan."

"Detective." He inclined his head, inexplicably relieved she hadn't lied about her first name. He'd taken one look at the sexy blonde and been smitten. At first they hadn't exchanged surnames or life histories, both wanting a no-strings hook up. But by the end of the night he'd wanted to know everything about her—except the one thing he'd discovered. He cleared his throat. "Your chief requested assistance from the BAU. I'm it."

Her boss, at the urging of the governor, had indeed called the FBI for assistance. None of the local cops needed to know the DOJ was also involved.

"BAU? You're BAU?" Her expression became less antagonistic now that she knew he wasn't a field officer who might try to wrest the case from her. But the question remained in her eyes—why lie about being a Marine all those years ago? A spark of apparent understanding lit her eyes, but he couldn't begin to guess what she was thinking.

"I guess we both lied to get what we wanted," she said in barely a whisper.

A night of burning-hot sex. The memory of it seared the air between them, and that pissed him off. As a trained sniper, he never made the same mistake twice—that went double for his personal life. He kept his voice to the same low whisper. "Only I didn't have a spouse back home waiting for me."

"Gold star for Agent Singh." She looked him in the eye, raised that stubborn chin of hers, and got back to the job at hand. "Serial crimes generally involve more than two bodies, and have a cooling off period between crimes. Why is BAU involved here?"

"Because after the rape trial last year this town doesn't need a killer on the loose." A little truth went a long way. "The faster you solve this thing, the better." They held each other's gaze, but he didn't back down. Neither did she. "You have anyone photographing the crowd outside?" Divert her attention. Give her a reason to value his input.

Her eyes widened, and she swore. "Geoff," she spoke to a man packing up his photography gear. "Get some more exterior shots and make sure you get plenty of the crowd in case the perp came back."

"Right, boss." The photographer unzipped his camera with the resigned air of a man not getting any sleep that night.

"We did it earlier, but I should have thought of doing it again a few hours later. The perp might have gotten curious as to what was going on. Thanks." She nodded curtly.

"The bodies are still here, correct?" He got a much better sense of the killer's mindset when he saw victims *in situ*. And this was a volatile situation and a sensitive case. The quicker they figured out who'd killed these girls, the better for everyone. He took a step toward the stairs, but she side-stepped, blocked him, and they collided hard. He grabbed her upper arms so she didn't fall on her ass and tried to ignore the fact her soft breasts were pressed up against the hard wall of his chest. The dilation of her pupils and flaring of her nostrils told their own tales, even as her jaw flexed and eyes narrowed. They stood glaring at one another like angry lovers—or a couple of wary dogs going head-to-head over territory.

CHAPTER THREE

DARSH WAS AMUSED. Was the detective really going to try to stop him from doing his job? Considering the top of her blonde head came to his chin, and he outweighed her by seventy pounds, it wasn't the smartest move. Although she did have a gun.

Evidence techs and other cops were watching with keen interest, and Darsh wasn't about to give them a show. He let her go and took a step away from her. Touching her made his blood heat, and he couldn't afford to get distracted.

"You have a problem with me being here, Detective?"

Something faltered in her gaze. She papered the cracks in her composure with a smile that said not only did she not trust him, she didn't like him very much either. But she'd liked him well enough in Virginia.

"I need to talk to my chief before I'll allow anyone near those bodies. I need to check you're not some reporter or whacko off the street with really good forged credentials. I owe it to the victims and their families not to take things at face value."

He regarded her quizzically. Technically he didn't need her permission, but he appreciated the thoroughness in checking with her boss, and he appreciated the fact she seemed to care about the victims—although that could cloud judgment when an investigator got too close.

"I'll wait," he said patiently.

She stepped away, already pulling out her cell. He wandered into the kitchen and looked around. A stack of washed dishes drained next to the sink. The place was clean if a little tatty and worn. Typical female student accommodation, except for the picture of Erin Donovan stuck to a dartboard, riddled with holes, and two darts carefully piercing each eyeball, the third sticking out of her mouth.

The woman in question followed him into the small room with its rickety table piled high with bills. She spotted his raised brows as he looked at the dartboard, and grunted. She put her hand over the microphone. "Cassie Bressinger wasn't exactly a fan of mine. I assume you know she was Drew Hawke's girlfriend?"

He hadn't. That put a whole new perspective on the case.

Conflict of interest, anyone?

The problem was the police department here was so small they probably didn't have anyone who hadn't been involved in the serial rape case last year.

He walked to the back door and surveyed the yard. A concrete path led to a gate in the back fence. The lawn consisted of a couple of strips of brown grass and some empty plant pots stacked to one side. It looked like someone might actually make an effort to cultivate a garden in summertime. Empty wine bottles sat in plastic recycling containers. A five-foot tall wooden fence enclosed the property.

A dog started barking next door.

Donovan came up beside him. "Okay. Chief Strassen vouched for you. Come on."

"Any sign of forced entry?" He bent down to examine the

lock closely but saw no scuff marks, no jimmying of the wood, no scratches on the metal. He straightened.

She shook her head, and a lock of pale blonde hair caught on his sleeve. The sight of it paralyzed him for a moment as the sensation of it drifting over his bare skin came back like an erotic tease.

Impatiently she caught her errant hair and tugged it into a ponytail away from her face. "Not that we've been able to tell." He had no clue what she was talking about. "Front and back doors were both locked when we arrived."

How the killer had gained entry. Locks. *Right.*

Not silky hair, or soft skin, or hot mouths. Not walls and floors and tables.

Darsh kept his expression stern and nodded. *Fucking hell.*

"Let's go." His voice was gruff from holding in his reaction to her. He wasn't here for this. He wasn't here for her.

He followed her through the house away from the murmur of other people working the crime scene. And as he trailed her up the stairs, he became aware of another undeniable truth that was neither professional nor appropriate. It was a God-given fact that some views had a way of distracting a man regardless of circumstance—Detective Donovan's ass turned out to be one of them.

He shook his head. He was working. Even if he wasn't working, he did not sleep with married women. What if he met her husband during this case? The idea made a cold sweat break out on his back. Damn Erin Donovan for putting him in this position and for making the experience so goddamn unforgettable.

He got to the top of the stairs and was plunged back into the here and now. In the room on the left, a female victim lay on the bed. The sight of her inert form snapped his focus back to the job.

She was a young adult, eighteen to twenty. Dark hair loose around her face. Fully clothed in a ruby red sweater and blue jeans. Her socks had Santa hats on them. Darsh flinched. He knew without a doubt she'd gotten them for Christmas—the same way he'd received Christmas socks from one of his sisters every year for as long as he could remember. The thought stirred his anger, and that was something he couldn't afford. He pulled himself into the zone where his family and feelings didn't exist. A place where red-hot sex with Erin Donovan had never happened.

During Operation Iraqi Freedom, getting in the zone had allowed him to stare through the scope of his M40A1 bolt-action sniper rifle and neutralize threats to his fellow Marines without a shred of remorse. He'd pulled the trigger and smoke-checked a target, time after time, without hesitation. Ghosts might visit him occasionally in a deadly roll call, revealing their humanity and his, but he didn't regret his actions. The lessons of dissociation had served him well in the past, and he drew on them now, trying to become the machine and leave the weakness and distraction of sentiment behind.

"Mandy Wochikowski. Twenty years old in her junior year at Blackcombe. Majored in criminology," Donovan informed him.

"What about registered sex offenders in the area?"

"I have an officer tracking down their movements. A lot of them moved away last year, when their addresses were posted on a student blog." She looked uncomfortable.

"Vigilantism?" he asked.

"There were no official complaints, but name someone

who wants to live next to a pedophile?"

"Good point."

He looked back at Mandy Wochikowski. The young woman appeared to have been strangled, but there were no obvious signs of sexual assault. It would be impossible to know for sure until the Medical Examiner performed an autopsy, and even then it might not be conclusive. The girl stared up at the ceiling with vacant eyes dotted with petechiae—a clear sign she'd suffocated, and her nail beds showed definite signs of cyanosis. Her limbs had been carefully aligned, arms laid close to her sides, legs straight and parallel. Feet together. Neat. Tidy. Coffin-ready.

He turned away and checked the pictures on the yellow-painted walls. There were some band posters: Nirvana. Cold Play. Fall Out Boy. A corkboard with her printed schedule mounted on it, surrounded by what he assumed were family photographs and a few photographs of friends. He recognized Drew Hawke in one of the pictures. The quarterback was a good-looking young man who'd had an NFL career waiting for him when college finished.

Blown.

Textbooks lay open on the desk. He recognized some from his own studies. A laptop sat there, the battery humming away loudly to itself. Older model. He tapped the touchpad with the tip of a latex-clad finger. Donovan began to make a sound of protest then stopped. Maybe she'd decided they were both on the same side. Or maybe she was picking her battles.

The computer screen opened to an unfinished essay. The girl had stopped halfway through a sentence about serial harassment and bullying.

"Her music is paused," Donovan noted. "Press play," she

instructed over his shoulder.

"Did Evidence dust this for prints?" He indicated the computer. Useable fingerprints were a lot harder to find than most people realized.

She nodded. "They examined it, but didn't see any. Didn't dust because of the risk to the computer itself. We'll bag it to check for contact DNA before the computer boys get their hands on it."

The detective rested her hands on her hips, and he forced himself not to notice the way the cotton of her shirt clung to the curves of her body. So much for the zone. He pressed play, and they both flinched at the volume. He recognized the band and the song—Halestorm's "In your room." A little too close to the bone.

He flicked it back off, and he and Donovan looked at one another in the sudden silence. "Was this music turned on or off when the first responders arrived?"

"Off."

"You sure?" he asked.

"*I* was the first responder, along with Officer Mason. We were called out on an intruder alert. The music wasn't playing then. You think the perp turned it off?"

"Someone called in an intruder alert?" This was news to him. He'd received the barest of details before he'd jumped into some tiny turboprop aircraft that had dumped him at the closest airfield.

Erin shifted uncomfortably. "Since Drew Hawke's arrest we've had a spate of false reports from this address. We responded as we always do, but we didn't take it too seriously. A third housemate arrived home when I was on the doorstep. She let herself inside. Found the bodies." And Donovan was beating herself up over not breaking down the door the moment she arrived.

"You thought they were prank calling?"

"Not prank." The expression on her face wasn't bitterness, but it was a close cousin—regret. "They were deliberately provoking the police, but my chief wanted us to go easy on them."

"Because their parents are loaded?"

Her blue eyes flashed. "Because I'd arrested one of their friends, and they seemed genuinely distressed by events. They were going through a bad time." She released an unsteady breath. "And their parents are loaded."

He looked at the body on the bed. She'd definitely gone through a bad time tonight. Had the fact they'd made a habit out of crying wolf gotten them killed? Or had the killer chosen them for some other reason—like being Drew Hawke's girlfriend?

"You think the Hawke conviction is solid?" he asked, testing the waters.

If Erin's teeth clenched any tighter together, her jaw would break. "It isn't up to me to decide. I just provide evidence—"

"Cut the bullshit, Erin. Do you think Hawke did it or not?"

Her eyes flashed blue mercury. "Yes. Yes, I think he was guilty of raping those two women, and probably two other cases that weren't prosecuted last year. But not because I have some vendetta against football players, which is what the papers keep spouting. It's what the victims and the evidence told me."

DNA in the form of a hair, witness testimony, even polygraphs. The case had seemed solid, but he needed to look at every detail. Darsh turned away and played the music again.

He lowered himself into Mandy's rickety chair, ignoring the way it creaked under his weight. Then he turned to face the monitor with his fingers hovering over the keyboard. Would Mandy have heard someone coming through her bedroom door with her music this loud? Would she have seen his reflection in her screen?

Or had the UNSUB burst in and quickly overpowered her, and then turned the music up to cover her screams? That didn't make sense given there was another girl in the house—unless the other girl was already dead.

He pressed "pause" again. "Walk up behind me," he instructed Donovan.

She did as he asked, but he didn't see much of a reflection against the white background of Mandy's Word file.

He glanced around the girl's room, taking it all in, trying to imagine her sitting here just a few hours ago, more worried about an essay than the predator who had her in his sights. There was no sign of a struggle. The room was neat. Clothes folded. Darsh got up and checked the clothes hamper. Almost empty after the Christmas break. The way the UNSUB had arranged the body suggested remorse, but he hadn't covered the face, which would have suggested the killer knew the victim.

"He caught her by surprise, didn't he? She was listening to music, working on a paper, and he crept up behind her." For one unguarded moment, anguish ravaged Erin's features. She thought she'd misjudged the situation, and now she had two dead girls on her conscience. "She never stood a chance."

Darsh forced himself to ignore her. "I'd like copies of Mandy's schedule and all her social media accounts and email. You have her cell phone?"

"Cell was on the desk. Harry Compton, the other detective in Forbes Pines"—*wow,* two *whole detectives*—"took it when he went to find contact information to inform both sets of parents."

Darsh didn't envy Harry that task on any level. Working with dead people had its merits.

Erin's lips pressed together as if keeping her emotions tightly under control.

Did she ever smile anymore? The way she'd smiled at him in that bar? The memory of it blazed through his brain until he shut it down. The fact that she was attractive and good in bed was not in question here. The question was, was she a good cop? He'd ask Brennan to do a little digging into her background and performance evaluations. See if she had a history of making mistakes.

"I'll make sure you're sent copies of everything we find," she told him as if he was going anywhere soon.

He ignored the supposition. Frankly he had no idea how long he was going to be stuck here, but he'd be lying if he said he wasn't praying for an emergency situation that needed his immediate attention anywhere other than Upstate New York. "Tell me about the other victim."

"Cassie was a junior majoring in sports psychology. Head of the cheerleading squad. Twenty years old." She grimaced. "She thought I was Satan's bitch."

"But you still think it's appropriate to work her murder?" he asked quietly.

The straightness of her spine was matched only by the sternness of her expression. "Unless I've become a suspect, Agent Singh, I'm the best hope she has of finding justice." Her gaze met his in a direct challenge. "She annoyed me because

35

she wasted police time, and we're all busy enough without that bullshit. But I understood her position. I never felt any animosity towards her."

"The chance of this being a random murder is pretty slim, which means someone targeted Cassandra Bressinger because of the Hawke connection. There's no way this isn't a conflict of interest," he argued.

"Not true," she said vehemently.

"You don't think you're too close?" he suggested.

"Too close?" If he hadn't been watching her lips so intently he wouldn't have noticed the subtle way they tightened. "We're talking about facts and witness statements. The Hawke case was never personal to me. I know it better than anyone."

"You must have gotten pretty friendly with the victims."

Pain flickered in her gaze. She rested her hands on her hips, revealing her nipped-in waist and a Glock-22 strapped to her side, and he stopped looking at her eyes. Lord have mercy. He was a sucker for a woman with a sidearm.

Had she done it on purpose? Distracted him away from a moment of vulnerability.

"There was never any doubt the women were raped, Agent Singh, so naturally I felt sympathy for them. It was the identity of the attacker that was in question. We found hair that linked back to Hawke, and the women reported it was Drew Hawke who raped them. They each took polygraphs when challenged by the defense and passed with flying colors. Excuse me if that doesn't sound like a slam-dunk."

They stared at one another for a few seconds. He couldn't afford to be distracted by Donovan's passion for her cause—he knew exactly how that passion translated into other areas of her life, and that wasn't good for his objectivity. He turned his gaze back to the bed and then stretched out his stiff neck. Maybe he shouldn't be thinking about Donovan's capacity to do her job. He should just concentrate on doing his own.

They headed across the hall to another bedroom with blue-painted walls and flowery drapes closed against prying eyes. The whole house was quiet now, not even the murmur of ghosts.

The victim was stretched out in a way that exposed her genitalia. Had the UNSUB imagined the cops seeing her like this? Had he thought about shocking Detective Donovan when she walked in the door and saw the degradation? Darsh ignored the part of his brain that wanted to hurt for the victim and concentrated on what he was here for. Getting into the mind of a killer.

Mandy Wochikowski's death had been clean and sanitary, whereas this one was violent, demeaning, and graphic. She'd been beaten. There was a definite sexual component to this assault. The lack of clothes, the overt sexual display. The mattress was bare. He peered closer at her blue jeans on top of the pile of bedding in the middle of the floor. The denim was ragged where they'd been cut with what looked like scissors. The fact her clothes had been cut off her body suggested the killer needed to subdue and restrain her before stripping her— hence the beating to the face? Would Mandy have heard the struggle in here if the doors were closed, and she was listening to loud music?

Probably not.

He looked around. "Did you find any scissors?"

Donovan shook her head; her silence speaking volumes.

Mandy's murder had seemed almost like an apology. This one...the UNSUB had clearly been punishing Cassandra

Bressinger, and had fun doing it. Darsh eyed the knots and blue climbing rope that tied her limbs to each corner of the double bed. It had been a long time since he was a boy scout, but some of the knots looked familiar. "Is the rope from the house, do you know?"

"I didn't see it anywhere, but I haven't talked to the other roommates yet."

He had a feeling the killer had carefully planned this murder, so he'd probably brought the rope and scissors with him. The rope might be the best physical link they had to this guy. Had Cassandra been the original target and Mandy collateral damage? Or had he planned to tie up both girls, maybe even all four of them, but had been interrupted by the cops before he could do his sadistic shit to Mandy?

Had he lost his nerve? His arousal? Maybe killing someone hadn't felt how he'd expected it to feel. Too messy. Too ugly? Maybe he hadn't meant to kill the woman at all. Maybe the UNSUB had pushed the strangulation factor too far and cracked the hyoid bone. Cassie's attack had been intentional, but maybe her death had been an accident.

"Who made the call about the intruder?" he asked.

"I haven't listened to it yet. It's first on my to-do list as soon as I get back to the station." Donovan showed clear signs of exhaustion, but there was no way she'd leave until he did.

"Make sure those knots are preserved when the ropes are removed." Knots could be very specific to offenders. "You have photographs of everything?"

She nodded.

"I want the rope and knots sent to Quantico for analysis."

Cassandra's wrists were bloody and raw where she'd fought her bindings. She'd been alive long enough to struggle.

Then again, why tie her up at all if he didn't want her alive for the main event? Darsh peered closely at the victim's unpainted nails. Then he leaned closer, drawn by a hint of a scent that didn't fit.

"Smell her hands," he told Donovan.

The detective leaned closer and sniffed. Her brow crumpled. "Bleach?" She swore.

Bleach destroyed DNA. Cassandra had probably scratched the guy.

"I'll go tell the techs to check the Clorox bottle for prints."

When she came back, he asked, "How similar is this to the method that Drew Hawke was convicted of using?"

Donovan cleared her throat. "No bleach was recorded as being used to clean the bodies. He used a yellow nylon rope to tie up his victims, but we never saw the knots because the victims were either untied or managed to free themselves after he left."

It was a difference possibly tied to the escalation, but still the crimes were remarkably similar. "The victims reported they were tied to the legs of the bed, correct?"

"Spread-eagled. Yes," Donovan said quietly. "He crept into their bedrooms in the middle of the night. Injected them with ketamine, gagged them and then tied them to the four corners of the bed where he raped them repeatedly. I haven't seen any injection sites on these victims, but we're waiting on the medical examiner."

"Ketamine *and* rope restraints?"

She nodded.

"Isn't that a little excessive for a large male athlete who probably outweighed them by a hundred pounds?"

Her lips pinched. "I'm just telling you the facts. I didn't get inside his head."

No, that was his job, as she'd meant to remind him. He checked his watch. It was nearly five AM. "Does it usually take this long for the ME to arrive?"

"The chief wanted the State Medical Examiner involved in this investigation from the start, and they're based in Massena about an hour away. There was a snowmobile accident last night and three people died—two children and their father. ME's been tied up with that case, otherwise you'd have missed your chance to see the bodies in place."

"As least the temperature here is the same as the morgue." If not colder. "Any other similarities between the other cases?"

If she knew he was testing her, she didn't show it.

"The pattern of bruising around the throat on Cassie is similar, although the other girls obviously survived. The fact it looks like she was violently raped? Yup, that's the same." Her gaze was sharp and penetrating. "And the bottom sheet is missing."

He looked at the pile of bedclothes tossed on the floor. "You're sure?"

She nodded. "That information came out at Drew Hawke's trial. No one knows what happened to the sheets, but it seemed likely Hawke took the bed linen to try to reduce physical evidence tying him to the crime."

Rather than as a trophy. The fact this killer had done the same thing…

"So this UNSUB arrived with a murder kit and took even more stuff when he left." Prepared. Experienced. Disciplined.

"So why not take the rope, especially if the girls were dead?" Donovan voiced one of the things he thought was inconsistent.

"You have people searching nearby dumpsters for physical evidence?"

"Yeah." She didn't sound optimistic. "Every dumpster in town. I called the garbage company and had them halt collections until we're done. But I don't think he'll dump the sheet anywhere obvious. He's probably already burned it." She stuffed her hands in her coat pockets and huddled into its warm depths. Darsh wished he'd thrown on something more substantial than a T-shirt and windbreaker before he'd started out. There was no snow on the ground in Boston.

"Did he know there were only two girls here?" she asked suddenly. "And if so, how? Was he stalking them? Does he know their routine? Is he a friend? Was he watching the house, maybe from a vehicle? Or does he live nearby?"

Darsh liked the way her brain worked. His thoughts had been traveling the same direction.

She continued. "Maybe he didn't care that the others could have come home at any moment. Maybe he was waiting for them to turn up until he saw me roll up? Did he have a gun or a knife that he used to control them? Is that how he subdued two smart women, then killed them both?" She started to say something else, then closed her mouth.

"What?" He wanted to know how she thought, and how she acted on those thoughts.

"He's not a novice. He's done this before."

Darsh agreed. The million-dollar question was, had he gained his experience on the women Drew Hawke was convicted of raping, or was he using that case to raise the stakes and increase his own notoriety? Or had Hawke had a partner? No one had ever mentioned the possibility, but Special-K was renowned for leaving users confused and disorientated. If the victim was conscious, ketamine could produce hallucinations, but didn't actually erase short-term memory the way some date rape drugs did.

Darsh glanced at the girl's walls. No posters. Just a shrine to the Hawke kid.

Cassandra's lamp was on. Computer off. A mug lay over-turned and broken on the rug, a brown coffee stain on the carpet. Crumpled papers were strewn across the mat. He leafed through a few boxes that sat on a shelf—receipts, university administration type stuff. Then studied the contents of the desk. Laptop. Headphones. Printer. Textbooks. Writing paper. Envelopes. And stamps. He opened a drawer. No letters.

"Did she correspond with Hawke?"

Donovan watched him move around the room. She seemed reluctant to let him out of her sight, and he doubted that was because of his irresistible good looks.

"I don't know. We didn't find any letters from him to her, but after her declarations of undying love? I'd be shocked if they hadn't written."

"We need to find out." If the killer had taken the letters, it would tell them something about his mindset.

She carefully stepped around the mess in the middle of the floor. "So you're thinking he takes letters but not computers or cell phones. This isn't a robbery gone bad."

"No," he agreed.

"Is he likely to stop killing if we don't catch him?" White teeth worried her bottom lip.

Darsh felt them on his skin and shied away from the tactile memory. "The suggestion that serial killers won't stop unless caught is a myth. Dennis Rader killed ten people between 1974 and 1991. He didn't kill anyone else before he was arrested in 2005. Sometimes they find a substitution for the buzz they get from killing. Sometimes they get scared and don't want to get caught. Psychopaths often offend less as they enter their mid-forties—no one knows why. Serial rapists, though?" He stared at the dead girl. "I doubt this guy is done."

Cassandra Bressinger had fought hard, but it hadn't mattered in the end. In fact, the more she fought, the more excited the killer had probably become. Rape was a crime of hate and dominance, not uncontrollable lust. This UNSUB had viciously attacked Cassandra Bressinger, using more force than necessary to overpower her and commit the act. It looked like the work of a classic anger rapist who used sex as a weapon. The UNSUB had wanted to humiliate and defile Cassie. Maybe the identity of the victim hadn't mattered. Maybe the guy hated women in general. But Darsh had a feeling the attacker had chosen Cassie deliberately, and that she was a message—and he needed to figure out what the message was and whom it was directed toward. That smacked more of a power rapist who used sex as a tool to compensate for feelings of inadequacy.

The nature of the sexual assault gave Darsh information on this guy's twisted psyche, but this attack was sending mixed messages.

"If he's driven by a desire for notoriety, this might be enough to sate him for now. But if he becomes addicted to the spotlight…"

"He's about to get the fix of a lifetime." Donovan nodded. "The media is about to descend on this town and make this guy a worldwide celebrity." And her a pariah.

"And if he's trying to make Hawke look innocent, or law

enforcement incompetent," he gave her a pointed look, "he might just be getting started."

She swore.

"Bottom line is I doubt he'll stop on his own." He clenched a fist. "I need to figure out his motive—"

"*We*," Donovan cut in sharply. "*We* need to figure out motive."

Her expression dared him to deny her the right to do her job.

"We." He conceded eventually.

He flicked the curtain to look out at the street. What he was really doing was avoiding the woman he'd never expected to see again. The one who'd lied to him and brought him to his knees. If he discovered she'd screwed up the Hawke investigation and inadvertently gotten these two women killed, she'd be off the case and off the job. Detective Donovan wasn't going to like that very much. Nope. She wasn't going to like it at all.

CHAPTER FOUR

Erin let the engine of her truck run for a minute and tried to pretend she wasn't floored by the fact her past had just collided with her present. Of all the men to walk into a murder scene… She groaned out loud and wished she could slink home and hide out in her bedroom for a week. Long enough for freaking *FBI Agent* Darsh Singh to be on his way.

God. She wanted to scream with frustration.

It took years to become eligible to even *apply* for the BAU, so he'd definitely been an agent when they'd last met. He'd known she was attending a course at the academy, and that's probably why he'd gone with the USMC story. Maybe he'd worried she wouldn't have hooked up with anyone she might bump into during her training course at the FBI. But she'd forgotten, until after it was too late, that adultery was a criminal offense in the military. She'd harbored years of guilt for putting him at risk and had understood why he'd freaked out when he'd discovered she was married. At that point, telling the truth about her situation wouldn't have made a difference, so she hadn't even tried to explain.

But he'd lied to her about being in the Marines.

The fact he was still furious about sleeping with a married woman spoke of higher morals than she possessed. He probably thought she was some bored cock hopping slut out for a good time. He was wrong, but she *had* been after sex when she'd walked into that bar, and she had been married, so maybe he wasn't completely wrong. It might have been a sin in the eyes of the church, and under military law, but the part of her that wanted to feel ashamed was quickly buried under a mountain of resilience and hard-won independence.

It was none of his damn business.

Hypocrite.

No one had the right to tell her how to act or what to feel. Especially not a man who'd done his own share of deception in the quest to get her naked. He'd never *asked* if she was married. She hadn't lied.

As the heater finally began to deliver hot air, she pulled out and drove slowly past the crowd of onlookers who lingered despite the hour and frigid temperature. She tapped her brakes just to make sure they still worked. Not that she was paranoid or anything.

Headlights pulled into the street behind her, and her shoulders slumped. Agent Singh was following her to the police station.

Why had her boss requested FBI assistance? Of course she knew. She was just trying to ignore the elephant in the room until it trampled her into a bloody pulp. The boss was worried Hawke might be innocent, and she'd arrested the wrong guy.

The fact she was a small cog in the criminal justice system wouldn't matter if they needed a scapegoat. She'd been the face of the investigation. It was her head on the chopping block. While her career wasn't much compared to the lives of those two women, it was all she had.

Had the high profile trial attracted a serial rapist to their affluent little town? Or *had* she been wrong about Hawke, and the real rapist had been free all this time and had now escalated from rape to murder? But the evidence against Hawke was solid. She hadn't pulled him out of thin air as a suspect, and the rapes had stopped after he'd been arrested. This didn't make any sense.

Her fingers tightened on the steering wheel as she thought about what had happened to Cassie and Mandy. She knew monsters were out there, and that her chance of crossing paths with them was higher than the average citizen. She knew they hid amongst the honest and polite, the good looking and earnest. Insidious evil lurking beneath seemingly normal veneers. She knew it all too well.

Her phone rang, and she used her hands-free unit to answer it. "Donovan."

"Are you all right, love?" her mother asked.

Erin checked the clock. Of course her mother would have heard the news and been worried. "Yeah, Mom, of course I'm fine. You unpacked yet?"

She'd taken her parents with her to Hawaii for their fortieth wedding anniversary. It seemed like a grand gesture, but the family wasn't fooled. She was still avoiding going home to NYC.

"We're fine. I just saw the news and wanted to check you were safe."

A pang of guilt hit her. Brigit Donovan's nerves were probably shot from worrying about all her offspring, not to mention her husband. Maybe that's one of the reasons Erin had become a cop. It was easier not to worry from this side of the blue line. "I've been up all night, Mom, working the case. I can't talk right now."

Erin heard the eye-roll in her mother's voice. "Of course

you can't. Stay safe, Erin. Get some rest and lock your doors. The idea of you all alone in that farmhouse—"

"Thanks for freaking me out, Mom. I'll call you when I get time." Which would be after they solved the case.

"Love you, Erin." It was how her mom ended every conversation. That and a quick prayer to St. Michael and a kiss of the rosary.

"Love you, too, Mom. Go back to bed." Another call came through as soon as she hung up.

"Erin." She recognized the voice. Professor Roman Huxley. "I just heard about the murders. If I can help in any way, please don't hesitate to call me."

Huxley was a leading expert on criminology. He was based at the university here and was an invaluable resource. She'd sat in on a few of his classes and even given a guest lecture in one of his courses before the Hawke case last year.

"Thanks—"

"I don't know if you know this, but one of the victims was in my sophomore class. Mandy Wochikowski. She was a bright kid. Did some work for me over the summer. I feel terrible."

"Anything you can tell me about her?" Erin asked quickly. She didn't know much about Mandy. Any information would be useful.

"She was a straight-A student who always attended lectures and handed in her projects on time. Those students are rarer than you think."

"Boyfriend? Girlfriend?"

"Not that I noticed."

So probably not. The professor was a bit of a player and had hit on her when they'd first met, and several times since.

Erin got hit on a lot—not because she was some raving beauty. But the more she said "no," the more of a challenge she became. Apparently being unattainable was attractive to a lot of men. It took some guys multiple knock-backs to get the message across that she wasn't dating anyone. Ever.

Thoughts of the sexy fed tried to intrude. He was an unwelcome reminder of the last time she'd said "yes."

"She ever mention the Hawke case to you?" she asked.

"You think the two crimes are related?" His surprise seemed genuine.

"Not necessarily," she said carefully. She didn't want to be the source of rumors that could jeopardize her career, but it wouldn't take the press long to start screaming the same questions. "The other victim was Cassandra Bressinger. I can't ignore the possibility of there being some sort of connection."

"Christ, I didn't know the other girl was Cassie. I'd forgotten they lived together."

Erin heard the change in his tone. "You knew her, too?"

"She sought me out during the trial. Wanted to know the recommended reading on serial rapists and if I could suggest any current research papers concerning their psychology."

Erin wasn't surprised. Cassie had been driven to exonerate her boyfriend.

"I'm very sorry to hear she was involved," the professor said softly. "She seemed genuinely convinced Hawke was innocent despite the compelling evidence to the contrary." There was a long pause. "As to your other question, Mandy and I discussed the Hawke case on several occasions in class. It was an incredible teaching opportunity as you can imagine."

She rolled her eyes because it was so much more than that.

"I used it as a demonstration about criminal behavior and

how criminals are often viewed as a consequence of their social standing. Needless to say the discussion degenerated into a fight between how the quarterback of the Blackcombe Ravens could have any girl he wanted and didn't need to rape to get sex *versus* football players are brainless meatheads too stupid and overindulged to understand a one-syllable, two letter word. I actually begin teaching material about serial rape next week. I expect the information will open some students' eyes to aspects of the crime they assume they understand. If it doesn't, they're going to flunk."

She had bigger things to worry about than narrow minds or failed grades. "Thanks for your help, Professor."

"I keep telling you, call me Roman."

The familiarity felt wrong, like calling the family priest by his first name. "Right. Well, if you think of anything else, feel free to give me a call."

"It would help if I could review the case notes…"

Erin checked her rear view mirror. "I'll talk to the FBI to see if we can consult with you on this one."

"The FBI is involved? Already?" The professor sounded intrigued.

"Yeah."

"That's what happens when you have lots of wealthy parents and murdered co-eds."

And an elite college whose enrollment was going to suffer as a consequence. She understood the stakes could be measured in dollars and lives—only the lives concerned her right now.

"I'll get back to you." Erin said goodbye and hung up.

She turned into the police station, Agent Singh following closely in his black rental SUV. She had a feeling he was going to be her own personal shadow until the powers that be decided whether or not to make her the sacrificial goat. Erin growled with frustration as she pulled into a parking space and turned off the engine. She got out and leaned against the warm hood of her truck as she waited for the fed to join her. He walked toward her, all muscled grace and professional cool. Her mouth went dry.

Get a grip, Erin. He thinks you're a cheating slut and is probably gonna get you fired.

He caught her gaze and raised a brow in question. She tried to keep her expression blank. The guy was gorgeous and looked more like an actor playing a role than a law enforcement officer with powers of arrest, but she didn't let it fool her. People often dismissed her because she was young and blonde. It made getting the cuffs around those thick wrists that much more satisfying.

She led the way, grateful there were no reporters yet. They'd arrive soon enough like a plague of flies.

"It's a long drive from Virginia," she noted, walking up the stairs toward the red brick building.

"Flew in from Boston."

"Murder case?"

He glanced at her sideways. "Suspected white slave ring."

"You shut it down?"

"It's ongoing." He carefully avoided her gaze.

So he'd been pulled off that case to come here. Damn. Her mood soured further as she held open the door for him. "Well, we sure do appreciate you dropping everything and rushing here to help." She didn't bother to keep the sarcasm out of her voice.

His glance flicked over her again as he held the inner door

51

for her this time. She'd made her point. Bottom line was she was stuck with the guy for a few days, and she was going to make good use of him. The Bureau had access to resources that their small PD could only dream of. And if this BAU profiler could help catch their killer, she'd put up with all the associated politics and bullshit from the rest of her department and city hall. She'd even put up with all the snide inferences from Agent Singh regarding her loose morals—as if she'd been the only one naked in that bed.

Protecting the people of this town was her main priority, even if they hated her for it.

She led him into police headquarters, which occupied the lower levels of the north side of the building. Courthouse was above. This corridor was lined with age-darkened oak panels and a gloomy atmosphere. Agent Singh seemed to be cataloguing every detail, and Erin had never liked being judged by anything except the work she did. The guy may have seen her naked, but he'd never seen her working. They headed into the squad room, which buzzed with activity. Every available body was manning phones, or out canvassing for information and running leads.

"You want a coffee?" she asked him. "It comes with a health warning." Law enforcement wasn't known for its baristas in the break room.

"Please." He nodded.

"I'll get you one. Wait here." She left him near the bullpen and went over to the coffee room that housed a couple of padded chairs, a fridge, a sink, coffeepot, and tea kettle. Hopes of finding a clean mug were futile, so she got out the scouring pad and did her best to make a spare one less of a biohazard.

Ully Mason walked into the room behind her. The ten-year veteran stood close to her shoulder.

"What's with the fed?" he asked in a low, urgent whisper. "He looks like a fucking terrorist."

She rinsed out the mug and grabbed a paper towel. "Spew that bullshit again, Ully, and I'll report you myself."

His cheeks reddened at the rebuke.

"He's a profiler from the BAU. Here to help us figure out who did this before the town erupts." Even though she didn't trust the FBI agent, she was not about to badmouth him to other people in the department. Her father had taught her to respect her peers, whatever badge they wore.

"Hey, don't get your panties in a twist." She rolled her eyes and wondered how much trouble she'd get into if she smacked him around the back of the head. Ully cleared his throat and leaned close enough his breath brushed her ear. "I need a favor. Can you keep quiet about the fact I stopped to give out a traffic ticket on the way over?"

She frowned at him. "You were doing your job. No one is going to think the worst of you for that."

He shifted, his equipment belt creaking like an old saddle. "Yeah, but I pulled over what turned out to be a very hot blonde in a very shiny sports car and let her off with a verbal warning after she ran a red. I was in a hurry to get to you, but it isn't going to look good in any report." He wouldn't meet her gaze.

"Especially when you got her number." Dammit. Aside from the occasional unexpected bout of assholishness, Ully was a good officer. But he liked the ladies, and his uniform and good looks meant they liked him right back. "You didn't have sex with her, did you?" she asked quietly.

"No." He took a half-step away, his expression affronted.

"Shit. I was on duty. I'm not that sort of cop."

She poured coffee into two mugs and grabbed the milk out of the fridge. It was kind of depressing that she remembered Darsh Singh took a splash of milk in his. "Fine. But I'm not covering it up."

"I never asked you to lie, just not hang me out to dry."

"Hang you out to dry?" *God.* She stood still and forced herself to draw in a slow deep breath before she spoke again. "I'm not that sort of cop, either."

"Yeah, well, we all make mistakes."

Low blow. Nausea coiled hot and low in her belly. Her fist clenched around the handle of the milk jug, but she forced herself not to react in any other way.

Through the glass window, she watched Darsh cross the room toward them. Whereas Ully Mason was good-looking in a powerful, blunt, hockey player kind of way, Darsh was the classic tall, dark, and handsome. No wonder she'd been attracted to him all those years ago. He had straight black brows, sharp cheekbones, full bottom lip. His pretty face didn't diminish his masculinity. The tall broad-shouldered frame and long legs filled out those tactical clothes in a way that made women drool. All the females in the office were casting him covert looks that thanked the world for hot guys.

Maybe *that* was Ully's problem. He didn't like competition.

She, for one, wasn't interested in either of them. Not even for a no-strings hook up. There were always strings, and they were usually wrapped around her heart or her pride. Either way, they strangled self-esteem.

Darsh's hair shone blue-black in the artificial light. His jacket rustled as he stood in the doorway.

She introduced him to Ully and held out a mug. "There's sugar around here somewhere if you need it." She pointed in the general direction of the countertop.

He shook his head. "This is good. Thank you." He blew on the top and took a sip. His light brown skin gave him a healthy glow, especially in a land of shockingly white winter skin. Even her tan looked wan less than twenty-four hours back in the land of snow and ice.

Ully's stare was resentful. "Where you from originally?"

A stillness came over Darsh. The expression in those black eyes so cold it made her nape prickle.

"Quantico," he said quietly.

Ully's expression grew mulish.

She hid a smile. Ully was right about one thing. They all made mistakes—he'd clearly underestimated the fed. As much as she enjoyed watching alpha males posture, she needed to get the investigation moving. "Any luck tracking down the other roommate?"

"I found her." Dispelling the tension, Ully turned and poured himself a coffee, then stood with his back against the sink. "Tanya Whitehouse. She was at a party that was still going strong at a frat house on campus. Had her tongue down Jason Brady's throat when I got there around eleven-thirty."

Jason Brady was Drew Hawke's best friend.

She grunted. "I saw Brady on the street outside his house when I drove to Cassie's house last night. Around 10:04 PM." He'd been wearing dark track pants and a zipped hoody. Sneakers. Considering the guy was on the football team he rarely wore anything else except his Ravens' uniform on game day.

Ully continued. "They hadn't heard about the murders

when I picked Tanya up. Otherwise things might have gotten hairy."

There could have been a riot.

"She still here?" Erin asked. The hot drink was thawing out her insides. It was the first time she'd felt even vaguely human in hours.

"I dropped her back at the sorority house a few hours ago. Romano took her statement. She was pretty shook up. I told her you'd be in touch today and to stay available." Ully looked pointedly at Agent Singh. "You going to reopen the Hawke investigation?"

Erin kept her expression neutral as she watched Darsh's reaction. People around here weren't much on subtlety. It was both a blessing and a curse.

"I'm here to help find this killer." Darsh straightened, and she realized he was taller than Ully.

"The sooner the better," Ully said grimly.

"As long as we nail the right guy." The fed took another sip of coffee.

She and Ully exchanged a look.

"What's your plan of action?" Singh asked her pointedly.

She finished her coffee and quickly washed up her mug. She did not want him hanging over her shoulder, but she needed to keep an eye on him. The fact they'd slept together and that he'd obviously formed an opinion of her based on that encounter made her uncomfortable, but that was the price she'd paid for taking back control of her life. She hadn't been about to waste that opportunity or let the memory of it derail her career.

"Priority number one, I want to listen to the 911 call. Then speak to the roommate. But first I need to update my boss and see what team has been assigned to work the case and make sure everyone knows what they're supposed to be doing." Would she be in charge? She didn't know.

As if he'd heard her mention him, her boss waved them over to his office.

"Agent Singh, thanks for coming." Chief Strassen reached out to shake the fed's hand with big meaty paws. Then he led them into his office and closed the door. "I'm grateful you could start working with us on this straight away. We need the public to know that we're doing a good job at keeping them safe."

"Two dead girls tell their own story, Chief," Singh said. "You know that."

Her boss nodded, not getting pissed the way he would have if she'd voiced the same opinion.

"We need to catch this person before he hurts anyone else. Everything we have is at your disposal, Agent Singh."

Which was a joke because the two things the feds brought to the table were toys and funds.

"I appreciate that," Agent Singh inclined his head, "but all I really need is Detective Donovan's full cooperation."

The chief glanced sharply at her, and her mouth opened in surprise.

"Which she's providing," the fed added somewhat belatedly.

Her grim smile revealed her fused teeth.

Her boss relaxed. "Erin's a good cop. The Hawke conviction was solid…"

A loud unspoken "but" hung in the air.

Dammit.

"I will need a room of my own to work from," Singh said.

A short burst of laughter escaped her. Space in the nine-teen-twenties building was at a premium.

The chief's glare shut her up. "We've arranged something. It isn't perfect, but…"

Erin's eyebrows stretched high. Not even she or Harry had their own office, and she didn't see the chief willing to give up his space or enrage the secretarial staff just because a fed was in town for a day or two. They needed their one and only conference room for briefings and meeting updates.

"Barry cleared out his office and put a desk in there." The chief ran a finger inside his collar.

Barry? The janitor. "There's no natural light in that space." She leaned forward, slightly horrified they were treating a visitor this way. Not that she wanted Darsh to get too comfortable, but…

"I'm sure it'll be fine," Singh said. "As long as the door has a lock." This time it was the chief's brows that rose.

"Barry has keys to all the rooms. And Linda, the adminis-trative assistant," Erin put in helpfully. She was enjoying letting her boss squirm for a change. "Come on, I'll show you where it is."

"Meeting in the conference room at nine AM sharp," her boss yelled after her.

They walked past the locker rooms to the end of the corri-dor. The linoleum was dirty and curled up in one corner. Arrestees never saw this part of the building. They were kept on the other side of the bullpen, away from where the cops worked cases and did paperwork. The holding cells were downstairs in the basement.

She stopped at the last door on the right. There was a discolored square of wood where Barry had removed the

"Custodian" sign.

"Here it is." She opened the door and turned on the single bulb that dangled from the ceiling. The room was scrubbed clean and smelled strongly of pine disinfectant. The shelves where cleaning supplies usually sat were empty. She pushed farther inside and had to squeeze through the gap when the door refused to open all the way. A black industrial mat covered the floor drain. A battered desk took up most of the space—God knew how they got it in here. A plush office chair that looked suspiciously like hers added a little class to the cramped quarters.

Darsh came in behind her. "At least it's cozy." One side of his mouth tipped up and, for the first time, his eyes held a gleam of humor.

The moment she'd seen him walk into that bar flashed through her mind. He'd been with a group of guys all dressed the same; a bit sweaty and rumpled, as if they'd been out playing war games all day. They'd all been fit, attractive men, but she hadn't been able to take her eyes off this man here, and they both knew how that had ended up. Her heart pounded, and her face flamed with heat, unfamiliar tingles of arousal stirred her blood for the first time in years.

His gaze touched her lips, but his expression was guarded. They were both pretending that sexual attraction wasn't charging the molecules between them. That path went nowhere, and she refused to follow it.

"I'll get out of your way and let you get settled in." She went to brush past him, but he held her by the shoulders, his hands like hot brands even through her jacket.

"Tell me something?" His voice was deep and smooth like whiskey after midnight. "Does your husband know about what happened?"

She jerked out of his hold as if she'd been scalded, and knocked her head on the shelf behind her. *Goddammit.* She rubbed the sore spot. "It doesn't matter. I'm not married anymore."

"You're divorced?" His hand shot out to stop her again when she would have run.

Being manhandled was not her idea of fun, so she pried off his grip and restrained herself from breaking his fingers. "No."

She ignored his initial look of confusion and the way his eyes changed from suspicious to interested with the knowledge that her husband was dead, and she was single. She didn't owe him any explanations. And it didn't change anything between them.

"You can get supplies from the secretarial staff in the office next to Chief Strassen's. When you're ready to listen to the 911 call, come find me."

"Erin—"

"No," she cut in sharply. "It's over. Done. It didn't mean anything, and there won't be a repeat performance."

His jaw hardened, but apart from that, he didn't move. When he spoke, the anger in his voice was barely restrained. "I wasn't asking for a repeat performance. I was trying to make sense of what the hell is going on here."

She raised a brow. His expression gave nothing away, but she knew he was lying. She tapped the gold shield he'd attached to his belt, and he jolted in surprise. Maybe he thought she was going after something lower.

"The only thing going on is a murder investigation." Then she squeezed through the doorway and fled.

Her problem, she decided, striding back to her desk, was

jet-lag combined with lack of sleep, plus a horrific double homicide and the absence of a normal sex life. A splash of cold water on her face and mainlining some caffeine could help with the first two enough to get her through the next few hours. Her lack of a sex life was something she'd just have to deal with, because she wasn't opening herself up for heartbreak again. She came to an abrupt standstill as she eyed the hard plastic chair under her desk.

Get over it. A day or two at most, and Darsh Singh would be gone. She just needed to forget their past and wring as much information from him as possible so they could put this killer away. That was the only thing that mattered.

CHAPTER FIVE

D ARSH SAT AT a small table opposite Erin and Officer Bickham, the same cop who'd let him through the police tape last night. He was glad for the buffer of another person's presence. The minute he and Erin had been alone together and he'd found out she wasn't married, his attraction had ratcheted up by a factor of a million, which wasn't convenient or professional. And if she wasn't married and hadn't been divorced, then the guy was dead, and that raised a multitude of questions all on its own. Erin Donovan was a walking-talking conflict of interest.

Donovan was in charge—for now—but the chief was pushing hard for results, as the brass always did. Darsh was curious to see how that shaped her actions over the next twenty-four hours. Would she cut corners or take the easy road? It was simple enough to do both while under pressure.

"Okay. We're ready, Cathy," Erin told the officer. The team meeting was in less than thirty minutes, and they both wanted to review the 911 call ASAP.

Any good cop would.

Bickham clicked a button on the laptop. The dispatcher's voice asked the caller to state the nature of their emergency. Heavy breathing filled the air.

"*Help.*" A sob. A gulp. More labored breathing. The air in

this small cramped interview room became electrified. *"There's s-someone in my house. He's—"* A sharp gasp cut the caller off. The hair on his nape lifted as if a ghost had kissed his skin.

He and Donovan exchanged a glance.

"Is that Cassie Bressinger?" he asked.

Donovan nodded. "Sounds like her, but we can compare voice analysis to the other 911 calls and media interviews she made over the last few months to confirm." Her hands were clenched into fists on top of the table.

"Where was the call made from?" he asked.

Erin checked the number. "Cassie's cell." Which had been found at the house.

"The 911 call came in at five to ten. Officer Ully Mason caught me in the parking lot just as I was heading home at ten p.m., and I decided to attend the scene."

Ully Mason was a bigoted asshole. Did he and Donovan have a thing going? Darsh pressed the nib of his pen hard into his notepad. None of his business.

"Ully needed to gas up. I decided to drive around from the southern perimeter, which is a longer route and took me about ten minutes." Her skin paled beneath the strip light. "If I'd driven faster, or broken the door down as soon as I arrived—"

"What time did Mason arrive?" he asked.

"Around half past."

He raised his brows. That was a long time to get from A to B, although like she said, he had to gas up. "Play it again," he said.

"Help. There's s-someone in my house. He's—" A note in the woman's voice clawed his heart. Had she known the attacker was going to kill her, or did she think he'd leave her alive like the other victims from last year?

"Turn up the volume." Donovan cocked her head to listen. "I think I hear something in the background."

Officer Bickham turned the volume as high as the laptop would go, and Cassandra Bressinger's voice filled the small interview room with tinny resonance.

His skin prickled. That level of fear couldn't be faked.

"He's there with her. He's forcing her to make the call, isn't he?" Erin asked suddenly.

She had good instincts.

"Yes. I think so." The way it cut off before she gave them any relevant information. The absolute terror in her voice and the level of control she must be exerting to just keep from screaming. Cassie had been forced to deliver her message, probably knowing she was about to die.

But he noticed what Erin obviously already had. The sound of Halestorm's "In Your Room" being just discernible in the background. His hearing range had been adversely affected by the amount of shooting he'd done in the Marine Corps. He'd worn ear protectors ninety-nine percent of the time, but it was hard to run around a war zone wearing earplugs. "Good catch," he told her.

Her eyes flashed in surprise, and he found himself staring into their depths—they weren't quite blue and they weren't quite gray. The color was unique and difficult to define, a bit like their owner. He looked away, dragging his fingers through his short hair. He wanted to impress his bosses, not embarrass the hell out of them by panting after a female detective whose work he'd been sent to assess.

"That song is the one paused on Mandy's computer," he said. "So presumably the UNSUB forced Cassie to make the 911 call, and then he went through and stopped the music."

Why?

Darsh blocked everything out. Put himself in the zone. "We know the one roommate, Tanya, left for a party around eight and the other one, Alicia, wasn't expected home until ten." Had the UNSUB studied the girls' schedule? Had he been watching the house? "During that two-hour time window, the UNSUB gets into the house, goes up the stairs. Attacks Cassie, ties her to the bed…" He shook his head. "I can't believe he would risk raping Cassie until he knew Mandy wasn't a threat."

"He didn't have time to rape and kill them both in the fifteen minutes it took me to arrive after the 911 call," Erin said.

She was right.

He checked the length of the song: two minutes forty-seven seconds. "And I have trouble believing he would call the cops until he was finished and ready to leave. So Mandy was probably the first victim, and the music disguised the attack on her, and also masked his preliminary assault on Cassie." The one where the killer had incapacitated and threatened her enough to force her to make the call. "He made her record the message, presumably using his cell phone." Darsh would bet his favorite rifle he'd recorded more than just that. "Then he called dispatch with Cassie's phone and played her message back just prior to exiting the crime scene."

Erin splayed her fingers on the surface of the table. "So they were already dead when we got the call?"

Darsh held her somber gaze. "I think so. The ME should be able to tell us more."

Some of the tension eased from her shoulders though her fingers clenched briefly. No matter how fast she'd driven, or whether or not she'd smashed down the door on arrival, she'd never had a chance of saving those young women.

Darsh didn't like the way he'd started to empathize with Erin on this. He was investigating her competence as an officer, not her emotional wellbeing. He couldn't allow his feelings to compromise his effectiveness.

"Maybe the ME can tell us which girl died first?" she said.

"Knowing which girl died first might help us pin down the killer's MO. Doesn't bring us any closer to motive aside from personal gratification."

She took a sip of black coffee, and he found himself mirroring her actions. Damn. He put the cup back down. So did she.

"It seems to me…" The rookie officer volunteered an opinion in the awkward silence.

He waited while Cathy Bickham swallowed noisily.

"Well, usually when someone reports a crime they go on the cops' radar as either a witness or a possible suspect. By making Cassie report the crime herself, he took that out of the equation."

"Good point," he said.

"But why call it in at all? A few minutes later Alicia would arrive home from the library and find the bodies," said Erin. "This seems like a deliberate taunt to law enforcement."

"Or he was punishing the girls by making them phone it in," Darsh argued. "We all know what's supposed to happen when you cry wolf."

"Everyone in town knew about those calls," said Erin. "It was reported in the local paper."

She shrugged out of her suit jacket, revealing a tight and fitted white shirt. The fact his gaze wanted to linger on the faint outline of lacy straps in the middle of a murder investigation pissed him off.

He'd always prided himself on his control. He wasn't driven by impulse or desire. He was meticulous, dedicated, and hardworking. But more than that, he knew how damaging it could be when people selfishly went after what they wanted regardless of others. It wasn't who he wanted to be. He forced his brain back to what was important—the job, the case.

"My being a law enforcement officer never slowed Cassie down any." Erin's voice dropped lower. "She was smart and strong, a fighter. I think she would have fought him before he overpowered her, which is maybe why he hurt her so badly."

Sometimes people didn't fight at all. They shut down and waited for it to be over. It was probably the strongest survival instinct when faced with someone stronger, and more violent. Survival involved many things—fight, flight, endurance, and chance. Many rape victims froze and berated themselves for it. Many acted in ways that made no sense to observers dissecting events afterwards. Often victims couldn't remember the details of the attack because their brain shut down so they could get through the experience alive. Losing the battle to win the war? Maybe. Whatever it was, defense attorneys loved it.

Erin checked her wristwatch. "Time to head to the team meeting."

Darsh needed to set up a detailed timeline of the crime but in the meantime, he jotted notes to himself. The rookie scooped up the laptop with the recording.

He pointed to it with his pen. "Cathy, I'd like a copy of that call sent to me, please." He fished a card from his wallet. "I'm going to submit it to our lab for analysis. In fact, I'd like all the evidence shipped to Quantico ASAP. I've been

67

promised it will get maximum priority."

"How long before we get results?" asked Erin.

"Possibly by the end of the week." Brennan had promised Darsh he'd put the burners under the lab techs and jump the queue.

"Well, thank God for the FBI. I might start a cheer club." Erin flashed him a quick smile, momentarily forgetting she didn't like him very much.

"We aim to please."

Erin's pupils flared. And suddenly there was that awareness arcing between them like lightning in a storm.

Bickham cleared her throat, oblivious to the sexual undertones simmering between him and Donovan. "That'll be great, Agent Singh, thanks."

"Call me Darsh." He gave the officer his best smile.

"Yes, sir." Bickham nodded and quickly left.

"Why's she so nervous?" he asked Erin after the rookie was gone, grateful to have something other than them or the case to discuss.

Erin tapped her pen on the table as she read some notes she'd made in her book. "I think she's a little in awe of the fact you're FBI," she said absently. "She told me once it's her ultimate dream to become an agent."

"I can give her some advice about the application process when she's ready. If she wants."

Erin smiled and Darsh stared like a fool. He kept forgetting how incredibly pretty she was when she wasn't spitting mad at him.

"I'm sure she'd appreciate that." She stood, leaning a hip against the table, crossing her arms, revealing cleavage, badge, and sidearm. His skin got tight. His neck hot. "She also tends to be swayed by pretty faces."

He stilled. Raised his chin. "You think I have a pretty face?"

"No." Erin gave him a smirk that told him she knew exactly what he was thinking before she gathered up her notes. "But she does." With that she left the room with an arrogant swagger to her hips.

He found himself grinning. Then he stopped smiling and climbed slowly to his feet. He was in danger of starting to like her all over again. *And you're investigating whether or not she screwed up badly enough to send an innocent kid to prison, not to mention get two girls killed.*

Yeah. And that.

———————

THE CRUSHING WEIGHT that had settled on Erin's chest when she'd first seen the two murdered girls had lifted a little at the knowledge they were probably already dead by the time the 911 call came in. But ten hours later, she came out of the team meeting no closer to finding this killer than when she'd first rolled up to the girls' front door.

The TV news blared in the background, rerunning the footage of black body bags being loaded into the Medical Examiner's wagon. Reporters had flocked back to town like vultures circling a kill. The smart money was on her for being the number one carcass of choice.

So much for that vacation.

Harry Compton, her fellow detective, was working through the social media stuff and contacting the cell companies for records of calls and voice messages. Physical evidence was being couriered to Quantico and fast-tracked for analysis. That alone told her someone higher up than Agent Singh was pulling the strings.

Everyone on the sex register list had an alibi for Monday night. There were no easy suspects.

No sheets had been found in any dumpster inside the town limits. Uniforms were continuing to canvass the neighborhood, talking to people who'd been out the first time they'd knocked on doors. That was the cornerstone of good police work—canvassing and asking the same question over and over again. Now she and Agent Singh were off to interview Tanya Whitehouse and Alicia Drummond, both of whom were staying at their sorority house. Then she had a date at the morgue, followed by another team meeting at three.

She was a little surprised she had the lead on this, but figured it would make it easier to fire her if she didn't make an arrest. How long would they give her to get results? A day? A week?

"We'll take your car," she informed Darsh as she caught up with him outside the chief's office. "They know mine on campus, and I wouldn't put it past someone to slash the tires."

He grimaced. "That popular?" He pulled out his keys and they headed down the steps towards the rental.

"As spare ribs at a vegan barbecue," she told him.

The reporters, who'd been made to assemble on one side of the parking lot, started baying for blood when they saw her. She ignored them and the biting cold that wanted to sink into her flesh. Darsh pressed his key fob, and she got into his vehicle, appreciating the comfort of the soft leather seats.

"Quite the fan club you have around here. How do you cope with all the adulation?"

Apparently she didn't have the monopoly on sarcasm. "It's easy. I have a badge and a gun, and I know how to use it." She pulled a face, needing a little honesty. "I do my job, even when no one likes the results." She put on her seat belt, uncomfortably aware of the proximity to the rock hard body she'd once investigated naked. To her consternation, she realized her backside and thighs were getting hot. Heated seats. Thank God. "This is a lot more swank than my truck."

"You don't seem like the truck type." He started the engine and backed out of the space.

"What do you mean?"

"More a hybrid SUV kind of person."

She snorted.

The press would be trying to run his plates before they got around the block. What would they make of the fact there was an FBI profiler on the case? The chief would probably tell them soon anyway. Anything to feed the maw of the beast.

She shrugged. "I needed a vehicle that was good in the snow and that I could use to transport furniture when I moved up here from Queens."

"When did you leave the NYPD?"

The innocent question brought back all sorts of painful memories. "Take a left out of here and a right on Main." She hoped he'd forget the question.

No such luck.

"So when you started working here is privileged information?"

"If I had a choice my whole life would be privileged information." The defensive edge to her voice gave away too much. He'd find out if he wanted to, and now she'd made it into a *thing*. Damn. "Three years ago."

"Not long after we hooked up?"

Fiery heat worked its way across her cheeks at the reminder. "Three months after my training course with the Bureau, yes. You turn right in about half a mile."

She watched his fingers handle the steering wheel. Long and tapered. Short, clean nails. She remembered them drifting over her skin.

She jolted when he spoke.

"I take it your husband didn't come with you?"

She fought the urge to retch. "No."

"How come?"

She glared at him in silence.

"You know I can find out." He shrugged those impressive shoulders, and Erin wished she was a better liar.

"Have fun with that." But all he needed to do was read the newspaper reports surrounding the trial. Reporters had had a great time digging into her "tragic" past.

"I'm not trying to be an asshole here, but—"

"But you have an issue with having had sex with a married woman. Trust me, I got it when you slammed out of the hotel room that morning."

"That's not what I was going to say—"

"You think anyone who cheats is inherently untrustworthy."

He drew in an audible breath. "You broke *vows*, Erin. Isn't that the definition of untrustworthy?"

She stuffed her hands in her pockets to hide the fact they were shaking. "Then you know everything you need to know about me. Let's leave it at that."

Another long, loud exhale suggested he was trying to hold onto his temper. "You're putting words into my mouth. That's usually a deflection tactic."

"Deflection from what? You asked why the man I married didn't come with me when I moved here? He died. Okay?" Shame rose up inside her. "And you want to know if he knew about the fact you and I hooked up?" She forced herself to say it casually, like one night stands were something she did all the time. "He didn't."

"Good."

He swallowed her explanation, which inexplicably made her resent him more. "I guess I should have picked one of your buddies to take home from that bar, huh? Someone with less of a conscience." She gave a sharp laugh. Jesus, he was going to think she was a lunatic.

His eyes narrowed, and his fingers tightened on the steering wheel. "I guess you should have." But the expression on his face told a different story. Anger drew his features tight. A vein pulsed in his neck.

A sane person would tell him the truth, but it was so ugly. And she didn't want forgiveness or understanding, especially from this man. The less he liked her, the less this attraction between them would be a problem.

"Maybe we should stick to discussing the case?" he said, finally.

Exactly what she'd wanted, except now she felt like her insides had been scraped raw. "That would probably be best."

"Tell me about the evidence you gathered from the other crime scenes."

She pressed her lips tight together. Reviewing the evidence for the other case didn't mean she'd made the wrong collar. "We found hair at the scene of one of the rapes last year that belonged to Drew Hawke."

"But no semen, right?"

"No semen," she agreed. "He wore a condom." The image of Cassie's naked body flashed through her mind, and she huddled deeper into her jacket. The idea of being that exposed and vulnerable destroyed her. "We might get luckier this time."

"Perhaps. Taking the sheet is a good way of removing trace evidence and shows some knowledge of forensics. Not to mention the bleach. Hawke never admitted taking the sheets?"

She shook her head. "And we never found them."

"It's an unusual MO," he said.

"Hawke didn't even admit to having ever seen the other women, let alone raping them. He didn't use the 'I thought it was consensual sex' defense, which is so much easier to defend against." And which led to so many victim-blaming situations and "not guilty" verdicts in court. The case had been such a landmark victory with the university and the establishment standing so firmly with the rape victims in this high-profile case. She didn't want to think what that would mean if she'd arrested the wrong guy.

"You sound like you have doubts." He shot her a sideways glance.

"I don't like having two dead women in my jurisdiction, and I'm not about to stick my head in the sand when there are obvious similarities between the crimes. Doesn't mean I don't think he did it. Take a left up here." She was a detective, and detectives looked at the evidence.

They drove in silence, each wrapped up in their own thoughts. Another five minutes, and they pulled up outside the sprawling pale green sorority house.

"The girls met here in their freshman year and moved out

together as sophomores," she told him.

Darsh stared at the building for a moment, making no move to get out of the car. "I've never understood the appeal of fraternities."

"Me, either," she agreed. "I lived at home all through college and shared a room with my younger sister. She's messier than a houseful of frat boys." She missed her family even when they annoyed the crap out of her.

"I stayed in residence," he said.

"The whole time?" She undid her seatbelt and put her hand on the door handle, pausing before she got out.

"I dropped out of college after two years. Joined the Marine Corps."

"So you really *were* a Marine." That amused her until she realized he'd probably joined up after 9/11. It had been a terrible time to be in NYC; the endless list of victims, many of whom she and her family had known. Firefighters she'd gone to school with. And a lot of people had gotten sick afterwards. It was a miracle her family hadn't lost anyone.

A lot of people had heeded the call to serve their country after that nightmarish day. It had changed the course of US history. "I guess the Marines are a fraternity of sorts."

"Ooh Rah."

"You miss it." She detected the affection in his voice, the fierce pride.

"The Corps was fun. War not so much." His expression closed down, and she knew better than to push it.

"Well, you didn't move far." Quantico wasn't just the home of the FBI, it was also a USMC base.

His smile was crooked. "I was based in California. Twenty-nine Palms but, yeah, I spent some time in Quantico for training courses."

She looked into those ridiculously dark eyes and that beautiful smile and found herself catching her breath as her heart did gymnastics in her chest. Then the air in her lungs seized, and she pushed her way out of the car before anything stupid came out of her mouth. God, she was so blonde sometimes.

So he was good-looking. So what? She rolled her eyes at herself. She had a job to do. Justice to serve. She led the way up the path to the front porch. Darsh joined her as she rang the bell.

The door opened, and an attractive woman in her fifties stood there.

"Mrs. Conway," Erin said. They'd met during her investigation last year. "This is FBI Agent Singh. We're here to see Tanya and Alicia."

"We've been expecting you." Mrs. Conway was the house mother and made sure the rules were followed, girls were fed, and curfew enforced. "They're in the dining room. Come in."

Even though it went against everything she'd been taught growing up, Erin didn't take her boots off at the door, and neither did Darsh. If the situation went south the last thing she needed was to be in her stockinged feet. She wiped the soles of her boots thoroughly and winced as she crossed the pristine floor in the wake of the trim figure of Mrs. Conway.

"We'd like to interview them separately if possible," Erin said to the woman's retreating back.

"Not without a lawyer, I'm afraid. If you want to wait, we can call one."

Erin eyed Darsh, but he shook his head. The girls had both made written statements and had enough time to share stories anyway. It probably didn't matter.

They walked into the dining room with its enormous table and about twenty chairs. Tanya and Alicia sat at one end of the table cradling steaming cups of coffee.

"Would you like coffee? Tea?" Mrs. Conway asked. "I have some made in the kitchen."

"Appreciate it," Erin accepted for them both, anything to get the woman out of the room.

Tanya was wearing pajamas and wrapped up in a fleece blanket. Alicia was still wearing the clothes she'd worn last night when Erin had met her in the street. Both girls eyed her warily. "This is Agent Singh from the FBI. He's helping us with our investigation."

Alicia's gaze sharpened, and both girls looked at Darsh with a mixture of trepidation and female curiosity. The guy was hot. You'd have to be dead not to notice.

Not where her thoughts wanted to go, on any level.

Erin sat down and retrieved her notebook from her pocket. Then held up her digital voice recorder. "Do you mind if I record this?"

Tanya shook her head.

"But it isn't admissible as evidence," Alicia insisted.

"Evidence? I'm just trying to piece together the timeline from last night. It'll be easier to refer to the recording than track you down every time I have a question. Yes?"

Alicia looked away and nodded. She obviously regretted throwing herself into Erin's arms last night. Erin wouldn't hold it against her.

"What time did you go out last night, Tanya?"

"I left just after eight. Probably five minutes past. My friend Jillian picked me up, and we went to a party across the road from here."

"Mandy and Cassie were both in the house when you left?"

Tanya sniffed and her eyes started streaming again. "Mandy was in her room writing a paper. Cassie was lying on her bed reading a magazine. She said she didn't want to come to the party because she had an assignment due, but really she didn't want to see anyone who reminded her of Drew."

Erin hadn't seen a magazine in her room. She saw Darsh's gaze sharpen. He was probably thinking the same thing.

"What frame of mind were they both in?"

"Mandy was desperate to get an A to keep up her GPA. She was hoping to get into the honors program with Professor Huxley."

"He's a criminology professor here at Blackcombe," Erin told Darsh.

"Cassie was down over Drew."

The glare sent in her direction was duly noted and ignored. "Did you lock the front door when you left?"

Tanya's mouth dropped open. "Are you trying to blame me?" She averted her gaze to the ceiling and muttered, "Fucking bitch."

"Tanya!" Mrs. Conway reprimanded sharply as she entered the room with a tray of fresh coffee and a glare for her charges. "That's no way to talk to the detective."

Tanya hunched down into her seat.

"Detective Donovan is trying to figure out how the UNSUB got into the house." Darsh's voice was velvet smooth. "There's no sign of forced entry so the door was either unlocked, picked, or the UNSUB had a key."

Both girls' eyes went wide, and matching expressions of horror stretched their features.

"I locked the door handle, but I didn't turn the deadbolt," Tanya admitted. "It's what we all did."

"The back door was also locked?" Erin asked.

"Yes. We always kept the back door dead-bolted. We don't go out there much in the winter except to put out the garbage."

"Was the party you went to last night common knowledge?" Erin asked.

Tanya shrugged and looked at her friend. "I dunno. I always hear about them because Jillian dates a guy who lives there. They aren't secret, but not everyone is allowed in."

Erin looked at Alicia. "You were in the library studying?"

The girl nodded. "We have exams at the end of January."

"Did you tell people you were going to be out of your house?" Erin pressed.

Alicia looked at her like she was crazy. "My study group knows, and my housemates. Who else would I tell? People see me there, sure, but I don't put my location on social media. I'm not an idiot."

How had the UNSUB known there were only two women to deal with, or had he gone in prepared to kill all four? Two showed a high degree of confidence. The idea he'd been willing to handle four scared the crap out of Erin.

"You often stay at the library until closing?" she pushed.

Alicia nodded. "Until 10 p.m. every weeknight. Not Fridays, Saturdays, or Sundays. It's about a fifteen-minute walk."

"You walk alone?"

"Only from the bottom of our street. One of my study partners lives a street over."

Darsh interrupted. "Did you see anyone in the street, or any cars you didn't recognize?"

Tanya shook her head. "I wasn't paying attention. I was happy to see Jillian after the Christmas break, and I was talking about Cassie, and how sad it was she was wasting her life on a guy who was stuck in prison." A harsh sob ripped out of her throat, and she covered her mouth as if trying to stuff it back inside.

"Did Cassie correspond with Drew Hawke?" Darsh asked.

Erin threw him a grateful look. If she brought up Drew's name, she was liable to be spat on. Having the fed around might come in handy.

Tanya cleared her throat. "Yes, she wrote him every day."

"He write her back?" Darsh asked.

Alicia sneered pointedly in Erin's direction. "He doesn't have much else to do, does he?"

"She'd got a letter from him that day." Tanya frowned as if remembering. "She was reading it on the bed."

So where were the letters? She and Darsh exchanged a look. Had the UNSUB taken them? Was he fixated on Drew Hawke? Or had they been partners?

"Is there anyone new in your lives? Friends, boyfriends, neighbors?"

Alicia crossed her arms. "No."

Tanya shook her head. "We've been pretty subdued these last few months. We haven't been out much."

Erin scrolled through some photographs on her phone and carefully found one of the rope. She zoomed in so Cassie's body wasn't visible.

"Do you recognize this rope?" First she showed Tanya, who shook her head.

Alicia blanched as she recognized it from the crime scene last night. "No. It's not from the house that I know of."

Erin nodded and slipped her phone back into her pocket. She turned off her recorder and snapped her notebook closed. "That's all we need for now."

"How long until the girls can move back home?" Mrs. Conway asked. Ever the practical one of the bunch.

Tanya huddled into her blanket. "I'm never living there again."

"It'll be at least a week until the crime scene is released." Erin addressed the house mother. "But I can have an officer escort the girls to pick up some of their belongings today if they like. I'd really like you to think hard about seeing anyone in the street or hanging around last night—"

"It's the same guy who raped those girls last year, isn't it?" Tanya turned accusing brown eyes on her. "Drew's innocent, isn't he? Cassie was right, and the bastard killed her to prove it."

Alicia covered her mouth and sobbed. "Poor Mandy. She wanted to help catch these assholes. But we all know Mandy wasn't the main target. I saw the bodies. She was collateral damage the same way Tanya and I would have been if we'd been home."

"Don't talk like that!" Tanya gasped.

"It's true."

The sound of the front door crashing open reverberated throughout the house. Erin braced herself when she heard shouting in the hallway.

"Where is she? Where's that bitch!"

Here we go. She went into the main hallway, conscious of Darsh at her side. Would he back her up or watch the situation play out? Jason Brady and a bunch of Blackcombe Ravens football players stood in the doorway. Brady spotted her and immediately strode across and leaned down until they were nose to nose. Stale beer saturated his breath.

"I just heard two girls were raped and murdered last night in the exact same way you arrested Drew for." He jabbed two fingers into her chest. She gave him that one. "Is that enough evidence that he didn't do it?"

She shoved his hand away. "You need to calm down, Brady. This is an ongoing investigation, and you were not invited to this interview."

"Back off, pal." Darsh pushed against Brady's shoulder.

"Who the fuck are you?" Brady swiped at his arm.

"Agent Singh, FBI." At least the fed sounded cool under pressure. "Let the detective do her job."

"If she could do her fucking job, Drew wouldn't be rotting in a fucking prison cell."

"Back off, Brady. That is your last warning," she told him.

Jason Brady played wide receiver and was six foot four inches of pure muscle. His pals were wider and meaner looking. Brady leaned so close his stale beer breath brushed over her face. "Or what, bitch?"

It was the spittle on her cheek that sealed the deal. Two seconds later, she had Brady flat on the floor with his arm pinned high behind his back as she dug the cuffs out of her pocket.

"Jason Brady, I'm arresting you for threatening behavior. Assault of an officer." She snapped the cuffs around one thick wrist. Jesus, the guy was strong. She didn't ease up on the grip she had on him even though it had to be excruciating. The knucklehead seemed oblivious to pain. She checked behind her and half-expected a riot, but Darsh stood planted in front of her, stance wide, weapon in hand in a come-and-get-some-if-you-dare challenge. A huge guy who played defenseman lay on the floor, out cold.

Mrs. Conway took control and started hustling the students out of her hallway—more effective than either the cops or the FBI in restoring order.

Erin radioed for backup and a cruiser to transport Brady to the station. She jerked the young man unceremoniously to his feet and marched him out the door into the frigid January air. A growing crowd of onlookers was forming on the grass outside; murmurs grew into yells of outrage when they spotted Brady in cuffs. The atmosphere became downright ominous.

No time to wait for backup. Darsh opened the rear door of his rental, and she stuffed Brady inside, secured his seatbelt, surprised when he didn't struggle. He glared at her with such intense hatred in his eyes it made her stomach clench.

"Get in," Darsh ordered her.

She glanced up to see some of the football players coming purposefully toward them. She slammed the door and walked calmly to the passenger door and climbed in. The fed immediately pulled away from the curb, and she turned in the seat to keep an eye on their prisoner.

"Were you born a misandrist or did you grow into it?" Brady asked with a sneer from the back seat.

"Fancy words," she said, eyeing him thoughtfully. "I always forget you're a smart guy under the Neanderthal. The only word I usually hear come out of your mouth begins with 'c' and rhymes with grunt."

"You're going to regret this. I haven't done anything wrong. Then again neither did Drew, did he?"

Darsh eyed him in the rear view mirror. "You crossed a line back there, pal. You received several warnings and still put your hands on a police officer. This is your own fault."

"You must be fucking her to defend her," Brady said bitterly. "I always wondered how any guy could get it up for such a cold bitch. Despite the hot little package, I bet it's like nailing a corpse."

Erin glared.

Darsh thankfully said nothing.

But Brady wasn't done. "Your husband couldn't stand it, could he?"

Erin's flesh turned to ice.

"Blew his brains out rather than face life with you."

Erin ignored the stiffening of Darsh's hands on the wheel and forced herself to hold the student's vitriolic gaze. Never show fear. She raised her chin. "Keep talking, Brady. It's all fodder for the police report."

At that he shut his mouth, but insolently looked her over like he could see her naked. He hated her all right. She stared right back as her brain ticked over. Her cell rang. She checked it and mentally groaned. The Dean of Students was on the line. The guy had been very supportive of the rape victims last year, but with two new murdered students and the fact she'd just arrested another of his football players, he wasn't likely to be happy.

She let the call go to voicemail.

It crossed her mind that Jason Brady had been in the courtroom almost every day last fall. He knew every detail of the crimes, and he would do almost anything to get his buddy out of prison. Would that include killing Hawke's girlfriend? The idea ticked like a bomb in her brain. If it went off, the whole town was gonna explode.

CHAPTER SIX

H E DROVE UP to the old farmhouse, careful to keep his tires in the established ruts. The snow was compacted almost to solid ice. The tires on his vehicle, even if they left tread marks, were so generic they weren't likely to be traced in the unlikely event Erin noticed them and became suspicious.

She'd be tied up for most of the day with the investigation, but he was still taking a risk coming here. A calculated risk.

Taking care of Mandy had been more difficult than he'd expected. As much as he'd wanted to cover her face afterwards, he couldn't risk it. Depersonalizing the victim revealed too much about the killer. Even so, he hadn't been able to strip her or touch her the way he'd originally intended. Thankfully, he'd been able to do the deed without her seeing his face.

Killing Cassie hadn't been hard at all—what a *bitch*. His waist still stung from where she'd clawed him with her inch-long nails. Hitting her had been surprisingly arousing—an unexpected result from his change in tactics. He'd taken out his anger and frustration on the irritating bitch and enjoyed every fucking moment. It had been messier than he expected. He'd made her pay for that.

The look on her face when he'd had her all tied up. The understanding in her eyes when she realized what he'd done, and what he was about to do. It was enough to make him hard all over again.

Smoke poured out of a chimney, telling him the furnace had kicked on. He turned off the car engine and got out. Raised his face to the perfect blue of the sky as the cold wind whispered across his cheeks. It was quiet here. Peaceful. He'd visited a few times. He liked it.

He walked up to the backdoor and inserted the key he'd had cut after he'd borrowed the original, and slipped inside. The floorboards creaked beneath his feet. The kitchen was large, but old fashioned, and Erin hadn't really touched this room yet.

He ran his hand over the raised grain in the old farmhouse table and glanced around. The mail was stacked on the counter. She probably hadn't had time to go through it yet after her vacation.

He belonged here. He'd help her with this case now that he'd forgiven her for ignoring him yesterday. She'd probably been tired after her long flight. Well, she'd be a lot more tired now.

It was a lesson, and he was the teacher.

He wandered into the dining room. Last Christmas she'd stripped out the lath and plaster and replaced the wiring and insulation, and her brothers had come up and put up drywall. She'd never entertained a boyfriend here that he knew about. The thought settled him. Reminded him it was just a matter of time until she realized they were supposed to be together.

Swatches of paint in various colors dotted the opposite wall. His favorite was a dark mossy green, but he had a feeling she'd go with the amber. In the living room, she'd gotten as far as gutting the place and inserting the insulation. Plasterboard was stacked on the floor, but she must be waiting for her family to visit again before finishing it off. The floors were hardwood, and they looked scuffed, but he had no doubt that by the time she was finished, they'd gleam.

She was building a home for them, she just hadn't realized it yet.

His foot hit the bottom stair and with it, a growing sense of anticipation. The bare wooden boards creaked. He listened to them and mentally catalogued which to avoid should he need to move silently around Erin's house.

He smiled as he pictured coming upon her in the bedroom while carrying a large bouquet of red roses. Her eyes would widen and soften. She'd invite him into her bed.

He'd been angry with her yesterday, but it had made him realize this was the way things needed to be. Soon, she'd have no one else to turn to. No one who believed in her, who loved her—except him. He'd be there for her. He'd love her. And she'd love him right back.

She'd renovated four rooms upstairs, the bathroom, master bedroom, a spare bedroom, and an office. He walked into her room and drew in a deep breath. Subtly sweet, like the almond shampoo she favored. Her bed was unmade. Nightshirt and panties scattered on the floor. Even the idea of touching them turned him on, but he ignored the sensation, letting it grow in the back of his mind.

Her suitcase sat on the floor, lid open against the end of the bed, belongings still inside. There was a fine residue of sand in the base. He touched the grit and then pulled out her sunscreen. Sniffed it and imagined himself lying beside her on the beach spreading this across her soft, smooth skin.

He hooked her bikini with one finger and dangled it in the air. It was grass green, and there was barely enough to cover the bases. He whistled appreciatively. She'd look good in that. Something red and shiny caught his attention. His erection nearly burst out of his jeans as he held a pair of satin panties to his nose and inhaled the musky scent of the most incredible woman on the planet.

She wasn't perfect. She was dedicated and driven, beautiful and compassionate. Even thinking about the shape of her lips when she frowned aroused him.

He knew he shouldn't take the risk, but he lay on the bed, undid his jeans, and wrapped the panties around his aching cock.

Lying in Erin's bed with her scent surrounding him, it didn't take long for him to climax. Afterwards, he lay staring at the ceiling Erin stared at every night, his head cradled by her pillow. His heart rate slowed as he thought about the flak she was going to get. His joy soured.

It was necessary.

She was going to get hurt.

But he'd be there to help pick up the pieces.

He cleaned himself up and stuffed the panties in his pocket. He should burn them, but he wouldn't. He'd wash them and bring them back another day, and it would be a thrill knowing they shared this secret connection.

A car engine roared in the distance, and he froze. Then the noise drifted away from the farmhouse, and he relaxed. He headed swiftly back downstairs. He needed to be careful. Not only was the FBI involved, the press were also sneaking around. He couldn't afford to get lazy or complacent. If this plan worked, he was going to be the hero *and* get the girl. Now was his time to shine.

JASON BRADY DIDN'T have a clue about women if he thought Erin Donovan was frigid, although the stubborn cop did try to convince the world she was a cold-hearted bitch. Darsh knew better. He glanced at her profile out of his peripheral vision, but she was staring straight ahead. *Had* her husband blown his brains out? Or was Brady spouting bullshit?

Darsh had a lot of questions. He'd spoken to Jed Brennan earlier and confirmed to his boss the unstable situation in the town with its simmering tension just waiting to explode. He'd also asked for whatever background information he could get on Erin Donovan.

The ME cleared his throat and brought Darsh back to the cool white room with its steel benches and incandescent lighting. The dab of Vicks VapoRub under his nostrils didn't mask the smell of death. The exposed corpses of the two young women made him wonder if he'd made a mistake joining BAU-4 investigating crimes against adults. God knew, he'd already seen enough death to last a lifetime.

It didn't help that every time he went near an autopsy room, he was reminded of his mother. She'd ended up on a slab in a cold room surrounded by strangers with some guy opening her chest and weighing her heart—assuming she'd had one.

The counterterrorism unit, BAU-1, played more to his strengths. Three years ago, just before he'd met Erin, the Washington Field Office had become aware of an active terrorist cell in DC. Darsh had been on rotation with BAU-1 and had volunteered to go undercover.

The major advantage of his less than pearly-white complexion was if he grew a jihadi beard and stuck a prayer mat under his arm, he could pass for someone of Middle Eastern origin. With his looks, language skills, and military experience, he'd been in his element. He'd just pretended to be on the other side of the Abrams tanks during the fall of Baghdad. He'd helped the FBI and Homeland foil a plot to blow up the DC Metro. They'd swept up those bastards in an operation that had taken the extremists by complete surprise. He'd taken great satisfaction in arresting the ringleader who'd "recruited" him.

Darsh had gotten happy drunk that weekend with the rest of his buddies, knowing they were lucky to have avoided a major catastrophe. Now he stared at the bodies of two young women, and the world once again felt off kilter. He rubbed his eyes. Maybe he should have joined HRT like they'd asked him to, but the idea of looking down his scope and taking more lives made him sick to his stomach. It wasn't an issue he advertised to his bosses or co-workers. He'd do his job, but he didn't get a thrill from handing out a death sentence every time he took a shot.

He averted his eyes from Mandy Wochikowski's chest as an assistant ME sewed up the Y-incision.

It was one thing to die as a soldier. You picked up your weapon and made your choice. But murder was a violation. Murder was inherently wrong. Murder was also his job—a job where he got to make a difference by taking bad guys off the streets. Bad guys who enjoyed raping and murdering men and women like these. He might not like dealing with victims, but he sure as hell enjoyed nailing the killers.

Erin stood quietly beside him, waiting for the ME to finish the post. Self-contained. Professional.

Personal considerations aside, she seemed like a good cop—smart, dedicated, not afraid to swim against the tide if that's where the evidence took her. But had she misread that evidence? Made a mistake? Maybe she wasn't as smart as he thought she was. He needed to be objective about her and not fall for the kickass cop in an angel's body.

That scene on campus this morning had blown up out of nowhere. No wonder the DOJ was worried about this situation being a tinderbox. Erin had handled Jason Brady with surprising ease, although Darsh was glad he'd been there to back her up. The situation was too volatile for her to be riding alone. Brady had been ready to light the fuse that the girls' murders had provided and had almost caused a riot. The asshole was now cooling his jets in holding. They'd probably release him with a warning.

"So to recap." The ME's voice once again dragged Darsh's wandering thoughts back to the impersonal sterile room. The steel top table. "We've found no semen. No ketamine in either girl's system. Scrapings from fingernails and swabs for contact DNA have been bagged and prepped to be shipped to the lab at Quantico. Cassie's fingertips were dipped in bleach and then rinsed in water. We might find something, but the killer certainly stacked the odds in his favor."

Other physical evidence had been a bust except for the hair they'd found on Mandy's sweater, which could have come from the killer or from a girl standing next to her in the line at Starbucks.

"He probably wore latex gloves *and* a condom," Darsh muttered.

"Unless he wore a rubber suit there are still some places we might find skin cells. Don't give up all hope, Agent Singh,"

Dr. Grice chided.

But even if they found DNA, it didn't mean they'd get a name. DNA profiles had to match a known offender in CODIS, and he had a feeling this UNSUB was too meticulous for that to happen. Or maybe this *was* his first rodeo. He'd studied hard and knew how to leave as few clues as possible…

"Cause of Death—asphyxiation. Note the petechial hemorrhaging in the whites of the eyes. They were both strangled, although in different ways. Mandy from behind, probably in an arm lock." Dr. Grice demonstrated the move holding his arm angled across his own chest. "Cassie was strangled from the front, the assailant wrapping his hands around her throat and squeezing hard from above. Her hyoid bone cracked. Trachea crushed. Cassie appears to have been raped, but Mandy showed no sign of sexual assault."

Just strangled.

Darsh's stomach churned. Maybe his dad was right, and this job was a way of punishing himself for all the people he'd killed.

"Manner of Death—homicide," the ME declared. Like there had been any doubt.

"TOD?" Erin asked.

"There's always room for error, but at an average temp of 72F, the body stays about the same temp for the first hour after death, then decreases 1-1.5 degrees per hour thereafter. I adjusted for when the cops arrived and the resultant decrease in ambient temperature when you guys left the doors open at around three. I took my own readings and compared them to the local weather station."

Math and death. Odd bedfellows. It reminded Darsh of all the bullet trajectory and windage calculations he used to do in his head on those rooftops in Baghdad.

"Liver temp suggests they both died between eight and nine last night. It's a guess, but it's an educated guess," the ME finished.

So the killer had spent some time in the house after he'd killed the girls. Cleaning up? Destroying DNA? Arranging the bodies? Finding letters? Having fun.

"Any idea which girl died first?" Erin asked.

Dr. Grice pulled a thoughtful face. "They both have similar body types. Mandy's temp was almost identical to Cassie's, but Mandy was fully dressed whereas Cassie was nude." The guy scrunched his face as if thinking hurt his brain. "Theoretically, Mandy would cool more slowly than Cassie. If I had to pick who died first, I'd say Mandy for the reasons I stated, but there's only an hour or so in it."

"So it's likely the UNSUB entered the house, killed Mandy, then attacked Cassie—"

"The music bothers me in this timeline. He recorded that message from Cassie and then walked through and shut off the music?"

Erin frowned, her hands resting on her hips. "Okay, so as soon as Tanya leaves for the party, he lets himself in, kills Mandy using her music to hide the noise of the struggle from Cassie. Then, still using the music to disguise his actions, he attacks Cassie, ties her up, makes her record the 911 message, and then goes and turns off the music? Why would he bother turning it off?"

Darsh put himself in the place of the killer. He'd already killed one girl and had the other under his control but wanted to play with her... "To make sure no one walked in on him unaware. So he could concentrate on what he wanted to do to

93

Cassie and not get caught."

Erin's lips pinched. "What's to stop Cassie screaming for help?"

"I found traces of rubber in her teeth," Dr. Grice put in.

"Ball gag?" Darsh asked.

"Probably," the ME agreed.

The skin between Erin's eyebrows tugged downward.

"Which he also took with him after he raped and killed her. So why not take the rope?" asked Darsh.

"He staged the scenes exactly as he wanted us to find them. Taking what he wanted from Cassie's room," Erin stated.

The letters from Drew Hawke. The magazine. The sheet.

"So he's careful, meticulous, and ruthless," Erin said. "Suggesting the rope wasn't an accident. It was a message. A clue? A taunt?"

Darsh didn't remind her that rope had been left behind after last year's rapes. He didn't need to. "Anything else, Dr. Grice?"

"Nope. I've taken multiple tissue samples and sent everything where it needs to go. These ladies can be released for burial unless someone requests a second autopsy."

They thanked the ME, said goodbye, and came to an abrupt halt in the reception area outside the autopsy suite. Five people sat in waiting room chairs. Three men and two women.

"Parents?" Darsh muttered under his breath.

Erin gave him an abrupt nod and approached the group. She introduced herself and him.

"The Medical Examiner has just finished the autopsies—"

"When can we see our children?"

"I'm not sure—"

"Who did this to my daughter?" A man with steel gray hair stepped close to Erin. "The same person who raped those girls last year?" The man's upper lip curled, and Darsh understood he was hurting, but Darsh wanted him out of Erin's personal space. Why did everyone treat her as an acceptable target? "People said you were going after Drew Hawke because you hated football players. After the trial I was inclined to believe you were right about him, but not anymore, not after this."

Erin straightened her spine as if bracing for more verbal blows.

Darsh intervened. "We are very sorry for your loss, sir. But we can't discuss details of an ongoing investigation."

He felt Erin withdraw from him, but what the hell was he supposed to do? Let her be ripped apart by anyone who wanted to take a shot? He'd been sent to assess her work and if she'd fucked up, he was going to expose her to her bosses. But it didn't mean he'd let anyone treat her like crap in the meantime.

The man drew in a jagged breath to say more, but a woman touched his arm. "Let it go, George. I want to grieve for my baby, not fight with the police who are only trying to do their jobs. Not today."

The guy sat down and put his arm around his wife's shoulders, but his gaze didn't lose the hostility. Darsh understood the grief process, but it didn't help them solve crime.

"You have my sincerest condolences." Erin handed each person her card, and he had to admire her tenacity. "Please call me if you can think of anything or anybody who might have wanted to hurt your daughters. A victims' advocate will be in touch soon as will the FPPD if we have any news we can share. The ME will be out to talk to you shortly." She strode out the front door of the municipal building in the small town of Massena and headed straight to her truck. She'd insisted on driving, because they had to be back in under an hour for another team meeting and snow was forecast.

She seemed distracted. He thought she was thinking about the accusations the father had made, but her next words proved she was thinking about the case. "The fact the UNSUB took Drew's letters to Cassie. What does that mean?" She turned the key in the ignition, and the engine roared to life.

"It suggests a fascination or keen interest with Drew Hawke. I don't think Cassie was a random choice."

"What if I *did* get the wrong guy?" she said suddenly. "What if it *is* my fault these girls died?"

"The only person to blame for their deaths is the asshole who killed them."

She gave him a look that said "bullshit." "That's a fine pep-talk, but we both know it doesn't fly in the real world."

"Did you do anything wrong? Did you suppress evidence or ignore a lead?"

She shook her head.

"Then you've got nothing to worry about." Which wasn't entirely true, and they both knew it.

She huffed out an unconvinced laugh as she pulled out of the lot. "What if Jason Brady killed his best friend's girlfriend in an effort to get Hawke out of prison?" She swore. "If I go after Brady it's going to look like I do have a vendetta against the football team."

Brady as a suspect had crossed Darsh's mind, too. It was a viable option. They needed to verify his alibi for last night. "As long as you have cause to investigate him, no one can blame you for the fact he's a Ravens player."

She scoffed. "Are you kidding me? I get blamed every time the team steps on the field."

"So why stay in a town that hates you?" The sun was low in the sky and starting to sink toward the horizon. Neither of them had slept the night before, and they were both exhausted. Maybe she'd give him a straight answer for once. "Why stay where you don't fit in?" He'd grown up with that sense of never belonging. If anyone understood not fitting in, it was him.

Her fingers tightened on the steering wheel. "I don't like running away."

"That's not what I heard." It was a gambit, but one that hit its mark. A ripple of light played over her cheek as her jaw flexed. She kept her eyes aimed straight ahead.

"Why'd you leave the NYPD?" he pushed, wanting the truth.

"None of your damn business."

"What's the big deal, Erin? Got something to hide?"

The skin around her mouth whitened. "You mean is Jason Brady telling the truth? Did my husband really blow his brains out because of me?" There was a hardness in her eyes when she glanced at him. "Yeah. He did. And, yes, that's why I left the NYPD. Satisfied?"

If someone kicked him in the face, he couldn't feel much worse. "Tell me again it had nothing to do with the fact you and I slept together."

"What do you need to hear, Darsh? That it's not your fault? Trust me, it wasn't your fault. You are absolved of all guilt."

It wasn't guilt he was feeling. It was something much more complicated—and that hadn't been a "no" dammit. He needed to find out exactly what happened in Erin's past and hoped to hell the fact they'd had sex hadn't contributed to her husband's death. He had enough ghosts to deal with.

"You're supposed to be the analyst." Her words were like shards of glass slicing his skin. "How about you contribute something relevant to this investigation rather than probing ancient history that has nothing to do with the case?"

Ouch.

She was right. He was ready to start looking at the old cases now, see if there was any linkage between crimes. But he'd seen enough of the town now to know that regardless of whether or not she'd got the right guy, or done everything by the book, public opinion would crucify her. And he was the one who was supposed to provide the wood and nails for the cross.

CHAPTER SEVEN

E RIN GLANCED AT the ever-increasing crowd of reporters as she strode toward the police station. The media was gathering for the statement the chief planned to make after their team meeting later. She wanted to tell them all to piss off and let her do her job. Probably why she wasn't in charge of public relations. Heads paused and lifted like raptors scenting blood on the wind. Coats flapped as they jockeyed for position.

A murder of crows. The collective noun had never sounded more appropriate.

A couple of cameras flashed, and she gritted her teeth. She pushed through the front door and didn't bother holding it for Agent Singh. He could fend for himself. He wasn't IA, but the way he was interrogating her about her past, he sure as hell felt like it.

"Did you know your husband was going to draw his weapon?"

"Did you know he was dangerous?"

"Did he try to kill you before he turned the weapon on himself?"

Anger moved through her as it always did as the barrage of questions they'd shouted at her three years ago pelted her memory. Anger, shame and sorrow—for all the things she couldn't change. She shook it off. There was no time for pointless recollections. This killer was slipping away from them, and Darsh was paying more attention to her history than to catching the guy.

She checked her watch and headed to the booking desk and leaned on it.

"Rodriguez," she shouted to the desk sergeant who was talking to a couple of officers off to the side. "Brady still here?"

Arnie Rodriguez walked over to the counter. He was a twenty-year veteran just serving out his time until retirement. He leaned his arm across the polished wooden surface and smiled down at her. "Why, yes, he is, Detective Donovan. His lawyer's been in twice, along with the team coach who said the kid needed to get to practice. I explained—very patiently if you ask me—I needed to wait to see if the arresting officer was going to press assault charges. You decided yet?"

Football was worth a lot of money to this college town, and she'd already cost the university its star quarterback. But just because they felt entitled didn't mean they got to threaten police officers. However, she didn't want to escalate the tension in the town, nor did she wish to give Brady ammunition for a harassment charge. She did, however, want to question the guy about his movements last night. "I'm still thinking about it. Get him into an interview room for me, will you?"

"Sure thing, Erin."

"Thanks, Arnie." She wove through the bullpen to the back of the room where she shared twin desks with Harry Compton. They had a corner partitioned off. It meant they could put up suspect photos, timelines, and theories out of sight of the general population.

The veteran detective was hunched over a laptop and

printing out Facebook posts. That had to hurt. She slipped out of her parka and hung it over the back of the hard plastic chair under her desk. Darsh Singh would be gone soon, and she'd get back her comfy office chair. Sooner the better.

"Got anything?" she asked.

Harry wasn't the touchy feely type. But he was a good cop.

"Apart from Bressinger's bordering-on-obsessive hatred of you?" His features twisted, and he stretched his spine as if relieving pressure there. He was only a couple of years from retirement, but the last year had been the busiest of his career. "Not much. If anyone challenged Cassie on the fact Drew might have been guilty she blocked them and deleted the comment. Problem solved."

"I wish I could block people from my life so easily," Erin muttered.

"Me, too." He pulled more sheets out of the printer. "There are a few names I'll follow up with, but I'm not seeing any drama beyond bitterness against the police for arresting her honey." Harry smiled, which was a rarity. "Mandy Wochikowski was much less active on Facebook, although she made a lot of social commentary posts on Twitter. And there were a few flirtatious exchanges with an anonymous user with the handle "@DarkMatter" who claims to be a Blackcombe student. I'm going to try and identify him, but don't hold your breath."

Only Harry could say things like "flirtatious" and "Dark-matter" and make it sound as exciting as stale bread.

"What about cell phone calls?"

"Still waiting on the warrant for the phone company."

Seriously? "We need that warrant."

"Yeah." Harry looked unimpressed. "Tell it to the DA."

The district attorney's office was probably trying to cover their asses should the Hawke conviction go sideways.

She should probably just paint a bullseye on her forehead and stand still so they could all take a shot at her, but the killer wasn't standing still, so neither was she. Erin bit down on her frustration. "I'll talk to Strassen, see if he can put some pressure on them. I'm going to interview Jason Brady. See what his alibi is for last night before I release him."

"Not pressing charges? I hear he went after you."

"I handled it." She shrugged. "It depends what he says during interview." Any other time, he'd be up on charges.

"Need any help?" Harry pushed back from his desk.

She grunted softly. "I appreciate the offer, but the FBI wanted in on this." She'd let Darsh see her weakness earlier when talking about her husband's suicide, now she had to pretend it didn't matter.

Harry looked unimpressed. "Let me know if you want a real cop in there. I can make time."

"Will do." She walked down to the cleaning supply closet and knocked on the door.

A muffled voice said, "Come in."

She found the fed completely surrounded by boxes.

"If there's a fire around here, you're toast." She forced a smile. He'd been pushing for information she had no intention of sharing, but she'd have been curious in his shoes, too.

Darsh laughed, and the sound was sexy as hell. "I don't think I can get out of here without a crowbar," he admitted.

The sheer volume of the information crammed into such a tiny room was overwhelming. She knew it all inside out, but that didn't matter. He'd want to see it for himself.

She had a murder to investigate. If he decided the cases

were linked then it would become her problem. "You said you wanted to sit in on the interview with Jason Brady or are you too busy?"

Dark eyes snapped to hers. "Yes, but I'd like to interview him alone."

"Er, no." Damn. So much for the olive branch. The guy had smacked her on the head with it. She backed away and started walking.

"Erin. Wait!"

She ignored him, but he caught her in the bullpen.

"He's not going to talk to you. He's not going to give you anything except grief."

Darsh got in front of her, and she had to put on the brakes or crash straight into him.

"What's more important?" he asked quietly. A hundred ears flapped in their direction. "Slapping him down to size, or figuring out if he had anything to do with last night's murders?"

She drew in a furious breath, taking a half-step back, and crossed her arms over her chest. "You know the answer to that."

"Which is why it makes more sense for me to go in there alone." He leaned close to her ear. "Look, despite what you might think of me, we're on the same team. We want the same thing—to catch Cassie and Mandy's killer."

Her teeth hurt as they ground together. He was right, but she wasn't happy about what it said regarding her ability to get the job done.

"Fine, but don't fuck it up." She checked her watch. "You have twenty minutes before our team meeting. I'm going to watch from the window." Erin pivoted around the guy and headed for the observation room. She wasn't about to let her ego get in the way of finding the truth—not that she had much of an ego left anymore. All she had was the determination to get the job done and memories of better days.

DARSH NEEDED TO get moving but instead, he found himself watching Erin Donovan walk into the viewing room with her chin held high. How could anyone not admire a cop who not only single-handedly took down a two-hundred-thirty-pound gorilla, but also knew the right time to back away—and actually did it?

Now they had to either charge the kid or cut him loose, and charging him for anything less than murder-in-the-first was a waste of time. Forget the fact the creep had physically threatened and assaulted a female cop. The public only cared about catching this killer, and didn't have patience for side shows or distractions. Erin Donovan appeared to be fair game in this town. He didn't like that anymore than he liked assholes who put their hands on women.

The ring of a phone jerked him out of his trance. The lingering smell of death clung to him like smoke, but there hadn't been time to shower or change after the morgue. He grabbed a blank legal pad and pen off a nearby desk and headed inside. Brady was slouched over the table, but sat up when Darsh came in. His eyes were bloodshot, face haggard. The smell of metabolized alcohol oozed from the guy's pores.

None of them had gotten much sleep last night, but at least Darsh hadn't been hammered. He grabbed the chair and sat. "Mr. Brady, I'm Agent Singh with the FBI. We met this morning."

"I remember." The accompanying eye-roll was worthy of a fourteen-year-old girl.

"Mind if I call you Jason?"

The guy shrugged enormous shoulders. Darsh didn't know why Erin wasn't intimidated by the sheer size of these guys. After his stint in the Marines, he could handle himself, but Erin was almost a foot shorter and seventy pounds lighter.

"You seem to have a problem with Detective Donovan. Is that an accurate statement?" he asked.

"Yeah, I have a problem with her." Brady straightened from his slouch. "She put Drew in jail for something he didn't do."

"It was the testimony of the women who'd been raped, the physical evidence, and the jury who put Drew in prison."

"That cunt had it out for him from the start." Brady folded muscled arms across his chest. "There's no way Drew would touch any of those bitches."

"Why not?" Darsh forced himself not to react to the hateful words. To appear not to judge, but instead to empathize. No one said it was easy.

Brady rolled out a soft snort. "Did you see them? They were fucking ugly. No way would Drew go there. Cassie did whatever he wanted in the sack anyway."

No remorse shown over Cassie's death. Did the guy even know who the latest victims were? Darsh wasn't sure when the names had been released, but the housemates, Tanya and Alicia, must have blabbed to friends.

"The only way Drew would have touched those cows was if he were the one being hogtied and raped," Brady continued.

Darsh suppressed his gut reaction, which was to slap the

guy in the face with his fist. Brady was either clueless or a stone-cold sociopath.

"You'd like to see Drew exonerated," he stated slowly.

"He's the best quarterback in college football. He's got a fucking NFL career just waiting for him when he gets out— why would he jeopardize all that for an ugly piece of ass? They were lying."

When he gets out? A slip of the tongue or wishful thinking?

Power, anger, sadism were the main reasons rapists raped. Sexual attraction was not generally a factor. Proximity and opportunity were more important. But in Cassie's case, Darsh figured the victim had been chosen because of *who* she was.

"Are you saying the women who accused him of rape were jealous of his success and resentful of his lack of attention?" he asked.

Brady nodded and leaned forward over the table. Darsh got a serious dose of fiery breath. "They couldn't have him, so they decided to bring him down."

"What about the polygraphs?" Darsh was curious how the guy would explain away the case against Hawke.

"Everyone knows you can fool a lie detector, you just need to figure it out."

Controlling your heartbeat and skin temperature was a hell of an exercise in self-control. Sure, some people could do it, but two young women with seemingly nothing to gain and everything to lose by telling the world they'd been raped? He didn't think so.

"What about the physical evidence in the case?" Darsh pushed.

"What physical evidence? A hair? A fucking hair? They could have got that from the locker room or in a frickin' bar.

106

Fuck, I don't know how they got it, but I know Drew. He's a good guy—better than me. *Way* better than me. He doesn't deserve this shit."

Brady clearly idolized his friend.

"He was your roommate, right? How you holding up without him?"

Brady swallowed noisily, looking vulnerable for the first time. "There's a new guy in his spot, same as we have a new quarterback on the team. It's not the same." Brady shot him a glare. "It sucks."

"You think the fact you had a few too many beers last night is the reason you crossed a line with Detective Donovan this morning?"

Brady shrugged and didn't seem capable of holding anything back. "I hate her guts. When I see her I feel like I'm going to explode. She doesn't give a shit that she ruined someone's life because guys don't matter. She hates men."

From what Darsh knew Erin didn't hate men. She had many male colleagues who appeared to like and respect her. But she was hiding something. Some wound or flaw or mistake from her past.

"It's a crime—what you did to her earlier? That's assault of a police officer. You could be convicted and lose your own chance of a place in the NFL for doing that shit."

"I barely touched her."

"Trust me, assault of a police officer is one contact sport you won't win." Darsh glared hard at the younger man.

Brady shrugged a shoulder, and his eyes glowed sullenly. "She's a shitty cop."

"Even though she took you down?" Okay, so Darsh wasn't acting so sympathetic, but this guy wasn't showing *any* remorse for his actions. Unease moved through him, unease for Erin. She'd handled Brady earlier, Darsh reminded himself. She didn't need his protection, and protecting her wasn't why he was here. "What time did you start drinking last night?"

Brady winced as if the memory hurt. "I dunno. I probably cracked a beer around seven, but we didn't open the keg until after the party started."

And if he had witnesses to verify his presence from eight to ten, this guy was in the clear for the murders.

"Has Drew Hawke been in touch with you from prison?" asked Darsh.

"What d'you mean?"

"I mean has he written to you?" The guy was stalling. Darsh already knew the kid was brighter than he was pretending to be. *Misandrist*—someone who hated men. What kind of twenty-year-old football player used that sort of word?

A smart one, that's what.

Exactly how smart was he? Darsh wondered.

Brady stuffed his hands in his sweatshirt's pockets and sat straighter. He cleared his throat. "He's written a couple of times."

"You write back?" Darsh asked.

Brady wouldn't meet his eyes. Shook his head.

"Why not? He's your best friend."

The kid blinked a few times. His eyes looked suspiciously wet. "What am I going to say? Team's working hard and still winning? Coach Raymond is on my back about being late for practice?" He checked the clock, and his nostrils flared. "And there's me late again." He looked back up. "I can't tell Drew that the world is going on as normal while he's stuck in a shit-hole until he's fifty. Merry Christmas, buddy, and 'fuck you' by the way."

"Did he write to Cassandra?"

Brady's shoulders bobbed, but his expression closed down. "I guess."

"You two don't talk?"

Brady's lips twisted. "We aren't really friends."

Present tense. He was either a genius or he didn't know Cassie was dead.

"So you were at this party last night—did you leave at any time? Go for a walk maybe?"

The door crashed open, and there stood a tall thin guy in an expensive suit. Chief Strassen's face peered over his shoulder.

"What the hell are you doing questioning my client without his attorney being present?"

"We're just talking," Darsh replied, unruffled.

"Anything he said is not admissible in court."

"Court?" Brady's brow corrugated. "She's really going to press charges? That bi—"

"Enough!" his attorney yelled.

When Brady shut his mouth, the lawyer stared Darsh in the eye. "They aren't worried about any trumped up charges regarding Detective Donovan, Mr. Brady. They're looking at you for the murder of Cassandra Bressinger."

"Cassie's dead?" The blood drained from Brady's face. The kid shifted suddenly. "You fuck!"

Fast reflexes saved Darsh from a punch to the jaw. He held on to the younger man's fist and squeezed. "Keep your dress on, sweetheart. We were just talking. You're free to go. Unless…"—Darsh smiled with all the annoyance he was feeling—"You wanna try that punch again?"

The lawyer dragged on his client's arm, trying to get him moving before he succumbed to temper. The young man stood, but Darsh blocked the exit. "And one word of advice, Mr. Brady. Steer clear of Detective Donovan. Next time, she will press charges, and that will be the end of a very promising football career. Do you understand?"

The guy's eyes were hot with loathing. He nodded slowly and shot a glare at the mirror. "Oh, I got it. I understand perfectly."

CHAPTER EIGHT

T REETOPS ON EITHER side of the road lurched violently in the strong gusts of wind. The three o'clock meeting had gone long, and they were still no further forward in the investigation. The chief had sent her and most of the other officers home to get a few hours' sleep. She lived just south of town on the edge of the Adirondacks and was so tired her eyes kept drifting shut as she drove home in the dark. Great. Wrecking her car would be all she needed. Another mile, and she'd be home. Jet-lag on top of a sleepless night meant she physically couldn't stay awake much longer. She stretched her eyes wide and pulled a face. The highway was quiet, not many houses out this way. She wound down the window, and it was like stepping inside a blast freezer.

Watching Darsh interview Brady had been interesting. He'd gotten far more out of the guy than she would have. And Brady's reaction when he'd been told Cassie was dead had been very convincing. Either the football player hadn't known she was one of the victims, or he was a hell of an actor. It didn't take him off the suspect list. Now they'd have to interview the people who'd attended the party at the frat house and make sure he'd been where he said he was. She'd seen him just after ten last night. Could he have run from Cassie's to the frat house between the 911 call being made and her seeing him there?

Her phone rang and startled her. God. The thing hadn't stopped all day. Her mother, her dad, public relations, the mayor. This was the last one for the day, and it better not mean she had to turn around. She clicked the button on the handsfree.

"Hi Erin, it's Linus. I was sorry to hear about the murders."

"Linus. Hey. How's it going?" Linus Hall was one of Professor Huxley's graduate students. "What can I do for you?"

"Roman wanted me to call and ask if you wanted copies of Mandy Wochikowski's essays."

She wasn't sure what they'd tell her, but she still didn't have a feel for Mandy as a person yet and hated the fact her murder seemed almost inconsequential next to Cassie's. "Yeah, sure. Send them to my email could you?"

"Actually I don't have digital copies. I only have printouts. You probably have access to them on her computer," he said hesitantly. But Mandy's computer had been sent to the FBI's lab at Quantico. "I can drop them off at the station tonight if you want?"

"That would be great, thanks. I won't be there, but you can leave them with the desk sergeant."

"Oh." He sounded disappointed. "No problem. Mandy didn't deserve this."

Erin's ears sharpened. Mandy had worked for Huxley over the summer, which meant Linus might have known Mandy quite well. And there was something in his voice… "You two were friends?"

"Yeah, well all of the lab hung out over the summer. Went for coffee and stuff."

Had they been dating? It probably wasn't okay for a grad student to date one of the undergraduate students in his class. "Anything you can tell me about her?" she asked cautiously.

There was a long pause. "Well, she kind of reminded me of you."

That sent a ripple of shock through her body. The fact Mandy was dead and no one seemed to care struck her as infinitely sad. She needed to keep the girl a focal point of the investigation.

"Dedicated. Always working, never really satisfied no matter how many straight-As she brought home. Never really believing in herself."

This kid obviously saw more than she wanted him to. "She sounds like she was way smarter than me." She laughed off her discomfort at being analyzed. "Mandy believed Drew Hawke was innocent."

"She did." He cleared his throat. "She actually got me thinking about how Hawke *could* have been set up."

An unexpected sense of betrayal hit her. Linus had been vehement in his belief the quarterback was the rapist. The turn for her driveway came up on her left. Nearly home. "Pretty elaborate scheme to set up the guy."

"Difficult, but not impossible."

Her lack of response made him stammer.

"B-but highly unlikely. This is most likely a copycat. Someone wanting to make Hawke look innocent and you guys look bad."

"Well, they succeeded." A wave of weariness washed over her as she pulled her truck to a stop in front of her farmhouse. "I have to go, Linus. I really appreciate the offer to look at Mandy's essays, and I'm sorry you lost a friend."

"Yeah. Thanks. Talk to you tomorrow." He hung up.

She slumped her head on the steering wheel, forcing herself to move before she fell asleep in the truck. She jumped out and ran to the backdoor. Her cell rang, but she let it go to voicemail. She didn't have the energy to talk to anyone else. Inside, she strode to the thermostat and hit boost because no matter how many layers she wore, or cups of coffee she drank, she still couldn't get warm.

Except when she was with Darsh Singh and trying to forget all the sins they'd committed.

Dammit. She didn't want to think about him.

Tossing her keys and bag on the table, she stripped off her coat and hung it over the back of a kitchen chair. Then she sat and yanked off her boots, dropping them to the hardwood floor with a loud thud.

She was hungry, but too tired to eat. Her footsteps echoed hollowly on the bare wooden treads as she headed upstairs. One day she'd find the time to buy some carpet. She went to the bathroom, palming her Glock, unbuttoning her slacks and dropping her pants along the way. She washed her hands and face, cleaned her teeth, and avoided the mirror. She dumped her clothes in the hamper and stumbled to her bedroom. She didn't bother with the light and didn't need one as the moon shone brightly through the thin drapes.

She snatched up her nightshirt off the floor and tugged it on, shivering as the cold cotton pressed against her skin. Her suitcase still sat on the floor ready to be unpacked. Tomorrow, before she left for work, she needed to toss laundry into the machine. Right now she didn't care if it crawled there on its own. She turned off her cell, put her sidearm on the bedside table, and slipped into oblivion.

DARSH BIT INTO his deli roll as he dialed Mallory Rooney's cell.

She answered on the third ring. "Hey Darsh, how's it going?"

He liked Mallory. She'd only worked in the BAU-4 for a few months but she was smart, driven, and had not only faced evil head-on, she'd fucking crushed it.

"Mal. You're not at the office, right?"

He'd been there when she'd had a scare with her pregnancy not long ago. She was officially on bed rest, but she'd declared that if she had to spend one more hour watching daytime TV, she would literally go insane. Hence his phone call.

"Nah. I have my feet up on Alex's leather couch, and he's hovering over me like a momma bear."

"He's worried about you. We all are." Her fiancé, Alex Parker, was a cyber security expert who now consulted for the BAU-4. The guy was cool. Darsh, Mal, and Parker had spent some quality time together before New Year. Mallory was a good shot—women often were—but at close-range, Parker was a frickin' virtuoso, practically putting a bullet through the same hole even when he was moving. Darsh had never seen shooting like it, and he'd met some excellent marksmen in the military. Darsh's talent was distance. Even Parker had conceded defeat with the long rifle.

Darsh's skills with a rifle had earned him a coveted spot in USMC Scout Sniper School. He touched the hog's tooth necklace he wore under his shirt. His good luck charm. He eyed Rosie, who he'd propped in the corner of his matchbox-sized office. He never traveled without the Remington sniper rifle and hadn't wanted to leave it in the back of his rental car. Going to the range was how he relaxed when he had downtime. Ironically, he hadn't touched a gun until he'd hit Parris Island for boot camp. His family had crossed the pond from England back in '82, and his father had embraced American culture in every way, except for firearms. He'd refused to have a gun in the house. But it turned out shooting was easy if you remembered the sniper's mantra—slow, smooth, straight, steady, and squeeze. It worked on women, too. Erin's face flashed through his mind. His mouth went dry, and he forced himself to swallow.

"So despite the fact there's been some interesting developments in other areas of our band of merry men, I've been digging into Erin Donovan's background like you asked," Mal told him.

"Other developments?" he asked.

"Nothing you need to know about unless you fancy a trip to the Caribbean."

"Has anyone ever said no to a trip to the Caribbean?"

Mallory grunted. "Ask me again in a few days—or better yet, don't ever mention it again."

The woman was confusing the hell out of him, but what else was new with females.

"Donovan's record in the NYPD was exemplary. She was a beat cop for five years before taking her detective's exam. She was one of the youngest officers to make detective in its history, let alone female."

He felt a weird swell of pride.

"Naturally, there were rumors of nepotism. Her dad and uncles are lieutenants, three of her brothers are detectives, and she has another brother who's the captain of his own precinct."

"So NYPD is the family business. Why'd she leave?"

"Like I said, her work record was exemplary, but her private life was a mess. She married in 2009 when she was twenty-six to a guy called Graham Price."

"She never changed her name?"

"No, she didn't. Maybe she liked playing off the family ties?"

"You going to change your name?" he asked, knowing he was delaying finding out about Erin's husband.

Mal laughed. "I haven't thought about it but, yeah, probably."

"You could always hyphenate."

"Mallory Rooney-Parker? I sound like a law firm or a production company. Although I guess you could call me a production company right now."

He could hear her grinning. Mentally he braced himself. "So what happened after they got married?"

"They met on the job. Donovan switched precincts so they worked in different places. All was quiet on the home-front until she filed for divorce in September 2011."

He blew out a short, relieved breath. They'd hooked up in October 2011, and while she'd technically been married, it wasn't quite the same as cheating.

"Why'd she file for divorce?"

"Irreconcilable differences was what she cited in the papers. She actually attended a training course at Quantico that October." Darsh kept quiet and hoped Mal couldn't read minds. "The real drama happened in December, just before Christmas that year. Price walked into her precinct while she was booking a suspect, pulled out his off duty weapon, and blew his brains all over the ceiling tiles."

Nausea swirled in his stomach. Fuck.

"She applied for the job in Forbes Pines that January."

No wonder she didn't want to talk about it.

"There's something else. Alex found it somewhere he shouldn't have been. There's a hospital report filed for Erin Donovan. Bunch of photographs and x-rays. Looks like someone beat her up that June."

"Anyone arrested?"

"There was no police report about the incident, just the hospital report. And, hell, he just found another one at a different hospital."

Darsh climbed to his feet, unable to pace in the cramped confines of his broom cupboard but unable to remain still. "That asshole *hit* her?"

"Or she was incredibly clumsy when she was married to him."

He thought of the woman who took down two-hundred-thirty pound athletes without blinking. The one who'd given him one of the best nights of his life. Had her husband taken his fists to her? Was that why she was so good at taking care of herself now? Rage burned through his mind and made him miss what Mallory said next.

"Sorry?" he said.

"I said how's the case looking?"

He rubbed his forehead. "Complicated."

"Where you staying?"

He laughed and looked around his six-by-six-foot office currently stuffed with boxes. "At the police station. The press descended and someone forgot to book me a hotel room." He rubbed the back of his neck. "Doesn't matter. I've got about a billion statements and pieces of evidence to go through tonight anyway."

"Anything we can do to help?"

"I might take you up on that tomorrow, after I've looked the evidence through. Right now I don't know my ass from my elbow. There is one thing. Can you check out the football team and coaching staff for any previous assault or rape allegations?"

"Sure, I'll get Agent Chen on it tomorrow."

Ashley Chen—a new agent in BAU-4. "How's she working out?"

Mal laughed. "She's difficult to read. A hard worker who doesn't like being told what to do, but I can't exactly talk."

Darsh took a slurp of hot coffee. "You're an excellent agent, Mal. A good team player. You're doing better than I did at your stage." Maybe better than he was doing now. The constant need to prove himself got old.

"Oh, please. We've all heard about your wicked undercover work."

Darsh grinned. "Sometimes prejudice works in the good guys' favor."

"You're a badass."

"Roger that."

"Alex isn't too keen on Agent Chen. Doesn't trust her. Says her background looks suspect."

"He isn't keen on anyone he hasn't personally vetted from their day of birth." It had made Darsh uncomfortable at first to realize Alex knew all about his mother's murder, but the guy had kept it to himself. Darsh didn't think he'd even told Mal—although if anyone understood, it might be Mal.

"That's what I told him."

119

"What do you think of her?" Darsh had only met Agent Chen briefly. She had classic Asian features and a New York attitude. He knew someone else with a New York attitude, and hell if he didn't like it.

"She's intelligent and hardworking…"

"But?"

"There's a wall there when it comes to her private life. She doesn't trust us yet."

He thought of Erin. She had walls too. Maybe he was beginning to understand why.

"I gotta go. Alex is tapping his watch. Hey, Frazer's getting out of the hospital soon, but he's taking two weeks leave."

"Leave?" That was a surprise. Darsh didn't remember the guy ever taking a break.

"I think there might be a woman involved." Her voice was full of intrigue.

Darsh's gut tightened. "Lucky bastard."

"Lincoln Frazer is many things, but lucky isn't one of them."

Darsh grunted. "Okay, true, thanks for the information. Call me if anything comes up, but *don't* stress." The last thing he wanted was to put the baby at risk.

"Gotcha."

He ended the call and slumped in his chair, tiredness pulling at his muscles so much he wanted to lay down his head and close his eyes. Then he stared at the piles of reports and dragged the first box closer. The sooner he could decide on whether the old rapes and new murders were connected, the sooner he could get out of Forbes Pines and leave behind the temptation of Detective Erin Donovan.

CHAPTER NINE

ERIN WORE LYCRA pants and a long-sleeved T-shirt with a thin fleece jacket thrown over the top and fine black gloves. Her blonde hair was hidden under a thin wool cap, which she pulled as low as it would go over her ears. She turned on her headlamp and pressed start on the stopwatch. She jogged down the alley at the back of Cassie's house and swung south. The cold air pierced her lungs. It was dark and dank with dense fog swirling in the rapacious breeze. She scanned the tarmac for patches of ice, kept up the pace, knowing a younger athlete would leave her in the dust.

She cut down another street and headed into a small park. There were a couple of lonely street lamps spread out at wide distances, their halos hovering over the ground just visible in the frozen mist. She ran through a small wooded area, branches rattling, making her nerves dance and her heart beat faster in eons-old fear. She'd checked the route on her phone before she set out, and this was the shortest distance from A to B.

Her blood was pumping now, her internal furnace firing up and combating the icy chill. Besides the woods, the only sound was her feet hitting the pavement, and her breath sawing in and out of her chest. She entered the college grounds, and the dense fog cleared a little as she weaved between Biological Sciences and Chemistry. Her foot skidded, and she threw her hands in the air, but righted herself before she hit the ground. She carried on running. It was six a.m., but there were already a few people around. Cyclists. Another intrepid runner. A campus security cop making his rounds. She glanced up as she ran, looking for surveillance cameras. She didn't see any, but she made a mental note to ask campus security if they had any that covered this area.

She ran past the gym complex and up onto the sports fields where the mist gathered in thick sullen patches. The grass was crisp under the soles of her Nikes. A group of guys appeared out of nowhere. The football team running drills. Morning practice. She veered away from them. Someone wolf whistled, proving they couldn't see her face. The last thing she wanted to do was encounter Jason Brady when she was trying to figure out whether or not he'd had the time to kill Mandy and Cassie the night before last.

She kicked hard and hit the rim of the fields, hooking a right as she crested the embankment, running along the top toward the frat houses, and came to a halt exactly where she'd seen Brady that night. She jogged on the spot and checked her stopwatch. Six minutes forty-eight seconds. She took a different route back, avoiding the sports fields by running along the road to where she'd parked her truck on Cassie's street. She checked her watch again. Nine minutes. She bent over and caught her breath. They needed to check Brady's alibi from that night, but at least she now knew it was physically possible for the guy to have made the 911 call from Cassie's house at 9:54 PM and run back to the frat house in time for when she drove past.

Her phone buzzed against her side. She reached down and

checked the number and remembered she'd missed another call last night, too. Rachel Knight. Damn.

Erin wanted to smack herself. How could she have not called Rachel yesterday? But no matter how urgent, she couldn't talk to her where someone might overhear. She'd call her back from the police station.

Her breathing and heart rate began to return to normal, and she stretched out her muscles. Slowly, she became aware of the sensation of eyes crawling over her body. It was particularly creepy standing outside the house where Mandy and Cassie had been brutally slain.

Erin never discounted her instincts—unless she counted her disastrous marriage. But Graham had never seemed anything except devoted during their courtship—maybe too devoted, she thought, looking back now. She searched her peripheral vision, but couldn't see anyone or anything out of the ordinary. Crap. She stretched a leg against the truck, then straightened and climbed inside, giving it time to warm up, using those precious minutes to check out nearby cars and houses.

Had the killer come back? Did he live nearby? Was he watching?

Nothing stirred. Not a soul was visible. After five minutes of nothing, she told herself she was being stupid. Paranoid. She couldn't sit here all day looking like a damn fool. She put the car in gear and headed off to work.

DARSH GRABBED A quick shower in the station then set off in search of Erin. He found her in the opposite corner of the building behind two room dividers, talking on the phone. She looked at him without comment and jammed the handset between her shoulder and her ear, rummaging through the stack of papers on her desk before pulling out a pen and a piece of paper. They hadn't spoken since he'd muscled in on the Brady interview yesterday, but after his conversation with Mallory last night, he now understood the woman a million times better—not that he could admit that. If she found out he'd been snooping, she'd be more pissed than ever.

Her blonde hair was tied up in a thick, wet braid that left a damp streak down the back of her blue cotton shirt. The subtle sweetness of her soap and shampoo caught him off guard. She'd obviously just showered, and he did not want to think about her being naked anywhere on the entire contiguous landmass of North America, let alone a handful of feet away from his office.

The shadows beneath her eyes were disguised with makeup, but at least she looked like she'd gotten some rest.

"What time?" She wrote something down. "Okay. See you then." She hung up and let out a long breath before glancing up to meet his gaze. "Find anything last night? Any blinding omissions or flashes of inspiration as to how we catch this guy?"

He grunted. Police work was rarely easy or speedy, and last night was no exception. He'd spent hours trawling through witness statements and trial transcripts. He rubbed the back of his neck. At least she was talking to him again. "Still working my way through the evidence and reports."

Those pretty eyes of hers weighed him silently, and he wanted to ask if her husband had ever hit her. He wanted to apologize for being such a judgmental asshole after they'd slept together. But this wasn't the place. And it wasn't the time.

"How'd you sleep?" She frowned then turned away, looking for something else amongst the mess of her desk.

His back felt like someone had hammered nails into it. "Let's just say it's a good thing the chair in my office is better than this piece of shit." He tapped the leg of the crappy chair she was using.

Her eyes widened in surprise. "You slept here?"

"All the motels are full." He grimaced because they were going to be full for a while. "You need a better office chair."

She laughed. It was the first time he'd heard that sound in three long years. It soaked into his skin like sunshine.

"No kidding."

"I'm going to have to find a couch somewhere or sleep in my car," he admitted, twisting his shoulders.

"Press are gonna love that. Homeless FBI profiler working case at elite college."

"No such job title as FBI 'profiler' as you well know."

She waved his comment away. They both knew the press would say whatever the hell they wanted regardless of the veracity of the statement. She gave a triumphant cry when she pulled out a candy bar from under some file folders. "Hallelujah." She tore it open and bit into one of the Twix bars, munching happily. "There's always the conference room after the boss goes home," she said between mouthfuls.

His stomach growled, and he hoped to hell she didn't hear it. "I've slept in worse places. Armored vehicles during a sand storm. Flat rooftops under the blazing Arabian sun."

"I'm more of a bed girl myself."

Images of her naked on white cotton sheets flashed through his brain. His blood rushed through his body like

125

steam. Oblivious, she nibbled the candy and didn't notice the way he shifted his stance.

This attraction was going to be a pain in the ass because he was still investigating her work on the Hawke case, something that could get her fired. For the first time, he thought about asking Brennan to send someone to replace him. But their unit was stretched to breaking point, and he didn't intend to be the weak link.

And so what if he actually enjoyed working with Erin and found her ridiculously alluring? He wasn't going to compromise his ethics because they'd once slept together. If she'd screwed up, he'd put it in his report.

She licked her lips.

Right. Great.

His stomach growled again, and he leaned over to snatch the second piece of the candy bar out of her hand to steal a bite before handing it back.

"Hungry?" The sparkle in her eyes sent shockwaves of lust rushing through his system.

She had no idea.

She handed him the remainder of the chocolate, and he consumed it in one gulp. "Thanks."

"I timed the run from Cassie's house to the frat houses this morning," she began, wiping her lips.

"What? When?" He glanced out the window. The sun wasn't even up yet.

"Before I came in. About six."

"You went alone?" He tried not to sound like her big brother. His feelings weren't even remotely brotherly.

Her spine stiffened. "Yeah. Why?"

Because most people on campus wanted to lynch her.

"Next time you do something at the college, let me know. I'll come with you."

Her brows rose skeptically. "I can look after myself. And you won't be around that long."

"Jeez, you're stubborn. Just pick up the damn phone."

"Seriously?" She smiled, but the way her eyes narrowed held a warning. "You're gonna do what? Ride to my rescue every time some asshole wants to take a potshot at me? I'm not a florist, Darsh. I'm a cop. And I don't need some fed to save me."

He tossed the wrapper in the garbage. She was right, but he didn't have to like it. "At least tell someone where you're going."

"I told Ully Mason before I left home."

Something ugly twisted inside him. "You two seeing each other?"

Erin's features hardened as she leaned back in her chair and took in his telltale body language. You didn't need to be a behavioral analyst to recognize jealousy. "Why do you care?"

He blew out a big breath and felt like ten kinds of fool. "I have no idea. But for some crazy reason I do."

"I *called* Ully at his house from my house. Despite what you might think, Special Agent Singh, I do not sleep with my coworkers. *Ever*."

And if *that* wasn't another warning, he was a card-carrying member of the Ku Klux Klan. "What about your ex?" Jesus, his brain had clearly left the building.

"First, I moved precincts when we started dating. Second, I didn't sleep with another cop"—she held up her left hand and wiggled her bare fingers—"until he put a ring on it."

He stared into those gorgeous eyes and wondered if she

knew how much she'd just given away. She'd been chaste, but she'd slept with *him*. No dating. No rings. Just fast and hard, then slow and sensual, and everything in between. She'd tried to shed her old skin, and the bastard she was divorcing had punished her for her newfound independence by blowing his brains out in front of not only her, but her entire precinct.

And they were the only two people in the world to know about that night, he realized. There's no way Erin would have told anyone else.

Her expression turned pensive, and she looked away. Maybe she could read whatever he was thinking in his eyes, which made him the worst kind of fool.

She pulled out some photographs of the knots of blue rope from her desk and put them in a yellow file folder. She grabbed her parka off the back of the chair. "I'm going to see Rachel Knight—"

"The first victim?" He pulled his attention away from Erin and back to the case.

She nodded. "The three other rape victims live out of state and didn't return to Blackcombe this year. If I'm not back in two hours send out a search party—"

"Won't need to. I'm coming with you."

"I don't need your protection," she bit out.

"I want to talk to her." The first and last victims always held the most clues.

Erin folded her arms over her chest in an age-old defensive move. "She doesn't like talking to strange men."

Dear God, some days life was easier looking down the barrel of a rifle than dealing with stubborn cops. "I'm trained for this sort of situation. And you'll be there to reassure her." He turned on his heel to go grab his stuff. He unlocked the door to his office and reached inside for his windbreaker.

A truculent voice followed him. "Fine. We should go in separate vehicles. I'm going to the local outdoors shop afterward to ask about the rope. I'll be gone until lunch. You'll miss the morning meeting."

"They sell outerwear?" he asked, shrugging into the thin layer of Gortex that was currently the only thing protecting him from the insane cold.

"What?" She looked at him like he'd begun speaking Punjabi.

"This outdoor shop. They sell jackets like yours?" he asked.

She raised her hands in what-the-fuck surrender. "Yes. Of course they do."

"Then I'm coming with you. Let's go."

CHAPTER TEN

ERIN DIDN'T KNOW what had changed, but Darsh seemed less angry and disapproving than he had the day before. She wished he'd go back to being bitter and judgmental because, no matter how good-looking the outer package, the former was an easy combination to resist.

The man in question looked up at the mullioned windows with English ivy creeping up the side of the chimney. "Pretty swank student accommodation."

Wearing a charcoal suit, blue tie, and crisp white shirt, gold badge on his hip and weapon in its shoulder holster, he didn't look like a guy who'd slept in a chair. He looked like a professional federal law enforcement officer and just as attractive in a suit as he was in tactical clothes.

Dammit.

Erin knocked on the red front door of the elegant brick house. They were on the west side of town, on a small hill where a lot of faculty and university administration lived. The door opened, and a woman with short, straight, dyed brown hair appeared. Her gaze went from Erin to Darsh and back to Erin. She didn't look happy.

"You spoke to Rachel?" she asked.

"Yes, Dr. Knight. About an hour ago. She asked if I could come see her today."

The woman's hand went to the cross she wore around her throat. "I thought you'd have called yesterday. To reassure her."

Darsh shifted on his feet.

"I'm sorry I didn't. I was swamped." And hoping they could arrest the perp ASAP so she could put this woman's daughter's mind at ease. "This is Agent Singh from the FBI's Behavior Analysis Unit. May we come in?"

Rachel's mother took a reluctant step back and opened the door. Erin stepped into the hallway with its elegant black and white tiled floor. She wiped her feet on the mat, and Darsh did the same, both on their best behavior. She'd told him to let her do the talking, and so far he was following instructions. She had the feeling he would cooperate for as long as it suited his cause—following the route of least resistance, or spinning her a line to get what he wanted. Like telling her he was a Marine rather than an FBI agent when she was at that training course at the academy. She should resent him for that, but as he'd reminded her on several different occasions, it was trivial in comparison to her deception.

"You can wait in the study. The fire's lit." The mother indicated they go on ahead. Erin had been here on several occasions and knew the way.

"Donald went to work. I stayed home for Rachel…just in case." The woman trailed off as if she didn't really know what to do. "I'll fetch her." She turned abruptly and left them alone in the hallway.

"The dad is a professor in the Physics Department. Mom is a prof in Ancient Languages," Erin murmured as she led them toward the study.

"But the attack didn't happen here, right?"

"No. Rachel was assaulted in her dorm on campus. She moved home afterward." Erin wasn't sure if he'd read Rachel's account of the rape yet or not. She assumed he'd at least read the courtroom testimony.

Damn, she hated rape trials.

They'd no sooner arrived in the father's study than she heard footsteps behind them, and they both turned. Rachel Knight wore pink pajamas, a purple dressing gown and fuzzy slippers—she looked about twelve. Her eyes were red-rimmed and her nose splotchy. Her footsteps slowed as she caught sight of Darsh.

Her mother touched her arm. "He's with the FBI. If you don't want to talk to him, I'll ask him to leave."

Rachel held Erin's gaze, silently asking if she should trust this stranger. Erin nodded. She knew what it felt like to have your confidence shattered. She'd never been raped, but she'd been attacked. You were never the same afterward. Never as trusting.

"It's okay, Mom." Rachel patted her mother's arm.

"Do you want me to come in with you?" her mother asked, clearly trying to figure out what was the best thing to do to help her daughter.

Rachel took her mom's hand and squeezed. Erin was relieved to see their relationship was still strong. "Erin's here. I'll be okay."

Her heart clenched.

Rachel skirted both Erin and Darsh as she entered the room, heading to a wingback chair that sat in front of an open fire. The girl curled up her feet beneath her and gripped the armrests like she was getting ready for a rollercoaster.

Erin chose the other chair and took a seat on the edge,

leaning forward. "Rachel, this is Agent Darsh Singh. He's a behavioral analyst from the FBI."

Rachel examined him as if she could see secrets if she probed the surface deep enough. Erin knew for a fact people didn't work that way.

"I'm sorry I missed your call last night," she began. "When I got home I basically passed out."

Rachel's fingernails bit into the worn leather of the chair. "I wanted to ask you how this could happen? I wanted to know if it was the same guy?" Her fingers flexed, marking the leather. "But that isn't possible. Drew Hawke *is* still in prison, right?" Fear shone bright in the girl's blue eyes.

Erin nodded.

"But did you *check*? Did you *actually* check? Because convicts sometimes get let out erroneously." Rachel's voice rose in agitation.

Erin opened her mouth to reply, but Darsh beat her to it. "I checked. He's still in Riverview."

Riverview was a medium security facility. Even though the DA had pushed, apparently two rapes weren't quite heinous enough to warrant a spot in maximum security. Some days, Erin wondered what was.

Rachel let out a loud whoosh of breath, and her grip on the armchair eased a fraction. "Okay. Good."

Erin cleared her throat. This was more difficult than she'd imagined. She shifted the folder she carried to the side. It had been so easy to grab the photos of the rope from her desk, but showing it to this girl who'd suffered so much at the hands, not just of her attacker, but the town and the justice system…she couldn't do it. Not yet. She couldn't disrupt the fragile peace that settled over Rachel's features.

Darsh moved closer to Rachel and introduced himself again. He stopped moving as soon as the girl tensed up. "I'm assisting Detective Donovan with the investigation into the murders, but wanted to ask you a few questions about your rape."

"So it's true?" Rachel's eyes widened. "He tied the girls to the bed the same way he did to me and Mary?"

Mary Mitchell was the other girl Hawke had been convicted of raping last year. Erin knew the women had been in touch after their ordeal on the witness stand. Erin cleared her throat. "I can't comment on an ongoing investigation, Rachel. I'm sorry."

The girl huddled deeper into her purple dressing gown, looking miserable and angry.

"What are you studying?" Darsh asked.

"I was in kinesiology but I switched after…" She swallowed noisily then laughed harshly. "I thought I'd gotten over saying the word. After I was raped. *Raped*. There. I said it. Twice." She pressed bloodless lips together. Her fingers released the chair to clasp one another in her lap. "I switched to biology because there were too many athletes in Kin and," her voice wavered, "they weren't very nice to me when they heard what I had to say about Blackcombe's star quarterback."

Darsh sank to the floor in front of her and crossed his legs. Erin knew what he was doing. Trying to appear as unthreatening as possible. But he was still six foot three inches of solid male, and Rachel Knight was still a fragile rape victim.

"I read the statement you gave the police and your testimony in court. They were pretty hard on you in there," he said. "You were very brave to do what you did."

The girl drew her knees up to her chin and wrapped her arms around her shins. "They made out I was so desperate for a boyfriend I'd say anything to get attention. They said I 'chose' Drew Hawke as my rapist because it was more acceptable to be raped by someone like him than some loser." Her lip curled with distaste.

"I'm sorry the process sucks," Darsh said quietly.

A smile flashed across the girl's face. "Me, too."

"I want to go over a few things, but only if you're comfortable. I'm not going to push you, but obviously our priority is finding the person who killed these two young women."

"I heard one of the victims was Cassie Bressinger?" said Rachel.

Darsh nodded. The names had been released to the media. "Cassie Bressinger and her roommate, Mandy Wochikowski. Did you know either of them?"

Rachel pressed her lips together and shook her head. "I mean, I saw them at the trial when I testified, but I didn't know them. I was thinking it must have been awful to know your boyfriend did that to another woman. Especially if you loved him. No wonder she didn't want to believe it."

Darsh agreed. "You'd never met Drew Hawke prior to the rape?"

"No." She huddled into her pajamas. "I saw him on the football field like everyone else, obviously. And I saw him at a party once. He and his football cronies were bullying this poor guy. A friend of my roommate Jenny's boyfriend. He was wasted, so they stripped him naked and wrote 'faggot' in black marker on his back with an arrow pointed downwards and 'Do Me!' printed on his buttocks." She shuddered. "They were horrible. I should have called the police then. I heard they did that sort of thing regularly. You know, stuffed guys in lockers. Bullied other kids, tried to get girls drunk so they'd have sex with them. Someone intervened and dragged the poor guy away. Jenny and I left and never went to another party at a frat house again." She pressed the cuff of her dressing gown against her mouth.

"Can you talk me through the night you were raped?" asked Darsh.

Erin held her breath.

Rachel's eyes went huge. "Reading about it wasn't enough?"

He gave the girl a sad smile. "I know it's hard, but it might give me a better idea exactly what happened to you compared to reading what the lawyers wanted to get out into the courtroom. Lawyers aren't normal people."

"And trials aren't normal places," Rachel agreed. "I'll talk to you, but only if you tell me something personal about yourself."

"Like what?" A curious smile played on his lips.

"The worst thing that ever happened to you."

He lost the smile.

Rachel had made Erin do the same thing. It was the only reason Rachel still trusted her. She'd told the girl her awful secret, the one few people knew. Maybe she should have lied, but for all Rachel's youth there was an earnest quality about her that was hard to resist.

Darsh looked thoughtful for a moment then he nodded. "But it's not necessarily the worst thing that's ever happened to me."

"It has to be," Rachel insisted.

"Some people have got more to choose from than others."

Erin sat up straighter. She'd forgotten this guy dealt with gruesome crime on a daily basis. "I can leave if you wish…" She went to rise from her seat.

Rachel's eyes went wide with alarm.

Darsh shook his head, and she knew he wouldn't do anything to risk losing Rachel's tenuous trust.

"It was just before the fall of Baghdad in 2003." Erin hadn't expected him to start there, but maybe she should have. War was grim and being a Marine was obviously very important to him. "I was in an overwatch position on top of an old warehouse beside the Tigris River. I'd just put one of Saddam's Republican Guard out of commission after he'd aimed an RPG—a rocket propelled grenade—at a bunch of Marines on the ground. He was totally out of the game, but that RPG was still on the rooftop available for any enemy combatant who wanted to pick it up, so I kept an eye on it while scanning for other targets."

Erin held her breath. She hadn't known he was a sniper.

The clock ticked loudly on the mantel. He paused, clearly back on that rooftop looking down his scope. "For a few minutes nothing happened, and I started to relax. Then this little boy comes running out onto that rooftop. He was about five or six years old, no shoes. Brown sweater, blue shorts, jet-black hair. Beautiful kid. Clothes and skin were covered in a fine dust from all the rubble." Darsh's eyes went very far away. "My scope was so good I could see a scratch on the kid's cheek that was still bleeding. I sat on the roof with my spotter and we're both muttering 'don't do it kid, don't touch that fucking weapon.'"

Rachel was mesmerized, holding her breath. Erin wasn't far behind.

"So I have my crosshairs centered on his small chest, and he starts dragging the RPG out of the dead soldier's arms. My spotter is silent. He knows I have all the calculations I need to make that shot. We both know that once I pull the trigger, that kid is dead, and no way am I going to let him kill Marines on the ground." He swallowed noisily. "The RPG is a heavy sucker, but that little kid is frickin' determined. His mouth is moving, but I'm too far away to hear what he's saying, and I can't read his lips.

"I'm praying for some sort of divine intervention. He doesn't try and lift it, instead he starts dragging the weapon to the doorway, and my spotter gets on the radio to our CO to see if we have permission to take him out." He laughs a horrible sound. "Of course, they say yes because that RPG is a deadly weapon, and they have troops pinned down in that area. I exhale, start the slow pull on the trigger. One pound. Two pounds. And this kid is a fraction of a second away from meeting his maker when my spotter points out that there's a guy hiding behind the doorway, shouting out instructions." Darsh caught Erin's gaze, and she saw the anger in those black depths. "Imagine using a child that way? Anyway, I can see the guy's arm. I know my bullet can penetrate the mud brick of the house, but it's a risk, and I'm weighing every aspect of this scenario between heartbeats. I take the shot, and the guy falls dead across the doorway. I move immediately back to the kid, finger taking up the slack as soon as I have him on scope. But he's dropped the RPG and runs over to the dead guy in the doorway and steps over him so gingerly." Darsh's eyes were far away, flinching with internal regret. He shook his head. "I doubt he'll ever forget the sight of blood and gore."

"The boy lived?" Rachel asked.

Darsh nodded. "For then at least. Who knows what happened to him later."

Erin realized her heart was beating so hard she could hear her pulse pounding in her ears. "Would you have shot him?" she asked, because she needed to know.

"Yes." Obsidian eyes regarded her blankly. "Those soldiers

and Marines on the ground were my friends. A lot of them had wives and kids back home. I wasn't about to let them lose a father or a husband because I couldn't do my job." He nodded sharply. "Damn right I'd have taken him out. Once he picked up that RPG he became the enemy. War isn't pretty. There's no time for sentiment." He blinked a couple of times, coming back into the room. "But I'm glad I didn't have to." He looked down at his clasped hands.

Rachel released a shuddering breath. "I think that counts as a worst memory. I'm glad you didn't shoot the boy."

Darsh nodded. He'd passed her little test. "Me, too." His lips moved into a smile, but his eyes didn't lose their haunted look.

This was a man who had layers upon layers of stories to tell about death if he wanted to—which he obviously didn't. No wonder he'd pretended to be something he wasn't when they'd met at that bar—he probably shed that skin on a regular basis just to avoid situations like this one. Maybe it had nothing to do with deception and everything to do with preservation.

"Will you tell me about the night you were raped, Rachel?" he asked.

Erin braced herself even though she'd heard the story many times before.

Darsh sat quietly on the rug in front of the fire, hyper-aware rather than relaxed.

Rachel started speaking. "I shared a room with Jenny—the girl I mentioned earlier—in Rathbone Hall. It's one of the older dorms, girls on one floor, guys on the next, so we were used to having people in and out all hours of the day and night. Students wedged the doors open all the time so they didn't get woken up by friends coming over and ringing the buzzer. Security was nonexistent." She glanced around as if cataloguing whether or not she was safe. The presence of two law enforcement officials didn't seem to calm her.

She licked her lips and blinked rapidly. "I went to bed at around ten. Jenny had gone to a party and was planning to spend the night in her boyfriend's room as his roommate had gone home for the weekend. They were going to have sex for the first time." This had all come out at trial.

"You weren't seeing anyone?" asked Darsh.

Rachel's smile was bitter. "Haven't you heard? I'm too ugly to have a real boyfriend."

The words made Erin bristle. "You know that's not true. It's what the defense team went with because there wasn't anything else for them to attack. Being raped is not a reflection on you." The words came out more forcibly than she'd intended, and Darsh looked at her with an odd expression in his eyes.

He turned away. "So you'd spent the evening doing what? Candy Crush? Facebook? Watching TV?"

"I watched a couple of episodes of *Friends* on Netflix. If Jenny was there we'd have watched a horror movie, but I was too scared to do that when I was alone. Ironic, huh?"

"I'm too scared to watch *World War Z*," Erin admitted.

"Me, too." Darsh drew up his shoulders in a mock shudder. "I don't do zombies."

Rachel laughed despite herself, and some of the tension eased out of the room. After a few moments she swallowed. "I must have dropped off. I woke up to the feeling of a needle stabbing into my backside. But before I could struggle or shout for help, he was on top of me, pressing my face into the pillow so no one could hear me scream." Her gaze became vacant. "He just lay there for ages not saying a word, and then my head started to spin. I thought I was going to suffocate. I went all limp and floppy, and then he let go. He stuffed a gag in my mouth." She stuck out her tongue. "I can still taste it."

"What kind of gag?"

"Rubber. One of those ball-gag things that some people think is sexy." She looked like she wanted to throw up.

Erin avoided looking at Darsh. She couldn't remember if that detail came out during the trial or not. She needed to look at the transcripts.

"It was dark?" Darsh asked.

"Yes, but there was faint light from my alarm clock and some from the streetlights outside the window near Jenny's bed. He turned me over and undressed me. I couldn't move, even though I wanted to. Then he tied me up, but I was so out of it I didn't have a clue…I mean, I *know* what happened," she said defensively. "There were flashes of clarity when I must have regained consciousness." Embarrassment made her avoid Darsh's gaze, but she looked at Erin. "I know all the things he did and made me do—although he might have done other things I don't know about. But it was like I was a rag doll and totally at his mercy." Tears welled in the girl's blue eyes. Erin's heart broke for her.

"Would you mind standing up?" Darsh asked.

Rachel got cautiously to her feet. Darsh moved a little closer, and Erin watched Rachel's eyes widen and breath hitch as he stood. Terror flickered in her eyes.

"What size did he seem to you, compared to me? Bigger? Smaller?"

Rachel blinked rapidly and inched a little closer until she almost touched him. She frowned in confusion. "Smaller than you, I think. But it's all so blurry. He seemed kind of huge sometimes and small at others." Special-K could do that. So could fear and panic. Rachel scooted quickly away and curled back into her chair.

"And you are positive you saw Drew Hawke?"

"I saw his face really clearly. He had these staring eyes, but his expression never changed. Just those horrible eyes staring at me as he, well," she swallowed, "you know, *raped me*. I passed out, and when I came to he was gone."

"The ropes were still attached to your limbs?" asked Darsh.

Rachel nodded. "But they'd come really loose I assume when he took the sheet from beneath me." Her glance darted up. "I did remember something the other night," she admitted almost guiltily. "Something I hadn't remembered before."

"What?" Erin asked gently even though a spurt of excitement moved through her.

"He combed my hair."

Erin's gaze shot to Rachel's head, but the girl blushed fiery red. "Not this hair." She brushed a hand over her head. "My pubic hair. I had this weird flashback to him doing that." She drew her knees to her chest again. "God, what a creep."

Erin didn't like that. She didn't like it at all. It showed a degree of forensic countermeasures on par with dipping fingertips in bleach. She pulled out her photographs of the knots in the blue rope. "Can you remember if this is what the knots he tied you up with looked like?"

Rachel looked at the photos, but her skin lost all color when she realized the rope was probably attached to a body. She held a hand to her mouth and started sobbing. "Oh, God. I don't know. I really don't know. How many monsters are out there?"

"Too many," Darsh said quietly.

Her eyes just got bigger. "I thought I'd beaten the bastard.

I actually felt free for a while. You told me it was over." The words held a bite of accusation as she looked at Erin.

The door opened, and her mother came in. She must have been listening at the door. "Please go now."

Erin stopped beside Rachel's chair and rested a hand on her shoulder. "I'm really sorry, Rachel."

Darsh thanked her, and Erin followed him out. Her mother opened the front door.

"I thought my daughter could get on with her life again after the trial, but it's not over, is it?"

Erin wanted to tell her that everything would be okay, but she was a lousy liar.

"We're doing everything we can to catch this killer, ma'am." Darsh spoke for her. "We'll keep you in the loop."

Erin said goodbye and strode to her truck, feeling like someone had just kicked the crap out of her. She started the engine and tried to find her inner cop. "Well, that sucked."

"She's a strong kid, but she's gonna need more counseling."

"What she needs," Erin commented angrily, "is for us to arrest this new attacker." She paused and looked at him as he buckled up beside her. "I didn't know you were a sniper."

"It never came up in the conversation."

Because they'd been too busy figuring out how fast they could get each other naked. She didn't appreciate the reminder, no matter how subtle. She eyed him narrowly. "And now you chase serial killers."

His dark eyes were once again unreadable. "I got a taste for hunting humans." He shrugged. "After that it's hard to hunt anything else."

A shiver whispered over her spine. She was pretty sure serial killers felt the same way.

CHAPTER ELEVEN

D ARSH HADN'T EATEN more than a sandwich and half of Erin's Twix in two days. His stomach growled so loudly it was like someone inside was trying to get out.

"Hungry?" Erin raised her brows at him as they strode past a stuffed elk that guarded the store doors.

"If I don't eat real food in the next ten minutes, I'm probably going to gnaw off my own hand," he admitted.

"It's almost noon." She checked her watch. It was an expensive dive number that Darsh flashed back to seeing on her wrist that night in Quantico. That, a pair of silver earrings, and a smile that had brought him to his knees. Not realizing his thoughts had once again sunk lower than the Earth's core, she gave him a sympathetic smile. "We can grab a quick lunch. Next team meeting isn't until three, and I could eat."

He grunted, hiding the fact he was finding it harder and harder not to wonder if her lips tasted the same, or remember the sound of her gasping his name when she came.

Not what he needed to think about right now.

Instead, he thought about Brennan and Frazer and the other members of the BAU and how much he didn't want to let the team down. They all pulled their weight, even Mallory who was barely out of FOA—first office agent—status. She'd bagged a serial killer, helped thwart an assassination attempt on the president, and played a major role in exonerating a wrongly convicted FBI agent and uncovering a Russian spy. And she wasn't just a rookie, she was a pregnant rookie, and if that wasn't overachieving, he didn't know what was. He wasn't a slacker, but he had to admit it would be nice to take one of these fuckers down for a change—except the person he might also take down was walking beside him to her truck.

The idea left a bad taste in his mouth.

Erin appeared to be a solid cop. He'd be shocked if she'd messed up the Hawke investigation, but these crimes were so similar in nature they automatically suggested linkage. He had to be impartial. He had to look at the facts and not just what he hoped to be true.

His father took great pleasure suggesting Darsh was the token minority hire for the BAU, but Darsh was good at his job. His only real problem was the constant need to prove it.

They climbed into the huge truck without speaking, each lost in their own thoughts. They'd talked to a salesman in the outdoors shop. The good news was Darsh was now the proud owner of a black down jacket, hat, gloves, and boots. He had a fighting chance of making it through the next few days without anything important snapping off. The bad news was that although the rope was good quality climbing rope, it was relatively common, and you could order it off the internet. He was going to ask Agent Chen to investigate that aspect. See if anyone around here had ordered any, someone who maybe didn't need it for climbing.

Erin pulled up outside a low-slung A-frame building constructed of dark gray slate and big wooden beams. The Belmont Inn. The parking lot was almost full. A classy place—not where he'd expected to go for lunch. Good thing he was wearing a suit.

"Belongs to a friend of my dad's," she told him, unbuckling her seatbelt. "It's pretty much the only place in town where I'm reasonably optimistic they won't spit in my food."

It was an issue for law enforcement in general, but he imagined for Erin in particular. They walked in the front door and were greeted by a balding guy in his sixties wearing a blue suit.

"Erin!" He enveloped her in a big hug and kissed her on the cheek. "How's the finest detective in town?"

Her laugh was warm as she greeted the man. "I bet you say that to Harry when he comes here, too."

"Nah, I say how's the best *male* detective in town to him. I'm not a putz."

"Nice distinction." She grinned, and the strain and worry around her eyes were temporarily replaced by humor. "Jerry, this is Agent Singh of the FBI."

Darsh shook the guy's hand and almost had his fingers crushed. "Cop?" he guessed.

"Retired from the NYPD with twenty-five years on the job. Feels like yesterday. Me and Erin's dad were partners in the bad old days."

"Miss it?" Darsh was curious. He often wondered how people eased back into civilian life. It was the same when leaving the military, which was why he'd had his eye on a federal law enforcement position from the get-go.

"Every day, but I also enjoy not dealing with crazies and people not taking random potshots at me."

"Not to mention owning the nicest family restaurant in town. His son's the head chef. Daughter manages the place."

Jerry shrugged. "I help out. I had a bit of a windfall and

decided to give my kids a head start in their chosen careers. Me and the wife always liked it around here."

"He retired and a week later got run-over by some rich guy in a Ferrari," Erin said bluntly.

"Best day of my life," Jerry said cheerfully.

"Luckily the driver couldn't get out of first gear."

Jerry grinned. "If you're going to get run-over make sure it's by an Arab sheikh lost in Manhattan."

"I'll keep that in mind," said Darsh.

"I'm assuming you're here to eat?" Jerry asked them both.

The smells out of the kitchen were making Darsh drool. They both nodded and Jerry grabbed menus. "Come on. I'll find you a good spot."

They passed an older couple dining. The guy turned to openly stare at him and Erin.

Darsh moved his jacket aside so the gold shield he'd attached to his belt, and his gun, were both clearly visible. The man's gaze rose to meet his, and a flush worked its way over his cheekbones. Those people who didn't believe bigotry was rife in the world should walk around as part of a mixed race couple for a day.

Not that they were a couple.

Jerry led them to a corner booth near the back of the restaurant. Darsh grabbed the seat facing the door before Erin could get there. She shot him a glare.

"I'll take whatever's on special," Erin said, not even looking at the menu.

"Me, too. With a side of fries and coffee."

Jerry nodded knowingly. Cops ate on the run. Speed was key. He tapped the menus against his palm. "I won't ask how the investigation's going, but I will tell you if this dickwad breaks into my home, he'll get my forty-five shoved up his ass, bullet first. Food won't be long. I'll make sure your order goes straight to the front of the queue." He walked away to the next customer.

"Nice guy."

Erin nodded. "He was a good cop, too. He's the one who suggested I come work up here."

"After your husband shot himself?"

Her mouth dropped open, and she looked away. "Yeah," she murmured. "After he shot himself."

He stared at her, willing her to say more, to talk about it, but she refused to even look at him. "You go home much?" He tried a different direction.

She shook her head. "I've been pretty busy. With the rape cases last year, and the farmhouse I'm renovating. It's taking a lot longer than I expected." She grimaced. "I must have suffered a blow to the head before I bought it."

"Needs work?"

She snorted. "And then some. But I'm getting there. I need my family to come up for another long weekend, and I might get the worst of it finished." She shrugged. "Should have bought an apartment in town but after growing up in the city, I liked the idea of being in the country and owning some land."

"Don't you ever get scared living out there alone?" Crap, he didn't know if she lived alone, but if this was a fishing expedition, he may as well make it deep and oceanic.

"Only when I watch scary movies," she admitted with a shudder. "But I'm armed and have good locks on the doors and windows." She shrugged. "Sure, I get creeped out sometimes and start imagining someone hiding in the closet, but that's no different from any woman anywhere in the world."

And sometimes monsters shared the same bed. "Is that why you know so much self-defense? I mean, you took down a guy twice your size without blinking."

She held his gaze with a flat stare, giving nothing away. "Yeah, that's why."

He wanted to call her on her words. Tell her he knew about the hospital visits buried in the system. But it wasn't his business. His business was finding this killer and making sure that perpetrator wasn't also responsible for last year's rapes. The fact he couldn't acknowledge the truth about what happened to her made him angry. Angry that he wasn't allowed to have an opinion or comment on what she'd been through or on how much it must have sucked. And, how, if she was his, she'd never have to worry about some abusive asshole messing with her again. But she wasn't his, and he wasn't supposed to know what she'd been through.

He had the feeling Erin would close down faster than a trapdoor if she ever found out he did.

A waitress brought them each a glass of water, and he took a drink, grateful for the interruption. He turned his mind back to the case and something he'd wondered about while listening to Rachel. "Why d'you think no one ever saw him on his way to and from the victims' rooms?"

"I wondered the same thing." She leaned closer, and he met her halfway. They didn't want anyone overhearing their conversation, but it brought him dangerously close to her mouth. "Drew Hawke was part of the student community, but it's kind of hard to miss the star quarterback skulking around the corridors."

"What was the theory?" he asked.

She shrugged. "The attacks happened in the early hours when it was quiet and no one was around. Maybe he wore a hat and a hoodie. The girls he attacked were always alone—most of them were in single dorms except for Rachel Knight." Her pink lips twisted. "Some of the girls documented their lives on social media like it was a college course. Every time they left their dorm, who they met, who was going to what party, when, and they kept their location apps turned on." Her gaze met his briefly. "I'm not saying that makes it their fault, but it makes it easier for the predators."

"How many girls in all?"

Erin's eyes clouded. "Four came forward. DA refused to prosecute two of the cases because the girls had…reputations."

He frowned. "Remind me which century we're in?"

"Yeah, I know. It sucked. Trust me, it sucked." She leaned back against the booth. "The DA's position was they felt they could secure a conviction using just Rachel's and Mary's testimonies whereas if they charged him with all four rapes, the defense might be able to muddy the waters. Persuading a jury is a lot easier if we can prove he's a serial offender, obviously, but the DA figured two victims were enough. The families of the other girls were livid." She frowned. "Think this could be some sort of act of revenge by a victim's family member?"

Darsh grimaced. "I hate to say it's possible, but it is possible. I have an analyst already running all the football players and staff for priors. I'll ask her to add the victims' male relatives to the list. Can you email me the names?"

She fiddled with the saltshaker then looked up at him with heat in her cheeks. "I, er, don't actually have your email address, or your cell number…"

And all the air was immediately sucked out of the room. The subtext was clear and made him feel like a jackass. They'd had wild and crazy sex, but she didn't know a damn thing about him. Why the hell would she confide in him? He hadn't made this situation easy for her.

He pulled out his card and slid it over the table. "My name is Darsh Singh. Thirty-five years old. Served in the US Marine Corps after 9/11. Got out, finished my degree in criminal psychology, and applied to the FBI. The rest, as they say, is history."

Erin smiled reluctantly, fingering the card before slipping it into her pocket. "You're obviously not married. Significant other?"

Not knowing how to interpret that question and afraid of all the reasons he wanted to, he held her gaze as he shook his head.

"What about the rest of the family? What do they do?"

"My dad's a pharmaceutical engineer, and my two sisters are website designers."

"Your mom?"

"She died." He took a drink of water, relieved when the arrival of their food interrupted that line of questioning.

Erin waited for the waitress to leave before saying, "I'm sorry."

He nodded, hoping she'd leave it at that. "It was a long time ago."

"How did she die?" Erin asked, because cops never left a damn thing alone.

Darsh bit down on the anger the question brought. He didn't want to talk about his mother, but if he wanted Erin to open up? He needed to play fair. "She was murdered." He popped a fry in his mouth.

"They ever catch who did it?"

He shook his head.

"Did you ever look?"

Sure, he'd looked. "There was no evidence."

"So you looked."

He wanted her to drop it. He shrugged and said nothing.

"I hear that sort of trauma drives a lot of people into law enforcement. Either you're born into it like I was, or you're dragged into it by the compelling need to serve, or to fight for justice. I'm not sure what I'd do if I wasn't a cop." Her expression clouded, and he wanted her to stop talking. "I don't remember a time when this wasn't the only thing I wanted to do."

Jesus. He couldn't respond or meet her gaze, he just stuffed his face with lasagna so hot it burned the roof of his mouth and wished he'd ordered a beer. Alcohol would be great right about now, but last time he'd had a drink in this woman's company things had gotten a hell of a lot hotter than his lasagna They ate silently for a few minutes, both hungry and needing to refuel. Both avoiding talking about personal things.

"You know," she said, wiping her mouth with her napkin and pushing a nearly empty plate away. "I never said sorry for not telling you I was married when we first met. That was wrong of me and put you in a difficult position. At the time I never considered your feelings. I'm sorry."

He stared at the table, and a thick wedge of emotion stuck in his throat. He'd acted like a dick and now he was stuck with that reality. If he said he knew she'd filed for divorce before they'd hooked up, she'd know he'd been digging into her background. It wouldn't take long for her to figure out that he also knew her ex was an abusive fuck.

"I was an ass. I owe you an apology." Some stupid part of his brain wanted her to trust him. To confide in him of her own free will.

A small group settled into the booth behind them. An older guy of about forty, another two guys in their mid-twenties and two younger women. Academics and students.

"Rachel Knight is a brave young woman," he said thoughtfully. "I get the feeling more things might come back to her the way that other new detail did."

Erin nodded. "I'm not sure how it will help us, though. Rachel was adamant it was Drew Hawke who raped her, and he's locked up."

"There's a connection between the cases. You know it, too."

She didn't look happy, but truth was truth. The forensic countermeasures told him that while he wasn't sure it was the same perp, he was singing from the same playbook. This was one smart UNSUB.

"Erin, is that you?" One of the guys who'd settled into the booth behind them stood and leaned over the divider toward them. He wore skinny jeans, a roll neck sweater, and a tweed jacket.

"Professor Huxley," she exclaimed, twisting in her seat. Darsh didn't miss the slight note of dismay in her voice.

"Roman," the professor corrected. The guy's eyes roved Erin's cleavage from his vantage point, but she didn't seem to notice.

Or maybe she did. She slid out of the booth to stand. Darsh folded his napkin and climbed to his feet, having inhaled his meal in record time.

"FBI Agent Singh. This is Professor Roman Huxley, a world-renowned expert in criminal psychology at Blackcombe. And this is Linus and Rick, his research assistants, and Rena and Kelsey, two of his other students."

"We had a lab meeting, but I decided to treat everyone to lunch." Huxley's voice dropped to a conspiratorial whisper. "We're trying to escape the rather maudlin atmosphere on campus."

"Murder will do that to a place," Darsh said sardonically.

"You're with the BAU?" Huxley asked him. The easy tone belied the intensity of the man's gaze.

"That's correct."

"Perhaps you'd consider coming in and giving a guest lecture while you're here?"

Darsh wasn't about to be interrogated about his job by a bunch of students when he was busy investigating a crime on campus. He threw enough money on the table to cover his and Erin's meal. "I doubt I'll be here long enough, Professor, and my priority is the investigation. You could submit a request through the public relations liaison at the FBI, though."

The professor's expression tightened. "Well, maybe if you come to me for help on the case I can twist your arm?"

Darsh shrugged and smiled. Yeah, not even if the man held a gun to his head. "Maybe."

The others watched them with rapt attention.

"Linus said you were all friends with Mandy Wochikow-ski?" Erin asked the group.

Darsh's gaze sharpened on the students.

"She did an honors project with us over the summer so we knew her quite well," one of the girls told them quietly. "It's hard to believe she was murdered. We all liked her."

"She was a bright student," the professor stated.

"Was she seeing anyone romantically?" Darsh asked.

The two girls shook their heads.

The blond male grad student, Linus, spoke up. "Like I told Erin." The young man's eyes watched the detective with a hint of reverence. "I don't think so. We'd go for coffee sometimes during the summer, and she never mentioned she was seeing anyone."

"She fancied Linus," the dark-haired young man, Rick, gave his pal an arched look.

"She had a bit of a crush on me, but I was dating another girl at the time," Linus admitted quickly, because they all knew romance was the quickest route to becoming a suspect. "We were just friends."

"Know any of her other buddies?" Erin asked them.

"I knew she hung out with some of the sorority girls, but they weren't really my scene," Kelsey said.

"There was a guy in computing she mentioned a couple of times in the summer," Rick said, his eyes lingering on Erin in a way Darsh recognized. The woman herself was oblivious. "She was pretty serious about her studies, not really a party animal."

"If you remember anything you think might be useful, please get in touch. You know how to reach me," Erin told them. She turned to the professor and nodded. "We'll be in touch, Professor."

"Look forward to it, Erin, Agent Singh." The guy grinned like he'd won a minor victory, but Darsh didn't know what the hell that might be.

He walked out of the restaurant feeling full for the first time in days. But the contentment didn't extend beyond his stomach. "Quite the fan club you have back there."

She rolled her eyes at him. "I've discovered the easiest way to make yourself more appealing to the opposite sex is to say you're not interested. The world is apparently full of masochists."

Darsh didn't quite know how to respond. She had a lot more going for her than that, but her ex had done a real number on her psyche. "He helped out on the last case?"

"Huxley?" Erin nodded. "He's assisted numerous police departments and has done some really great studies."

"I don't like him."

"Because…"

"Because he wears skinny jeans and hair gel." And looked at Erin like he wanted to undo her shirt buttons.

"*That's* how the FBI forms opinions? Very scientific." She climbed into her truck cab.

He walked around the front and got in the passenger side. "Never ignore your lizard brain. They teach you that in the Marines."

"I'll try and remember that next time my lizard brain decides to chat." She started the engine and pulled out of the parking space. "I owe you for lunch."

He closed his eyes and leaned his head against the padded headrest. "You can get it next time."

Considering where his thoughts strayed whenever he spent more than five minutes in her company, he owed her more than lunch. If he were a Catholic he'd be on his knees begging forgiveness and *that* picture conjured a whole new array of sins, so he tried to distract himself by pretending to sleep while she drove back to the station. The sound of something smacking against the glass jerked him back into awareness.

"What the fuck was that?" Something gooey slid down the front of her windshield. He turned and saw a crowd of demonstrators on the front steps of the courthouse.

"That would be the sound of someone egging my truck." She squirted wiper fluid over the glass and eventually the screen cleared. The resigned tremor of anger in her voice told him she was pissed.

Fury curdled in his stomach. "Don't you ever get tired of it, Erin? The bullshit, the hatred?"

The corners of her mouth tightened as her chin came up. "I guess I'm used to it."

"Why would you ever want to be used to it? Is it some form of penance? Because of you and me and your dead husband?"

She pulled up outside the station, her expression studiously blank. "Well, like you, I have a lifetime of regrets to choose from." Her eyes held his for a moment—long enough for him to know he was one of those regrets.

He gritted his teeth together to stop from telling her that he had no regrets about that night, none at all. It had been one of the best nights of his life. But Erin did what she always did when he said something she didn't like. She got out and walked away, and he sat there like a damn fool.

CHAPTER TWELVE

THE TEAM MEETING started at three PM sharp, but Darsh was nowhere to be seen. Neither was Ully. Erin stood at the front of the large table in the conference room and tried not to speculate on what that meant. She had enough things to worry about.

"So where are we on the door-to-door canvassing?" she began, despite Chief Strassen frowning at her.

"We spoke to someone in every house in a two block radius," said Bill Youder, another senior patrol officer. "No one recalls seeing a strange car parked or a stranger lurking in the area on the night of January 5. But it was the first day back after the winter break, and students had been arriving on and off all day."

"You spoke to the neighbors on either side and opposite?"

"Yep. No one heard any screams from that address on the night in question. Apparently there was often loud music playing in the house, but the guy in number seventy-three said the girls were never noisy after about nine so it didn't bother him."

"You think that was why the attacker turned the music off after he'd recorded the message from Cassie?" Cathy Bickham asked. "He didn't want to disturb the neighbors?"

"Possibly, or to make sure no one caught him by surprise

when he was raping Cassie." Erin nodded. Was this someone close to one of the girls? Did he know their routine? "What's the neighbor's name?"

"Raymond Butcher."

"Any priors?"

"A parking ticket about three years ago."

She stretched the tense muscles in her shoulders. "This morning I dug into the rope used. It is good quality climbing rope, but not uncommon. The FBI is looking to see if anyone local ordered it online."

"Where is the fed?" Harry asked with a disdainful expression on his face.

"Not sure." Erin gave him a wry look. No matter how much she was attracted to Darsh, these were the people she had to work with on a daily basis.

"Any word on the evidence we sent to Quantico?" the chief asked.

She shook her head. "They've only had it twenty-four hours." Not even.

Strassen rubbed the back of his neck as if that were her fault, too. "So we're still no further forward?"

His disapproval sank into the pit of her stomach like an anchor. "Not really, sir. I did time a run this morning between Cassie Bressinger's house and the frat house where Jason Brady lives."

The chief's eyes bugged. "You think *Brady* did it this time?"

Crap. "I only know that I saw him on the street as I drove to the call. I timed the run this morning, and it took me seven minutes. Theoretically he could still have committed the murders, therefore I am not ready to rule him out as a suspect."

Youder leaned forward to look at the chief. "Me and Bickham interviewed the partygoers, including Tanya Whitehouse—Cassie and Mandy's roomie. Turns out no one remembers seeing Brady between eight and ten. No one knows where he was, and he's not talking." He leaned back in his chair and held her gaze. "You think he might be trying to make his BFF look innocent?"

Erin nodded. "It's an idea, but I'd rather have a suspect from the evidence or a witness."

"The witnesses are all dead," said Cathy Bickham.

Erin's stomach knotted.

"Except the neighbor's dog," Harry said glibly.

"Pity the mutt doesn't speak English. He might put us all out of a job," Youder joked.

Erin got that black humor was a way of dealing with terrible situations cops often found themselves in, but for once she couldn't join in. She was too emotionally invested.

"I finally got the subpoena for the cell records," Harry said after the moment of levity. "I'm going through phone numbers and names looking for connections. I can't get anything on the @Darkmatter handle who was flirting with Mandy. Account was set up anonymously and is only sporadically active and nothing posted recently. I did notice some pretty vocal complaints about the police investigation in general. There're talking about asking the governor to bring in the National Guard to keep the women safe in their beds at night."

Erin grimaced. The egg on her car had been an apt expression of what the people of this town thought of her ability to crack the case.

"So what's the plan for solving this thing?" Strassen asked

impatiently.

"Harry's still working social media and cell phone angles. I'm going to go talk to campus security and see if they have surveillance footage from Monday night," Erin told him. "Then I'm going to the offices and stores in the Fairfax Road area and see if they have any footage I can look at."

The chief nodded. "Bickham, give Detective Donovan a hand."

Erin pushed away her natural resentment at the implication she needed help.

"Yes, sir." The rookie piped up.

The chief dismissed them, rubbing his stomach like he'd developed an ulcer overnight.

Erin packed up her notes and headed to her desk. Where the hell had Darsh disappeared to? Part of her wanted to go see if he'd fallen asleep in his office, but the desire felt like a weakness, and she wasn't giving in to it.

She glanced over to the chief's office and saw the Dean of Students staring at her through the glass. She gave him a smile, but the guy ignored it and turned away with a sour expression on his face as the chief arrived. They shut the door.

There was no doubt the dean wanted the killer found and her off the case, not necessarily in that order. She was pretty sure the chief felt the same way.

Damn.

As she was grabbing her coat to head off to find video surveillance, a furor erupted next to the booking desk.

A homeless guy they all knew as Stinky Pete stood there in handcuffs. Usually he was a law-abiding citizen who kept to himself. Today he was shouting and carrying on.

Ully stood nearby grinning like a fool.

161

"What's going on?" she asked.

He was holding a large plastic bag, which he held open for her to look inside. It was full of material. Material that looked suspiciously like that of the bedding from Cassie Bressinger's bed.

Her gaze shot to his. "Where'd you find it?"

"Under the bridge down by the river, wrapped around Stinky Pete."

"Hey, that's mine!" The guy, who was only in his forties but looked more like seventy, lunged toward it. The patrol officer held him back.

She dragged Ully farther away so they could talk out of earshot. "You call the evidence team down there?" Erin's heart was banging about a hundred beats per minute.

"Yup. They pulled up before we left." He grinned and put his hand on her shoulder. "We got him, Donovan. Now get your ass in the interview room and nail the sonofabitch."

THE INTERVIEW ROOM had gray linoleum, beige walls, a faux-wood table screwed into the floor, and two uncomfortable looking plastic chairs either side of it. There was a window covered with a metal grill with a view of a small courtyard and a cement wall opposite. The sky was overcast, depressing and bleak.

Darsh figured looking at that view everyday would be a fine line between incarceration and torture, but prison wasn't supposed to be a picnic.

He heard the clang of a door and then footsteps. He hadn't told Erin he was coming here, and he wasn't sure why. A guard appeared in the doorway. The man was huge—six-six and heavily built with the sort of face that made you remember your manners. The prisoner behind him was prettier, about Darsh's height. Wider across the shoulders, lean through the torso and hips—classic quarterback physique clad in bright prison orange. Drew Hawke. He had his hands cuffed in front of him.

"Take a seat," Darsh offered.

Hawke eyed him warily but slid his ass into the chair.

"Keeping in shape I see."

Hawke's lip curled. "I don't have a lot else to do. May as well workout."

"Just in case?"

"Just in case, what? I get out and get drafted?" Hawke snorted. "I gave up all hope of my old life a long time ago. I'm stuck in this shithole for good."

He was a good-looking kid, but there was a hardness around his eyes now that went beyond being tough on the field. Doing time in the big house was a little different than living it up in a fraternity.

The kid held Darsh's gaze. "What do you want?"

The young man didn't know about Cassie yet, Darsh had made sure of it. The governor, at the request of the DOJ, had called the warden and asked to have Hawke placed in solitary yesterday. The prison officers had used a cell search to justify their actions and had found a homemade shiv. It could have belonged to either of the guys in the cell so they'd punished them both.

"Have you found more delusional girls who swear under oath I tied them up so I could nail their asses? Or maybe I crossed state lines to do it this time?" His eyes held dark amusement and a hint of fear. He shook his head. "I don't know where you find these women. I mean, I have an amazing girlfriend and groupies lining up to suck my dick, but it wasn't enough for me, apparently." He rolled his eyes, went to cross his arms over his chest but was stopped by the handcuffs. "Fuck," he muttered quietly and some of the steam seemed to go out of him.

"You and Cassie still dating?" Darsh asked.

"Sure, we're '*dating*.'" Hawke's expression said it all as he glanced around the holding room. One shoulder rose. "I'm going to break up with her when she comes to visit with my dad in a couple of weeks though. I don't want her wasting her life waiting for me."

"Thirty years is a long time. You think she'd wait?"

"I know she'd wait." Hawke swallowed repeatedly, and even then his voice came out hoarse. "Cassie's the best thing that ever happened to me, and I didn't even know it until I was arrested. Breaking up with her is gonna hurt, but it's better for her in the long run. She'll find someone else eventually."

Darsh was trying hard not to like the guy. Genuine psychopaths could be a lot of fun to be around when they thought you had something they wanted. But genuine psychopaths didn't worry about other people wasting their lives on them— they actually expected nothing less. He eyed the guard. "Can you release the restraints?"

The man nodded and came forward with the keys. He removed the cuffs and waited over by the door again.

"I have some bad news for you," Darsh said quietly. He rarely had to do death notices, and they sucked.

Hawke leaned forward over the table. "Something happen to my dad or mom? My sister?" His face was pinched with worry. Mouth tight.

Darsh shook his head. "Your family is fine as far as I'm aware."

Hawke frowned, then his expression dropped. "Cassie?"

Darsh nodded.

"Where is she? What happened?" Hawke got louder, and the guard moved into the room as if to subdue him, but Darsh waved him away. He'd given up his weapon and credentials before they let him through the door. The kid might get a punch in, but being a Marine, not to mention a federal agent, meant he could hold his own.

"I'm sorry to tell you, Drew, that Cassandra Bressinger was murdered along with her friend, Mandy Wochikowski." Darsh braced himself for anger, but the guy in front of him dissolved into tears.

"What?" Hawke sobbed. "Murdered? Who would want to murder Cassie?"

"Someone broke into their home."

Hawke looked aghast. "A robbery?"

"It wasn't a robbery."

His eyes went wide. "Oh, God. Oh, Christ. This is because of me, isn't it?" Tears dripped onto the orange cotton of his coveralls. "I told her to stop fighting for me." His voice hitched. "I told her over and over to drop it and move on with her life, but she wouldn't listen." He used his big hands to wipe his wet cheeks. "It wasn't worth it. I'm not worth it. Did you catch the fucker who did it?"

Those weren't the words of a psychopath, although the fact he'd assumed it was all about him was slightly narcissistic. Then again, under the circumstances, he was probably right.

"Not yet," admitted Darsh.

"Did they hurt the girls? Cassie and Mandy?"

Whatever was on Darsh's face must have given the facts away.

"No. No. Noooo." Hawke shook his head in denial. "They were not raped."

"I'm sorry." Darsh pressed his lips together. "Cassie was raped during the attack."

Hawke looked dumbstruck. "Was this some revenge thing? Did someone rape and kill her because she was my girlfriend, and they thought I'd raped those other girls?"

It was a possible theory, but more telling was Hawke hadn't slipped from his stance of innocence even once. Maybe he'd convinced himself he was innocent. Or maybe the kid was doing someone else's time.

"I don't know who did it or why. I'm looking into it. That's why I'm here."

An angry snort replaced the tears. "You think I had something to do with this, too?"

Darsh didn't miss the way the young man's fists clenched. "Do you know of anyone who might want to hurt Cassie?"

The fists relaxed. He shook his head. "Just everyone who thinks I'm guilty. Those girls who were attacked maybe—or someone who loves them?"

"Anyone care about you enough to have done this to try and get you out of prison?"

Hawke's eyes widened, and his expression turned incredulous. "You mean do I have any friends who are twisted enough to murder the woman I love—someone who has stood by me through this entire nightmare at great cost to herself—just to try to throw my conviction into question? Well, shit, yeah, actually my dad is pretty shaken up by the whole deal. Maybe he did it. Or Coach Raymond—because he fucking loves to win no matter the cost." Hawke's face was turning red with rage, but he made no move toward Darsh.

Darsh had watched video of the guy playing football, and he was incredibly disciplined even under extreme pressure. But what happened when he lost his cool? How did he channel his rage, or was it bottled up like a volcano ready to blow?

Darsh pushed. He wasn't here to make friends. "What about your teammates?"

Hawke held his hands wide. "You want me to throw another player under the bus? You have some insane hatred of the Blackcombe Ravens?" The young man took in a calming breath and fixed his gaze on the ceiling. "Look, I read the stats on student athletes. I know on average they commit nearly twenty percent of reported college sexual assaults and I know people think we're entitled assholes. I *was* an entitled asshole," he paused, his chest pumping heavily, "but my teammates are solid."

"What about Jason Brady? You and he are best friends, right?"

Hawke blew out a tired breath and shook his head. "Jason isn't that sort of guy."

"He's pretty torn up about you being locked up—"

"Because he knows I didn't do it."

"He written to you in here?"

Hawke shook his head.

"I thought you guys were best friends?"

"I wrote to him a few times. I told him not to write back. And not to visit. Just to concentrate on his game. To do his best for me."

"He seems pretty angry."

TONI ANDERSON

"Why the fuck wouldn't he be angry? He knows I didn't do it!" Hawke's voice rose in fury. Then he froze, staring hard at him. "This is the same guy, isn't it? The same guy who raped those other girls last year, but somehow got them to say it was me." His eyes gleamed.

Darsh kept silent.

Hawke carried on talking. Maybe this was why his lawyers had kept him off the stand. The kid wouldn't shut up.

"There's no way Jason is the rapist."

"Why's that?"

Hawke shook his head in disbelief. "He's my best friend. We lived together, played together, traveled together, got drunk together. I know he's not the rapist same way as he knows it's not me. I *know* him."

"He had his tongue down Tanya Whitehouse's throat at a frat party on Monday night."

Hawke winced. Darsh didn't know if it was because he'd mentioned Cassie's roomie, or reminded him that life went on even as he rotted in here.

"Jason likes sex. A lot. He's not in a relationship. He's a star athlete at an elite college and girls dig him. Doesn't mean he can't control himself."

"He likes hurting people on the field."

Hawke shook his head in disgust. "It's *football*. Fuck."

Darsh watched the guy carefully but saw nothing except a frustrated young man.

Hawke leaned forward again, eyes intent. "Did she suffer? Cassie?"

If the kid *was* a serial rapist he might get off on the details, but hopefully he wouldn't be able to hide it. Darsh needed to test him.

"He beat her up. Tied her to the bed, and raped her. Probably more than once."

Hawke lost every vestige of color.

"Then he strangled her with his bare hands."

Hawke veered away, put his head between his knees, and puked all over the floor. Darsh stood and stepped back. Hawke stumbled away and sank against the far wall, wiping his mouth with the back of his hand.

It was tough to fake that sort of visceral reaction.

The guard glared at Darsh then left—presumably to grab a mop and bucket.

"Did you write to Cassie?" Darsh asked. His own stomach was roiling, and not just from the smell. He was starting to have serious doubts about Hawke's guilt.

"Yeah, I wrote to her." He swallowed repeatedly. He sat shaking with his knees tight to his chest—he reminded Darsh of Rachel Knight earlier. "Dear God, I hope they put me back in solitary."

"Why?" Darsh said sharply.

Hawke's lip curled. "There's a group of guys biding their time to nail my skinny white ass." His eyes were desolate. "If they see this weakness, they'll figure it's time and try to fucking destroy me. Then I'll have to fight back to survive, and if I fight back it hurts my chances of appeal and parole."

Darsh ignored the sympathy he was feeling. "What sort of letters did you write to Cassie?" He wanted to know what the UNSUB knew.

Hawke blew out a big breath. The guard came in with a mop and metal bucket, handed it to the kid. He climbed slowly to his feet.

"I described what it was like in here. The other inmates.

169

The guards. The fucking walls." He raised his brows at the guy at the door who didn't crack a smile. "I tried to keep it light." He wiped his face on his shoulder, even as he kept mopping up the mess off the floor. "I should have broken up with her when I was arrested." His hands twisted on the wooden handle. "I should have ignored my lawyers, and her. Made her hate me." Hawke held Darsh's stare. "He chose her because of me, didn't he?"

Darsh nodded. "Probably."

"Did he rape Mandy?"

Darsh shook his head.

"Isn't that unusual for these perverts?"

"'Unusual' and 'pervert' seems to go together." Darsh shrugged his shoulders. "Detective Donovan was the first officer on scene." He waited for a reaction.

"Oh, man, Cassie hated her. She'd have hated that Donovan was on the case." The kid pressed his eyes shut against a fresh onslaught of tears.

"You don't hate Donovan?"

"She's just doing her job. Despite what you may have heard, I have a great deal of respect for women in general." Hawke glared at him. "Was I happy she thought I could do this to another human being after she'd interviewed me a couple of times? No, I was pissed. But after hearing those girls testify in court? I'd have convicted me, too."

"So what do you think happened?"

His breath came out in a soft snort. "Someone set me up, Agent Singh. And they did a bang up job of it, too." Hawke's expression turned cold. "And they're not done with me yet or they wouldn't have murdered Cass."

Darsh's gut was telling him the same thing, but that

wouldn't look good for the Forbes Pines PD. And Erin in particular because everyone wanted to make her the scapegoat for a failure within the system.

But what was more important? Putting the right bad guy behind bars or the reputation of the local cops? He knew, he just didn't like the fact he was going to put a good cop in a bad position. "Do you know anyone who hates you this much?"

Hawke rinsed out the mop one final time and pushed it to the side of the room, propping it against the wall. "I used to think I was a good guy, but looking back? I was a jerk. I drank too much, bullied people, even though at the time I told myself we were all having a good time. Before I started seeing Cass I had hundreds of girls and never bothered to even learn their names. I trash-talked every member of any opposition I ever met. I was a fucking jerk."

"You remember the names of people you pissed off?"

Hawke spread his hands wide. "You got a few hours?"

"Write them down. Ask to have the warden send them to me. I'll make sure you're kept in seclusion from the general population." A phone call to the governor should help with that.

Hawke shook his head. "Pretty ironic that I'm safest locked up with the rapists and pedophiles." He stared down at the floor. "Can I ask you something?"

"What?"

Hawke looked up. "Can I go to Cassie's funeral?"

Darsh could read the wretched grief on the kid's face, but doubted it would happen. "I'll talk to the warden."

The kid nodded, and Darsh walked away, wishing he didn't have that terrible feeling in his gut that the justice system had failed this young man.

CHAPTER THIRTEEN

ERIN LET THEM finish booking their homeless suspect, which thankfully involved stripping and hosing him down before she started to question him. Someone found him some coveralls to wear when they took his clothes for evidence. He'd waived his right to an attorney.

Harry was sitting in with her. Darsh was still nowhere to be seen. She had no idea what to make of his absence.

She opened the file in front of her. "Your name is Peter Zimmerman?"

Stinky Pete—AKA Peter Zimmerman—wouldn't meet her gaze. His hair was a straggly salt and pepper gray. Grooves cut deeply into the skin of his forehead and around his mouth. His cheeks were hollowed out beneath prominent cheekbones. There was a fresh cut on his face as if someone had recently hit him. His hands lay on the tabletop, wrist bones too big for his scrawny arms.

"Is your legal name Peter Zimmerman?" she repeated. That's what AFIS had come back with when they'd run his prints. The guy had an open warrant down in Texas for DUI back in 2010. He'd been a Marine before that. Erin ignored the pity she felt for a man who'd fallen on hard times. This was exactly why justice needed to be blind.

Pete stopped trying to ignore her questions. "Yeah."

"You live under the bridge near the river?"

His eyes jerked around the room as if blinded. "Got a spot there. You guys better not wreck it," he growled, suddenly focusing on her.

"Isn't it cold?" she asked. How the hell did he bear it in winter?

"The mission gives me a bed and shelter when it gets real bad."

"You been there this week? To the mission?"

Peter shrugged. "Maybe. Not sure what day it is," he admitted.

He sniffed loudly, and she pushed a box of tissues towards him. He ignored it and wiped his nose on his sleeve.

"Peter, do you remember what you did on Monday? Today is Wednesday."

He gave her a goofy grin showing broken teeth. "Sure. I was at the shelter for a while."

"What time did you leave?"

He shrugged. "I forgot to check my Rolex."

She didn't respond to his sarcasm. "You sleep in the mission that night?"

He scratched at his head, and Erin shuddered to think what might be in his hair.

"Don't remember."

"Were you drinking?"

His eyes slid away. "Maybe." Clearly alcohol was his demon, but he'd never been pulled in for drunk and disorderly. He did his drinking alone or at least quietly. Probably because he didn't want the cops to find out about the arrest warrant.

"What were you drinking?"

He scratched his chin this time, and Erin heard the sound

of bristles scraping against his fingernails. "I got hold of a bottle of vodka."

"Someone gave it to you?"

His gaze looked sly. "Maybe. Don't remember."

"Did you steal it, Peter?"

His shoulders hunched. "Don't call me that. Call me Pete. Stinky Pete. That's what I like to be called."

Erin hardened her heart. Being upstate for the past three years had made her soft. Back in NYC, she dealt with ten drunks or homeless people a day, each with stories more heartbreaking than the last. There was no American Dream for these individuals. They were stuck in the sewer and some of them were determined to stay there, others were constantly being dragged down by circumstances they couldn't control.

"There's an outstanding warrant for your arrest down in Texas."

He wouldn't meet her gaze.

"DUI. Want to tell me about it?"

He crossed his bony arms over his withered chest. "Nothing to tell. You got the wrong person."

"They think it's you."

His eyes got hard. "They're wrong."

"Guess we'll leave that up to them to figure out."

His Adam's apple bobbed. "I ain't going back to Texas." His lower jaw pushed forward.

"Where'd you get the bed sheet they found wrapped around you?"

"It's mine," he snapped.

"How long have you had it?"

He cocked his head. "Not long."

"Where did you get it?"

His gaze narrowed further, and a calculating light entered them. "This about those girls that were murdered in town on Monday?" His body might be addicted to alcohol, but there was obviously still a razor-sharp brain in there when he was sober. "That why you brought me in?"

"Where did you get that sheet, Peter?"

He rolled his shoulders and straightened his spine. "Took it when I killed her."

Erin's heart stumbled. Could it really be this easy?

"Is that a confession, Peter?" Harry asked.

The man who wanted to be known as Stinky Pete nodded. "Sure. I killed her. I killed them both."

"How did you kill them, Peter?" she asked.

He held his hands in front of him and acted like he was wrapping them around something and squeezing.

"What else did you do?" Erin held her breath.

One side of his lips curved into an emotionless smile that chilled her blood. "I raped one of 'em. Didn't get time to do the other one though."

Erin nodded at Harry to take over and stepped out of the room. Ully high-fived her, but after a moment, she walked to her desk feeling unsettled and pensive.

She tossed her folder on the desk and wanted to go home and sleep for a week. At least she'd get rid of the federal agent who was pushing her for answers she didn't want to give, but the thought didn't bring the joy she'd anticipated. Instead she felt hollow and empty and depressed. She picked up the phone to call Rachel. At least she could improve one person's day.

———————

HE SAT ON Erin's bed and wound the rope around and around his forearm, tighter and tighter. He unfused his jaw and twisted the cord until his fingers throbbed from lack of blood and pain screamed along his nerves. He released the tension on the rope, and the blood rushed back through his starving veins with a flare of exquisite agony. That's what giving in to the hunger felt like. Starvation followed by a feast.

He climbed to his feet, knowing he couldn't linger because it had started to snow, and he couldn't afford to leave tracks. But he was frustrated. He wanted to see her, but she was *too* busy. Too *preoccupied*, hanging out with that federal agent who thought he was God's fucking gift.

Prick.

So what would be the best way to punish her? What did she care about most?

He glanced at a family portrait that sat on the chest of drawers. She had four brothers, but only one sister. He used his cell phone to take a snap of the photograph. He'd turned off all the locational trackers the day he'd bought the thing. Didn't want his electronic footsteps to be traceable.

Should he take the sister?

He pressed his lips together. She was hot, although not as hot as Erin. But, no. The sister was too obviously linked to Erin. It showed his hand. She was also in Manhattan. He sucked in his lips and narrowed his eyes.

It was time to set another plan in motion. Fuck with the system and maybe eventually someone would realize how broken it was. Hadn't he been trying to tell them that all these months? What would it take to get them to listen to him?

Maybe this had always been the path he'd been meant to walk. Showing how easy it was to manipulate anything as long as you were smart and knew the rules others played by.

He checked his wristwatch. Almost time to go. He took the laundered red panties out of his pocket and slipped them into Erin's lingerie drawer. He ran his fingers slowly through the silky material, picked up a black lacy bra, and let it dangle from his fingers.

He imagined it against Erin's ivory skin.

Pretty.

Very pretty. But not what he wanted.

He let it drop back into the drawer and closed it without making a sound. The top of her chest of drawers was cluttered with knickknacks, perfume bottles, candlesticks. The lid of her jewelry box was inlaid with walnut. He opened it and picked up a silver cross on a chain. He ran it over his skin, enjoying the cool touch of the metal. He let himself get aroused even though he didn't intend to do anything about it. Sometimes denying himself a simple pleasure produced much more intense results later. And he still had the little freshman dangling on his string. He was enjoying her naiveté and her eagerness to please. He pocketed the cross, even though it was one Erin wore often and might miss. He liked to have something of hers on him at all times. The tangible connection gave him something to hold onto. It would have to be enough until she realized they were meant to be together.

He smiled grimly.

She was a smart girl. She'd get there eventually.

He was going to make sure of it.

———————

THE MOMENT DARSH walked back into the police station, he

knew something significant had happened. The atmosphere had shifted—the tension eased. He spotted Erin talking to the chief by his office door and went to meet them.

Strassen wore a wide smile. "You hear the news?"

"Which news?" Darsh said carefully.

"We found the killer."

"Really?"

"Tell him, Erin." Strassen instructed her.

Erin's expression was less joyous. The corners of her mouth were drawn tight. Her eyes guarded. "A couple of patrolmen found a homeless guy by the name of Peter Zimmerman—AKA 'Stinky Pete'—under one of the bridges wrapped in what looks like the sheet from Cassie Bressinger's bed."

"He say where he got it?"

"He says he took it when he killed the two girls and raped one of them."

The fact that only one of the girls had been raped wasn't a detail that had been released to the media, although the rumor-mill was rife with speculation after Alicia Drummond had posted online about how she'd found her friends dead and feared she might be next.

"And we found blue rope consistent with the crime scene tying his tarp in place," she told him.

Darsh stared hard at Erin, but her expression was shut down, revealing nothing. "Can I question him?"

Erin opened her mouth to speak, but the chief cut in. "Not a lot of point under the circumstances."

Circumstances being that his job was supposed to be determining whether the previous series of rapes were related to the new murders.

The chief continued, "He only moved into the area around last summer. Right, Erin?"

Even though this vindicated the police department he didn't see jubilation in Erin's gaze. He saw mistrust and indecision.

"First time he was reported to the cops was back in September. It's doubtful he was here for much longer before that." Her smile gave him chills. "Forbes Pines isn't too fond of vagrants, but this guy kept to himself and didn't cause any trouble. Pretty much flew under the radar."

"I'd still like to talk to him," Darsh insisted. A homeless guy wasn't who he'd profiled as the killer, but that didn't mean it wasn't true. They obviously had a lot of physical evidence tying him to the crime.

The chief looked pissed, but Erin nodded. "I think you might be better served doing it tomorrow when we know more about him. He has an outstanding warrant for a DUI down in Texas. I have a call in to the detective involved in the case, but he's not back at his desk until morning."

"This Peter Zimmerman have a family?" asked Darsh.

"That's one of the things I'm trying to find out." Erin dragged her hair back from her face.

"Okay." Darsh nodded.

The chief reached out to shake his hand. "So I'm guessing you'll be leaving soon. Thanks for your help with this one." Strassen checked his watch. "I have to go make a statement to the press. Hopefully they'll leave us alone now." The chief went into his office, dismissing them both.

Darsh followed Erin back to her desk. Harry Compton wasn't anywhere to be seen. Darsh checked his watch. It was nearly seven, and they'd all been working overtime for the last few days so it wasn't that surprising the station was quiet.

"So…" He left the sentence hanging.

"So?" She eyed him narrowly.

"You don't think this guy did it?"

Erin slumped in her chair and looked away. "That's not what the evidence is telling me."

"But…"

"But this time I don't want to listen to the evidence, and if that isn't bias, I don't know what is." And he could tell from the light in her eyes that it pissed her off. Or maybe her cop instincts were starting to ping the way his had been since he'd seen Cassie Bressinger tied to that bed.

"Where were you, anyway?" There was a glint of suspicion in her eyes.

"Working." He put his hands in his pockets, not ready to tell her he'd been to see Hawke. "Did you check the surveillance cams yet?"

She shook her head. "I was just leaving to do that when they brought Zimmerman in." Her mouth twisted. "He was a Marine. You might be able to get more out of him than I could."

An arrow of denial hit him, but he ignored it. Marines were more than capable of fucking up. It gave him a useful avenue to pursue, a way of bonding with the guy. The hog's tooth necklace he wore around his neck suddenly felt warm against his skin.

"What are your plans now?" It wasn't his business, but he wanted to know anyway.

"I'm going to read witness statements to see if there's any mention of seeing a homeless guy in the area on Monday night." She grabbed her mug off the desk and shoved to her feet. "The thing is," she muttered quietly under her breath as if afraid of being overheard, "when the evidence pointed to Drew Hawke, I readily accepted it."

Darsh shrugged. "You had two victims who were willing to be polygraphed about the identity of their attacker."

"I know." She blew out a big sigh. "But now I have a confession and physical evidence and yet I still want to follow up on Jason Brady's alibi for Monday night, and if I do that, I'm screwed." She gave a humorless laugh. "Maybe I do subconsciously hate football players unless they play for the Giants." Her voice lowered even further. "The Dean of Students was in Strassen's office earlier. If Stinky Pete hadn't been brought in right at that moment, I'm pretty sure I'd be clearing out my desk." The muscles in her jaw flexed. "So if I push for more digging into Brady, I'll be out on my ear. I don't like this. I don't like it at all."

She strode away, leaving him standing there. He watched her go and wondered if it was part of the abusive ex thing where she always had to be the one to take control and walk away. Maybe she just wanted to be alone. Whatever it was, he wasn't chasing after her. Not today. He headed to his office.

This guy, Peter Zimmerman, didn't fit the profile of the UNSUB who'd committed these murders, but profiles were only guidelines as to whom the cops should be looking at. They were often wrong... But the locals were rushing their assumptions, probably in an effort to calm the fears of the local community. Removing some of the seething tension wasn't a bad thing.

He frowned as he remembered Drew Hawke's assertion someone had set him up. Was there some sort of conspiracy? Or a dirty cop on the force? It wasn't difficult to plant evidence, not in a situation like this, but that didn't explain the witness statements.

Outside of Erin he hadn't looked at any other members of Forbes Pines PD—maybe he should start. He also needed to talk to Agents Rooney and Chen about looking into Zimmerman's background. False confessions by the mentally ill or people seeking attention were always an issue when investigating high profile cases. This confession didn't feel right, and Donovan obviously felt it too.

Would she let it ride? Or fight for the truth?

The answer to that question would tell him a lot about her integrity, but it might also cost her her job. She was damned if she didn't and damned if she did. He pushed inside his crowded office and dialed Brennan, hoping he could stay long enough to figure it out.

CHAPTER FOURTEEN

E RIN READ EVERY witness statement taken over the last two days, and not one of them mentioned seeing a homeless guy near the scene of the murders. She'd also called the evidence techs, and they hadn't logged any cell phones, scissors, or letters found in Peter Zimmerman's camp. There were some magazines and newspapers the guy had used for warmth when it got really cold. She ran her hand through her long hair, which had fallen out of its braid and kept getting in her face.

The idea of being out in this cold was mind numbing and reminded her that no matter how hard things had gotten, she'd always had a roof over her head.

She pulled Peter Zimmerman's mug shot out of the file. The eyes were staring, the face haggard. It could easily be the face of a murderer because that was what they looked like, right? Unclean, straggly, wild-eyed, slightly deranged? *Sure.* If they were so easy to spot she wouldn't have a job.

She tucked the photo into a folder and pushed to her feet, grabbing her jacket off the back of her chair. She bumped straight into Darsh.

"Damn. You move quietly. You scared me." She backed up quickly and pressed the palm of her hand against her thumping heart. His eyes followed the movement and skimmed the vee of her shirt; they were almost black when his gaze met hers, and the tingle of arousal shimmered across her skin.

They were both trying so hard to pretend they weren't attracted to one another. Thankfully they wouldn't need to pretend for much longer. He'd be gone, and she'd go back to the uncomplicated, celibate life she was used to.

The idea didn't bring the comfort it should—just the sense of an opportunity lost and a chance not taken.

"Heading home?" he asked.

"No," she admitted, almost changing her mind as the idea of dragging him back to her place hit her in the solar plexus. But last time had ended badly. Very badly. "I'm going to check out the homeless shelter. See if anyone remembers seeing Peter Zimmerman there on Monday night."

Surprise flicked over his features, then something else she couldn't identify. He checked his watch. It was nearly nine. He had dark circles under his eyes and probably hadn't had a decent sleep in days.

"I'll come with you."

"You don't have to. I can look after myself."

He tilted his head, assessing her. Trying to figure out how good a cop she was. She put a little steel in her spine.

"Erin," he said slowly. "I saw you take down Jason Brady, remember? I know you can take care of yourself, but you have a target on your back and backup isn't a bad idea under the circumstances"—*i.e. two dead girls and a town that hates your guts*—"and I want to take a look at this shelter if I'm going to interview the guy tomorrow. Hear what the people who run the place say about him. See where he lives in relation to the crime scene."

She'd known from the look in his eyes earlier that he hadn't bought the confession any more than she had. Damn. The chief was going to bust her ass if he found out they were trying to prove the guy was innocent. "Fine. I'll drive."

"Shocker," he muttered, but there was a twinkle in his eye. She hated how his humor warmed her.

She turned away. She couldn't afford to drop her guard. He was charismatic and handsome—which was why she'd picked him up in that bar all those years ago. But she didn't want him to see the reflection of that night in her eyes, or the renewed feelings of lust. The only thing she had left was her integrity. If she lost that, she'd have nothing.

"Meet me outside. I'll go warm up the truck." She watched him walk away and tried not to admire the view. Darsh Singh wasn't safe, she reminded herself. He wasn't her friend, and he still had the power to destroy her career. But she'd rather go down searching for justice than rolling over because the truth had become inconvenient to the people in power.

On the back steps of City Hall, she paused long enough to pull on her gloves. It was quiet out. A layer of fresh snow three inches thick shrouded everything in sight—she hadn't even noticed it was snowing. It was still falling softly, large, fat, lazy flakes drifting out of the air. She raised her face to the beauty of it, enjoying the relatively warm temperature and lack of an arctic breeze.

She hadn't checked the forecast since Monday. All she'd cared about was this murder investigation.

The quietness told her the news vans were gone. Barring a disaster, they'd be back in the morning ready to peck at the details of Peter Zimmerman's life and try the guy on live TV. She didn't want him to go through that if he was innocent.

He'd never be safe on the streets if people thought he'd had anything to do with a rape and double homicide.

She trudged down the steps, watching her footing on the slippery pavement. Her attitude toward the press probably wasn't fair, but they'd impinged on her privacy at a time when she'd desperately needed to be left alone, and often hindered rather than helped investigations. Sure the public had a right to know what was going on, but only if it didn't get in the way of catching a perp. Free speech could be a bit of a bitch.

Her truck was parked a row over behind two patrol vehicles. As she got closer, she noticed the hood listed slightly to one side. Crap. She had a flat. Front left. The slash in the tire wall said it was about as accidental as the egg that still coated her windshield. Weariness tugged at her shoulders. The last thing she felt like doing was hauling out her jack and replacing the tire. Footsteps sounded behind her. She whirled and there was Darsh bundled up in his winter gear. The fact he looked sexy whatever he was wearing wasn't lost on her.

She kicked her hubcap. "Looks like we're taking your car."

His breath came out in an icy cloud as he rubbed his hands together. "Want me to change it for you?"

She shook her head. "I could do it myself, but one of the guys on patrol owes me a favor. He's on the graveyard shift tonight. I'll text him later."

"You don't like being on the other side of that equation, do you?" He dug out his keys and tossed them in the air before catching them with a flourish.

"What d'you mean?" She tried not to sound defensive.

"Owing people favors."

"I like being independent." That's what happened when your husband turned out to be an abusive, controlling prick. "I don't like being the weak simpering female asking for the big strong men for help—unless it's my dad and brothers." She thought about all the jobs she had lined up for their next visit. "I work them as hard as they'll let me."

"So you feel like you can rely on family?"

She stopped herself from saying *duh*. Not everyone had the kind of backup or support she did. She tilted her head at him. "Yeah. I do."

They headed a few cars over to where his black SUV was parked. He used the fob to unlock it and she got in. Within seconds the seat started heating beneath her, and she was fast becoming a convert to all the mod-cons.

He pulled out of the parking lot, and she gave him directions to the mission about a mile away.

"What was it like growing up in such a big family?" he asked.

She huddled into her parka. Talking about them made her homesick. "I loved it. They're nosey and loud. We're a typical Irish Catholic family full of NYPD cops."

"All of them?"

"Pretty much, except my mom and my baby sister, Siobhan. She's an actress off off Broadway."

He stiffened, which was an odd reaction.

"It was her dream even when she was in diapers." Erin shrugged. "I never understood the pull of the limelight, but it's all she ever wanted."

"My mother always wanted the limelight, too. I never understood it either."

"Yeah?" He'd said his mother had been murdered, and she wanted to know more, but didn't want to push.

He nodded. "Yeah. We moved from the UK in the eighties

with Dad's work. She was thrilled, because she thought she had a better chance of becoming famous."

"You're *British*?" She grinned at him.

"Born in Nottingham, not Delhi."

"Why didn't you keep the sexy English accent?"

He sent her a sideways glance. "There's only so much sexy people can handle."

His expression sobered, and one side of his mouth drew back in a wry smile. "People think my identity is somehow rooted in my family being Indian, but it's not. I've never been to India. I speak the language, but I also speak Farsi and French. I grew up in Britain and moved to the US. My cultural identity is wrapped up in soccer and Coronation Street, baseball and in necking with a hot blonde in the backseat of my daddy's car. The only time I ever realize I'm different is when other people point it out."

"Bias can be subtle," Erin agreed carefully. "I was lucky. My mother was a teacher and intolerance and inequality are her hot button topics. She wouldn't put up with it from anyone. I guess it rubbed off on us kids which made us all much better cops." She watched his hands on the steering wheel. Strong and capable. Thought of them on her body and had to look away.

"The only thing my mother cared about was making it as an actress in Hollywood."

"What did your dad think of that?"

"He encouraged her to act with local theater companies and audition for TV parts. He even paid for acting lessons, but his heart wasn't really in it. He was just trying to make her happy."

"It sounds like he loved her a lot."

He shrugged. "He did. She didn't love him back."

That statement made Erin flinch, but he didn't notice.

"Right here?" He checked directions.

She nodded.

"They had an arranged marriage, knew each other for about a month before the ceremony. Her parents thought he'd settle her down. She was looking for a way to escape the stranglehold they had on her. I've visited them a few times in England—they're pretty traditional in their values."

She rubbed her hands together and adjusted the heater. Damn, but she really needed to move to Hawaii. "Arranged marriages always seem barbaric to me."

"And yet, statistically, the divorce rates are about the same as non-arranged marriages."

Erin pressed her lips together at the gentle rebuke. She wasn't about to give lectures on the subject of matrimony. "I didn't know that."

"Obviously there are cultural differences, and I'm not endorsing it, but I'm not condemning it either. Most people judge it without knowing anything about it."

"Is that how you plan to find a wife?" she teased, but the idea caused something painful to contract inside her, even though she had no hold on the guy.

"Hell, no. I'm too much of a control freak. My dad would probably choose a real witch to spite me."

"You two don't get along?"

Darsh smiled and was so frickin' gorgeous her toes curled. "We got along just fine, right up until I quit school and joined the Marines." Her brows rose in surprise. "Indian parents— even those from Britain—seem to believe that if their kids aren't doctors, they're failures. 'I thought you were going to learn to *save* people, not *kill* them.'" He gave an imitation of an older man, presumably his father. "Now he spends his days telling me I'm the token minority in the BAU. And I spend my time trying to prove him wrong. As for marriage…" He shrugged. "The job has me on the road almost every week and after what happened between my mom and dad, I'm not a big believer in compromise. A woman would have to be crazy to want a relationship with me." His eyes raked over her, and her skin burned. "Long-term, anyway."

But short-term might be a lot of fun—that's what the gleam in his eyes was telling her.

Dangerous territory, so she kept it light.

"I think it depends on the compromise. I mean, a 34-inch TV rather than a 55-inch? I could live with that."

He gave a mock shudder. "Sacrilege."

Then her mood shifted, and she said seriously, "But when it's a choice between suffocating your own dreams and freedoms versus staying home and putting a nice dinner on the table every night…" Her mouth went dry.

Her husband had tried to get her to give up the job she loved, even though he'd known she was a career cop when they got married. It had been the first step in him trying to take over her life, and she'd had to fight for freedom every step of the way. The cost had been his life, and it could easily have been hers. She should have seen it before they got married. She should have figured out some way for him to move on and get help.

Jesus.

She was never going to get over the guilt of his death, and that was probably the suckiest thing about surviving an abusive relationship. Somewhere deep inside you always took a portion of the blame, even when it wasn't your fault.

She didn't want to think about it. "What happened to your mom's acting dreams?" she asked gently. She knew the story had a sad ending.

His fingers tightened on the wheel, and she noticed they were pulling to a stop outside the mission. He switched off the engine and lights, and they sat in silence. "She left us without a word in May 1987. I was seven. My sisters were four. In September we were notified by a detective in Hollywood that she'd been found dead in an alley. She'd been turning tricks for money."

"I'm sorry."

His face was in the shadows. His voice hard. "She chose that life over having a home and family. The fact she ended up dead was almost irrelevant."

Shock hit her. "You don't mean that."

"I do. My dad was a good man. He treated her well, bought her nice things, and respected her. If she'd asked for a divorce he would have given it to her, but he'd have tried to make it work first. Bottom line is she didn't love us. She dumped us." His eyes glittered in the darkness. "They're always telling kids that there're consequences to their actions and sometimes those consequences aren't very nice. She left us, not because she was abducted or needed to work, but because she didn't want us anymore. It's a hard thing for a kid to accept and once I did, I wasn't wasting any more emotion on her. Consequences."

"Maybe she was suffocating on the inside," Erin said carefully. What would he think of her walking out on her marriage and then using him to reclaim her body?

"She should have found some other way." His voice

cracked. He wasn't as dispassionate as he wanted her to believe. But if his mother's ghost haunted him the same way her husband's did, then he was a long way from not caring.

Erin couldn't imagine how she'd have felt if her mother had walked out when she was seven years old. Would she have walked away from Graham if they'd had a child?

In a heartbeat, she realized. But she'd have taken the child, too. "You loved her."

"Of course I loved her. I also hated her." That statement made her bite her lip. "And I'm damned if I know how to forgive her."

The words put a vise on Erin's heart and squeezed tight. She reached out and laid her hand on his warm wrist. "I'm sorry she left you. I'm sorry she died."

He placed his hand over hers, and they held each other's gaze with all of the pain from their past naked in their eyes. Someone opened the door of the shelter and made her jerk her hand away and push open the car door. Jeez. They were working, not out on a date.

"Get a grip, Erin," she muttered, although not quietly enough. She caught Darsh hiding a grin.

Inside the shelter was a small reception desk leading into a cafeteria with a dozen round tables. No one was on the desk, so they headed through toward the dining area. Half the tables were occupied despite the lateness of the hour, or maybe because of it. People looked toward them and seemed to shift almost imperceptibly when they realized they were cops. Only one or two looked homeless, but she knew a lot of people slept in their cars, and on a night like this that would be as cozy as snuggling down in the deep freeze. She sniffed. The place smelled of boiled rice and some sort of fragrant curry.

"Can I help you?" The man who approached them was tall, but stooped, with sunken eyes and a wisp of gray hair on his head.

Erin couldn't help the shudder that ran through her. If she was casting a film and needed someone to play a serial killer, she'd pick him. "Yeah. We're looking for the person who runs the center."

"That's me. Randolph Cane." He smiled, but for some reason the guy made her skin crawl.

"I'm Detective Donovan from FPPD." She held up her badge so she didn't have to shake hands. "This is Agent Singh with the FBI. We'd like to ask you a few questions about Monday night."

He blinked, slowly. "Well, come on through to the kitchen. I'm finishing off the dishes. We can talk there."

Before she could ask for somewhere more private, he'd turned and was walking away. She looked at Darsh, and his expression was amused as he waved her ahead of him. Fine.

She marched into the kitchen where Mr. Cane was pulling on bright yellow rubber gloves. "Were you working on Monday night?"

He paused in the act of scrubbing a big stainless steel pot. Frowned. "No. I don't work Sundays or Mondays." He looked up and smiled at her. "Sunday is my day for the church, and Monday I catch up on my household chores and then usually go to the movies."

Something about those sunken eyes freaked her out. She usually liked old people, but this guy made her want to back away with her hand on her weapon. She pushed the irrational feeling away and asked her questions. "Do you recognize this man?" She held up the photo of Peter Zimmerman.

"Of course. That's Peter. He wasn't in today. Is he okay?" Mr. Cane's brow furrowed. Soapy water splashed on the drainer as he turned the huge pan upside down and placed it on the drying rack.

"He comes here regularly?" Erin persisted.

Cane nodded. "Yes. To eat and shower occasionally."

Very occasionally, judging by the odor when they'd booked him.

"He ever sleep here?" asked Darsh.

Mr. Cane shook his head. "He could, we have twenty beds, and we are rarely full, which is a blessing, but he usually refuses unless it's dangerously cold outside. Says he doesn't want people stealing his patch." Cane hunched up bony shoulders. "Like many people who've fallen on hard times, he isn't very trusting as to other people's motives for wanting to help him."

"Know where he came from?" Erin asked.

Mr. Cane shook his head, and his eyes grew sad. "I don't ask for more than people want to volunteer."

"If you weren't here on Monday, can you tell us who was working?" she asked impatiently. The guy was giving them nothing.

He moved his lips to form an "o" as he thought about her question. "It varies a little. I can check the schedule, but I think Roman was in charge of dinner duty that night. Roman Huxley."

"Professor Huxley?"

"You know him? Wonderful man. He and his students help out regularly. We always need volunteers," Mr. Cane said, not so subtly.

Erin and her family had often helped out in local shelters

and food banks when she was growing up. It was part of the community spirit in Queens, and also a big part of the church they'd attended. She hadn't done that here, and she rarely went to church anymore. She hadn't tried to integrate into the community at all, which might explain why she felt like she didn't fit in. All she'd wanted was to be left alone and, eventually, that's what happened.

Erin checked her watch. It was too late to call the professor now. She'd check in with him tomorrow. Soothe the ego Darsh had ruffled at lunch.

"Thanks for your help, Mr. Cane." Erin handed him her card. "If you think of anything else…"

"Peter's not in any trouble is he? He's a gentle, if tortured, soul. Wouldn't hurt a fly."

"Thanks again," Erin said. "We'll be in touch."

"There's a donation box on the wall on the way out. Feel free to contribute," Cane called after them.

Erin dug out a twenty and stuffed it in the box. Darsh did the same.

They headed back to the car and as they climbed inside, Erin leaned her head back against the headrest.

"So we've still got nothing."

"I've got some people digging into Zimmerman's background," Darsh told her. "We should know something by morning. Where's the bridge from here?"

"Keep heading east." Even though she was tired, she needed to figure out if Peter Zimmerman could actually be their killer. The idea of another person becoming a victim because she was too tired to do her job pushed the sleepiness away.

Darsh drove through the gathering snow, flicking the wipers on slow.

They stayed silent except for Erin's directions. After a couple of minutes, she saw the single span suspension bridge. "Pull up over there." She pointed in the direction of a turnout just up ahead on the right-hand side of the road. There were tracks in the snow but no vehicles.

He turned off the engine and they got out. The snow was growing steadily thicker now. Dark woods edged the highway.

Darsh walked around to the back of the SUV and pulled something out of his bag. He flicked a light on and off. Flashlight. She didn't think they'd need it, the snow was so bright.

"How long would it take him to walk from the mission to here?" Darsh asked.

"It's about a mile. Ten minutes, assuming he was sober."

"Was he?"

She shook her head. "He said he had a date with a bottle of vodka, but it isn't clear where he got it from or when he started drinking." They needed to trace his movements. Fast. But no one had reported seeing him. Maybe Huxley could help.

"There's a path over there." Darsh led the way, keeping the flashlight off as they followed the footsteps of cops and crime scene techs who'd visited earlier.

It was deathly quiet in the forest, the only noise the creak of branches and the groan of ice on the river. The occasional whoosh of a car along the highway reminded her they weren't that far from civilization, even though it felt like a million miles away.

She slipped down a small incline, and Darsh turned in time to catch her against his body. "Steady."

The connection sent shockwaves through her. She backed away and struggled to find her footing.

The path curved away from the bridge, and she thought they must have gone the wrong way when Darsh suddenly stopped in front of her, and she came up beside him. The path forked, and when they looked left, the riverbank was cordoned off with yellow tape. He flicked on the flashlight, and they both ducked under the flimsy barrier. The crunch of snow beneath their feet marked their progress. A few moments later, they got to the bridge. The void beneath it looked black as hell and just as welcoming. The bank was slippery, and she almost went down again, but Darsh grabbed her under the arm and hauled her up the slope in front of him. "Careful."

Her heart pounded, and she wished her body didn't enjoy the touch of his hands quite so much. They stood under the bridge, and it was like entering a different world. Out of the wind, the air was dank, damp, stale, and the smell of urine so strong she grimaced. She looked around as Darsh shone the flashlight into every corner.

"Looks like the crime scene people removed everything they thought might be related to Peter Zimmerman's camp." Darsh's expression was disbelieving. "I have a hard time knowing veterans live this way."

"He was running from a DUI charge down in Texas."

Darsh shook his head. "He might have been running, but it wasn't from the DUI charge."

Her eyes shot to his.

"Demons."

"From his time as a Marine?"

"Who knows." He looked up from his perusal of the dirt and snow and concrete. "We all have demons, Erin. Sometimes we chase them, sometimes they chase us."

"What about you?" she asked.

He smiled. "I'm here aren't I?"

She huffed out a laugh, wishing she wasn't so interested in what made this guy tick.

"Did they find a handgun?" he asked.

"No. Just a pocket knife." She was sure the crime scene techs would have alerted her if they'd found another weapon.

He frowned. "So where'd he hide it?"

"Why do you think he had one?"

"Because he was a former Marine, and he was vulnerable. He'd have a gun unless it was stolen or he pawned it for booze. Why'd the cops check him out anyway?"

"I have no idea. I guess they were searching the area for Cassie Bressinger's missing sheet."

"We still within the town limits?"

She nodded. "Bridge is the line."

Darsh studied the ground and frowned. He walked all the way under the bridge and came out in the forest on the other side. She didn't know what he was thinking, but she followed him anyway. She hated to admit it, but being alone out here in the woods gave her the creeps.

They followed a natural path between the trees. During spring this part of the bank flooded, and it was littered with fallen logs. Darsh shook his head and then headed towards the frozen river. Erin grabbed his arm. "Careful," she warned.

One side of his lips curled as he grinned at her. "Worried about me?"

She let go of his arm and swallowed uneasily. Dammit. "Just don't expect me to jump in and save you."

He clambered down the bank. "I think it's well and truly frozen." He eased out onto the smooth surface, tested it with his foot, and then stamped on it and grinned at her.

"Please." Her voice trembled. "Don't. I hate the ice. What are you doing?"

"Looking for his weapon." Her question had him running his flashlight over the surface as he walked back towards Peter's camp. She followed his progress from the bank. Then she spotted it. A dark metallic sheen between several lumps of ice.

"Over there." She pointed.

"You got an evidence bag?" he asked in a calm voice.

Reluctantly, she eased down onto the ice sheet and edged towards him. Her heart vibrated with fear. "The idea of this freaks me out so much I'm pretty sure my body is actually standing on the bank watching. I'd never be this foolish."

"I got your back, Erin." He grinned at her. "I'd dive in and save you."

His words hit her unexpectedly, because for some reason, she knew they were true. And she figured, just this once, she wouldn't mind being saved by this handsome federal agent.

She handed him the bag, and he used it to ease an old revolver from its hiding place.

"Saw the cops coming, and he didn't want to get caught carrying a gun," said Darsh.

"Because of his outstanding warrant and desire not to call attention to himself," Erin agreed.

"Which he'd pretty much fucked up by admitting to murdering two coeds." Darsh sounded angry.

"That would do it."

Darsh started walking towards her. The sound of ice cracking had her grabbing his arm and shoving him onto the bank. He lay there in the snow, laughing, as she glared up at him from her position down on the frozen river.

Her chest rose and fell rapidly. If her pulse went any faster, she was likely to stroke out. "I hate you."

He held out his hand to pull her up to the path. "No, you don't."

"Yes, I do."

"It was good police work. Admit it."

She stood over him as he lay there, her hands braced on her hips. "It was okay police work," she conceded. "But I still hate you for scaring me."

He stood up, and she was grateful it was too dark for him to see her expression. He leaned close to her ear, and she felt his breath on her neck. She shivered, but it wasn't from cold.

"Damn good police work," he said.

She raised an unimpressed brow. "You trying to impress me?"

He laughed. "Is it working?"

She shook her head in exasperation.

"Here, hold the flashlight." He placed it in her gloved hands and then retrieved the weapon from his pocket. He checked the gun, which held six rounds, then unloaded it, all through the plastic of the evidence bag.

"What you going to do with it?"

"Confront him with it tomorrow, and see if it's linked to any other crimes. Who knows, maybe he is our guy."

They began the walk back to his SUV. The cold air sank farther into her lungs, making the climb harder than it should have been. The ache at the base of her skull told her it was time to go home and get some rest. "You got anywhere to stay tonight?"

He moved easily, clearly unaffected by the cold or the terrain. "Just a date with my office chair."

She smiled but didn't tell him it was *her* office chair. If she did, it would be back under her desk tomorrow, and he'd be riding the plastic monstrosity she'd been saddled with.

And he'd be gone soon—if not tomorrow, then in a few days.

"You can stay at my place." The words popped out before she could stop herself.

He slowed and half-turned, brows raised.

"Don't get excited. It's not an offer of rampant sex."

He caught her hand to pull her up another steep section. The moon shone through the trees, and she had to drag her eyes away from his lips. She unzipped her jacket, suddenly hot and definitely bothered.

He let go of her. Didn't answer.

"I have two spare rooms, but no transportation. You'll be doing me a favor by giving me a ride." Why was she pushing this? Because it made sense, and she wasn't quite ready to say goodbye to him yet.

"I could give you a ride home and pick you up again in the morning."

"While I let you sleep in your office, and I have two un-used beds at home? Not very hospitable. But if you don't want to stay with me... Crap, for all I know you lied before and do have a girlfriend who wouldn't appreciate you staying overnight with someone you once slept with."

"No girlfriend." The long pause made her hyperaware of the crunch of their footsteps through the fresh snow. "And I don't remember much sleeping going on three years ago."

Heat flamed in every part of her body. They got to the car, and he started the engine with a roar. The revs matched the rhythm of her heart, and she was grateful for the dark interior of the car even though the air had been sucked out of it. She wasn't going to have sex with this guy. He already thought she had dubious morals, and she'd vowed to herself she'd never be vulnerable or weak again.

But he was leaving soon…

She closed her eyes. For the first time in years she was tempted, but she wouldn't be stupid enough to act on it. She'd learned her lesson the last time the two of them had gotten together. The sex itself had been amazing, but the aftermath had been painful and humiliating. She wasn't going there again.

CHAPTER FIFTEEN

D ARSH KNEW EXACTLY what he wanted when he followed Erin into the lonely isolated farmhouse she called home. It didn't involve sleeping in the spare room. Cold moonlight shone through the thin kitchen drapes, casting an eerie light over an almost austere setting. She flicked on the light switch, but nothing happened.

The hair on his neck stood up as she swore.

It probably wasn't healthy that his mind immediately went to "serial killer," but his line of work tended to make him inclined to assume the worst.

Erin cocked her head, listening intently. Her right hand rested on her weapon, proving he wasn't the only one who was paranoid. "Furnace is still on, so electricity supply to the house is good. One of the breakers must have blown."

He heard the sound of a drawer being opened and saw a flashlight beam track across the floor.

"This happen a lot?" he asked.

"No."

Tension crackled between them. Sexual, personal, professional. You name it. They were wading neck-deep in it.

"Got another torch around here?" He'd tossed his in with his vest in the back of the car when he'd grabbed the go-bag he'd brought in with him.

"Torch?" she asked curiously.

"Flashlight," he translated.

She snorted. "You can take the boy out of England, but you can't take England out of the boy?" She dug into the drawer again, and something hit him in the stomach.

He grunted as he took it from her. "Thanks." He turned it on and shone it around the huge kitchen. "Doesn't it bother you, living so far from other people?"

She headed toward a door on the opposite side of the kitchen. It creaked when she opened it. "It took a bit of getting used to after growing up in Queens, but I'm okay now. The house shrieks and groans in the winter, but *this* doesn't normally happen."

"You think it's a coincidence that there just happens to be a killer on the loose?" Darsh asked softly.

"Chief says we have the killer in custody." She headed into the black pit of her basement.

"Which you don't believe." He followed her down the steep steps, not ashamed to have his SIG Sauer in hand.

She walked over to a fuse box, and he shone the flashlight into every crevice, behind every packing box.

"Got it." The light in the kitchen came on and flooded down the wooden steps. "The kitchen lights and the clothes drier are on the same electrical circuit. I left the drier running this morning after I washed the sheets and headed out. Must have tripped."

He nodded. "Maybe we should clear the house anyway?"

"Afraid of the boogey man?"

"They exist," Darsh told her sincerely.

"You don't really think someone would target me, do you?"

"Why risk it?"

"There were no tracks in the snow."

"It only started falling this afternoon. Someone could have broken in earlier in the day and waited for you to come home." Snow was both a blessing and a curse. It might tell someone about recent visitors to their door, but it wouldn't tell them whether or not someone was hiding in a cupboard—or sitting a kilometer away in a tree with their crosshairs lined up on your center mass. People got complacent, and then they died.

"Fine. Okay." She pulled her weapon. "Now that you've freaked me out, I won't be able to sleep until we check anyway."

They worked their way through a massive dining room, which had a fancy light fixture and not a lot else. Paint splotches were on the wall, but she obviously hadn't decided on what color to go with yet. A treadmill sat in one corner and a music system next to it on the floor.

His footsteps echoed across the bare wooden boards. "I like what you've done with the place," he noted dryly. "You just move in?"

There was a defensive pause. "Three years ago."

Silence was his best option here. The living room had a couch in it but also a dozen panels of sheetrock stacked against the wall. She had told him it had been a lot of work. She hadn't been lying.

They headed upstairs, and he kept his eyes high rather than getting distracted by Erin's shapely backside. At the top of the house, the attic was bare, aside from insulation. From there they moved down to the second floor and went from room to room, weapons drawn, reaching out with heightened awareness, checking for signs someone else was in the house. Training kept him calm and alert, even though there was probably no one here except the two of them. He'd learned in Scout Sniper training never to ignore his instincts, especially those relating to survival.

They ended their search in the master bedroom. He looked under the bed while she cleared the walk-in closet. No one here. Just the two of them. Standing in the bedroom with the light shining in from the hallway. He holstered his weapon and looked around. The room was finished and the walls painted. A big bed dominated the room, massive wooden headboard and crisp, white sheets. *Don't think about the bed.*

"Looks good up here."

"Thanks." She placed her Glock on the bedside table and then sat on the bed and pulled off her boots, dropping them on the floor with a tired thump.

She looked really good, on that bed he wasn't looking at.

"Like I said, I had great hopes of being the next Mike Holmes. It turns out I'm better at demolition than construction."

He ran his eyes over the high ceiling, knowing he should leave. Not wanting to. "Why'd you buy something so big?"

This time she actually laughed, and it gave him a warm feeling inside. "I grew up in a three-bedroom house in Queens. I have four brothers and one sister and literally thought I'd suffocate from the lack of privacy and personal space when I was a teen." She grimaced and looked around. "Turns out you can have too much of a good thing."

"You could sublet. Get a roomie."

The moonlight streamed through the open drapes and made her look like an ice princess. "As the most unpopular person in Forbes Pines last year I think finding a roomie is pretty unlikely. Plus, I like my privacy."

She stood up and walked toward him. "Let me show you where you can sleep."

He didn't say anything. He wanted to stay here. With her. He hadn't realized quite how much he wanted it until he saw her sitting on that bed. His thoughts must have been written plainly on his face because she swallowed tightly and veered away from him. She walked to the window that overlooked her yard.

"It's not a good idea." She hugged her arms around herself. "Last time didn't end well."

"So let's give it a better ending." His voice sounded rough even to his own ears.

She laughed, a small bitter sound that dug into his gut. "You just want to get laid."

"No."

She looked at him doubtfully.

"No. I'm more than capable of getting off any time of the day or night if I want to." He held those big eyes of hers that looked so unsure and so uncertain. "You *know* I'm attracted to you. I've been attracted to you from the moment we first met. Nothing's changed."

Lines appeared between her brows. Suddenly she seemed delicate and almost ethereal in the moonlight. "I don't want to get involved, Darsh. I've got enough going on in my life." Her voice was small. Almost a whisper.

She didn't sound like the Erin Donovan he'd come to know. She sounded beaten, like she'd given up on relationships—even purely physical ones. "Because of your ex?"

Her lips pinched. "Maybe," she admitted.

It pissed him off that she was letting the bastard ruin her life from beyond the grave.

"Chances are I'm going home tomorrow, so I'm about as uninvolved as it gets." Okay, he'd asked to stay longer, but she didn't need to know that. Regardless of whether or not the DA thought this vagrant was guilty, there was an expiry date on his time here.

And even if the cases were related, even if Hawke had been set up, he didn't believe Erin had been at fault during the last investigation, and he was willing to go on record saying so. She'd done everything by the book and was a damn good cop. The fact she'd been heading to the shelter when he'd caught her leaving earlier proved she didn't take things at face value. But he didn't think this was about her job. "When was the last time you had a relationship with someone?"

She rubbed her arm, and he watched a ripple move down her throat as she swallowed. "I wouldn't exactly call it a relationship."

"Another hook up?" Jealousy shot through him, which was garbage as he'd had hook ups and short-term relationships with other women since Erin. Three years was a long time, and he'd never expected to see her again.

Her gaze rose to meet his. "Not *another* hook up."

He frowned, not getting it at first. Then his mouth went dry. "You haven't had sex since we were together?" And he'd accused her of being the one with shaky morals?

She bit her lip and turned away.

"Why the hell haven't you dated anyone?"

Her shoulders bumped. "It's not illegal to be celibate."

"It should be, for someone who looks like you." He tried to keep it light. There was a deep well of hurt beneath Erin

Donovan's beautiful exterior, hurt he'd added to by being a judgmental asshole.

She turned and rolled her eyes. "That's the stupidest thing you've said to me, and trust me, you've said some zingers."

He shrugged out of his heavy jacket and draped it over a nearby chair, then went to her. Outside was a winter wonderland. Inside was warm and snug and private. He reached out to gently touch her upper arm. "Why haven't you been with anyone? Look at me." He wasn't about to drop this. She was too young and too much of a fighter to run away from such an important aspect of life. "What did your ex do to you?"

She flinched.

"Tell me, because I know what you and I did together didn't leave you with any scars." He lowered his voice and hooked her hair behind her ear. "I still dream about our time together."

She stared at him, searching for the truth in his statement. He let her see it on his face, in his eyes.

She drew back and pulled in a shuddering breath. He thought she was going to tell him to mind his own business like she usually did. Instead she wrapped her arms tighter around herself and leaned against the wall.

"Graham was the macho type—you know, loved beer, guns. One of the guys, but always with an eye for the ladies. A bit like you."

He raised his brows. It might be true on the surface, but there was more to him that that.

"He was a good guy, or at least he seemed to be at the start. It was a whirlwind romance. Intense. He was completely devoted to me, and I felt like the luckiest woman alive. Things changed after we got married. At first it was my job. 'Why

209

didn't I quit and have a baby?'" Pain crinkled her eyes at the corners. "I wanted kids one day, but I was committed to my career at that point. I wanted to make detective before I even thought about having a baby."

Darsh let her talk. Finally talk. The dam had broken and everything was rushing out.

"Then he started getting pissy about my buddies who were mostly guys from the job. I ignored the warning signs, even when he started telling me he didn't like me spending so much time with my family, and then he started tracking my every move. But the first time he hit me was devastating."

Darsh wanted to haul her close. He had to force himself to hold back, to not scare or smother her.

"The first time?" Rage moved through him, but he shoved it aside. It wasn't about him. "Why didn't you leave him? Report him?"

He put his arms around her, and she leaned against his chest, her cheek pressed next to his heart. "He'd have lost his job and I...I was ashamed." She gave a laugh that sounded like a sob. "How many domestics had I attended? Hundreds, if not thousands. The stupid woman always fails to press charges, and the cops end up back there week after week until one of them kills the other, or one of them gets arrested for something else."

Her breath was warm through his shirt, stroking his skin. "After Graham hit me, he broke down crying. I mean he was a tough macho guy. I'd never seen him cry before. He was devastated to have lashed out. He came from a poor working class family where his dad solved all his problems with a fist. I'd known that going into the relationship, I just hadn't realized Graham dealt with things the same way." She pulled back, wiped tears from her eyes but wouldn't look at him. "I told him that if it ever happened again I'd leave him, but I should have done it then, that first time. I knew it, but the damn Catholic guilt got to me."

Darsh held his silence and just let her talk. Let her get all the ugliness out.

"So one beautiful September day he comes home after a shitty day at work, and he starts picking a fight. I knew it was going to be bad, but something inside me needed it to play out. He finds my cell and goes through my texts like some overprotective father. One of my buddies had sent me a heart smiley just as part of the conversation, harmless. It didn't mean anything, but Graham lost it." She shook her head, and he couldn't resist sliding his fingers into the silken tresses of her hair, trying to soothe her agitation.

"He hit me again. Tried to force himself on me,"—*good thing the fucker was dead*—"but I didn't hold back this time. I fought back with everything I had. He broke two of my ribs, but I'd upped my training with a martial arts instructor I'd been going to. I gave him as good as I got, and he wasn't expecting that. I kicked his ass and when he was down, I ran out of that house faster than you can say 'divorce proceedings.' I got patched up by a doctor I knew from high school and went home to my parents."

His fingers clenched against her waist, pulling her closer.

"He came around the next day with flowers and some made up story about our 'little' argument. But I'd told my parents the truth about what happened by then—he hadn't expected me to do that. He'd expected me to be too ashamed to admit it, as if *I'd* done something wrong. My dad and my brothers were all there waiting for him in our little front room.

Five badass cops with a personal grudge." Humor touched the side of her mouth. "Let's just say he was lucky to make it out of there alive, and he knew it. After that I started getting incessant messages about how he was sorry—like when I was in Quantico that night." She'd gotten a dozen texts at four in the morning, which was how the subject of a husband had come up. "Then, when I was obviously not falling for it, the messages started saying if I didn't come home to him he was going to kill himself." There were tears in her voice. "And then he did."

He hugged her close again. She felt good there tucked in beneath his chin. Like she belonged.

"So what was I?" he asked after a few moments of silence. "Some sort of declaration of independence?"

She laughed, but the way she clung to his shirt and refused to look up made something in his chest tighten. "That's exactly what you were. I went to that bar determined to reclaim ownership of my life and my body. When you walked in…" She finally looked up and met his gaze. "Well, you know what happened next."

She licked her lips, and his eyes tracked the movement. Three years ago he'd been blindsided by the beautiful blonde smiling at him in that bar. Now he knew the kind of person she was, hardworking, smart, dedicated. She blew his mind.

"This is why you connect so well with the victims, you know," he said.

The shadows in her eyes flickered. "I don't like being thought of as a victim."

"You're a survivor, not a victim. There's a difference." He brushed a finger across her cheek. Every particle in the room seemed to ionize and electrify.

"This is a really bad idea," she said hoarsely.

"I don't care if you don't." But he wasn't taking any part of the decision-making process away from her. It was more than obvious he wanted her. The proof was pressed against her stomach and evident in the way he couldn't leave her alone. He'd been circling her like a planet around its star since he'd arrived, and no matter he told himself it was about the case, that was a lie. And he wanted to get closer. *Much* closer. But he wasn't going to pressure her in any way. As a woman who liked to walk away, it was important that she chose to come to him.

She leaned back in his arms, and he braced himself for disappointment. He wasn't about to try and change her mind. Not today. Not after what she'd told him about the asshole she'd married. There were a million reasons for her to reject him and most of them made way more sense than acting on this ill-fated, ill-conceived attraction.

She slid her hands over his jaw and rubbed her thumb across his bottom lip. "Okay."

"*Okay*?"

She nodded.

Green light.

He lifted her up and brought her eyes level with his. He wanted her mouth, those sweet lips. Wanted her naked in his arms. But he didn't want to rush this. She wrapped her legs around his hips, and he secured her in place with a hand on her ass and pressed her tight up against the wall.

"You're sure about this?" He palmed her breast, and she arched up into his hand.

"Only if it's as good as last time." She sucked in a breath as he found her nipple unerringly through the fabric of her clothes and gently pinched the sensitive tip.

"Nothing could be as good as last time."

"Then we better brace ourselves for disappointment. Or die trying." She nibbled closer to his mouth. Small kisses getting nearer to his lips, but never quite hitting the mark. Driving him crazy with want.

Finally he captured her jaw in his hand and held her while he took her mouth. Her lips were warm, soft. She opened them slowly, making him work for a real taste of her. He ran his tongue around the inside of her bottom lip, and she groaned, pressing her center against his arousal. He sank deeper against her, searching her lips with his, stroking her tongue, taking it deeper, tasting the sweet essence that was all Erin Donovan.

And suddenly need burst through him like a supernova, and she felt it too.

Frantic fingers unbuttoned her shirt, and he pushed it off her shoulders, trapping her arms behind her back as she tried to get it off. The lacy white bra that had teased his senses all day looked incredible against pale smooth skin. He pulled the cup of her bra down to expose a rosy nipple. He plumped it between his fingers and sucked.

"You don't play fair." She moaned, gripping him tighter with her legs, still struggling with her cuffed sleeves.

"Why would I?" he asked honestly, enjoying the taste of her, unable to believe they were doing this again, and so far it was just as good as last time.

He noticed an even paler strip of skin. "Tan lines?" He ran his tongue over them.

"Yes," she gasped.

"Let me know if you don't like anything." He smiled against her skin. "And I'll stop."

"I will." Her fingers clutched at him. "But please don't stop."

He dragged the second cup of her bra aside and played with her other nipple, loving the way it hardened and glistened in the moonlight. So beautiful. He blew across the dampness and she trembled. So responsive.

He wrenched at the sleeves of her shirt until it fell away. She reached behind her for the clasp on her bra, and he dragged it from her body and tossed it to the floor. And there she was, half-naked in his arms.

"We're taking this very, very slowly."

"No." She sank her fingers into his hair and kissed him open-mouthed, before breaking apart. "I don't want slow. I want it hard and fast against the wall. Right." She nipped his lower lip. "Now."

Her words made him so aroused his hands shook, but who was he to argue with a woman who hadn't had sex in three years? She slid her feet to the floor and reached for his belt, jerked the leather free. "You have protection?"

He swallowed and nodded.

Heat spread through his body as he watched her free him from his pants. The feel and sight of her small hands stroking him almost drove him over the edge. He found a condom in his wallet and handed it to her. He made short work of her pants, and she kicked them off, along with her socks, until she was standing there in only a pair of white lace thong panties. She went to slip them off, but he stopped her with a firm grip on her wrist. "Leave them on."

He took the wrapper from her shaking fingers and covered himself. He was almost entirely dressed, but she leaned almost naked against the wall looking like the sexiest thing he'd ever laid eyes on.

Her gaze held his, begging him to give her what she'd asked for.

He stepped closer, and she wrapped a leg around his waist. She was so tiny and so perfect. He knew she was resilient, but he didn't want to hurt her. He moved her panties aside and slid a finger into her hot wet core. Then he lifted her up, and she wrapped both legs around him, and he buried himself so deep he went blind from pleasure.

He thrust inside, over and over, straining into her soft willing body, feeling her arousal grow, feeling her *need* burn through her natural reserve. This woman who hadn't had sex in three years wanted it hard and fast against the wall. He almost grinned, but it was too much effort. Her fingernails bit into his neck, sweat making them both slippery, but he wouldn't let her fall. He ground against her, lifting her higher and hitting the spot she needed until she cried out, muscles rippling around him, squeezing him tight.

He wanted to hold back. Wanted to treat her with reverence, but he was beyond slowing down. Her gaze met his. Urged him on. "Do it."

Part of him wanted to curse her for reducing him to a rutting animal, but the expression on her face wasn't sordid or dirty. It was lust and want and desire.

He held her steady and rammed into her, over and over, feeling her arousal build again, hearing her cries of passion as she crashed over the edge, and his climax exploded and blew out his brains even as she pulsed and spasmed around him.

After a few moments of being strung out following one of the best orgasms of his life, he rested his forehead against hers, his hammering heart slowly steadying.

"You're beautiful," he whispered, nuzzling her ear.

She laughed. "Gravity made a few adjustments over the last three years, but thank you for not noticing."

"Gravity looks good on you. Thankfully it doesn't affect guys in the same way." He rocked his still hard cock inside her.

"Thank God," she murmured, dragging his mouth back to hers with a tug on his hair.

He kissed her again, savoring the flavor of her, the heat of her flesh, the playfulness escaping her usually tightly controlled demeanor.

Truth was she looked better now than she had three years ago. She'd been skinnier back then—stress, he realized with new insight. Her curves were softer, sweeter. She ran her hands over his shirt and started loosening his tie. He was still wearing his suit jacket. The view of them still joined together made him want her again. In a bed this time. Slowly. Thoroughly. Lazily.

He eased out, lowered her carefully to her feet, and got rid of the condom. He fastened the button of his pants, forcing himself to slow things down, to savor and enjoy. He shrugged out of his suit jacket and let it fall to the ground. She undid the knot in his tie and drew it in a slow glide through his shirt collar. His skin buzzed where she touched him. She bit her lip as she undid the first button of his shirt, then the next.

Finally when they were all undone she smoothed her hands over his bare chest. She touched the bullet he wore around his neck. He usually took it off before a date, but he hadn't exactly planned this encounter.

"Spare ammo?" she questioned. She made a joke, but there was curiosity in her eyes.

He captured her fingers and wrapped them around the

217

warm metal. It was hard to put into words exactly what that talisman meant to him. "Old sniper superstition."

"You weren't wearing it last time."

The fact she remembered proved that night had meant something to her. The fact that she hadn't been with anyone since meant it was special.

"It's a hog's tooth," he said.

"Hog's what?" She frowned as she examined the 7.62 mm bullet.

"Acronym. You know how the military loves acronyms."

"What's it stand for?" She looked up at him between her lashes. The fact she was pretty much naked kept distracting his small brain.

This probably wasn't the best time to remind her he was a bona fide trained killer. He hesitated, cleared his throat, wondering how she was going to react. "Hunter of Gunmen. It's a tradition for those who graduate Scout Sniper School."

Some women got excited by the idea of his having killed. Others were repulsed.

Erin looked somber, but not horrified. She carried a weapon too.

"You know that old saying about everyone having a bullet with their name on it? This is supposed to be mine." He brought it quickly to his lips. It represented more than that to him, though he'd never admit it out loud. Hard work, brotherhood, sacrifice, and honor. "Helps us believe we're invincible."

Erin's pupils widened as she looked up at him. "You were good at it, weren't you?"

"For a while, but it wasn't what I wanted to do with my life." His throat got tight. Ironic. Being a sniper was all about leaving emotion behind and becoming a killing machine.

Her touch lingered on the necklace for another moment, then she smoothed her palms over his chest. "I love your skin." She pressed her lips above his nipple.

He cupped her breast. "I love *your* skin."

"But you're so smooth and hot." She ran her fingers over his abs. "All these fine muscles I want to explore."

He tweaked her nipple between thumb and forefinger just hard enough she gasped.

"And I like your hands," she laughed.

He grinned. "Is that so?"

"Definitely."

He lowered his mouth to her breasts again. Her nipples were ripe, sweet, succulent, like raspberries. The hollow of her collarbone was ridiculously appealing. He nibbled his way over her body, not sure which part he liked best. Body? Or brain?

"And I'm very fond of your mouth." She leaned back against the wall, her hair falling like a cloud around her shoulders as he held her up. She looked at the ceiling and closed her eyes as he began making slow love to her body. She started to whimper, her fingers digging into his scalp. "I want you inside me again."

He scooped her up and carried her to the bed. He sat on the edge of the mattress, and she swiveled in his lap, pressing him back against the cool cotton covers. Her hair brushed his skin and in an instant he was catapulted back three years to the first moment he'd seen her. She'd been the most beautiful girl he'd ever met. That hadn't changed.

He moved them both farther up the mattress and reached for her, but she dodged him. "Not yet. I want to take it slow."

"You're going to destroy me." He held her gaze. "And I'm

219

going to beg for more."

"That's the intention." She tugged on his pants, and he shifted his hips so she could remove them and his boxers. He toed off his socks so he lay completely naked on the bed, at her mercy.

She kissed his chest and played with his flat nipples. A sweat broke out on his brow. He wasn't sure he'd be able to last if she put her lips on him, but damned if he wasn't willing to give it a shot. By the time she'd kissed her way down his body he was trembling. The memories had faded compared to the reality, and those memories had kept him company on many a lonely night in anonymous hotel rooms.

The moment that hot mouth wrapped around him, he knew he was doomed. He started reciting windage and distance calculations in his head, trying to recall the Coriolis force at this latitude, easing away from her when she took him too close to the edge.

"Did I do something wrong?" Her lips curved into a wicked smile.

"You're perfect. You should know that already." He drew her up to lie beside him, tracing his fingers over the pale skin of her breasts, over the tanned skin of her arms. "I want to make the most of tonight." He cupped her jaw again. Leaned forward until he could brush his lips over hers. "I'm glad I found you again. I'm sorry I was such a jerk last time."

Her smile was sad. "I *could* have told you I'd served him with divorce papers."

"Why didn't you?" He tucked her hair behind her neck, absorbed in the play of light over her face.

"I guess giving you a reason to walk out on me made it easier to end things."

"You let me believe the worst," he admonished her.

"You said you were a Marine and I was still officially married. I was terrified you were going to get into trouble and it would be my fault."

He winced. "I shouldn't have lied to you, but I was supposed to be keeping a low profile for an undercover op—infiltrating Islamic terrorists."

"Ah, that old 'national security' saw. Now I feel even more guilty." She ran her hands over his body, clearly enjoying touching him. He let her explore even as he ached to bury himself inside her again. "I used you for sex," she murmured. "I'm Catholic. Trust me, I'm still not over the guilt."

"You used me for empowerment. And I'm all for female empowerment." His fingers went to her panties, and he tugged the scant material down her legs. She kicked them off, and he pressed his hand over her mound, just touching her opening. "Use me again."

He kissed her as she opened for him. He turned them so she straddled his body, and she pressed her core against his rigid flesh. He bit back a groan.

"Are you sure?" She was teasing him.

He grabbed her wrists as he stared up into those shadowed eyes. "I'm sure, baby. Take whatever you want. As much as you want. For as long as you want it."

CHAPTER SIXTEEN

H E STOOD IN the shadows long after they'd disappeared from view. His palm pressed against the rough bark of the maple, using the tree to hold himself together as his life and plans unraveled. Her betrayal traveled through his bloodstream, pain resonating with every heartbeat.

To do that with another man in their home…she couldn't have hurt him more if she'd taken a blade and stabbed him in the heart.

Nausea rolled inside his stomach, and he had to swallow repeatedly so he didn't vomit.

He'd thought she was saving herself for him. After what she'd gone through with her husband he'd assumed she needed a long, slow, romantic courtship. Not to be fucked against the wall by a near-stranger.

A scream roared through his mind and emerged as a high-pitched keening noise that he shut down before it could travel on the wind and give him away. *They* were supposed to be together.

He looked up at the window and pain morphed into anger. He'd wanted to be the one to save her. To worship her. He smashed his fist against the bark. She was supposed to be working on a fucking homicide, not fucking the FBI.

Fury vibrated through his muscles. God, he wanted to

punish her. To hurt her. To make her *see* him. Beg him for forgiveness. To tell him he was the only one she wanted—the only one she'd ever want. The temptation to go in there and kill them both was almost overwhelming. But he held himself back. The fed wouldn't be here long.

If he could kill the bastard and get away with it, he would. But murdering an FBI agent would bring down the wrath of the federal authorities, and then he'd never get Erin.

He wasn't stupid. Or impetuous.

But he was done waiting.

She was *his*. And she deserved to be punished.

He closed his eyes, and the memory flashed through his brain like a retinal scar. His father screaming at his mother a split-second before he killed her. He swore he could feel the spatter of blood hitting his cheek as his mother's head exploded.

That's how he'd known Erin was the one. To share an experience so profound had been a sign that she was the woman he'd been waiting for, and he'd do everything it took to win her.

But first he was going to make her wish she was dead.

Blood dissolved on his tongue as he sucked his battered knuckles. How did he get her attention? How did he make her hurt as seriously as he was hurting? An image from the trial flashed through his brain, and he knew exactly what he needed to do. Make her regret taking her eye off the prize. Make her realize mistakes had repercussions, and repercussions could hurt just as much as any whore's betrayal.

ERIN COULDN'T BELIEVE how her entire being buzzed with a strange mix of satisfaction and arousal. She'd been nervous that she'd forgotten how to do this, and that it couldn't possibly be as amazing as she remembered. But it had been.

Every sensation felt brand-new and mesmerizing. She trailed kisses down his throat, nibbling the thick cord that ran down the side of his neck. The contrast of the darker tone of his skin against her much paler body made her think of sandy beaches and hot sun. His body was honed and fit, showcasing muscles that made her want to touch and taste. She ran her fingers through silky hair, over powerful shoulders, strong collarbones, and defined abs covered in warm tanned skin. Even his navel made her want to dip her tongue to taste.

Her fingers skimmed a rough spot. A scar. She hadn't noticed it last time, but that night had been about reclaiming her life, and she hadn't thought much beyond Darsh's wicked smile and crazy good looks.

She'd used him without any thought as to his emotions.

"What happened here?" Her voice was gruff.

He shifted his arm to see what she was looking at. "Bullet."

"I can see that." She kissed the scar and rolled onto the side, lifting his arm to see the exit wound. *Ouch.* "Marines? Or FBI?" She kissed the puckered flesh. He reared up and tried to grab her, but she pulled away.

"Baghdad. Small arms fire."

She wanted to know more about him, about what made him get up in the morning and strap on his federal armor.

"Thankfully it wasn't bad enough to get me sent home." His grin sliced the air.

"Why not?" she asked.

"Because the team medic sewed me up in the field, and I

didn't tell my CO until it was almost healed. It was just a flesh wound." He dismissed it.

He'd been inches from death but had been more worried about losing his place in the fight than the prospect of dying. There was something ridiculously attractive about people prepared to sacrifice themselves in the service of their country. Something that melted a woman's heart no matter how impermeable she tried to make it.

Death could happen to anyone on any given day, especially to soldiers, cops, or firefighters, but it was slightly more of a hazard in battle. She found another scar on his hip and kissed that, too. Teasing him with her hair because she could tell he liked the feel of it against his skin.

His cock twitched, and he tensed when she kissed along his length. Though she wanted nothing more than to take him inside, she didn't.

The first time with Darsh had held an element of risk and danger, like walking on hot coals or touching an open flame. This time she wanted to take it slow. She tested them both by delaying what they each so desperately wanted again. She tugged on his shoulder until he rolled over and lay on his front. She traced the strong column of his spine and the indents around each vertebra, the sharp angles of his shoulder blades. It was so unusual to have access to another body, and his was so finely made. She wanted to enjoy every inch. She kneaded her fingers into his tense shoulders, and he groaned.

"You're so stiff." She dug her thumbs into a knot of muscle.

His big hand reached back to cup her thigh. "I've got something else you can massage—"

She pressed deeper into the tight muscles, and he growled

and sank into the bed. "You're killing me."

"Suck it up, G-man. I dated a physio back in college who took some massage courses. He taught me a few things."

"I bet he did." He laughed but sounded almost in pain.

"About massage." She stilled. What did he actually think of her? That she did this every other week? That her bedroom had a revolving door? Sure, she'd told him she hadn't had sex in three years, but why should he believe her? "I never had sex with him. We got close, but…"

He sat up, and she fell back onto the mattress beside him. He stretched out on top of her and brushed her hair back from her forehead with both hands. "You don't need to give me a blow-by-blow of your love life. I'm not judging you for hooking up with me that night in Quantico—or tonight for that matter. In fact, I'm not judging you at all."

The way he stared at her was like he could see all the way to her soul.

She bit her lip. "I know it's stupid. I know I should own it. But, gah, I don't want you thinking I sleep around."

"I don't, but even if I did, I wouldn't judge you for it. You think I'm a saint?" He dipped his mouth and captured her bottom lip, tugged, and then kissed the sting better. "You need to get over it."

She laughed. "I can't. It's ingrained—like the blonde hair and blue eyes." She tensed, painfully aware of the irony of her laying here naked and telling him she wasn't easy.

"Okay, let me guess, you've slept with, hmm," his eyes narrowed as he stared at her face, "three guys in your entire lifetime. The first was some guy in college. The second was your husband. And the third was me…"

"How'd you know that?" She frowned. "About the guy in

college? I never told anyone about that loser."

"I'm a behavioral analyst." He laughed at her expression. "Look, it's obvious you don't just dive into the sack with anyone. Cops talk. I've already had two guys tell me not to bother hitting on you unless I want my ego crushed. And you're too hot for someone not to have pulled every trick in the book to get you into bed, and college boys are good at it—not as good as Marines though." His dark eyes shone with humor. "That's an open secret in the military. Don't fall for all the Special Forces hype. Those guys are more in love with their tools than with women"—his eyes brimmed with amusement—"but, getting back to your sordid exploits, when you realized the college kid was a worthless piece of shit, you dumped him and waited until you met someone you thought you could fall in love with, only he turned out to be another piece of shit. God,"—he rubbed his nose against hers—"you have lousy taste in men." His hand moved lower and made her gasp. "I should be insulted," he said, drawing a finger over her slick flesh and making her back arch off the bed in shocked pleasure.

"I'm trying to improve my batting average," she managed to get out. "No pressure."

"Pretty sure I can beat two duds." He ran his tongue over the tip of her breasts, and she knew he was right. She couldn't believe how easily he brought her to a state of frantic arousal, like he knew exactly how she needed to be touched before she did.

As long as she didn't fall in love with this one, she told herself sternly. She didn't want to think about the dark abyss that had been falling in love with her husband.

She caught Darsh's face in her hands and kissed him deeply. She'd forgotten how good it was to feel a man's weight on top of her. She planted her heels on the bed, and her hips arched. His mouth was on her breast, his hand stroking over her, arousing, but never really touching her. Paying her back with some of her teasing and making her want to groan with frustration.

Her body felt like someone had poured gasoline all over her libido, and he'd just lit the match. The slight grain of stubble on his jaw scraped over her skin, the sensation incredibly erotic. He shifted, and she thought he'd gone to grab a condom, but instead, he moved between her legs and his mouth brushed her inner thighs. The rasping of his beard added a layer of sensation to the experience. A thousand pleasure points exploded over her skin. Her orgasm ricocheted through her so fast she was spinning through the universe and screaming out his name.

He smiled against her thighs and then he picked up a condom that he'd pulled from God knew where and covered himself. He crawled up her body, kissing every inch along the way before the tip of him was pressed against her entrance. He kissed her deep and carnal, and she tasted herself on his lips.

He paused. "You sure about this?"

That he was asking this again, when he was cradled between her open thighs, made her want him even more. "Yes."

He pushed inside, and she dug her nails into his back, reveling in the feeling of being completely full. God, she'd missed this. Missed the weight, the friction, the delicious glide of skin against skin. Slowly he pulled out and entered her again, hot and slick. Her body clung to his like he was the only safe place in a storm-tossed sea.

He thrust deeper until he was buried all the way inside. He

rested his forehead against hers, then propped himself on his elbows and stared deep into her eyes. "All right?"

She hadn't realized how desperately she was clinging to him until he asked. Hesitantly she nodded and let go of some of the tension. "Incredible."

He kissed her again, slowly, as if letting her get used to their intimacy. Sex against the wall had been thrilling and exciting, but this was letting him even closer, and he knew it. He was moving unhurriedly, kissing her over and over, stretching his body over hers without giving her too much of his weight. Teasing her nipples with the rough hairs on his chest. His hands held her face in place so he had full access to her mouth. Controlling the kiss, plundering her lips, taking what he wanted and giving her everything he had. It should have scared her, but it didn't.

Moonlight struck the side of his face, outlining the masculine brow, the sharp nose. He looked so tense, so focused…

"You're so beautiful," she told him.

"That's my line." He rolled them so she was on top. Ran his hands down her sides and then up over her breasts, cupping their soft weight in his palms. She loved how he made her feel, like she really was beautiful. Slowly he started moving beneath her, small thrusts driving her insane with the need to take more. Stretching her, filling her, making her toes curl with pleasure, but not enough to push her over the edge. The callouses on his fingers grazed her skin in a way that made her back arch. *So good.* She'd forgotten. She'd forgotten the long, winding path that could lead to the perfect climax.

He reared up and tugged her hair back, exposing her throat and taking advantage of the position to thrust just a little bit harder. His other arm banded her waist, pulling her against him as he drove her insane. Moving not quite hard enough or deep enough to tip either of them over the edge, but feeling so good she never wanted it to stop. Her body knew the rhythm, and she matched him perfectly. She put a twist into the shift of her hips, and his fingers dug deeper.

"The first time I saw you, I thought you looked like an angel." He held her hair bunched tight in his fist, and she desperately tried to get closer even though he wasn't letting her move as much as she wanted. "There was no way I was leaving that bar without you." His voice was gruff when he admitted that.

"Unless you'd known I was married."

His gaze held hers even as he kept driving her upwards on that elusive hunt for release. "You're not married anymore." He let her hair go and shifted them again so she was on her back and he was on his knees. His movements became faster, deeper. A fine layer of sweat formed on his forehead.

"I can't wait much longer," he gritted out.

"What are you waiting for?" she gasped. It felt so good. *So good.*

His eyes heated. "You."

He hit the spot that made her cry out again in panicked pleasure. Suddenly she was flooded by sensation, each nerve bursting like a firework through her body as white light exploded behind her eyes. His shout of completion chased her as she catapulted through some alternative dimension before landing right back in his arms.

He gathered her to him, holding her close for a few heartbeats while the world righted itself. Then he gently extricated himself, got rid of the condom, and came back to bed, pulling her tight against his body to combat the sudden chill in the room.

"You should sleep in the other room," she murmured, but she snuggled closer anyway.

He kissed her ear, spooning her body like he'd been made to fit. The pulse in his wrist throbbed against her ribs as he cupped her breast.

"Go to sleep, Erin." He nuzzled her ear. The heat of his body soothed her, and exhaustion swept over her like a calming wave before dragging her beneath the surface.

CHAPTER SEVENTEEN

RACHEL CREPT OUT of the front door, careful not to make a sound. Her car was right there, and she started the engine, all the while checking the windows of her home to make sure her parents hadn't woken up. She doubted they'd heard her leave. They slept in separate bedrooms at the back of the house. Pretended it was because of Dad's snoring, but no one was fooled.

Their marriage was another victim of her rape.

Her throat knotted as she drove away. What had happened to her had destroyed them. So much remorse. So much shame. She wished she could go back and do something differently— not moved from home into a dorm, screamed louder, fought him off—or maybe just never told anyone…

The secret might have destroyed her, but so had the truth. She never went out except to the crisis center or classes. She didn't sleep. She was scared all the time. She saw his face above her every night. Hurting her. Every night. Like a devil in her dreams torturing her all the way from the depths of hell.

She'd felt empowered when the verdict had been read. After Hawke was sent to prison. After the jury told her and Mary that they believed them. That they believed they weren't lying to get some boy's attention. The town said otherwise, and the wall of hatred had driven her off social media and made her change her accounts to ones she only shared with her closest friends.

She wiped at the tears. She hated how weak she'd become. How untrusting.

Snow drifted out of the sky in indolent spirals. Another big fall was forecast for today. She loved snow—or rather, she loved being tucked up beside a roaring fire surrounded by her parents, and their house. Safe. She shuddered. What did that even mean? Safety was an illusion for the foolish. And the fact she was arguing with herself about it showed exactly how crazy she'd become.

They said two-to-eight percent of rape allegations were possibly false. The figure was low, but who in the world would lie about being raped? Who'd make up that sort of vicious desecration just to get noticed? Certainly not someone who'd been raped. Forget the pain and terror of the attack itself, the aftermath was worse. It was like stripping away everything you thought you knew about yourself and reducing it to ashes, lies, illusion.

Rachel knew she was considered one of the "lucky" ones. She'd studied the stats. Eighty percent of rapes were never reported to the cops. Less than five percent of those were prosecuted, and of *those*, only 0.2-2.8 percent resulted in convictions where the attacker went to jail. Erin Donovan had made that happen with her belief in Rachel's statement and dogged police work. It had made Rachel believe in miracles, made her believe that her community had triumphed, at least in legal terms. She'd hoped it had been a sign that the rest of the country was getting serious about the issue of rape on college campuses, but only time would tell.

And now these murders had brought back all the old fear

and insecurity. She shuddered and pushed the uncertainty out of her mind.

The only positive thing was she'd discovered she could use her experience to help others. Sure she was scared to death, but she was also more empathetic than she used to be. She was damaged, but she had practical knowledge in how a victim could get help. If that was all she took with her from this awful chapter of her life, at least it was something.

She put on her blinker to head toward Fox Creek Park. She had classes at nine, but she had something very important to attend to first.

It was quiet, which she preferred. People were either spit-in-her-face hateful, or overly-friendly sympathetic. They all looked at her like they knew her. They didn't *know* her.

Earlier, she'd received a call from one of the guys who helped out at the crisis center. She clenched her fingers around the wheel. Another girl had been attacked, but she was too scared to officially report it. The girl needed to go to the clinic and get checked out. The problem was she was so traumatized she was reluctant to seek treatment.

The woman needed to think about STDs. Pregnancy. UTIs. Physical damage. A rape kit in case she changed her mind about wanting to nail the bastard at some point in the future. It was important, or Rachel wouldn't have agreed to get out of bed before the crack of dawn.

It scared her that this was happening again in her small town. Hawke was in prison. She should feel safe now, but she didn't.

Maybe it was time to move away? Or for plastic surgery. The last made her laugh. People went through worse things, she reminded herself. That's why she asked people to tell her the worst thing that had ever happened to them before she'd talk about her own experience. You couldn't tell what people had gone through by looking at their faces, though Rachel tried. And no matter how terrible, at least she was still alive.

She clung to that.

She drove into the parking lot and found a space near the fence posts that marked the entrance to the footpath. She left the engine running as she tapped her bitten-to-the-quick fingernails against the steering wheel. He'd said they'd be here at six AM sharp.

Rachel checked her watch. Hopefully the clinic wouldn't be busy at this time of day, but they still needed to hurry if they all wanted to make class.

The big SUV he sometimes drove pulled into the parking lot. He slid into the empty bay next to her and got out. She rolled down her window, and he leaned inside.

"She's in the backseat." He jerked his head toward the SUV. "She needs another woman to talk to. Someone she can trust." Concern etched his features.

Rachel couldn't see the young woman through the tinted-glass, but she had no doubt she'd be crying, replaying what had happened over and over in her head. Still, she sat there, paralyzed. Could she really listen to the details of another girl's ordeal without imploding from misery?

"Look, maybe I should just take her home. Sorry I wasted your time—"

"No," Rachel said softly, undoing her seatbelt. "Let me talk to her."

He pressed his lips together and shrugged as she got out of the car. She went to the passenger door of his vehicle, and he followed, hands stuffed in his pockets.

She opened the door and looked inside, frowning in confusion as she stared at the empty seat. "I-I don't understand."

He grabbed her hair in one hand and slammed her head against the metal of the door. An explosion of white light was followed by blinding pain above her eye-socket. Something hard jabbed into her lower ribs. "You don't have to understand, Rachel. You just have to do what I say."

She cried out as he dragged her backward, shoved the door closed, and force-marched her toward the woods.

"What are you doing? Let go of me!" she yelled. She tried to get away, but he was so much stronger than she was. The pain in her scalp when he hauled her against him made her eyes bleed.

He laughed.

"Let go! I mean it." She kicked out at him, but he shoved her onwards. She grabbed at his wrists to try and ease the pressure on her head, to reduce the searing pain in her skull. "Why are you doing this?" she screamed. It was hard to think. Hard to ignore the pain and panic to try and figure out what the hell was happening.

She'd trusted him. He shoved her onward. She screamed, but there was no one to hear, and her cries echoed uselessly through the forest.

"We're just taking a walk. I need to tell you something."

Bullshit. "Tell me now."

"In a few minutes. It's important." She didn't believe him. Her heart raced so fast it felt like a buzz saw in her chest. Why was he doing this? He knew what she'd been through. Why had he lied to her about another victim?

It was so cold she started to shiver violently. Or maybe that was the fear taking hold and shutting down her function.

Her eyes darted into the shadows of the trees. If she could get out of his grasp, she could run. She could run forever. The grip on her hair tightened as if he read her mind.

They kept walking into the heart of the park.

"Where are we going? This is stupid! You're scaring me." Her voice got small when she needed it to be strong. It was happening again—the utter loss of control, the overwhelming sense of powerlessness. They'd walked for ages off the path into the forest, trudging through snow that soaked her jeans. "I don't understand," she sobbed.

"Of course you don't." He gave her a violent shove, and she fell, face-first.

She scooted onto her back and started crab-crawling away from him, through the snow. "Why are you doing this to *me*!"

"Oh, please, Rachel." His tone was condescending. "I'm putting you out of your misery."

"W-what?" She could barely breathe she was so scared.

He eyed her with mock concern. "I'm giving you a choice."

"W-what choice?"

"Take your clothes off and lie down on the ground."

Her throat felt raw from clawing back emotion. "Or?" she rasped.

A smile touched his lips, so callous and evil it eased between her ribs and into her heart like a blade. "Or I'll do to you what I did last time, except there won't be any drugs to block the reality of what's happening this time. No convenient black outs."

Pain streaked through her chest, and it took a moment to realize she was hyperventilating. "It was *you*! But that's impossible. I saw Drew Hawke—"

"You saw what I wanted you to see." He glanced at his

watch as if bored.

"I know what I saw!" But there were so many pieces of broken information that didn't fit together.

He pulled something large from his jacket pocket and placed it over his face. Blue eyes glittered from behind small holes in a facemask.

"You made a mask of his face?" She flashed back to that night, and it suddenly made sense. The utter lack of emotion shown by her attacker. The fact he hadn't said a word.

She was going to throw up. Hawke was innocent. She'd helped send an innocent man to prison, and no one knew. A high-pitched squeal sounded inside her head—like her sanity was escaping her skull. Her only hope was to outrun this monster who'd taken so much from so many people. Who'd convinced her so thoroughly it was Drew, she'd taken a polygraph to swear he was guilty.

She had to tell someone.

He put the mask carefully back in his pocket. "You should have seen the look on Cassie's face when she saw it."

Rachel's stomach knotted. He'd killed Cassie, and now he was going to kill her.

"Hypothermia isn't supposed to be a bad way to go. It doesn't hurt—you just fall asleep."

She bolted. She scrambled under a pine and around a silver birch. She was small, but fast, and she would not let this twisted creature win.

She dodged right, but her foot hit a root, and she sprawled into the snow. A heavy weight smashed into her back before she could get up, shoving the air from her lungs so she lay there wheezing desperately, trying to draw in oxygen.

The weight of him behind her brought back a myriad of

powerful memories from that night last year. A barrage of emotions—fear, rage, confusion. When she was finally able to haul in a breath she saw he held a rope, blue rope, just like Erin Donovan had shown her in photographs. Terror beat out revulsion.

She bucked against his weight, but he didn't budge. Tears welled at the unfairness of it all.

"You killed those girls, raped the others. Framed Hawke. Why?" She screamed as long and as loud as her lungs allowed. Only silence answered. She drew in another breath, but he shoved her face into the snow.

"Shut the fuck up. No one's going to hear you out here, and you're giving me a headache." She almost choked. He grabbed her ankles and dragged her to a nearby tree. The icy ground scratched her face.

"Why are you doing this?"

"To punish her." He took in a deep breath as if winded.

Her? "My mother?"

He laughed, a horrible sound. "How can someone whose parents are so smart be so incredibly dumb?"

She flinched. "Who, then?" He was looking up as if searching for a place to throw the rope. He was looking for somewhere to set a noose… "Who are you trying to punish by doing these awful things to me?"

"Will you just shut the fuck up." He cut off a short length of rope and wrapped it around her head, tight, forcing the knot between her teeth. The edges of her lips split, and she tasted blood.

"Better." He smirked.

She was trembling with cold and fear, but she edged onto the balls of her feet.

"Detective Donovan. I'm punishing Detective Donovan."

She frowned in confusion. What did the detective need to be punished for? And why attack her, not Erin?

He leaned close. "That's who I'm punishing. Because she's a cheating whore."

Rachel didn't understand. But maybe it didn't matter. He stood back to throw his rope over a nearby branch, and she pushed up from the ground and ran.

She didn't look behind her, didn't pause. She forced her legs to move faster than they'd ever moved before. She heard him thrashing through the bushes, but she was losing him. She felt elation. She'd won. She'd won! Then she realized she was running straight for a cliff, and he was closing in from behind. There was no escape. She heard his laughter. He knew she was running to her death like some stupid lemming.

And as the cliff loomed she realized she had a choice. Grab hold of life and take control—even if it meant certain death. Or suffer at the hands of a monster who wanted to destroy her over and over again. She took control and threw herself over that precipice, her heart soaring free as she sailed through the air.

DARSH CRACKED HIS eyelids apart at the sound of the shower. It took a fraction of a second to remember where he was and what he'd been doing for most of the night. He checked the clock. Six. Rubbed his eyes and rolled out of bed and walked buck-naked into the bathroom. Thick, billowing steam filled the air, but he could just make out Erin behind the frosted glass. All his good intentions about getting an early start evaporated.

He didn't stop moving, just walked into the shower and grabbed the woman who'd filled his head with lust from the moment they'd met. He pressed her against the cool glass.

After a moment's hesitation she kissed him, open-mouthed and sensual. Then she ran soap-slick hands over his back and shoulders. His body couldn't get enough of her. His brain was struggling too. He lifted her up, and her legs went around him and he slid home. Then he froze.

"Fuck. I don't have any condoms left." His teeth were fused together in the effort not to move.

Her ankles pressed into the back of his ass, and she held his gaze. "I'm on birth control. I'm safe."

She felt so good with no barrier between them. "I'm safe too, but…" He'd never done this before. Too many of his friends had become early parents, even the ones using condoms.

"We don't have to. There are other ways." Her smile told him she had plenty of ideas, but her muscles clamped around him, rippling in the early stages of orgasm.

"No, I want this." Wanted it so much it was scary. And he sank into her, finding a rhythm that had her gasping and clawing at his back, trying to ride him, holding onto his shoulders. He watched her face as she teetered on the edge before crying out and crashing over. His own release swept over him like a wildfire rushing through parched grassland, obliterating everything before it. She collapsed against him, and he held her there, letting her breath settle as he watched water pour down her spine.

She raised her head, eyes no longer bright and febrile, but pensive and shadowed. "We need to get to work, and pretend we didn't stay up most of the night having sex."

Carefully he let her feet slide to the floor. She looked a little shell-shocked. Rather than pleasure on her face, there was sadness. He'd promised her a better ending than the last time, but she knew reality would rip them apart. They'd broken the rules. Hooked up when they should have been keeping it professional and working the case. He grabbed some shower gel, which he smoothed on her body then his, washing her, cleansing her.

"What if this didn't have to end?" he said.

She tensed beneath his fingers.

"I thought three years ago was the best sex I'd ever have in my life, but last night blew that away. What if it keeps getting better?" *What if they were meant to be together?*

She looked away. "It's just sex."

He knew better. Their "just sex" was like comparing an incendiary device to a party popper. But Erin had been through hell. She was obviously gun-shy when it came to relationships.

"What if we carry on seeing each other after this is all over and actually find out?" Darsh willed her to meet his gaze, but she kept those blue eyes steadfastly fixed on the floor and tried to sidestep him. "What if we give this craziness between us a chance?"

She gave a harsh sounding laugh and stepped out of the shower, slipping into a robe. He followed, and she handed him a towel. He rubbed his hair dry, and he watched her watching him naked in her bathroom.

Despite the look of female appreciation on her face she wasn't throwing him any positive vibes about seeing each other again.

"We can't." Her throat moved as she swallowed.

"Why not?" Another thought occurred to him. He bristled. "Is it the fact we're from different backgrounds?"

Her mouth rounded in shock. "What? Are you insane? If you're good enough to go to bed with then you're good enough to date, jackass. And if you're insinuating there's a race agenda here, you aren't as smart as you think you are."

He'd had plenty of women who wanted him for a one-nighter but hadn't wanted to be seen in public with him. It had started in high school and happened numerous times since. But if race wasn't the issue for Erin, what was?

"We live in different states, and you're investigating my work on the Hawke case, remember?"

Like he could forget. He scrubbed the towel over his back and down his legs. However much he hated it, she was right.

She marched past him to get dressed, and he followed, digging a clean T-shirt and black pants out of his bag. He wasn't ready to give up. "What about when this is all over?"

She snapped on her weapon and pulled on her boots. Her lips pressed together in an angry line. "We'll still be in different states."

"You could move?"

"Ha! Where've I heard that before? Quit your job and your friends—"

"Hey, I'm not your ex." Rage rushed through him. "Don't *ever* compare me to him."

"Or what?" She put her hands on her hips, spoiling for a fight. He got that now.

His chin went up. "I meant quit Forbes Pines PD. Join the FBI or some bigger police department. You'd make a hell of an agent."

Her eyes went wide, and her arms dropped to her sides. She took a deep breath. "Oh."

"Yeah, 'oh.'" He pulled on his holster and checked his SIG. Made sure he had all his clothes and belongings in his go-bag because chances were this was his one and only night in Erin's bedroom.

He'd tried. He'd put himself out there, and she'd rejected him. At least he hadn't walked away without trying to explore whether or not this explosive chemistry between them meant something more than just sex.

He swung his bag on his shoulder, but paused on the threshold of the bedroom. "One of these days you're going to stop running away from the fear of being hurt again." He looked back to where she stood frozen in place. "I just hope there's a little bit of life waiting for you when you do."

CHAPTER EIGHTEEN

ERIN WALKED BRISKLY up the stairs to the Department of Psychology and Professor Huxley's office. She and Darsh had shared a silent ride to work where she'd found her car with the tire replaced and a note from her buddy Manny on the dash.

At least she had friends in the department. That might change if they found out that after three years of rejecting every guy who'd asked her out, she'd hooked up with the first federal agent to pass through. Waking up in his arms had brought on a strong hit of remorse. If their bosses or co-workers found out they were involved her career would suffer. She'd devoted too much of her life to her job to lose it over one night of reckless passion. And the idea they had more than that going for them? That was Darsh's conscience talking. Or leftover lust.

He'd get over it. Hell, he'd be thanking her before long.

She ignored his barb about always running away. She'd needed to put some distance between herself and NYC, that was all. Being alone wasn't a damn crime.

She reached the third floor, searching for Huxley's office, which had moved since the last time she'd visited. Signs directed her left. The hallways were quiet except for her footsteps, which echoed on the parquet flooring.

The idea of joining the FBI teased her mind. But she wasn't uprooting just because some guy made her come more times than she could count. *Yeah, reduce it to sex, Erin, and you might just convince yourself that's all there is to it.*

She found Room 345 and knocked on the door.

There was a rustle of papers and the screech of a chair from inside. Then a hesitant, "Come in."

She opened the door and there was Huxley with a female student standing at his shoulder clutching what looked like an essay.

"Erin! Come on in," Huxley said jovially. Too jovially for this time in the morning, but that was just her personal opinion.

"Thanks, Monica. I'll see you in class. If you have more questions about your essay, email me or talk to Rick or Linus."

Erin waited for the girl to walk past her. Her cheeks were flushed. Was that guilt in her eyes? Had they been doing something they shouldn't? Or was the inability to meet her gaze and anxiousness to disappear based on personal dislike, which seemed more prevalent when it came to Erin's dealings with anyone on campus?

Erin didn't know, but Huxley wouldn't quite meet her gaze either. His hair was mussed. Lips reddened. It crossed her mind that he and the student might have been doing more than an essay review before she'd rapped on the door. Right now, Erin didn't care about moral turpitude. As long as they were both over the age of consent and no one was breaking any laws then they could go at it like rabbits for all she cared.

And it was possible she was seeing things that weren't there—especially regarding sexual relations. Her mind flashed back to Darsh finding her naked in the shower that morning when she'd been trying to do her best to remove herself from him and re-establish their professional boundaries. Instead they'd had unprotected sex.

A mix of hunger and remorse sifted through her veins as she thought of all the unprofessional things they'd done together over the last twelve hours and how she couldn't afford to do them ever again. So, really, she wasn't about to give lectures about who people chose to have sex with—as long as it was consensual. That was her only line drawn firmly in the sand.

"Roman," she said as the student closed the door behind her with a firm snick.

He leaned forward and dragged his coffee mug to his lips. "Sorry, it's chaos around here at the start of term, and I'm lecturing at nine. What can I do for you, Erin?"

She pulled out a picture of Peter Zimmerman. There was another knock and before Huxley could say anything, the door opened. Rick Lachlan, the prof's TA, stood there with a surprised expression on his face.

"Can you give us a few moments…?"

"Actually it's fine for Rick to be here." Erin sent the guy a smile. He was shorter than Huxley, but good-looking in a clean-cut way. Rick and Linus were Huxley's shadows and might prompt the professor's memory, which could be remarkably vague at times. "I'm wondering if you saw this man at the mission on Monday night?"

She handed the professor the photograph, and he stared at it with a frown. Rick strode around the desk to look at the picture.

"Is this the fellow who confessed?" Huxley asked.

Rick's brows rose sharply. "I didn't know anyone had

confessed."

"Last night." She confirmed. "Did you see him at the shelter on Monday night?"

The professor picked up a pair of reading glasses and put them on. "Yes, they call him Stinky Pete, although I'm not sure what his real name is. He was there. We started serving dinner promptly around six PM, right, Rick?"

"You were there, too?" she asked the research assistant in surprise. Not for the first time she wondered if they had some sort of sexual relationship. Then she rolled her eyes at herself. She was seeing sex everywhere this morning. The ache between her thighs reminded her why.

"The whole lab helps out at least once a month. Not only is it our civic duty, it's also a good way to meet possible test subjects of people with various psychological issues."

Rick plucked the photo out of the prof's hands. "He was there when we opened the doors. I asked him if he was going to stay in the shelter that night because it was bitterly cold out, but he just glared at me. I took it to mean no."

"Any idea what time he left?" she asked Huxley, but it was Rick who answered again.

"I'm thinking around seven-thirty, maybe quarter to eight?" He frowned. "I'm not absolutely certain."

"Professor?" she asked.

His cheeks flushed slightly, and he took the picture back from his assistant. "I'm not sure. I was elbows deep in washing suds so I couldn't swear to anything in court."

"You were both there all night?"

"Yes." Huxley nodded decisively.

Rick's eyes widened, and his lip curled slightly.

"What is it?" she prompted.

Rick shook his head. "He just doesn't seem like the type, that's all."

"You know better than most that people don't wear their crimes on the outside," the professor admonished.

"Yes. I do know that." Anger flashed in the research assistant's eyes. "But you'd think with our knowledge and expertise we'd be able to see some psychological red flag to warn us about dangerous individuals—or liars. I mean we served him dinner and then he went and raped and murdered two young women?" He put his hand over his mouth. "What good is what we do if that happens?"

"Knowledge is key," the professor argued, leaning back in his chair. He had an irritating habit of reducing crime to intellectual statements. "I'd be more worried that he's confessing just to get a warm place to sleep and three square meals a day." He handed the photograph back to Erin and checked his watch. Time for his lecture. She got the message.

"Okay, thank you both for your time. I'll let you get to work."

She headed out and was surprised to find the corridor now full of students milling around. She paused just outside the office to jot in her notebook about the timeline. The sound of raised voices seeped under the door though the words were indistinguishable.

The professor burst out of the room, looking furious, and almost ran into her.

"Excuse me." He paused and then brushed past her. "Late for class."

Surprised, she watched him stride purposefully away. Rick followed more slowly, locking the door behind him.

He watched his boss with a pensive expression on his face.

"He's under a lot of pressure," he said quietly.

Erin narrowed her eyes. She wondered what kind of pressure a professor might be under.

"Fancy a coffee?" Rick asked, checking his watch as the students in the hallway started to dissipate into lecture theaters.

She was woozy with fatigue and gave a tired laugh. "I'd love to, but I can't. I have to go talk to campus security."

He smiled and nodded. "Next time, then."

"I look forward to it." She said goodbye and headed down the hallway and pushed through the heavy door to the stairwell. She smacked straight into something solid—Jason Brady. The impact was so forceful, she almost fell on her ass. He grabbed her by the upper arms and in the same moment seemed to become aware of who she was. Immediately he lifted and slammed her into the wall at the top of the stairs. The air left her lungs, and she gasped for oxygen. A wheezing sound escaped her lips as her eyes watered.

His eyes burned with hatred as he stared into hers, pressing his body forcefully against her, pinning her in place. Her heart raced. Sweat bloomed from every pore. She struggled, but she couldn't reach her weapon or move her arms and legs more than a few inches. Her glance slid left, and she realized how easy it would be for him to pick her up and throw her over that balustrade. He could toss her onto the unforgiving concrete steps and from this height she'd be dead. He followed her gaze, and the expression in his eyes hardened, as if he was weighing the implications. His grip tightened until pain streaked along her arms and her lungs seized.

No one was around. No one would ever know.

Finally, he came back into himself. He drew in a shuddering breath and stepped back, letting go of her as if she was poisonous. Then he strode away, slammed through the massive door, making it hit the wall with a crash, the noise echoing like a gunshot through the entire building.

Her legs buckled. She collapsed to the floor, trying to draw breath into her scorched lungs, surrounded by the stench of fear and sweat.

Was her job really worth her life?

She pushed up against the wall and gripped tight to the banister as she hobbled down the stairs like some drunk. She thought about Cassie, and Mandy, and Rachel, and Mary, and all the other girls in this town who she'd been there for when they'd needed her.

They were worth it.

Every one of them was worth dealing with assholes like Brady. She straightened her backbone and drew in a tight breath.

Darsh had been right about one thing though, she conceded. She needed backup while working on campus. She put in a call to Cathy Bickham and told the officer to meet her over at campus security.

———

DARSH SAT OPPOSITE Peter Zimmerman. Waiting. Ully Mason cleared his throat, but Darsh didn't say a word. He knew a way to a Marine's heart.

Unfortunately, that gave him time to think about last night.

The fact Erin could turn it all off as soon as the sun came up had him questioning everything he knew about sex and women. He tried not to let it bother him. She was right that no one could know about their night together. But the reminder that what they'd done was a dirty little secret pissed him off. He wanted more, but she wasn't willing to give it a try. She wasn't cold-hearted, but she was a coward.

She'd disappeared on him this morning. Told him she didn't want to sit in with him on this interview because she had something important to do. Truth was she was avoiding him. It had been the intimacy, the exchange of confidences and trust that had scared Erin enough to make her back away so completely. She'd made herself vulnerable, and it had scared the crap out of her.

He got it, but he didn't like it.

Finally someone came in with the coffee and bacon roll he'd requested. He nodded his thanks and they left. He pushed the savory snack across the table. Zimmerman didn't wait for an invitation. He dug into the fragrant sandwich and grabbed one of the three coffees that now sat on the table. He swallowed a mouthful of food, then drank greedily.

"Mr. Zimmerman, my name is Agent Darsh Singh. I'm with the FBI."

"Don't answer to that name no more," the guy said around a mouthful of food.

"I'm not about to call a US Marine 'Stinky Pete,'" Darsh told him honestly.

The blue coveralls the prisoner had been given to replace his confiscated clothing were so large they hung off one shoulder. Bones protruded against skin, indicating years of poor nutrition.

"When'd you leave active duty?"

Zimmerman wiped the grease off his face, but it coated his

beard. Ully Mason thrust a napkin across the table. Zimmerman scrubbed at his face with the cuffs of his clothes and thanked Officer Mason with a glare.

He turned his attention back to Darsh. "Two thousand ten. Did five tours." A hint of pride snuck through the resentment.

Five tours, but he was living on the streets? Darsh believed in personal responsibility, but what the fuck? What was wrong with this country that they didn't take care of their veterans better than this?

"I did three years with the Thundering Third," Darsh told him quietly. "I obviously wasn't in for as long as you were."

Something sparked in Zimmerman's eyes. A sense of shared experience, the brotherhood of the US Marine Corps. Pride. Darsh was going to need that to connect with this man and discover the truth about what had happened on Monday night.

"Fall of Baghdad?" asked Zimmerman.

Darsh nodded.

"I heard it was a good fight." Zimmerman paused in his eating to wash down his food with another mouthful of coffee. "See the statue topple?"

The towering statue of Saddam Hussein that had dominated Firdor Square until the Marines had arrived to pull it down. "My buddies were the ones who tore it down." Almost started another battle by raising the wrong flag afterwards. The actions of a good officer had averted disaster. At least they had that day. It hadn't been long until the locals became less friendly.

"You were part of all that?" Ully Mason was suddenly interested in more than his skin color and FBI job title. Or maybe the antagonism had more to do with his obvious interest in Erin—personal and professional.

"A small part." Darsh conceded. "With a big rifle."

There was no way around getting personal in this interview or revealing things about himself that he generally didn't talk about. Maybe it was just as well Erin wasn't here.

"I was part of the mobile sniper units. What did you do?"

Zimmerman's eyes flashed. "I heard about you guys. First time they'd done it that way. Worked a treat."

Darsh nodded, resigning himself to the conversation. The USMC snipers had deployed as fast reaction units on the battlefield, rather than hunkering down and waiting for targets to come to them.

"You guys saved my buddy's ass when the Republican Guard attacked that hospital."

Darsh remembered the incident. The hospital had been commandeered to treat the wounded, but Saddam's men had attacked, even though the place was teeming with their own people. Snipers had picked off the Republican Guard through the windows and saved a lot of lives. They'd gotten lucky.

"That was my job. What was yours?" He was trying to remind this man who'd fallen so low that he'd once been a proud Marine with a worthy cause.

"I was a gunnery sergeant." Zimmerman wiped his mouth again. Stared into his coffee.

"What happened?" Darsh asked quietly.

"Usual." Those bony shoulders bobbed, but he pushed the empty plate away and rested his elbows on the table. "Went to war. Came home to find my wife fucking my best friend. Got out. Started picking fights. Started drinking. Fucked up. Ran away like a baby."

"Why'd you run away?" Darsh asked.

Zimmerman's bloodshot blue eyes met Darsh's. Intelligence shone in the depths. Intelligence and pain. "You know why."

"I want you to tell me."

Zimmerman leaned back in his chair and for a moment looked like he was going to clam up. Then he leaned forward again and laid his fingers on the tabletop and stretched them wide. "DUI."

Darsh knew there was more to it. "Getting a DUI was worth an outstanding warrant?" Darsh made it sound like the most stupid decision ever. He wasn't far wrong.

Zimmerman's expression hardened, and his lips compressed. "Not just a DUI. I ran over my little girl." Darsh watched Zimmerman struggle to swallow. "She was playing on her bike in the driveway, and I ran her over."

"She wasn't badly injured. You took full responsibility for your actions at the time."

The guy looked up with devastation in his eyes. "I crushed her bicycle. You should have seen it, the wheels all mangled and twisted. That could have been her. I called the cops and the ambulance, but we were lucky, she barely had a scratch on her." The look in his eyes was far away. "Even then I couldn't stop drinking. The idea I'd hurt her one day when I was too drunk to know it…ate at me. So I left. By the time I remembered I was supposed to be in court I was already in Illinois."

"You never went back?"

He shook his head. "It's easier to be a bum where people don't know you."

"You were ashamed," Darsh stated.

Anger flashed. "Of course I was ashamed! Still am. And

the idea of them seeing me like this?" Self-loathing etched his features. "Can you imagine the horror of having a father like me? A husband? It's better for them if they think I'm dead."

This guy was a decorated soldier who'd gone to war for his country. Frustration ripped through Darsh. He knew the military was tough on families, but Jesus, did circumstances really have to come down to this? "Tell me what happened Monday night."

His eyes shifted again. "I told the detective yesterday. The pretty one."

"Tell us again," Darsh demanded.

Unease filled Zimmerman's eyes. "I had a meal at the shelter and then took a walk. Saw one of the girls and followed her into her house." He raised a shaking hand to his brow. "I was drunk. I don't remember much."

"You don't remember the rape and murder of a twenty-year-old girl?"

Zimmerman's skin blanched an even unhealthier shade, but he kept quiet.

"Where'd you get the handcuffs?"

Zimmerman squinted at him in confusion, then his expression cleared. "Found 'em."

"What, just lying around with keys?"

He shrugged. "People leave all sorts of shit around. They dump it over the bridge. I pick it up."

"Did you pick up the sheet when someone tossed it over the bridge, Peter?"

"Nah, I told you. I stole it from that girl's bed."

"After you raped her."

Zimmerman nodded, eyes hard now.

"Did she remind you of your daughter, or your wife?"

256

He blinked. "What the fuck is that supposed to mean?"

"She had long black hair, like Maria, and Katy." Darsh shrugged. "I thought you were maybe substituting—"

Zimmerman went for him then. Darsh dodged and held his hand out to Ully Mason so the officer didn't interfere.

"Did you handcuff her and rape her on the floor to get back at your wife and daughter? Maybe for not rescuing you from your shitty life after you went to war to protect their freedom? I mean, you come home from a tour, and she's doing your best friend? What sort of bitch does that?"

"Don't say things like that about my wife." Zimmerman stood, shaking with rage, his frame ravaged by starvation and years of heavy drinking. "My family are good people. They don't need to know anything about this. I handcuffed and raped that girl because I was drunk, horny, and she was there. No other reason." His voice broke. "They don't need to know anything about this," he repeated. "Just put me in front of a judge and lock me up."

"You'd rather do life in prison than go back to Texas and face your family for a DUI? You are one crazy motherfucker."

The guy glared at him. Ully Mason shot him a disbelieving look but kept quiet.

Darsh opened the file that sat in front of him and pulled out two head shots of the victims. He slid them across the table. "You like hitting women?"

Zimmerman started to shake his head and then realized that a man accused of rape and murder wouldn't mind hitting a woman. "Sure."

"Why'd you hit that one?" Darsh pointed to Cassandra Bressinger.

"She got mouthy with me. Must have said something I

didn't like." Zimmerman's fingers hovered over both photographs before pulling away. He curled his fingers in his lap.

"But the other one didn't, so you raped her?"

"I don't remember why I did it. I just did it." Zimmerman closed his eyes, tears streaming down his face as if the weight of what he'd confessed to had finally sunk in.

There was no way this guy was guilty. No fucking way. But someone out there was smart enough to set it up to look like he was. And the idiot Marine had taken the fall rather than reveal the depths to which he'd descended to the people who mattered to him most.

Darsh placed the clear evidence bag on the table with a thump. It held the gun he'd found last night. "You threaten them with this? That how you controlled them?"

"That's right."

"So why didn't you shoot them?"

"Because I know you can match the bullets, dickhead."

"So you confess instead? Now who's the dickhead?"

Zimmerman glared at him. The pride beneath the ragged surface wanted to fight back. Darsh wanted to make him.

"Did you think that if you confessed, pled guilty, no one would ever hear about this down in good ol' Texas?"

Zimmerman's eyes popped. "What do you mean? Why would anyone care about this down in Texas?"

Darsh sneered. "Don't be a dumbass. This case has made international headlines. You think the press isn't going to be knocking on Maria's door once they find out your identity? You think Katy isn't going to find out what her daddy did to these girls? Or her friends at school?"

The man's eyes were growing wider and wider. His mouth

opened and closed without anything coming out.

"What about the men who served under you? What are they going to think about their old gunnery sergeant killing two innocent women?"

Zimmerman dropped his face into his hands. "Oh, hell."

"Did you rape and murder Cassandra Bressinger and Mandy Wochikowski?"

Zimmerman shook his head, and Ully Mason looked ready to spit nails.

"Where did you get the sheet? And the rope that tied your camp together?"

"Someone tossed it over the side of the bridge. Like I say, people dump stuff all the time."

"Why'd you confess?"

Zimmerman looked defeated now. "I didn't want them to see me like this." He drew in a deep breath that seemed to rattle in his chest. "Fuck, I need a drink."

Last thing this guy needed was a drink.

Darsh stood and collected his photographs and file. "You're being charged with interfering with a police investigation." Zimmerman looked shocked at that. Maybe it was harsh, but it might be the one way for Darsh to start the ball rolling and try and get this guy the help he needed. He'd talk to the judiciary in Texas and see if they couldn't work something out involving rehab. He also had friends in the Corps who would help. "You confessed rather than face the truth about what you've been doing with your life. That's a dick move, pal. The real killer is out there and probably lining up his next victim as we speak."

Zimmerman sobbed.

Darsh nodded to the guard to take him back to the cells.

When they were alone, Ully stood and turned to face him. "You know you just talked our prime suspect into retracting his confession." Brown eyes weighed him.

"You think he did it?" asked Darsh.

Ully let out a big sigh and shook his head. "I did. Now we're back to square one."

"Not really."

Ully's gaze sharpened.

"We know whoever is doing this is smart and focused and two steps ahead of everything we do."

"Great." Ully pushed away from the table. "Perp smarter than the police. Gonna make a great headline. You got anything useful to add to the investigation?"

"Let's call a team meeting."

CHAPTER NINETEEN

ERIN WALKED INTO the precinct to a symphony of chaos. She found Ully in the break room.

"What's going on?"

Ully raised a mug to his lips. His eyes were bloodshot, and he looked like he hadn't slept last night either. Knowing Ully, he'd been doing exactly what she'd been doing. "Stinky Pete retracted his confession after talking to the fed."

Erin hid her relief by busying herself getting a coffee. "You think he did it?"

"I did," he admitted. "Right until Agent Sing-along started talking to him."

"Don't do that."

"Do what?" Ully looked confused.

"Make fun of his name. You're called Ulrik for God's sake. If anyone should understand what that kind of mockery feels like it's you."

"I'm joking," he said with exasperation.

"Doesn't sound like joking when the person you're laughing at isn't here."

He muttered something unintelligible. "Did you know he was in the Marines?"

Erin raised her brow, more at the fact he did.

"He started talking a little about it during the interview, so

261

I called a buddy of mine in the Corps. Apparently Agent Singh was a badass with a sniper rifle. His call sign was Specter."

People around here liked guns so she had no doubt Darsh had raised his cool quota by a factor of a thousand. The boys would all be comparing the length of their barrels later. She rolled her eyes. "So what's happening?"

Ully checked his watch and finished his coffee. "Agent *Singh*," he pronounced the name very carefully and precisely, "ordered a team meeting. Conference room in five. Find out anything at the campus?"

She thought about her run-in with Brady and wondered why the hell she hadn't had him arrested for assault. Because he'd pulled back? Changed his mind? Because she'd seen something in his eyes that looked more wounded than angry? Weren't wounded animals the most dangerous when cornered?

She could feel bruises forming down her spine and the knot on the back of her head where she'd hit it against the wall. She was failing in her duty by not reporting it, and she was also scared it was an echo of her past, showing her how weak she truly was. Truth was she didn't even know if anyone would believe her.

Brady could wait, unless she could tie him directly to the murder. For now.

"Not much." She finished her coffee and washed up her cup, spotting Darsh across the bullpen, talking to Chief Strassen and one of the lawyers from the college. The chief shot her a look, and she knew they were talking about her. Her lips tightened, and she ignored them all, heading to her desk to drop off her coat.

Harry sat there with two laptops perched on his desk.

"You survived the trip to campus?"

Erin sent him a sharp glance. "Why wouldn't I?"

"Didn't you see the headlines this morning?"

Erin peered over his shoulder as he pulled up the website of the local paper. "Murdered girls' housemate says detective sat outside the house while victims were slain."

Erin grimaced. It was close enough to the truth to hurt, and no way would she give away vital information about the fact the women were dead before the 911 call just to save her reputation. Her reputation was shot anyway. "Why do you think she does it? Desire for notoriety? Money?"

Harry shrugged. "And why are they all so focused on you? I mean, you got there before Ully, and you weren't even on duty that night."

She shook her head and shrugged. "Just lucky I guess. It'd be nice if they just let us get on with our jobs without the hourly appraisals. Got anything else?"

He gathered up his files. "I'll give you the rundown at the meeting. Come on. We're late."

DARSH WATCHED ERIN take a seat near the front of the table. The lawyer for the university had heard they were dropping the charges against Peter Zimmerman, seen this morning's headline, and come gunning for Erin's badge.

The fact Darsh had been the one to vouch for her, rather than her boss, told him she was on shaky ground. They needed to solve this thing fast if they wanted to save Erin's job.

She stared down at her notes, refusing to look at him. He wiped down the whiteboard, determined to forget they'd gotten way closer than colleagues should, and to stop trying to figure out how to get closer still. He'd told her what he wanted, she didn't feel the same. It wasn't like he could push it considering the shit her ex had put her through.

He consciously unlocked his lower jaw before it fused permanently shut.

Strassen came in and sat at the other end of the table. There were two senior uniform officers, Ully and Bill Youder, Bickham, and both detectives present. He figured the fewer people here for this session, the better.

He checked his watch and began. "I was brought into this case to help you find this killer as fast as possible, and also to assess whether or not these murders were carried out by the same person who committed the college rapes last year."

"And what have you decided?" Strassen asked. The tension in his body was palpable.

"There are too many similarities for me to say they aren't connected."

Strassen closed his eyes. The other cops bristled.

"You saying we messed up the Hawke investigation?" Ully asked belligerently.

Darsh shook his head, eyes on Erin, who now met his gaze with steely blue eyes. "I don't think you messed it up."

A line cut between her brows. "I don't understand," she said quietly.

"The average IQ of a serial killer is 94.7. Bundy was a 136. The most intelligent serial killer ever tested is Kaczynski, who tested at 167." He looked at Strassen. "I think we're looking at someone in the same range as Kaczynski—genius level and someone who understands criminal investigations."

Ully swore.

Darsh wrote "SMART" on the whiteboard.

"So we didn't fuck up, the perp is just cleverer than we are?" Erin's lip curled in disgust.

"Exactly." Darsh could have called her ugly, and she'd have been less insulted. "We're looking for a narcissistic predator, someone with a tremendous sense of entitlement and a callous disregard for the feelings of others. Let's look at other factors."

Erin started taking notes. She was pissed, but she was engaged. She never gave up unless it was to do with her personal life.

"This is someone who moves freely amongst the student population. It could be anyone from another student, to a custodian, to campus security. Bottom line is they fit into life on campus."

"What's the average age of a serial killer?" asked Ully.

Darsh hesitated. "I'm not a big fan of inductive profiling even though it's faster than deductive."

"Why?" asked Ully.

"Because data is only collected from killers who've been caught, or unverifiable sources, which biases the sample." Darsh grabbed a quick mouthful of coffee. "If inductive profiling was really valid, we'd approach every case by rounding up all Caucasian males between 18-32 with an above average IQ. We'd find the ones with some sort of child abuse in their history and unstable family life—he'd have been abandoned by his father and raised by a dominant female. We'd have evidence of the McDonald triad—bed-wetting beyond the age of twelve, animal abuse, fire setting. The killer would work alone and rarely cross racial barriers. Based on inductive profiles we'd pick up all those guys in the vicinity and the chances are we'd have our man.

"But if we'd only used inductive profiling we wouldn't have caught Joseph Ball, John Wayne Gacy, Ray and Faye Copeland, Jeffrey Dahmer, and a whole slew of others."

The quiet in the room was contemplative.

"In the rapes last year, the attacker was very careful for the victims not to see him until after he'd subdued them, or their faculties were inhibited by alcohol or drugs. Rachel Knight—he pressed her face into the pillow until the ketamine kicked in. Mary Mitchell—he held a pillow over her face until the drug kicked in. Jayelle Rouseau was drunk to the point of passing out. Paula Gruber, again drunk, but not as drunk. She'd willingly had sex with one guy. He leaves and she wakes to find someone penetrating her from behind. It was dark. Once she figured out this was not her earlier lover she started to fight and had her face pressed into the pillow and then a jab of ketamine in the ass until she passed out."

"But Drew Hawke is instantly recognizable. He wouldn't want them to see his face if he was raping them," Ully argued.

"Agreed. So why didn't he blindfold them? Stick a pillow-case over their heads? Duct tape their eyes closed for chrissake? Hawke's a smart guy. The women all say they saw his face clearly at some point during the attack. Why? Why let them see him?"

Silence crackled.

"So either it *was* Drew Hawke raping them and assuming the women were too out of it to recognize him because they were drugged. Or..." Erin swallowed.

"Or," Darsh finished for her. "It was someone purposefully pretending to be Hawke to women who were already either inebriated with alcohol, or who he'd drugged with ketamine which—interestingly enough doesn't wipe short-term memory unless they're unconscious."

"So, assuming your theory is correct, the UNSUB wanted them alive so they could implicate Hawke. He purposely set up the quarterback to take the fall." The twist of her mouth was bitter. "But now he kills because he doesn't need them to identify Hawke. Hawke is already in prison." Erin's eyes were huge.

"Or maybe this is a different guy who learned from Hawke's mistakes and offs the victims so he doesn't end up in prison the way Hawke did?" Ully suggested, across the table.

"Maybe," Darsh said carefully. "But I have a feeling he's stopped using Special-K because he's grown more confident in his abilities. He's figured out how to control the women without drugs. Maybe a knife or a weapon? Maybe just fear? They fight back more when they aren't drugged, they're probably a lot more fun to torture."

"But they can identify him now," Ully said quietly.

"And he doesn't intend to get caught," agreed Darsh.

"So he kills them," said Erin. She looked up. "You think he wore a mask of Drew Hawke's face?"

"That's my guess," Darsh said. "It wouldn't look perfect, but when you're drunk, drugged, and traumatized, maybe it doesn't need to look perfect. Maybe the image just needs to be imprinted on the victim's brain for a few seconds to be fixed in the memory."

"Which is why those girls could swear on the polygraph that Drew Hawke raped them, when in fact it was someone pretending to be Hawke. Setting the guy up." Harry Compton chewed his lip thoughtfully.

"So Drew Hawke might be innocent?" Erin's voice was

thin.

"Or," Harry interrupted. "Someone might be setting these murders up to make it look like he is."

"Someone smart," Erin agreed. "Really smart."

"Who not only understands how to destroy or contaminate evidence, he also understands exactly the sort of evidence that the cops look for that will stand up in court," Darsh said.

"Could he be law enforcement?" asked Erin. "Or someone studying criminal justice at the college?"

"Definitely." Darsh nodded. "The fact that Mandy was treated so differently makes me think he knew and liked her." And she was studying criminal psychology.

"Or campus security—I went there this morning, but the tapes from that night had been 'accidentally' wiped clean." Erin rolled her shoulders. She looked so defeated he wanted to put his hands on her in reassurance. She wouldn't appreciate that though. Not surrounded by her peers. "We need to run more thorough background checks. Anyone with law enforcement experience within a ten-mile radius of the town. Anyone who's studied criminal psychology or criminology."

"That's a lot of people," argued Harry.

"I know." Darsh rubbed at his eyes, trying to wake himself up. "That's why I asked for another agent from the BAU to come and work with us on this. She'll be here in a few hours. She's a computer whiz and is going to look for red flags in the background checks."

"Are you looking at football players and coaching staff, too?" asked Erin.

Darsh nodded again. "I want them included in this more detailed background check, yes."

"But they were a great team with Hawke as the quarterback. The only person who might want to take him out is his replacement, Johnny Weber," Ully argued.

"Dammit, if he is innocent," Erin said, "and I'm not saying I think he is, not yet—but I feel like this has to have a connection to the football team in some way—"

"Detective," Chief Strassen broke in.

"No, sir, because if Drew Hawke is innocent he's as much a victim as those girls are, especially with Cassie's murder." She looked away from her boss and straight at Darsh. "This is personal. This is hatred."

He nodded curtly. She was not a cop who'd cut corners to get a result. He had no doubt Detective Erin Donovan had performed her duties well, and come up with the same conclusions any officer would. He just hoped he could persuade her boss she was worth fighting for. "That's why we're going back to basics."

"Victimology?"

"Yes. I want to know everything there is to know about each victim, including Hawke. And we're setting it up in here. Just the six of us know about this, plus Agent Chen, when she arrives. We're running this dark because we can't afford for it to leak that we're onto him. The guy might be one of us, and he might bolt." He went and closed the blinds of the conference room. "We'll conduct future meetings in here and not discuss our findings or the direction of the investigation with anyone. Understand?"

Chief Strassen looked pale. Erin didn't look much better. Then she dug her phone out of her pocket and put it to her ear, obviously getting a call.

Ully came up to stand next to him and spoke quietly. "The town finds out we think these cases are related, Erin will be thrown to the wolves."

Darsh looked over at her. "Another reason to keep our mouths firmly shut until we find this killer."

Ully followed his gaze, then must have seen something on his face. "You've got no chance there, G-man."

Darsh held Ully's stare. "I'm more concerned about her career."

Ully smirked. "Sure you are. But don't feel bad when she knocks you back. She hasn't dated anyone since her asshole husband shot himself."

Darsh couldn't help the satisfaction that sliced through him at that. They'd shared something special. Then he remembered that she wasn't interested in anything beyond the bedroom, and his mood soured.

Erin's voice got louder.

"Have you reported it?" She had her phone in a death grip. She looked first to the chief and then to him. "Rachel Knight's mother is on the line. Rachel is missing."

———

ERIN HEADED TO Rachel's house, even though her boss had told her that they couldn't treat her as a missing person until the girl had been unaccounted for a full twenty-four hours, which was bullshit. What if Rachel harmed herself?

The truck groaned going uphill in the steadily falling snow. They'd had two more inches already, but a lot more was in the forecast. Darsh sat beside her, talking on his cell. Neither of them had mentioned last night, nor their argument this morning. They were back to being professional and working the case. She was grateful. Oddly, his presence bolstered her courage and security. She wasn't sure how to feel about that, but worry for Rachel overwhelmed everything else.

He hung up, and she glanced toward him, then had to correct for a slight slip of the back tires. She needed to keep her eyes on the road unless she wanted to end up in the ditch.

"I just spoke to a friend of mine who co-owns a security firm in DC. They're sending some extra security guards up to help on campus. The college contacted them for help."

Which was a waste of time considering how many young women were around here, but the college wanted to look like it was being pro-active until the cops caught the killer. It couldn't hurt. "Any news on the evidence?"

"Not yet. Lab said they'd have some results by the end of the day."

She bit back her frustration. Where the hell was Rachel? Had she been suicidal or had she been abducted? Had Erin missed something yesterday? Had she let Rachel down? The thought made her stomach knot with anxiety. The truck skidded again, and she forced herself to focus on driving, otherwise she'd cause a wreck and maybe put both her and Darsh in the hospital.

"She probably just went to a friend's house," he told her quietly.

She gave him a curt nod. He was trying to help, but until she spoke to Rachel, the overwhelming sense of guilt would continue to stack up inside her mind.

Finally they reached the Knights' residence. She pulled up into the driveway, and Rachel's mom opened the door and stood there waiting for them. The worry in the woman's eyes broke her heart, but Erin snapped her spine straight and got out of the truck. She had a job to do and getting emotionally compromised wasn't going to help.

She strode up the path with Darsh at her side. The temptation to reach out and take his hand for reassurance was huge. And completely inappropriate.

"Dr. Knight." She nodded and walked inside the door. "When did you last see your daughter?"

The woman crossed her arms over her chest. "Last night. I kissed her goodnight around ten."

"You didn't hear from her again, or see her leave?"

She shook her head.

"Can we see her room?" Darsh asked.

Erin knew this was the real reason Darsh was here. He wanted to snoop and gain insight into the victim in a way that wasn't possible when Rachel was here. She shouldn't resent him for it, he was just doing his job.

Rachel's mom turned on her heel and jogged up the stairs. "She wouldn't have gone off anywhere without telling me. She always told me where she was going and what time she'd be back."

Rosemary Knight strode down a carpeted hallway and opened a door into a large pale blue room with a big four-poster bed in the middle of it. The bed was made. A computer sat on the desk.

"Does she have her phone with her?" Erin asked as Darsh made a beeline for the laptop.

"Yes." The shoulders were narrow and tight. "At least, I assume so. It isn't here."

"What's the number?" Darsh asked. Pulling his cell from his pocket he speed-dialed someone.

Rosemary told him, and he gave it to whomever was on the other end of the line and asked them to try to ping it and call him back. He hung up. "Was the security system armed?"

Rachel's mom nodded. "Always. Someone turned it off to leave the house around six."

Darsh went back to reading email on Rachel's computer. There was no password.

"And no sign of a break-in?" asked Erin.

"No."

There hadn't been at Cassie and Mandy's house either, but how would the perp attack and kidnap Rachel without someone hearing? And how had he known the code for the alarm? "Would you have heard if she'd disarmed the security system and left?"

She let out a breath, and her features sagged. "Maybe, but I doubt it. I took a tablet to help me sleep." She put her hands over her face, hiding tears. "A terrible part of me wants to believe she's been kidnapped. It would be easier than knowing she ran away of her own volition."

"Rachel is a grown woman, Dr. Knight. Maybe she just needed a little space."

"You think I smother her?" The words were bitter and biting.

"No," Erin hedged. "After everything she's been through I realize you feel compelled to protect her, but maybe she just went to talk to a friend? Or drove out of the state because she was scared about these murders." Erin was praying with every lapsed-Catholic cell in her body. "Maybe she'll call you in an hour, and she'll be standing on a beach in Maine." Erin was trying to be optimistic for the other woman's sake. Rosemary Knight didn't need to hear her other theories.

Darsh's phone rang, and tension shot through the room. "Send me the address, and I'll Google it. Thanks." They all braced themselves.

He hung up and a few seconds later, his phone dinged with incoming email.

"Where is she?" Rachel's mom asked.

"Agent Rooney managed to ping her phone off a few different cell towers and got an approximate location. Fox Creek Wildlife Park?"

A wash of relief swept over Rosemary's features. "She sometimes likes to walk there." Then her eyes darted to the windows and the growing snowstorm. "What if she got lost?"

Erin's thoughts were darker, and she tried to stop herself from assuming the worst. "We'll find her, Rosemary." Erin clasped her arm. "We'll bring her home." She hoped she wasn't making promises she couldn't keep.

"I'm coming with you."

"Someone needs to stay here in case she calls or turns up."

"Donald's here. Stuck in his study, pretending he's not scared witless—although really, it would be hard to tell the difference." She laughed bitterly, proving all was not well in the Knight household. Then they were walking down to the foyer where she grabbed her coat and slid her feet into her boots. "I'm coming with you," she insisted. "I need to find my baby."

Erin drove, glad they were in the truck as the snow grew thicker. Her wipers lazily slashed at the snow on her windshield. Fox Creek was about four miles east of town and formed the entrance to over two thousand acres of National Park. *Please be here. Please be crying in your car because fate dealt you a shitty hand and you needed some space.*

She pulled into the small parking lot, and a swell of relief burst through her at the sight of Rachel's car. But it was obvious the vehicle hadn't moved in some time, and snow covered it in a thin shroud. The engine must be cold. She drew to a halt a few spaces away, and Darsh sent her a quelling look as he got out.

"Stay here," he ordered.

Erin stayed because it meant Rosemary Knight would be more likely to stay too, and she didn't want the mother to be the one to find Rachel if she'd decided to take her own life.

Darsh carefully brushed snow off a side window of Rachel's car and peered inside, taking what seemed like forever. Then he went to the passenger door and tried the handle. It opened. Erin held her breath and felt Rosemary Knight's fingers curl into the back of her seat. Darsh ducked inside and then pulled off a glove and dug into his pocket for an evidence bag. He came out holding a cell phone inside the plastic. Then he checked the trunk, but Erin could see it was empty. He strode back to them, shaking his head.

"She isn't here." Snow whirled around his shoulders, white crystals landing in sharp contrast to his black hair. He held up the cell phone and showed it to Rosemary in the back. "Is this hers?"

Rosemary reached out, but Darsh withdrew the phone. "I have an agent arriving in less than an hour who might be able to get key information off it, but it *can't* be compromised if there's a chance this might turn out to be a crime scene. Do you understand?" His voice was gentle, but firm.

Rosemary covered her mouth and sobbed, nodding.

"Do you know the screen pass code? I'll see if there's a text readily visible."

"It's four, four, four, seven." Then she folded into herself and seemed to just hold on.

Erin looked from Rosemary to Darsh. "Even though she hasn't been gone twenty-four hours, I'm calling Search and Rescue."

He nodded, tapping the code into Rachel's cell. "It's a good idea. They can look for her. We need to get back to the station."

Rosemary Knight thrust the door open and started running toward the forest.

Erin shook her head. "Dammit. Look, call in S&R, then call the station. Get someone to give you a ride back to town. I'm staying here."

"Erin—"

"I can't leave her." She pointed to the woman who'd dropped to her knees in front of the vast expanse of wilderness. "Look at her."

His expression grew tight. "Your job depends on catching this killer, Erin, not tracking down a lost girl who is more likely to have committed suicide than been abducted," he said angrily.

"You don't know that." Her eyes flashed to his. "And don't tell me how to do my job, Agent Singh."

His expression was disgusted, and Erin shriveled a little on the inside.

"Lady, I wouldn't tell you how to do a damn thing." He slammed the door closed and stalked away, already on the phone. Erin got out. When she reached Rosemary, she pulled her up out of the wet snow and hugged her tight. "We'll find her. Don't give up hope."

But the woman collapsed, and Erin could barely hold her up as her sobs rang out in the deadening silence.

CHAPTER TWENTY

T HE NEXT SIX hours were a blur to Erin. Search and Rescue arrived, mostly volunteers who knew their way around the backcountry even when the weather was hostile. At least a foot of snow had fallen since morning, and Erin didn't know how anyone out in the woods without the right equipment could survive.

Rosemary Knight sat in the back of Erin's truck, wrapped in a blanket. Donald Knight was out there somewhere searching in the forest for his daughter. He'd come when Rosemary had called him, but the two hadn't spoken. The strain between them was palpable.

Erin swallowed tightly against the sadness that welled up inside her. It wasn't just the victim who suffered—although they suffered the most—but the people who loved them floundered too. Wanting to help. Failing through no fault of their own. She knew her own parents had been horrified by the knowledge her husband had beat her. And bereft when she'd picked up sticks and moved away. She'd done what she had to for her own survival. But looking at the devastation wrought on Rachel's parents' faces, Erin realized she needed to go home and face her past. They needed to see she was whole, not broken. That she'd come through the experience and was happy again.

Okay, *happy* was stretching it. Content maybe.

She thought of Darsh, and him saying he wanted more, and wrapped her arms tighter around herself. She'd dismissed it. Dismissed him when he'd taken that leap and asked her.

Had she refused to consider more because she wasn't interested? Or was he right about her running away from the potential to be hurt again? She had a horrible feeling it was the latter because even the sight of the darkly handsome FBI agent sent a quiver through her, not just lust, but something else too. Something too small and frightening to bring out into the light.

She leaned against the hood of her truck. The engine was running to provide heat for Rachel's mother and a warm refuge for anyone else who needed to defrost. There was a fire going over on one side of the parking lot, close to the entrance. Movement caught her eye, and she straightened. A group of searchers tromped out of the shadows of the forest. Erin recognized the team leader, Greg Thompson, from previous searches. Some had ended well. Others had ended badly.

She had no idea how this was going to end.

They'd put out news bulletins for anyone seeing Rachel Knight to get in touch with the cops immediately. There had been a few calls, but nothing had panned out.

The group headed toward the fire. She trudged over to meet them, her toes frozen nubs inside her boots. Someone had their rear door open with a waterproof map laid out inside.

"Anything?" she asked.

Greg turned to her and shook his head. "No sign of anyone out there. No tracks. Snow covered everything before we got here." His breath came out in a frosty cloud. Someone handed him a drink from a thermos and he took it, looking grateful.

Another group arrived back, Prof Huxley leading the way. He'd been out since noon when his class had finished.

He shook his head as they approached, though it was obvious Rachel wasn't with them. One of the men broke away and headed over to Erin's truck. Donald Knight. He opened the door, said something to his wife, then slammed it before walking away to his own vehicle.

"Must be hard." Huxley leaned close to her ear.

She glanced up. "What?"

"Not knowing where your child might be, whether they're even alive."

Erin shivered. "No sign of her at all?"

Huxley shook his head.

"Are you guys done for the day?"

"It's dark." Huxley accepted a warm drink from one of the volunteers. His skin was pale, cheeks ruddy. "We're all sweaty and exhausted which is dangerous when it's this cold. Can't afford for the rescuers to become liabilities when they succumb to hypothermia." His lips firmed. "I'm sorry, Erin. Very sorry. I know you're close to the girl." He eyed her with concern. "You look terrible. I bet you haven't eaten all day. Let me take you to dinner."

She shook her head. "I can't leave yet." She hugged herself harder.

He nodded thoughtfully and then turned away. Erin stood watching them all pack up their gear and start to leave. She went over to Greg. She pretended to be calm, but she felt shaky inside. "What's the plan?"

"There's so much ground to cover it's like searching for a

needle in a haystack while wearing a blindfold. I've arranged for a tracking dog to join the search tomorrow." Regret flickered in his eyes. "But even a seasoned outdoorsman would struggle in these conditions. I don't want to sound pessimistic but…"

Erin nodded silently. She understood, even though she didn't want them to stop searching.

"We'll be back at dawn."

"Thanks, Greg. I know the family appreciates it. *I* appreciate it."

"We all know what she went through last year…" He glanced over to Erin's truck and Donald's car. "Unless she took off and just left her car behind." He grimaced. "I'd be pissed but relieved. It'll be a miracle to find her alive in this weather, that's for sure."

Erin thanked him and the others and walked back to her truck. She opened the back door. "There's no news yet."

"They're not giving up, are they?" Rosemary asked. The whites of her eyes glowed pink she'd been crying so much.

"They need to rest and recoup. They'll be back at dawn," Erin told her firmly.

"But what about Rachel?" The woman's voice rose.

"They need to rest, Rosemary. And so do you. Do you need me to drive you home or will you go with your husband?"

The expression on her face was a mix of anger and deep longing. "I don't know if I can face him."

"Don't you think he's as upset as you are?"

Rosemary nodded. "He just buries himself in work to get through it, whereas I bury myself in looking after Rachel." Her eyes welled with fresh tears. "I've been so awful to him. I don't think he'll ever forgive me."

And yet he was sitting in his car, waiting.

"There's only one way to find out," Erin told her firmly.

Rosemary dragged the blanket from her shoulders and tossed it on the back seat. "I'm not giving up on her, Detective."

"I'm not giving up on her either, Dr. Knight."

Erin stood back as the woman climbed gingerly down and waded through the thick snow to reach her husband's car. She got in and closed the door. Nothing happened immediately, but after a few minutes they drove away.

Most of the other vehicles had already left.

Erin's phone rang. Darsh had been calling her on and off all day, telling her to get her ass into the police station. But she couldn't abandon Rachel. She'd promised the girl she'd help her and not being here felt like the ultimate betrayal.

She snapped herself out of her funk. There was nothing she could do here now. It was time to get back to work. She had no idea if Rachel's disappearance was in any way connected to the case or just a depressing coincidence. Her phone stopped ringing as she was about to answer the call. She figured she'd see him in person soon enough.

Drawing in a deep breath, she pulled out of the parking lot and up onto the highway, driving slowly. Her headlights met a wall of white, and she could barely see ten feet in front of her grill. She dropped her speed until she was crawling down the mountainside.

Today had started badly and gone downhill from there. She thought about what she'd done with Darsh—okay, maybe it hadn't started so badly if you counted multiple orgasms.

A pair of headlights appeared behind her. The snow

cleared enough so she put her foot down, speeding up, the back wheels losing a little traction and then regaining it, making her heart race. A few seconds later, she realized she was approaching a dangerous curve that she needed to slow down for. She tapped the brakes gently. The lights in her rear view went full beam, and she swore as they blinded her. Then the vehicle zoomed around to overtake her on the sharp bend. Her heart skittered at the insanity of the move. "Jackass."

But he wasn't overtaking her. Instead, the giant SUV slammed into the side of her truck and she was so surprised, the road conditions so slippery, that she lost control and started to fishtail. Another slam in the side panel had her gritting her teeth and holding on for grim life. She smacked the brakes, but they didn't do anything as her tires slid smoothly over ice. The inevitability of it killed her—she wasn't even going that fast. The truck crashed through the barrier and went over the edge in an avalanche of snow. A scream wanted to rip through her throat. Instead, she swore viciously, holding tight to the wheel as if she could somehow control the car as they flew down the steep slope. Time slowed, each second stretching to ten as adrenaline stormed her bloodstream. Her heart rammed her ribs so powerfully, it felt like it was about to explode from her chest. A tree sat directly in her path. She jerked on the wheel to try and avoid it, but momentum and gravity were more effective than the steering wheel. She was going to hit that giant monolith and chances of surviving the impact were slim to none. And, goddamn, there was nothing she could do about it, except pray.

HE SAT IN the car shaking.

Erin was dead. She had to be dead. No one could survive that crash. He'd killed her.

Sweat coated his body, and cold swept over his skin and down his torso, chilling him to the point that his bones felt like ice picks.

He rested his head on top of his leather gloves on the steering wheel. It had been a long day, and Rachel had made him so furious when she'd escaped that morning he'd had a hard time concentrating on anything else.

His teeth chattered.

Dead.

The searing hate he'd felt earlier was softened by remorse. He hadn't meant to kill Erin. He loved her. But when he'd watched her leave the parking lot, frustration and anger over what she'd done with the fed boiled over, and one thought had flashed through his mind—if he couldn't have her, no one could.

His mouth was so dry his tongue stuck to the roof. Regret wrenched his insides and made him want to weep. But he shook it off. Regret was for losers. His gloved fingers slowly unclenched from around the wheel.

He looked around the garage and knew he had to get out of here. A cop had been killed and once they found her—*if* they found her—the town would be swarming with law enforcement.

He had three choices.

Give himself up—*not in this lifetime.* Disappear—which would make him look like another victim or guilty as hell. Or set up the next most likely candidate.

Good thing he was always three steps ahead of everyone

else, which was what he'd been trying to tell them all from the start. They'd never catch him. He was too smart. He knew the system. And if you knew the system anything was possible. He opened the door, carefully closed it behind him, then slid into the darkness and disappeared.

———————

DARSH PRESSED THE disconnect button on his phone and refrained from throwing the thing across the room. *Damn* that woman. Stubborn didn't begin to describe her. He was doing everything he could to stop her performing career suicide, but she was hell bent on doing it anyway. And while it was one thing to care about victims, it was another to waste a whole day standing around in a frozen parking lot while other people searched the woods, especially when a killer was on the loose and your boss told you not to.

The chief was looking for an update on the murder investigation. Darsh had been covering for her, but time was running out. He checked his watch. It was dark outside. What the hell was taking her so long?

It wasn't that he didn't feel for the Knight girl, but he knew they'd both be more effective here.

He'd finished writing out the timeline of the rapes last year, then the trial, and added in the two new murders. Hopefully the dates themselves would rule out some suspects.

Darsh had moved the boxes from his office into the conference room and set up Agent Ashley Chen in there too. She was his excuse for relocating and keeping things on a strictly need-to-know footing because of cyber-security issues.

"Got everything you need?" he asked her.

"Everything except peace and quiet." She sent him a quelling glance.

He shrugged, unrepentant.

Chen was an interesting character. Quiet. Studious. Definitely self-contained. Determined to prove herself. She was far superior to him with computers and technology, and that's what her background was rather than law enforcement. She'd examined Rachel Knight's phone but didn't find any ominous texts or emails. The list of callers was small, and Rachel had received a call around five AM from a payphone at the university. They'd subpoenaed the landline information.

Had someone enticed Rachel Knight to meet them in that secluded park in the pre-dawn? She was so skittish. Darsh was surprised she even left the house alone. It was more likely she'd spiraled into depression and lost all hope, then purposely walked into the forest on the brink of a major snowstorm.

He hoped they found her alive, but he couldn't make it his priority when they had a killer to catch.

"Got anything on those background checks yet?" he asked Chen.

She paused and looked at him like he was an idiot. "I'm still entering the names of all the people you want checks on. The list is long. This isn't television where you think something and the next minute it's magically done."

He winced then muttered, "Alex Parker would have done it by now."

Her eyes narrowed further. "Unfortunately for you, Agent Singh, Mr. Parker was busy handling some details for ASAC Frazer while he's on leave. You'll have to resign yourself to dealing with me."

Another ballbuster. God he loved working with strong

women, but he was grateful he was only attracted to one of them—even if she was driving him crazy by not answering her cell. "Anything on the rope?"

Agent Chen's fingers paused over her keyboard, and he could almost hear her beg for patience. "I've requested the buyer information from all online retailers. When I hear back I'll cross-reference that with this *giant* list of background checks. Is there anyone who isn't on the list, by the way?"

He pulled a face, but she didn't smile back. He looked at his watch again. He was tired and hungry. He hadn't gotten much sleep last night and had spent most of the day worried about Erin. Dammit. He gave into the urge and grabbed his coat. "Want me to pick up some dinner?"

"Sure." She didn't look up this time, and her fingers moved at lightning speed over the keyboard.

"Chinese?" He said it to needle her and was rewarded with a glare.

"Hmm…why don't you track down a good curry instead?" Her arched brow said she got the dig even if she didn't find it funny.

"Gonna kick my ass with your crazy Ninja skills?" He allowed himself a smirk. He was winding her up, looking for a sense of humor that made putting up with the attitude worth it. Not everyone had one, not when it came to race and gender issues.

She stopped working and turned to him. "I'd rather just shoot you and be done with it." She eyed him, assessing. "I take it that's your way of breaking the ice? Or are you always an ass?"

"Depends who you talk to." He thought of Erin. "Anything you don't like?" At her confused gaze he added, "To eat?"

She stretched out her neck as though she'd been sitting in the same position far too long. "I like everything except tomatoes."

"Tomatoes?" he asked. "Who doesn't like tomatoes?"

"Crazy Asian-American chicks apparently."

He grinned. "You added the 'crazy,' not me. I'll be back in an hour."

She nodded, already back to her bionic typing. Maybe she wasn't as uptight as they thought. Maybe Alex Parker unnerved her because, for all the self-deprecating humor and easy grins, the guy was more than just some cyber-security expert. Maybe Agent Chen had something to hide and knew one of the few people capable of uncovering it would be Parker.

Everyone had something to hide.

Darsh headed to his car, trying not to think about how pissed he was with Erin. Didn't she care about her job? Hadn't she told him she didn't know what she'd do if she couldn't wear a badge? What the hell did she think would happen if she neglected this investigation?

On the top step of the building, he paused and stared around in shock. At least a foot of snow had fallen since he'd come into work this morning. The idea of Rachel Knight being lost in the wilderness made him swallow back the feelings of anger. But the idea Erin was voluntarily out in this also pissed him off. People were trained for this shit. She was a detective, not Super Woman.

The snow had pretty much abated, except for the occasional straggling flake.

He headed out of town toward Fox Creek Park, lucking out when he tucked in behind a snowplow and gritter going up the hill. He hung back, headlights cutting through the darkness into a wall of winter white. It took twenty minutes until he got to the parking lot, only to find the place completely deserted. Rachel Knight's Jetta had been taken to the cop shop on the back of a flatbed truck that morning.

He sat staring at the pitch-black forest. Could Rachel be a victim of this killer? Had he changed his MO? Or had she succumbed to the despair and fear he'd seen in her every action yesterday?

He tried Erin's cell again, and her landline. Dammit, maybe she was just avoiding picking up his calls, which would be unprofessional as hell. Another thought unsettled him. What if she started to think of him as being as obsessed as her ex had been?

Darsh gritted his teeth. He refused to go there. Erin was a good cop. They were working a case. They needed to communicate.

He did a big circle of the parking lot and came out back onto the main highway. This side hadn't been plowed yet so he followed the ruts and crawled back up the hill and then around the corner to go down the mountainside. He concentrated on his driving and almost missed the impressions in the snow at the side of the road. From the look of the tire tracks someone had recently gone off the road.

His heart thundered.

He pulled over onto the shoulder and put on his hazards, grabbed his flashlight. No way would Erin have slid off the road, but the fact she wasn't answering her cell... Nah, she was a good driver. Experienced in snow with a heavy four-wheeler. But distracted, he thought. Very distracted. And tired.

But this couldn't be Erin.

Whoever this was could be seriously hurt so he needed to get a move on. He got out of the car and hoped the plow didn't come back this way in the next five minutes and bury his car. And, he realized with a feeling of dismay, if the plow *had* done this stretch of highway he'd never have seen the tire marks. Never have known someone might be in need of assistance. He jogged back to the spot and clambered through the knee-high snow bank.

Peering over the edge down the steep slope, he saw a huge trench of snow had been churned up. Fuck. Something had definitely left the roadway in the last hour or so. He shone his flashlight beam into the darkness, but there was nothing visible from up here. He pulled out his cell and called it in to the dispatcher. She told him to wait on the line, but he ignored her. Pocketing his phone, he started down the steep bank and had to hold onto pine tree branches to stop himself from sliding down the improvised ski run. He continued cautiously, hoping he didn't end up going over the edge of a cliff hidden beneath a foot of snow.

The land leveled out a bit, and he skidded down the slope, hanging on to damaged branches, telling himself over and over that it wasn't Erin down here in this ravine. He believed it right until the moment he saw the backend of a white Ford F-150 crushed against a sixty-foot fir. Every cell inside his body warped, and he felt like he'd been thrown through space. He slithered his way down to the mangled wreck.

"Erin. Erin!"

Fear shot through him and made it impossible to think. He got to the passenger side of the truck, which was closest, and grabbed the door handle, tried to wrench it open, but it was buckled and not going anywhere. He fought his way up the hill and around to the other side of the truck that seemed half the length it should be. The door was wide open. Glass showered the area, glistening like ice, air bags deployed. But no sign of the woman he'd come to care about.

"Erin!" He swung around, searching the area with his flashlight beam. "Where are you!"

There was a sound on the wind. He tilted his head toward it, starting back up the slope even though it could have been something up on the road playing tricks with his crappy hearing. He jogged uphill now, desperate to find her. How could anyone have survived that crash? Where the hell was she?

"Over here," came the sweetest gravelly voice he'd ever heard.

He swung the beam across the pale snow and found her propped against the trunk of a pine tree. Relief burst through him so intensely he could barely speak. She was in the well of the tree, surrounded on three sides, out of the wind. He scrambled toward her, almost unable to believe she was actually there. Her skin was pale as bone and there was blood on her chin. He'd never seen a more beautiful sight.

He fell to his knees beside her. "Are you okay? Stupid question, don't answer that, but tell me if anything really hurts." He ran his hands over her limbs.

"I'm fine, except cold and shaken up." The hitch in her voice told him exactly how 'fine' she was feeling. "I did, however, recently discover how desperately I don't want to die."

"The only good thing about near-death experiences."

"I can't believe you found me," she whispered.

He swallowed. "I can't believe I found you either." He was

having a few epiphanies of his own. Like how the idea of losing her tore his insides to shreds. "Where's your phone?"

She waved her hand toward the truck. "Somewhere."

He wanted to haul her against him but didn't dare move her. He touched her cheek. "Jesus, even though you survived the crash you could have frozen to death out here."

"Nah." Her voice cracked. "Once I survived the wreck I knew I was going to be fine. Believe it or not, I was making my way slowly—very slowly, I admit—up the bank." She smiled tiredly, her eyes huge and haunted. "And as I was crawling up this goddamn hill, I made a few decisions."

"Like what?" Talking was good for her. The last thing he wanted was for her to pass out.

"I decided to stop being a coward."

"Coward? You're one of the bravest people I've ever met." There were no obvious broken bones, but she could have internal bleeding or a head injury.

"Not with relationships. Even before I married Graham I was always afraid of making a mistake and falling for the wrong guy. Caution got me nothing but heartbreak. I'd like to carry on seeing you. To give us a chance like you said." Her smile aimed for cute but went a little wonky at the edges. "Unless you changed your mind."

He touched her cheek. "It takes a car accident to have a chance with you, huh?" His voice was gruff. "Maybe next time I can try flowers and dinner?"

"Let's just say my life flashed before my eyes, and my only regret was being too chicken to see if this thing between us could work out." Her eyes twinkled with humor although Darsh was worried she had a concussion. "I mean even if we fizzle out after a few months, we'd still have the great sex, right?"

This was a big step for her. Hell, it was a big step for him, too. If she wanted to pretend it was mainly physical, then he'd let her. For now.

He gently lifted her chin and kissed her on the lips, careful of her cuts and bruises. "It'll be worth it."

Her eyes watered, and her teeth chattered. Where the hell were the EMTs?

"I'm sorry I pushed you away this morning." Her mouth turned down at the edges. "Like you said, I'm a bit of an emotional coward."

He tried to stop her as she crawled out from beneath the tree and pushed to her feet, but apparently she was done waiting for help. "You were wrong about one thing, though."

"What's that?"

"This was no accident."

He frowned. "What do you mean?"

"Some bastard drove me off the road, and I'm going to figure out who so I can put his ass behind bars."

He steadied her as she insisted on trying to climb back onto the road. It wasn't just independence, it was what she was used to since marrying her asshole ex. Doing it alone, relying on no one but herself. He glanced behind them at the totaled truck, and rage grew inside him, gaining momentum. When she fell to her knees and started crawling, he'd had enough of her stubbornness. He ignored her complaints, picked her up in his arms, and carried her.

CHAPTER TWENTY-ONE

R ACHEL STUMBLED TO her knees in the snow. It was nighttime. The rope chafed her lips, but her numb fingers couldn't unpick the tight knot in her mouth no matter how hard she tried. The miracle of being alive was slowly fading into despair. She was lost. She'd been struggling through the snow for hours. She was cold, sore, and so incredibly frightened of dying out here alone.

They might never find her. Her parents might never know what happened, or the truth about Drew Hawke.

She'd helped falsely convict the quarterback.

She'd attached electrodes to her body, and sworn under oath he'd raped her.

But he hadn't.

It made her a liar and a fool—or maybe just a fool, because she'd believed she'd been telling the truth at the time. She needed to find someone and tell them what really happened. They were going to think she was crazy, but she didn't care as long as she survived.

She swiped her nose. Her chin was raw with frozen drool, lips chapped and bleeding.

Using a sturdy branch she'd found as a walking stick, she struggled to her feet and trudged onward.

She'd woken to complete silence, cradled in the arms of a

tall fir tree. Contrary to expectations, landing in a tree hurt like hell, but probably not as much as hitting granite from a height of seventy feet. She'd been so surprised she was still alive, like an eagle had swooped and plucked her to safety. There was a gash on her right arm and something bad had happened to her knee, because it had swelled to the size of a cantaloupe inside her jeans. Her arm was still bleeding, a steady drip that wouldn't stop, probably because of the cold. Inexplicably the blood trail gave her hope. It marked her path. Maybe someone with a bloodhound would eventually search for her and find her. Hopefully she wouldn't be dead.

It was nighttime, but the moon reflected off the snow so brightly she could easily see where she was going—she just didn't know *which* way to go.

She sucked in a hoarse breath. Her tongue was numb, the back of her throat raw from drawing in icy air that settled deep into her lungs.

She hacked out a cough and had to pause for a moment, leaning heavily on the stick, her heart racing as it adjusted to another obstacle to survival. When the coughing fit was over she straightened. She seemed to be in some sort of gully that was winding its way slowly downhill.

The snow had melted on her jeans and, even though she was wearing good winter boots, her feet were numb.

Keep going, Rachel, you don't need those toes anyway.

The sound of crows cawing in the trees drew her toward them. She was so tired and thirsty and hungry. How could she have walked for hours and still found no sign of human life?

Because you're going at about a quarter of a mile an hour, idiot, and probably walked in circles all day. She stumbled through the trees and came upon a ribbon of ice. At first she didn't know what it was, but then she realized it was the river.

She eased to her bottom and slid down the bank, testing the thickness of the ice with her stick. It felt solid. The snow seemed less deep here, the wind scouring it off the surface.

A loud groan made her glance nervously around. Then she realized it was the creak of the ice responding to the super-cooled water that raced beneath it. She'd studied ice formation in one of her classes. There was more going on beneath the surface than most people realized. Then another noise caught her attention. A weird, rushing hum.

She edged toward the sound, taking small uncertain steps, using her stick to probe the way. She reached a curve in the river and peered into the darkness ahead. Headlights swept in front of her, and her heart stuttered. A bridge. She hobbled toward it, her right leg not really bending as it should. She forced herself to keep moving, through the pain, through the exhaustion. *Don't stop.* She was too close to salvation to stop now.

Sweat was frozen on her back, her body wracked with fierce tremors. Slowly, slowly, she made it the quarter of a mile to the bridge. She dragged herself up the rise and crawled on all fours until she was clear of the bank. It took forever to find her way through the forest onto the road. She was almost there when the hum of tires caught her attention. A car. She stumbled and dragged herself upright using the trunk of a tree. The car was getting closer. She started running. She was so close to safety. So close to telling everyone what had happened to her, to the others, to Drew. She clambered over a pile of snow and stumbled out into the road. The car coming toward her slammed on the brakes, but Rachel skidded to a halt just as the vehicle did.

She screamed as it hit, pain exploding through frost-deadened nerves even as darkness engulfed her.

———————

ERIN'S HEAD THROBBED so viciously she thought her skull was going to burst. The TV was on in the background, running a bunch of stories around a large oil tanker that had been freed from hijackers near the Panama Canal. She must have seen the footage five hundred times.

Harry Compton stood at the end of her bed, his woebegone expression mixed with underlying resentment. "Can you describe the vehicle?"

"Not really." She frowned, eliciting fresh slivers of pain that sliced into her skull. "Big SUV. Dark color. They had their full beams on. I couldn't see the driver."

"Pretty bad conditions on the roads out there tonight." His pencil hovered over his notebook, but didn't connect with the page. Obviously she hadn't said anything useful yet.

"Especially when someone rams into you and forces you off the road," Erin grated.

"I'm just saying that considering the amount of strain you've been under, what with the disappearance of this girl and all—"

"You suggesting I pretended to get run off the road so I don't have to admit driving through the guard rail like a fucking moron?" She flicked off the news. This was all she needed.

He backed up a step as she pushed herself upright in bed.

"The road hadn't been plowed. It was dark, you maybe hit an icy patch—"

"My truck can handle a patch of ice, and I can handle my truck. That is until someone smashes into me on a sharp bend in the middle of a fucking snowstorm." She dragged a hand through her hair. Losing her temper with Harry wouldn't get her anywhere.

He shoved his notebook in his pocket. "Jesus, Erin. I'm just doing what you'd do if the situation was reversed."

She grunted. She hated that he was right.

"I'll put out a BOLO for someone with a damaged front fender or passenger side door. Forensics should be able to find paint on your truck and give us a make and model of the one that hit you."

Erin nodded. The fact she was damn near naked except for some paper-thin hospital gown didn't help matters. Darsh had disappeared after the doctors had taken her for a CT scan, and it was foolish to feel disappointed. They still had a killer to catch and a lost girl to find, and she didn't need anyone holding her hand.

Someone came into the room, hidden behind a large bunch of carnations. "I heard about what happened." Roman Huxley appeared behind the flowers. "I just helped Search and Rescue get ropes and lines on your truck to winch it back onto the main road. From the state of it, I'm surprised you're alive."

She forced a smile even though it hurt. "Thanks, I'm fine. I'm not even being admitted overnight."

Harry's eyes widened.

"But I appreciate the thought. You poor S&R guys must be exhausted." She hoped this didn't mean they'd be too tired to search for Rachel tomorrow, but as she looked out of the window into the sub-zero night, she knew it was hopeless. Without shelter, Rachel would freeze to death. Erin would have, too.

"Tell the other guys 'thanks,' and I appreciate the flowers." She pressed the buzzer to call the nurse. "Now you two need to get out of here unless you want to see me naked." She swung her legs over the side of the bed. She was bruised and battered but by a miracle hadn't broken anything. She'd thrown herself from the truck about a second before it hit that tree. It had felt like ten lifetimes.

Neither man moved.

"That's your cue to leave, guys." She didn't soften the bite in her tone and thankfully, they both jerked into action. Jesus. She was busy searching the cupboard for something to wear when the door opened again.

"What the hell are you doing out of bed?"

Darsh.

The flutter in her chest both warmed and scared her. She'd decided to stop running from relationships, but she'd be lying if she said she wasn't terrified of letting anyone past her defenses. "Getting outta here. What do you have in the bag?" She eyed it hopefully, thinking it was something she could wear.

He walked up to her, tossed the plastic bag on the bed, and caught her face in his hands. Then he kissed her, thoroughly, and although her lip stung she kissed him back, stretching her aching body against his because she'd so nearly lost her life today and the need to reaffirm she wasn't dead was overwhelming. He cradled his big hand at the back of her nape and angled his mouth, taking the kiss even deeper.

A noise behind them had them both freezing in place before guiltily moving apart. "Is there a line-up? Because I'm game." Ully Mason's tone was scathing.

Erin stepped away from Darsh. "Don't be a jackass." She grabbed the bag off the bed. A pair of flannel pajamas. Not exactly a pantsuit, but they beat the hell out of a paper dress with a slit from ass to neck.

"What do you want?" she asked Ully.

"Just came to see a fellow cop who got hurt on the job today—"

"To give me a hard time?" she snapped back.

He had the grace to look ashamed. "No. You just caught me off guard sucking face with a fed only a couple hours after totaling your truck, that's all. Didn't know you guys were involved."

"Fuck you, Mason," Darsh bit out.

She gritted her teeth. As much as she planned to give a relationship with Darsh a go, she hadn't wanted it to be public knowledge before they'd wrapped up this investigation. Now she was going to be the subject of every piece of gossip in the department for the next month. She already knew how awful that felt.

She dragged on the pants under the hospital gown and then turned her back on them both. Pulling the T-shirt from the bag, she checked to make sure there were no windows or glass doors to give them a happy reflection and tore off the gown, letting it fall to the floor before she slowly eased the long-sleeved shirt over her head. She heard a sharp inhalation from Ully, and Darsh swore. If her bruises looked like they felt, she was sure they were spectacular. Tomorrow she was going to look like a punching bag.

Once she'd pulled the top down, she turned and picked up a pair of fluffy white socks, Darsh had bought. There was no way she could bend down to put them on.

"Here. Let me." Darsh held out his hand, and she sat on the edge of the bed while he rolled the material gently over her cold toes.

When he was done, he held back the covers, but she carefully shook her head. "Doc says that I'm fine to go home."

Darsh eyed her. "He told me he'd advised you to stay in overnight. You have a minor concussion."

"Same thing." She shrugged.

Ully started smirking. "I just decided you two being together has actually made my day." He crossed his arms. "Not that locking lips with Erin Donovan isn't on every guy in the department's fantasy list—aside from the chief," he grimaced, "but putting up with that sharp tongue and smart mouth? Definitely not for the faint of heart."

Erin blew out a noisy breath. "Thanks for the approval. It means a lot." She rolled her eyes and found her boots on the opposite side of the bed and eased her feet into them. Darsh just shook his head. He reached up into a tall locker and pulled out her clothes.

"Why didn't you tell me they were there before?" she asked in exasperation.

He held up her parka so she could slide in her arms. "Because I didn't want you disappearing before I got back."

Her cheeks flamed, because she would have left an hour ago if she'd known.

"And I already knew there was no way you'd stay in here overnight." He shot a grin at Ully, who grinned back. They both thought they had her number. "This way I got you to walk out of here in pajamas and intend to make you go straight home to bed, unless you want me to call your parents."

"Oh, I'm definitely liking this." Ully scratched the back of his neck.

Darsh handed her her Glock from his pocket. The reassuring weight made her feel a lot better.

She wanted to bitch at them, but she was too tired. She gathered up her belongings, including the flowers Professor Huxley had brought, and walked to the door without a word. As they headed down the corridor, Darsh stood on one side and Ully bracketed the other. A bunch of patrol officers were milling around the waiting room. When she appeared, they all swarmed her, wanting a hug.

Ully shouted at them not to squeeze too tight. "Careful guys, I've seen her naked, and it wasn't a pretty sight." Erin was so grateful for her colleagues' well wishes that she thought she might start crying.

There was a sudden buzz of activity when a gurney was rushed past them.

"What is it?" she asked Darsh. She had to hold on to his sleeve to stand up straight, and she knew he wanted to carry her. If he tried in front of these guys, she'd kick his ass.

"Wait here, and I'll go find out," Ully told them. Two minutes later, he ran back across the waiting room and kept his voice low. "They found Rachel Knight."

Erin couldn't speak.

"Alive?" Darsh bit out.

"Yeah," Ully exclaimed. He was holding his jacket shut as if hiding something. "She made it onto the highway only to be run over by a Honda Civic. Driver realized who she was and didn't waste time waiting for an ambulance. He brought her straight in."

"How is she?" Elation filled Erin. "Can I see her?"

Ully shook his head. "She's unconscious and in bad shape. Hypothermia on top of all her other injuries. They're going to induce a coma and warm her up slowly. Going to be a few days until she's able to talk. They just stuck a tube down her throat."

"Do her parents know?"

"On their way."

Erin felt suddenly like she was made of glass and might shatter at any moment. "Does anyone know what happened to her?"

"Well, it wasn't an accident."

Her eyes snapped to his.

"What makes you say that?" Darsh asked.

"The rope gag I just watched one of the doctors cut from around her head." He opened his jacket, and Erin saw a piece of blue climbing rope coiled in an evidence bag. Ully shut his coat again as he scanned the crowd. He was right. If the press got hold of this story, there'd be hell to pay.

"Get guards on her door. She needs protection at all times," Erin ordered. From the press and the killer.

"Ully's got it handled." Darsh pressed a card into the patrol officer's palm. "Call that number if you need anything. Time for you to get home to rest, Detective."

"She needs protection, too." Ully spoke to Darsh as if she wasn't there.

"I'm on it," he answered.

"I don't need protection." She patted the Glock in her pocket.

"Some good that'll do you if you're seeing double," Ully snorted.

Erin rolled her eyes and winced from the way it hurt.

Dammit.

Darsh's hand tightened around her upper arm. "Courier that evidence to Quantico. Tell them to run a match on the other rope. Call me as soon as Rachel wakes up. I'm going to catch a few hours' sleep while I can." Erin opened her mouth to argue, but he spoke over her, which would have made her crazy, except she was so exhausted she was swaying on her feet. "And so is she."

Ully nodded as Darsh helped her out of a side exit. She hid her face as she realized the press had already caught wind of a good story and were waiting at the front. Or maybe *she* was the story. Darsh wrapped his arm around her waist and helped her to his vehicle.

She turned to him when he got inside and started the engine. "I can't believe she survived."

The look on his face was grave. "I can't believe *you* survived."

It hit her then, how close she'd come to dying. She reached out and clutched his fingers. "Did I thank you for finding me?"

He drove slowly out of the parking lot, keeping as far from the reporters as possible. "Thank me by getting into bed and sleeping through the night like a good girl."

Her ribs hurt when she laughed. "No crazy monkey sex?"

His features were stark when he turned toward her. "I thought you were dead, Erin. I thought I'd never get to hear your voice again." His mouth was a grim line. "I know you don't like anyone thinking you're weak or vulnerable, but all I want to do is wrap you up in cotton wool and keep you safe."

She bristled.

His eyes swept over her features. "Because that's what decent men do," he said, clearly reading her disgruntled expression. "But I know your ex fucked you up when it comes to normal relationships, so I'll content myself by making sure no one else hurts you tonight. It's not just about sex."

There was hurt in his tone. And anger. It was a combination she knew well, but maybe she had to stop comparing everyone to Graham. Graham had been sick. She touched Darsh's arm, felt his muscles coil beneath her fingers. "How about you just hold me while I fall asleep?"

His mouth twitched. "I can do that."

She closed her eyes, wondering if he knew what a big step this was for her. Trusting him. Trusting anyone.

ERIN FELL ASLEEP in the car, and Darsh didn't want to wake her, so he lifted her out and carried her. She didn't stir. It reminded him of when he'd been a child, falling asleep somewhere and then magically ending up in bed. An echo of his mother's voice singing him to sleep came to him and, for the first time in years, he felt a little of her love cross the barriers of time.

He used keys he'd found in Erin's pocket to awkwardly unlock her back door while still holding her in his arms.

She trembled, and he wished he could wipe the terror that must have overwhelmed her when her truck had been forced off the road. He pushed the door closed with his heel, flipped the lock, carried her up the stairs and eased her onto the bed before removing her boots. Gently he tugged the parka off her shoulders, grabbing the Glock and putting it in the drawer beside her bed. She lay watching him with tired eyes. Not asleep, but too exhausted to protest.

There was a bruise on her cheek. A cut on her lip. Her back when he'd seen it earlier had looked like a two-year-old had gone crazy with purple and red paint. Darsh had wanted to hit something. Had wanted to shout and yell and pound, but he held onto his temper. You didn't yell around people who'd been abused. He wasn't a dick.

"I'm going to make a hot drink. Want something?"

"Just water, please." Her voice was croaky.

He covered her up with the bedclothes, kissed her, then systematically cleared every inch of the house. Maybe he was paranoid, but he sure as hell wasn't taking chances. An asshole had run her off the road and when they found out she was still alive, they might try something else. Was it the killer, or just another member of Erin's fan club taking advantage of an opportunity? Or just some fuckwit too inebriated to realize what he'd done?

Except for a few spiders in the attic, the house was clear, so he went and got her a glass of water—the hot drink had been a ruse so as not to freak Erin out as he searched the place—and headed back to the bedroom.

Putting his SIG on the nightstand, he stripped to his boxers and climbed in beside her. Something clenched inside his chest when she snuggled into his arms. After a few minutes of silence, she spoke.

"I can't stop thinking about it. I just see this rush of trees flying past me. If I hadn't managed to throw myself out of the truck before impact…"

Her head rested on his chest. He held her hand tightly in his.

"It used to be that every time I closed my eyes I'd see Graham raising that gun to his head, grinning at me before pulling

305

the trigger. As if he'd finally figured out a way to invade my life forever. I suppose he did."

The things people did to one another never ceased to amaze him.

"I see my mother," he confessed. "The last time she kissed me."

"Did she really not tell you she was going?"

"She just kissed me goodnight, and I never saw her again." He rubbed his chin gently against her silky hair. "Experiences like that—like Graham, like my mother walking out without a word—they make it hard to trust anyone. Harder to let anyone get close."

Something wet hit his chest. Erin's tears.

"The thing is, there are never any guarantees." Because they both knew better than most, death could take them at any moment. A bullet, a dangerous curve in the road. A madman having them in his sights. "We either take a chance and try for happiness, or…"

"We miss out on the good stuff."

"Did you ever think about us? About that night in Quantico?" He needed to know.

Her fingers clenched his. "All the time. Whenever I got lonely I thought about that night. Whenever memories of Graham became too much, I'd remember the two of us together instead."

Her blonde hair formed a cloud around her head. He took a lock and smoothed it between his fingers. The enormity of what he was feeling, of what he'd almost lost today hit him like a meteor. The words he wanted to say lodged in his throat. All he could manage was, "You're beautiful."

She huffed out a disbelieving laugh. He leaned down and kissed her slowly, gently, hoping she could feel what he wasn't brave enough to say out loud.

"Go to sleep," he said.

She smoothed her hand up his stomach to rest it against his heart. Gradually her breathing quieted. He hoped she fell asleep and got some rest. They were both exhausted.

Oddly, her curled up against him in sleep felt more intimate than all the sex they'd shared. He and Erin hid their feelings behind desire and passion, but she meant more to him than that.

He was in love with her, and probably had been since the moment they'd met, which was why he'd freaked when he'd found out she was married. He was in love with a woman who guarded her heart as carefully as most men guarded their balls. She snuggled deeper into his embrace, and he pulled the cover higher to ward off the chill. He knew enough about psychology to wonder if maybe he was one of those people who set themselves up to fail at relationships—that way he could constantly relive the pain of his mother's abandonment. Or maybe he just had a thing for hot blondes with independent streaks the size of the Mississippi. Either way he was going to have a fight on his hands to make this, to make *them*, happen.

First they had a case to solve. They needed to figure out why the killer had wanted Rachel dead, and whether the same sonofabitch had run Erin off the road. Hopefully Rachel would wake up tomorrow and tell them everything.

One of the things Darsh had learned from being a sniper was it wasn't always easy to spot your enemy, but once you had them in your crosshairs you better damn well be prepared to pull the trigger. The other thing he'd learned was patience, but that was something the town and the chief of police were running short of.

Time was running out.

CHAPTER TWENTY-TWO

RACHEL WAS ALIVE. How the hell had she survived that fall yesterday? And a whole day wandering alone in the wilderness in the middle of a fucking blizzard? Stupidity always managed to find its way into the gene pool, and he had no doubt that, in a normal world, she'd go on to have at least fifteen children. But this wasn't a normal world. He'd helped forge the woman she'd become, and he didn't intend to let her live long enough to add to the population.

He'd already visited the hospital in the hopes of catching her unprotected. A cop had guarded the entry, and her parents had been inside.

His fingers drummed his thigh. He had time.

She was in a coma right now and would be for days according to what he'd overheard at the nurse's station. But eventually the guards would get lax. The parents would need to rest or get an urgent phone call. Maybe there would be a fire in one of their offices? Or drugs would be spotted in plain sight in one of their cars. Something. Anything. He didn't need long. Just long enough to stick Rachel with a fat ass needle.

Erin was also alive. At least that made him happy.

He looked at his prized possessions. His wall of devotion. Photographs. All of her. In her house, in her car. At work. The naked ones were the most precious. The idea of handing those over to someone else was killing him, but he didn't have a choice. He'd baited the trap. Now he needed to set the hook. Wearing gloves, he began pulling the pictures off his wall, pushpins flying around him.

He held up his favorite picture of her. He'd taken it with a zoom lens through her bedroom window and had climbed a tree to get it. He slipped the print into his back pocket. He'd buried the memory card of his camera and wiped the hard drive of his computer. He'd downloaded the images onto someone else's laptop.

He smiled.

It gave him a perverse sense of satisfaction to do that. Apparently, he enjoyed revenge, even for minor slights or insults. Getting back at people was addictive. Now he put the prints in a plastic bag and placed that inside his backpack. He dug into his pocket, removed the one remaining photograph, and shoved it inside with the others. He couldn't afford to be weak or sentimental. He was smarter than most people on the planet, but he knew he could trip up if he grew overconfident. Rachel needed to die. The investigators needed to follow the breadcrumbs and believe what he was telling them.

He included Cassie's letters from poor pathetic Drew Hawke. What a loser. He smiled grimly as he cinched the top of the pack and fastened the snaps.

Chaos provided its own kind of opportunity, and he intended to take full advantage of that over the next twenty-four hours.

AFTER A SHORT fight about whether or not she should be at

work, Darsh had helped her get dressed in yoga pants and a loose tunic-style blue sweater. He'd even zipped up her boots and helped her into her jacket.

She forced back the emotions that swelled inside her whenever she thought about him. She'd awakened wrapped in his arms, and she couldn't remember the last time she'd felt that happy. Even if it was just a reaction to careening down that hillside and then managing to escape alive, the fact she wanted to hold on tight to him whenever she saw him was disconcerting. She barely knew the guy, but ever since the murders, her confidence in her own abilities seemed to be eroding. She didn't like it. Didn't like it at all.

Her sidearm was in a shoulder harness that made the bruises on her back ache. But she'd rather hurt wearing it than get hurt without it. The chance of her pulling her weapon in less than thirty seconds? Small to zero. Whatever. At least she felt like a cop rather than a victim as she walked stiffly down the corridor.

The sight of a broad-shouldered guard outside Rachel's door made her very happy. Darsh had said they'd arranged additional security. She got to the opening, and he stopped her with a hand on her chest. She squeaked in pain.

"Sorry, ma'am." Bright blue eyes looked her over. "No one's allowed inside except medical staff."

She pulled her badge out of her pocket. He leaned closer to inspect it thoroughly.

"Donovan?" His eyes lit up in recognition. "So that's the reason you're looking a little peaky today, huh?"

She laughed at 'peaky' and then winced as she held onto her bruised ribs. "And I thought I'd used enough makeup to hide any side effects."

He tilted his head. "When you go sledding down a mountainside in a truck there're going to be consequences." He looked over his shoulder into the room. "The patient is still in a coma. Parents went for a coffee. I think it would be okay for you to go in for a couple of minutes if the nurses don't object." A nurse walked by at that moment and gave him a sweet smile. He cleared his throat. "My name's Jack Reilly. I'll need to come in too, just to keep an eye out. Not taking any risks with my client."

She nodded slowly. The guy was good. Really good. He opened the door, and she eased inside, careful not to jar herself by bumping into anything or moving too quickly. Everything hurt. Every muscle, every bone, every strand of DNA.

The room was dimly lit. The bodyguard left the door open and stood quietly to one side, watching her without making her feel like a criminal. Doing his job. She got closer to the bed so she could see Rachel's face, and gasped. The girl was so pale, and her injuries made Erin feel like a weenie for complaining about a few bruises. There were deep scratches on her face that were going to scar. Both her eyes were swollen shut. Cuts streaked around her lips. Her arm was bandaged. One leg was set in a cast. She was intubated, and on a drip. The sight of all that equipment and all those machines keeping this girl alive made Erin's heart break.

Tears welled up. She didn't usually let herself get this involved with victims, but this was *Rachel,* and she'd held her hand through the aftermath of her ordeal and promised her things would get better.

She touched one delicate finger that appeared to be the only unharmed part of the girl's body. "I'm so sorry I let you down. I'm so sorry you got hurt." She'd tried so hard not to cry about her own accident, but seeing this young woman like this, who'd been through so much. It felt like someone put a fiery rock in her throat. Her eyes watered, and she couldn't breathe properly. She swallowed tightly, looked back at Reilly standing near the door. "She's scared of strange men." The expression on his face tightened at the implications. "She might be scared of you when she first wakes up. It's nothing personal."

He blinked twice and raised his chin. "I'll keep her safe, Detective. No need to worry. We'll figure it out."

She took a last look at Rachel and hobbled to the door, passing the bodyguard with a grateful smile. Rosemary Knight and her husband, Donald, were just walking down the corridor.

They both seemed surprised to see her.

"Detective, you look terrible." Rosemary acknowledged. Her attitude was a lot chillier than it had been yesterday when she'd been crying in the back of Erin's now deceased truck.

Erin was going to make a comment about having felt worse, but she realized she hadn't. *This* was the worst she'd ever felt. Her lowest point. Even getting beaten by her ex didn't compare to how she felt after being forced off the road and seeing Rachel lying there looking so broken.

"Do they know yet who did this to our daughter?" Donald asked. He stood behind his wife and held onto her shoulders. Maybe they'd found a way of getting past their differences. It was all about coping strategies, Erin knew. Hers had always been to isolate herself, figure things out, make a plan and then deal with it. Darsh called it running away. She called it thinking things through.

"Not yet, but—"

"It's the same person who killed those girls on Monday

isn't it? It's a miracle Rachel isn't as dead as they are."

Erin flinched. "We're doing our best—"

Her cheek rang from the slap Rosemary landed on her. She reared back. *Dammit.* Erin rubbed her cheek, shaking her head at Reilly as he stepped in to intervene.

"Your *best* isn't good enough. Your *best* got my baby in here on a ventilator," Rosemary hissed.

"I am sorry about Rachel. Call me when she wakes up. You better get back to her." Erin skirted past them, ignoring her stinging cheek and bruised pride. Anyone else and she'd have hauled them downtown, paperwork be damned. But with these people? Goddamn it, what did they want? Blood?

She forced back the tears that wanted to fall. No way. No way was she gonna cry when she still had to run the gauntlet of the press. She felt vulnerable, emotional. Falling for someone when she felt like this was not a good idea. She needed to rein in the feelings Darsh was pulling out of her. Now wasn't the time to get involved in something that would probably lead to heartbreak.

She was a good cop, but she wasn't a magician. This perp had so far outfoxed them, but that couldn't last, and the guy must be starting to panic with Rachel still being alive. Maybe it *was* him who'd run her off the road yesterday, and not some football fan who hated her guts. Hopefully they were only the first of many mistakes, and it wouldn't be long until he was cornered like the animal he was.

———————

DARSH STARED AT the timeline he'd taped to the wall. He forced worry for Erin out of his mind. She was a professional and needed space to do her job. She'd only gone to the hospital, which was probably safer than staying home alone.

"What am I missing? What the hell am I missing?"

Agent Chen ignored his grumblings. She'd just got back in the office and looked immaculately dressed and freshly showered. He wasn't sure where she'd slept last night, but it wasn't in here, and it wasn't in an office chair. Mad Ninja skills.

He checked his email. There was a team meeting in five minutes. The good news was they got DNA from the hair on Mandy Wochikowski's sweater. The bad news was there were no hits in CODIS.

His cell rang. "Agent Singh."

"DOJ called. They want an update," Jed Brennan said without preamble.

"Nothing definitive, but I'm leaning more and more toward the cases being related."

"By the same UNSUB? You think Hawke is innocent?" Brennan asked with a hint of disbelief.

"Yeah, but don't tell it to the DOJ just yet. I have no evidence." This had been the DOJ's fear when they requested the BAU's assistance, but they'd still resist the idea that they'd helped send an innocent man to prison. Miscarriages of justice happened—look at Richard Stone, one of the FBI's own agents, who'd been wrongly imprisoned for the last fourteen years. "The rapes last year and these murders seem to have been orchestrated by an individual or individuals with some serious smarts." Darsh rubbed his brow. "I'm not sure there can be more than one genius level predator in a town this small."

Brennan swore. "The shit is going to hit the fan if you're

right. I take it the local cops missed something?"

"That's the thing." He thought of how hard Erin worked on behalf of the victims and how diligent they'd been. "I don't think they missed anything. I think they had more than enough for an indictment, and the jury had more than enough for a conviction. And I still don't think he did it."

"What about the witness statements?" asked Jed.

"We both know they're notoriously unreliable. I think the drugs and alcohol were used to confuse the victims and distort reality. I'm guessing he wore a customized mask of Drew's face that he ordered off the internet."

"Those things freak me out. Now you can fool biometric security systems for under $300 plus shipping. *Mission Impossible* has got a lot to answer for."

Darsh rubbed the knot of muscle tying up his neck. "He wore the mask when he raped women who were either shitfaced or high, and absolutely terrified. He was imprinting Hawke on them during a period of great stress."

"So the witnesses thought they were telling the truth."

"They *were* telling the truth as they understood it." Darsh didn't like being taken for a fool. "Hawke believes he was set up, and I think he might be right. It's this UNSUB's thing. He likes twisting the evidence, knowing exactly how the justice system will react." The bastard wasn't infallible though. He'd already made a crucial error with Rachel Knight. "I meant to call you last night. Someone tried to kill the first victim yesterday."

"You think it's the same guy?"

"Seems a stretch to think it was anyone else."

"Why did he try to kill her? Does he get off on torturing people, or does she know something?"

Darsh flashed back to his conversation with Rachel the other day. Had she told other people what she'd told him and Erin—that she'd started to remember things from her attack? "Probably both."

He looked out the window. There were press and demonstrators milling around in the parking lot and out front. So far no one had leaked the fact a rope had been tied around Rachel's mouth like a bridle bit. The exact same type of rope that had bound Cassie Bressinger to the bed during her murder.

"The Knight girl hasn't woken up yet and won't for a few days at least. It's a miracle she survived." Frankly if it weren't for what she might know, the doctors said they'd let her sleep for weeks in an effort to let her body heal. Darsh had insisted it was urgent they talk to her as soon as possible. They'd told him there was the very real possibility of brain damage from the car accident. That was the only reason he wasn't trying to make them wake her up now. He wasn't big on prayer, but he was praying Rachel Knight woke up with the name of her attacker on her lips.

Jed was talking… "I'm going to request field agents be brought in. The New York Field Office has a team—"

"Not yet," said Darsh. He wasn't ready to let this go yet, and he didn't even want to think about leaving Erin in the middle of the fallout this shit storm was bound to bring.

"I need you back here." The irony of Brennan asking him to drop the case was not lost on either of them. Jed had a reputation for becoming too emotionally involved in his work. "I've only got Henderson, Barton, and Walker fully operational. We're swamped. Tate is helping us out, as is Rooney, who's working from home even though she's not supposed to be working at all. Lazlo reports back on Monday."

Matt Lazlo was a former Navy SEAL whose boat and home had been destroyed on Christmas Eve. Matt and his pretty girlfriend had barely escaped with their lives. Rumor was the Russians had been trying to eliminate Scarlett Stone before she could prove her father's innocence. Naturally, they'd denied any involvement.

"Lazlo found somewhere to live yet?" asked Darsh, stalling for time.

"He's working on it. We need you back here, D," Brennan told him.

Darsh pulled at the shirt collar that suddenly felt too tight. "Look, Chen only just arrived. We're actually getting somewhere. This town is a powder keg. Some guy was beaten up yesterday when he entered the wrong dorm room, and the cop in charge of the investigation was forced off the road and almost died." He closed his eyes, and the horror of seeing her mangled truck infused him with fresh determination. "Give us another seventy-two hours—"

"Twenty-four, and then I need you back. The locals can deal with it."

"Forty-eight, and I *promise* I'll bring this thing to a close." He locked gazes with Chen who grimaced.

Jed laughed on the other end of the line. "I'm glad this gig is a temporary assignment. I'd rather deal with bad guys than stubborn agents any day. Keep me informed. I need to call the DOJ by the end of the day." He hung up.

Erin knocked on the door and came into the room. Ully Mason followed, as did Harry Compton and the chief. They shut the door and sat down at the table facing the white board.

Erin looked exhausted, and her mouth was strained.

"The Knight girl still with us?"

Erin's lips pinched into a thin smile. "Yeah."

"She's in rough shape, though," Ully added. "Don't hold your breath waiting for her to wake up."

Darsh willed Erin to look at him, but she was avoiding his gaze just like she had yesterday morning. Despite the fact he didn't think she should be at work today, he'd thought they'd been okay. She'd woken up in his arms, and it was the best thing he could remember happening in a long time.

Maybe she was pissed because she'd been replaced as lead investigator by Harry, mainly because she'd almost died yesterday. He knew it rankled, but it was an understandable decision. She hadn't been taken off the case, although he could tell the chief was tempted.

"Where are we in finding the vehicle that forced Detective Donovan's truck off the road yesterday?" the chief asked out of nowhere.

Harry answered. "Techs pulled black paint from the panel of Erin's truck. We're sending it to the lab, but from what Erin said, it was a large black SUV. We've put out calls to all body shops in a thirty-mile radius to contact us if they come across a vehicle matching that description with damage to the front passenger side."

The chief nodded. His eyes were narrowed and face pinched. He was chewing gum like it was a race.

"You've all met Agent Chen?" Darsh introduced Ashley and noticed Ully checking her out. Considering Darsh was sleeping with a fellow member of the team, he couldn't exactly judge him. Damn. That was a first.

"So I've been going over the timeline, and Agent Chen is conducting background checks on numerous people with law enforcement or criminology training, as well as anyone connected to the football team or the families of the victims," he began. They went over the case in detail like they had numerous times.

"What I still don't get," Erin said after twenty minutes rehashing details. "Is how the perp knew Rachel Knight was alone in her room the night of her rape? And the other thing that bothers me is how did he get into Cassie and Mandy's home without forcing the locks?"

"I think he has a key." Harry's eyes gleamed. "I think our guy gets close enough to the victims to steal their keys or keycards and make copies before he attacks."

Erin nodded. "Still doesn't explain how he knew Rachel was alone when every other night, Jenny was there with her."

"Rachel said her roommate was going to a party," Darsh recalled. The same way Cassie and Mandy's roommate had been going to a party. "Is it possible the attacker knew the other girl, or was at that party? Maybe he knew she shared a dorm with Rachel and went after her when he knew she'd be alone?"

The spark in Erin's eyes flashed to life. "I interviewed Jenny. Her and her boyfriend weren't at the party for long that night. Planned the whole first time thing with a lot more care than most college romances."

"Could the UNSUB be a friend of the boyfriend?" Agent Chen suggested. "Guys talk about sex, too, right?" Her brow questioned them all.

Ully smirked. Darsh gave him a quelling look.

"We trash-talk each other about sex, but we don't *talk* about sex," Darsh argued. "But if they knew he was a virgin?" He frowned. "Yeah, he'd probably have mentioned the big night to someone."

"It's a good idea to track him down and ask. He lived in Kelvin Hall. It's possible the perp was a friend of his or another student who also stayed there." Erin agreed. "But we seem to be introducing more suspects, not less." She dug her fingers into her scalp. She was moving stiffly. But Darsh was grateful she was moving at all. "What about the rope? Any hits on people buying it online around here?"

Agent Chen slid a piece of paper across the table to each of them. "I've highlighted the people on the list who don't belong to the local climbing club, but they don't cross match with any of the people on the other list of background checks Agent Singh asked me to run. I'll search to see if any of them stayed in Kelvin Hall."

Darsh ran his eyes down the list, but an unhighlighted name had him pausing for a moment.

"Roman Huxley?"

"Yeah, he's big on the outdoors," Erin confirmed. "Climbs, bikes year-round. He's on the Search and Rescue team."

Darsh frowned, thought aloud. "He's also super smart, arrogant, and up on current forensic methods in criminal investigations." He looked up and caught her eye. "He's a little old but apart from that he fits the profile."

"Seems a stretch. He's a world-renowned academic." Erin frowned. "I did overhear him and his research assistant having words when I left his office yesterday."

"Know what it was about?"

She shook her head. "No. He has an alibi for Monday night, remember?"

"Where's Bickham? I want her to double check exactly who was working at the shelter on Monday."

"I'll call her," Ully said, writing in his notebook.

"I spoke to the people at Quantico. Those knots are proper climbing knots." Excitement started to tingle the back of his neck.

"And he knew both victims of the homicide on Monday. Mandy worked in his lab over the summer, and Cassie went to him for information on serial rape." Erin shuddered. "You really think this guy might be involved?"

The more he looked at it, the more he liked the professor as a suspect. "Dig into his background, can you?" he asked Ashley Chen. She immediately began typing. "See if he has any alibis for the rapes last year."

"We need to interview him about the murders first, before you mention any connection to the rapes," Erin argued. She was right.

"Think we can get a warrant to search his house?" Ully asked.

Darsh drew in a deep breath. "On this? I doubt it."

Erin stood and walked stiffly to the whiteboard. She grabbed a marker and wrote *Peter Zimmerman*. "Okay, assuming it is the professor, I get he might try and frame the homeless guy, just to see our puny cop brains in action," she said sarcastically. Then she wrote Drew Hawke's name on the board. "But he has no connection with this guy."

"Yeah—if Hawke isn't guilty why frame the guy?" asked Ully. "Is he just jerking our chains? Or are we some sort of real-time social experiment?"

"What was your take on Hawke when you interviewed him the other day?" the chief asked Darsh.

Erin's gaze swung to his, angry enough to leave bruises.

Dammit he should have told her.

He cleared his throat. "He seemed genuinely upset when he heard about Cassie. He never once slipped from the point of view of an innocent man."

"Prison's full of innocent men," Ully shot back.

Darsh eyed him stonily. "I'm aware."

Agent Chen interrupted. "With the raised awareness of college rapes in the US, could we be someone's testing ground? The accusations against Hawke occurred during the turn of the tide when people stopped automatically believing top athletes were innocent just because they made their colleges a lot of money and scored a lot of points. If you wanted to look at a giant social experiment in action, look at how many ways you can screw with society and the justice system."

"He'd also have loved the insights contained in the letters about Hawke's life in prison. *And...*" Darsh pointed a finger at Erin. "He was in the booth behind us when we grabbed lunch the other day." He held Erin's gaze, but she kept her expression neutral. "He might have overheard us discussing what Rachel told us about her memories coming back. He might have worried she'd remember something incriminating."

"It's all circumstantial." Erin eased down into the nearest chair. "I don't buy it. Hell, we consulted with him on the rape case last year." She dragged her hand through her hair. If anything, she looked even more exhausted now than she had last night.

The chief rose to his feet and glared at Erin. "You gave him access to all the rape files?" His chest rose and fell and rose again. "And now he's a freaking suspect?"

She opened her mouth to argue and so did Darsh, but the chief cut them both off. "You're fired."

She blinked and sat there, visibly stunned.

"Clear out your desk immediately and don't breathe a word of this to anyone, got it?"

"Detective Donovan has done a good job on these investigations." Darsh stepped forward. "Firing her is not necessary or appropriate."

"Neither is sleeping with the detective you're investigating, Agent Singh." The chief glared bitterly.

Darsh felt his face flush, but it was anger, not embarrassment.

"That has nothing to do with the case." Darsh glared back even as Erin's eyes widened.

"Oh, really? Did it ever occur to you that maybe she was sleeping with you so she didn't get fired?"

Erin barked out a laugh. "Maybe Harry should ask if you have an alibi for when I was run off the road yesterday, Chief?" she bit out. "Just to be thorough."

Chief Strassen pointed his finger angrily at her. Darsh forced himself not to grab the guy and snap it in two. "She was the one obsessed with the football team—"

"Because the rape victims told me the quarterback was the one who raped them!" Erin lost her temper, and Darsh couldn't blame her. The witch hunt was over. The chief was ready to build the pyre.

"You were the one going after Jason Brady's ass again this time," Strassen spat out while Erin sat and fumed. "And all the time it was your pal over in the Psychology Department?"

"He's not my pal," Erin said with bitterness. "And I don't think it's him."

"The professor's a suspect—nothing more," Darsh interceded. "We need a real reason to get a warrant to search his house, his car, office. Anywhere he may have hidden the letters taken from Cassie's house on Monday. And we don't even have cause."

"He owns two cars. A smart car and a black hybrid SUV, and he volunteers at the rape crisis center from where Rachel received that phone call at five o'clock yesterday morning," Agent Chen cut in.

Strassen stared at him stonily. "Write it up. I know a judge who'll sign it."

Darsh wanted the warrant, but he couldn't let the guy just sack Erin for no reason. But the fact that they'd slept together made it look bad when he tried to defend her. Shit. "If we're wrong about this we're going to stir up a riot in this town and at the university," he warned.

"There are demonstrations going on every goddamn day outside my office window, Agent Singh. The town's already stirred up." The chief walked to the door. "You have thirty minutes to leave the premises, Ms. Donovan."

———————

"ERIN."

Darsh's voice followed her to her desk, but she didn't slow or wait for him. She grabbed her bag and jacket off the back of the chair. Her fellow cops were standing around, watching her collect her things. They'd heard the chief fire her—they'd have to be deaf not to—and even if they disagreed, they could hardly go on strike when the town needed them more than ever. Anyway, she fought her own battles.

"Erin."

She slowly swung to face Darsh, schooling her features into indifference because the alternate was screaming until someone wrestled her into a straightjacket. "You didn't trust me enough to tell me you'd spoken to Drew Hawke a couple of days ago?"

"It didn't seem relevant."

"Not relevant?"

The light in his eyes changed, as if he recognized she was gearing up for a fight and didn't need his sympathy. "I was sent to look at both investigations and see if there was any connection."

"You were investigating me. I'm the one everyone had their eye on if we got it wrong last year." She tried to keep the volume down.

"You knew what my job here was, Erin," he told her. "You always knew."

She pursed her lips as she nodded. "Which is why I shouldn't have slept with you. Sleeping with you put you in an untenable position."

And now he looked angry. Really angry. "We slept together after I'd examined the cases and knew you'd conducted a thorough investigation and hadn't committed any wrongdoing." Fury burned in his eyes. "I can look after my own integrity, Detective. I know how to be impartial."

"But you're not, are you?" And this was what made everything that had felt so right between them so damn wrong. "Unless you weren't counting that night we spent together in Quantico three years ago that you said you couldn't forget."

She saw the realization hit him, but he shook his head. "I'm perfectly capable of being objective about a woman I've had sex with. If anything, I'd have been more likely to condemn you after Quantico. All I knew back then was you were willing to cheat on the one person in life you'd sworn to love and cherish."

"I did cheat," she insisted stubbornly.

"You'd served him with divorce papers after he attacked you." He clenched his fists, clearly struggling to hold onto his temper. "That isn't cheating. That's wising the fuck up."

Tears pricked her eyes as emotions pricked her heart. She turned away. "I need to get out of here before Strassen has me bodily thrown out."

"I'll shoot any fucker who tries." He put his hand on her arm, holding her in place. She tried to shake him off, but he wouldn't let go. It was the first time he'd treated her with anything except kid gloves. "Fight this, Erin. You didn't do anything wrong. You're a damn good cop, and he's looking for a scapegoat so he doesn't look like an incompetent ass."

She kept her gaze on the knot in his necktie. She'd watched him tie it that morning through a haze of foolish optimism. She swallowed. "If I fight this, I'll take you down with me. No way am I dragging down a respected FBI agent and former Marine sniper."

His expression was bitter. "Don't use me as an excuse," he said in disgust. "I can fight my own battles, and I will. You need to go to your union rep. We didn't break any hard and fast rules, Erin. We just bent them a little when we fell for each other. That isn't against the rules."

She shook her head and pulled away from his grip. "I'll talk to my rep, but Strassen doesn't want me here, so I'm gone."

"Erin—"

"No." She cupped her forehead. Fatigue was making her want to sink to the nearest flat surface and just sleep, but she had to get out of here first. She couldn't deal with this. She felt too raw, too emotional, too battered. "We're done, too, Darsh. You'll be heading back home soon, and I have no idea where I'm going next, except maybe home to visit my family like I should have done years ago. This isn't a good time to start a long distance relationship."

He opened his mouth to argue.

"No." She swallowed the awful feelings of heartbreak that were starting to pierce her composure. "I don't want to get involved again. I don't want to get hurt again. It's just easier being single."

She tried to move past, but he wouldn't budge.

"You think I don't know that? You think I don't know exactly how much it hurts when someone you love turns out to suck? I won't do that to you, Erin. I won't let you down." He bent down to meet her at eye level. "We don't have to repeat old patterns. We don't have to keep suffering because other people are assholes."

She shrugged out of his grip. "I can't. I just can't. It's not worth it." She pushed past him, and this time he let her go. Someone would hopefully clear her desk, because she wasn't hanging around to do it. She pulled out her service weapon and shield and dropped them with the desk sergeant, not meeting his eye. She kept her back straight the way her dad had taught her and walked out the building with her chin high as her fellow cops remained silent and watched her leave. She was almost in the parking lot when she realized she didn't have a ride home.

Ully Mason pulled up in a patrol car. "Get in," he told her. "Where do you want to go?"

Home. She wanted to go home. "I need transportation."

He nodded and took off.

She didn't bother looking backwards. She was done with this town and with the FBI agent she'd fallen for. He'd stolen her heart, and she'd broken his. How the hell could anything be worth the pain that was bound to follow?

CHAPTER TWENTY-THREE

Darsh stood behind Harry Compton and Officer Bickham as they knocked on Professor Roman Huxley's office door. Darsh was trying to get his mind off Erin. It wasn't working.

"Come in," the man shouted.

Harry went in first, holding out the court order. Darsh went around the opposite side of the desk and stood near the window.

Huxley climbed to his feet. "What can I do for you all?" He was wearing a purple skinny-rib sweater, and his hair looked like it had been ruffled by a professional hair stylist. One of the grad students Darsh met a few days ago stood behind his boss, mouth open in shock.

The professor's gaze landed on him in question.

"Roman Huxley?" Harry asked.

The professor's head swiveled and he nodded.

"I have a warrant to search the contents of your office and your home, including computers, phones, any outbuildings—"

"What? This is outrageous!" Huxley snatched the sheets of papers out of Harry's hand and scanned them. "This is nonsense."

"Step away from the computer, please, sir."

"But I have to give a lecture in five minutes."

"You can give your lecture while we search your office," Darsh assured him.

The professor eyed him like he'd lost his mind. Maybe he had. Since Erin had told him they were over without even giving them a chance, he wasn't exactly feeling sane. But he had a job to do and damned if he'd prove anyone right by not doing it perfectly.

"Rick," the professor said slowly, turning his head to look at the young man behind his shoulder. "Would you mind going down to the lecture theater and giving them a spot quiz on the memory module we covered last month? I think I'd better stay here and keep an eye on the police officers before they destroy twenty years of research."

"Yes, sir. Want me to contact the dean?"

"That would be wonderful of you, thank you. And cancel any other classes for the day. I'm going to call my lawyer."

The kid nodded and left hurriedly.

Darsh's phone rang.

"You need to get over here." Ully Mason was on the end of the line.

"Why, what have you found?"

The professor frowned even as Harry and Bickham rolled on their latex gloves and started going through his desk. Huxley dug into his pocket and tossed his keys on the desk. "You'll need those if you don't want to break any of the locks." He rolled his eyes, bored with them and obviously considering them idiots. Was he innocent, or over-confident?

"Let's just say I think you nailed it," Ully continued. "Get over here. You need to see this." The guy hung up.

Darsh was both grateful and pissed Ully had been there to look after Erin after the chief fired her. Strassen was an asshole, happy to pile the pressure on his people to get results and then bail when there was even the slightest hint of a mistake that might reflect poorly on the department. As far as Darsh was concerned, Erin hadn't made a mistake. The witnesses had been manipulated by someone who understood that things like memory and perception could be altered.

"I need to go." Darsh turned to leave.

"Sir?" Bickham called out as he was leaving.

He jerked his chin in question, and she pointed down into the drawer she'd been busy searching. Darsh went over and peered down. Huxley came to stand beside him. Darsh kept his weapon away from the guy's reach, just in case. They all stared down. At the bottom of the drawer was a stack of letters held together with an elastic band. They were addressed to Cassie Bressinger.

Huxley's eyes bugged. "I-I don't know how they got there." He scanned the room wildly as if looking for an escape.

Darsh raised his brows at Harry.

"Roman Huxley," Harry began. "I'm arresting you on suspicion of murder…"

"I'm going over to his house," Darsh told them after a couple of uniforms led the professor away in handcuffs. "Send Chen the laptop. Keep searching."

WHEN ERIN SAW Darsh had texted her telling her to call him about the case, she picked up the phone, even though what she really wanted to do was hurl it into the snow.

"You need to get over here. Fast."

Her heart skipped. "Where are you?"

"Roman Huxley's house." He rattled off the address and hung up.

She swore. Dammit, she didn't need to do a damned thing he said. She wasn't on the force anymore, she was just your average Joe Blow citizen. Even as these thoughts ran through her mind, she grabbed her jacket and headed out the door. Had they found something? Had they caught the guy?

Ully had lent her his personal vehicle, a Ford Mustang GT. She knew how much it had hurt handing over the keys, and she appreciated more than any words he could have spoken that he had her back. Still, she decided to go to the insurance office and sort out her claim and a rental car on the way home from whatever the hell Darsh wanted her to see at Huxley's.

Ten minutes later, she pulled up and parked on the road. Darsh was waiting for her on the front step, a glint in his eye, but he didn't speak. Rather than taking her inside, he took her around the side of the house and opened the garage door. Huxley drove a SMART car around town or rode his bike. She hadn't known he also owned the SUV parked there until Agent Chen had mentioned it. She circled the car.

"Well, hello, friend." She shook her head as she examined the five-foot long scrape along the passenger side of the vehicle. "Did he admit to running me off the road?"

"Not yet." Darsh watched her intently, but she couldn't tell what he was thinking.

So she'd been wrong about the professor. "Find anything else?" she asked, looking up and pretending it didn't hurt to be this close to him.

Darsh nodded, and his eyes gleamed.

"Can I see?"

"You might not want to."

"I'm not afraid of the truth, Agent Singh."

He drew in a breath that made his shoulders seem even wider, and his expression changed as if he'd remembered they weren't together anymore. Not that they ever really had been. That reality gouged something bloody from her chest.

She went to brush past him, but he caught her arm. "Erin—"

Her body responded to his touch, even as she forced herself to say, "Don't."

She stared at his chest, knowing she was being a coward, knowing she'd promised him more.

"I can't believe you aren't fighting for this." He wasn't just talking about her job.

"For what? A short-term fling with no future?" She looked up and met his onyx eyes.

"You're the one saying we have no future. I'm the one saying you need to give us a chance. I'm coming over later, when I wrap things up here. We can talk—"

"I won't be there."

His head snapped up like she'd slapped him. "Why? Where are you going?"

She hardened her heart. "Queens. Not sure when I'll be back."

"Call me when you're not so upset and we can talk this through like two adults."

She backed away and shook her head. "Let it go, Darsh."

"Call me," he insisted.

"Fine." She shrugged and nodded, but they both knew she was lying.

———————————

TEN MINUTES LATER, she got back in Ully's car and drove away before the reporters turned up. The photographs on the wall of Huxley's spare bedroom made her skin crawl. That he'd been watching her for months, photographing her even in her own bedroom. And now her fellow cops on the case got to see photos of her naked. Jesus. The sooner she got out of town the better.

He'd been in her house…the one place she'd seen as a sanctuary, a haven. A silver cross her grandmother had given her years ago was on his dresser, along with a recent credit card statement.

Darsh hadn't tried to stop her from leaving. Why would he? He'd swooped in and saved the day, and now the town was finally safe from a monster who'd fooled her as easily as a two-bit street magician. Her stomach clenched.

There was no direct evidence to suggest Huxley had raped those girls last year. She wasn't sure what to think about that. She knew the case was being passed on to the FBI field office to be re-examined.

She would have bet her life savings—a paltry amount admittedly—that Huxley wasn't a killer. She must be losing her instincts, or maybe she'd never had any. Maybe she just knew how to walk the walk and talk the talk but had the actual investigative skills of one of the rodents who lived in her barn.

Her fingers clenched on the leather steering wheel of Ully's muscle car. She couldn't stay in Forbes Pines anymore. Not only did she feel violated from Huxley's creepy trespass, but the town hated her. And the idea of seeing Darsh again…

Seeing him ripped her heart out, because he was right. She was the one giving up on them. She was the one running away. But how could they possibly have a future when she didn't have a clue about what she was going to do with her life?

No.

She checked her watch. She had a million things to do before the close of business today. The first was visiting the realtor, which had become her overriding priority since she'd realized someone had been inside her house, the second the insurance office and getting a rental sorted out until her claim was settled. Ully would need his car back ASAP. At least having tracked down Huxley's damaged SUV meant the insurance people wouldn't fight her over that.

She passed a media van as she headed along Main Street. News was starting to leak out. It wouldn't be long before reporters were stacked knee-deep around her house, and she wasn't going to give them the satisfaction of trapping her inside. The sign for the travel agent caught her eye, and she swung into a parking space outside the shop.

The lie she'd told Darsh earlier suddenly seemed like a good idea. She was getting out of town. She just had one more thing to do before she left.

———————————

HUXLEY SAT WITH his legs crossed, foot tapping the air impatiently. Darsh eyed him as he walked in the room. He didn't look like a man who'd been arrested for the crime of murder. He looked like someone whose day had been inconveniently interrupted.

"Where's your lawyer?" asked Darsh.

Huxley shrugged. "In the bathroom or somewhere."

"Want me to come back later?"

"No. Get in here so I can go home."

"Home?" Darsh frowned. "You really think you're going home?"

Huxley leaned forward. "Look, I have no idea how those letters got into my desk, but my office is generally open so someone obviously put them there."

"In a locked drawer?"

Huxley shrugged. "I often leave my keys on my desk, too. I'm not very good with security."

Darsh said nothing and let him talk. Letting suspects talk was the best interview technique you could have as long as they kept on track.

"I have an alibi for Monday night," Huxley said with a condescending raise of his brow.

"The soup kitchen?" asked Darsh.

The professor shifted. "Actually, not the soup kitchen, no. I left the mission early on Monday because I-er, had a date." He pulled at the tight neck of his sweater.

"But you lied about it to Detective Donovan."

"I don't believe I lied directly."

"A technicality." Darsh kept his expression neutral. "Who was this date? Where'd you go?"

Huxley licked his lips. "We didn't go anywhere. We stayed at my house. We can't really go out in public…"

"Because?"

"Because…she's one of my students."

"So when you said 'date' you meant you were having sex with one of your students?" Darsh asked evenly.

The professor nodded. "But if the university finds out, well, let's say they won't be very happy."

The guy was definitely fucked. "What time were you and this student—I will need her name to verify your alibi, naturally—engaged in sexual activities?"

Huxley's expression turned angry. "I left the grad students at the mission about 6:45 PM. I picked up the young woman in question on campus, and we got back to my place about seven. We had sex, watched some TV, and ate. Then we had sex again before I gave her a ride home."

"The girl's name?" Darsh poised his pen over his notebook. And maybe he used the word 'girl' deliberately. So sue him.

"Monica Ripley. Ripley with an 'e.' I can give you her address if you like," he said, in a patronizingly helpful tone. Darsh wrote that too and hoped one of the officers watching this was now tracking this Monica Ripley—with an e—down.

"Where were you last night?" Darsh asked.

The question seemed to take the professor back for a moment. "I was exhausted after being out on the search all day. I got home around six. Monica came over with take-out and we…"

"Had sex?" Darsh took a wild guess.

The professor nodded, and Darsh wanted to tie his dick in a knot. And maybe he was bitter because Erin had dumped his ass despite the great sex. He should just let her go. Let her run and hide from any pesky emotion she might actually feel.

"You didn't leave the house again?"

He shook his head. "I did. I got called out to help attach ropes to Erin's truck. Popped in to see how she was doing at the hospital and got home about nine. Monica had already left. I went into work early this morning. I had a lot to catch up on after being out of the office all afternoon yesterday."

Darsh slid a photograph of the back of the hybrid SUV parked in Huxley's garage across the table. "This your car?"

Huxley nodded, looking wary.

"How do you explain the damage to the vehicle?"

Huxley frowned. "What damage?"

Darsh slid a second photograph across the smooth surface of the table.

The professor leaned forward, staring at the photograph. "When the hell did this happen?"

"You tell me, it's your car."

Huxley shook his head. "I don't understand?" His expression was openly confused.

Darsh wasn't about to spoon-feed him information. The professor pressed his lips together, staring at the photograph of the vehicle.

"What about this?" Darsh showed him a photograph of the montage of images of Erin, some of her naked, others candid shots when she obviously didn't know she was being stalked.

The professor glanced at the images, and his eyes widened. "Seems like someone has an obsession with the lovely detective." He frowned. "I assume you warned her?"

Really? He was going to pretend these weren't his when they were stuck to his walls and the originals were on his computer. "She saw them. She knows."

The guy nodded as if reassured.

Wow, if Darsh hadn't seen them in the professor's house with his own eyes he'd have believed the guy didn't know a thing about them.

Darsh frowned. What was his defense going to be? Someone else put them there? Or was he going to pull some multiple personality disorder mumbo jumbo?

"So why am I here?" the professor asked.

Darsh produced a picture of a coil of blue climbing rope and pushed it toward the other man. "Is that yours?"

Huxley nodded.

Then Darsh slid a picture of Cassandra Bressinger naked, tied to the bed with that same rope. The professor said nothing for a moment. Then Darsh showed him a photograph of the bedroom wall of his spare room from a distance so the man couldn't pretend not to recognize the space.

Huxley's gaze hardened as he stared at the pictures. When he finally looked up all he said was, "I want my lawyer."

CHAPTER TWENTY-FOUR

ERIN WALKED ALONG the corridor wearing a pair of sweats, sneakers, and her parka worn loose over a Blackcombe College sweatshirt. This was her disguise for blending in and being as inconspicuous as possible. A pale gray beanie covered her long blonde hair, and dark shades covered her eyes. She hit the second floor of the hospital and walked as swiftly as she could along the corridor. There was no way she could leave without checking in on Rachel, despite the girl's mother's actions earlier.

Up ahead she saw a doctor and two nurses hurry into Rachel's room. Erin's mouth went dry. Had she coded? Was she in trouble? She hurried to the doorway and caught Reilly by the shoulder just as he was about to follow everyone inside.

"Is she all right?" Erin demanded.

He removed her hand gently but firmly and gave her a friendly squeeze to show it was nothing personal.

"She woke up. A bit panicked from the tube so the medical team has come in to remove it. I need to get in there."

She gave a skeptical quirk of her brow. "You worried one of them is going to hurt her?"

"No." He smiled, the corners of his eyes crinkling. "But keeping her safe is what I get paid to do. Their job is to keep her alive."

With that, he left her standing in the hallway.

Often cops on bodyguard duty at the hospital got distracted by the pretty nurses. Reilly looked like he was more likely to start cross-dressing than let anything distract him. She wondered what he'd done before he did this. The guy practically screamed "military." As much as she wanted to go in there and make sure Rachel was okay, she realized with a faint pang that the girl was no longer her responsibility. It wasn't her job anymore. Erin had no place here. The idea left a raw spot in her soul. What the hell was she supposed to do now? How did she stop acting like a cop? It was all she'd known for the last nine years. How else could she help people like Rachel?

The questions and uncertainty ran through Erin's mind on a seemingly endless loop. She leaned against the wall and closed her eyes.

Had anyone told Darsh Rachel had woken up yet, she wondered suddenly. Erin doubted it. She dialed his number before she could second guess herself.

"Erin?"

The velvet tones of his voice did something to her every time she heard them. "Rachel Knight woke up. They're removing her breathing tube in the next few minutes. You might want to get down here."

"Wait for me." He hung up before she could make an excuse. Tears threatened.

She owed him an apology but knew she couldn't face him. Didn't want to look into those intelligent brown eyes and see the knowledge reflected there that she was running away again. She was a coward. Suddenly she needed to get out of here before Darsh turned up, and she made a complete fool of herself by throwing herself at the man.

She took a last peek and saw Rachel's bed surrounded by a crowd of people. She hoped the young woman made a full recovery. Recovering from this trauma might be the hardest thing the girl ever did, but she'd already proved she was a survivor.

Erin turned on her heel and saw Jason Brady stepping out of the elevator with another Blackcombe Ravens player. Their eyes locked, and her heart thumped crazily against her ribs as he moved purposefully toward her. It was gutless, but the last thing she wanted to do was face the student when she'd been kicked off the job and her entire body ached from yesterday's crash. It was time to pop another pain pill and then catch her flight home to visit her family. It was time to lay that particular demon to rest. She slammed through the exit into the stairwell and smacked into someone else. All her injuries screamed as they collided.

"Erin!" It was Rick Lachlan carrying an array of blooms.

"Rick. Hey."

Jason Brady opened the door of the stairwell, then paused when he spotted Rick. He opened his mouth to say something, but changed his mind and backed away. She couldn't read his expression. Maybe he didn't want any witnesses when he hurled his latest round of abuse.

"You visiting a friend?" she asked Rick.

"Yeah, but she must have been released early so I was going to leave these at the nurse's station for anyone who didn't have any visitors. What're you doing here?" Lines formed between his brows. "You didn't have any complications from your accident, did you?"

If losing her job and her nerve could be called complications then, yes, she was having them.

"I came to visit Rachel Knight. She just woke up." Suddenly overcome with emotion, she let out a sob and tried to cover the sound with her fist. Yesterday she'd been so certain Rachel was dead. Her waking up represented a miracle all of its own.

He handed the flowers to a nurse who was passing.

"Hey." He rubbed Erin's back in a friendly gesture. She refrained from flinching when he touched a bruise on her shoulder. There were bruises everywhere. "That's great news." Rick tilted his head to one side. "You look like you could use a drink. Wanna go grab that coffee we keep talking about?"

Tears gathered in her eyes, but she fiercely blinked them away. "Sorry." She wiped her eyes. "My allergies must be flaring up."

"Erin," he admonished. "You've been through a terrible few days, and you just got fired through no fault of your own."

She winced. Obviously that news was now public.

"Give yourself permission to take some time off. Decompress. Chill. Drink coffee, maybe go wild and have a cookie."

She laughed reluctantly. "I suppose." All she really wanted was for Darsh to wrap his arms around her and tell her everything was going to be okay, but she'd stopped believing in fairy tales the day her husband had used her as a punching bag. They started walking down the stairs, taking it slowly in deference to her injuries. Every muscle in her body ached, but most especially her heart. The betrayal by her boss hurt, but it wasn't unexpected. Strassen tended to look out for number one. What had really knocked her sideways was the fact she'd fallen for a man who'd contributed to her tumble from grace, helped get her fired, and then had gone and solved the damn mystery.

He was a hero, and she was a whore. No double standards at play at all.

"Come on. I've had a shitty day too. Hard to discover a man you idolized is in fact a sadistic killer. No wonder he was so good at teaching criminal psychology."

She tried to smile because he was trying to cheer her up, but her heart wasn't in it. "I guess he fooled us all."

They headed to the parking lot. She checked her watch again. "Actually, I don't really have time for coffee. I'm catching a flight at five."

His eyes flashed, and he checked his own watch. "How about I drive you to the airport? I know you don't have a truck anymore. We can grab a coffee before you catch your flight."

"I guess I could leave Officer Mason's keys under the visor and text him where I left his car." Erin pulled the keys out of her pocket.

"I expect he's going to be here soon talking to Rachel anyway," Rick said helpfully.

Of course he was right. She looked at him. "Are you sure you don't mind?"

He shrugged with his hands in his pockets. "I have nothing else to do with myself today except watch reruns of *The Big Bang Theory*."

It seemed churlish to refuse. "Okay, then." She opened the passenger door of Ully's Mustang and slid the keys behind the visor. She grabbed her small travel bag out of the trunk and made sure the car was locked before she shut the door.

She hefted the bag across her shoulder though Rick offered to carry it for her, and walked carefully over the trampled snow to his small sedan. She looked at the hospital and thought wistfully about Darsh. He'd be here soon. Mad and disappointed in her. Nothing she could do about that right now, although, for the first time, the idea she was making a big mistake teased the edge of her mind.

Rick was in the driver's seat waiting for her to get in. "It's just coffee, Erin."

She nodded and climbed inside.

ERIN'S PHONE CALL had Darsh striding into the bullpen and tracking down Ully Mason. "Rachel Knight just woke up. Let's get down there."

The other man nodded and got off the phone. "I'm coming."

They took the cruiser, Ully driving while Darsh checked his incoming mail. Monica Ripley was proving impossible to track down, and he hoped she hadn't become another victim of this ruthless killer. Ully shot out of the parking lot with the sirens blasting.

There was an email from the warden of Riverview, forwarded from Drew Hawke. The list of people who might have a grudge against the quarterback was long, but Professor Huxley wasn't on it. He frowned, then forwarded it to Agent Chen to crosscheck with the other lists. The evidence against Huxley was piled as high as the snow at the side of the road, but there was nothing to link him to the campus rapes last year.

What if he was wrong about Hawke, and the quarterback wasn't innocent?

What if Erin had been right about Hawke, and Strassen had fired her anyway?

Had Huxley enjoyed the attention he and the college had received last year and decided to continue it, to manipulate the cops and dabble in some practical application of his academic interests? He was denying everything.

"You serious about Donovan?" Ully asked, turning off the sirens as the traffic thinned.

"Yeah." Darsh didn't want to talk about this. "But she's not interested."

Ully's eyebrows hiked. "She's interested all right. She hasn't looked twice at a guy in all the time she's been here, so she's definitely interested."

"We knew each other before." Darsh admitted reluctantly. "A few years ago when she did a training course at Quantico."

"When she was still married?" Ully asked in surprise.

"She'd filed for divorce. Guy was an asshole."

"Obviously," Ully agreed, and he didn't know the half of it. "Look, she's a good cop, but we've had a hell of a year. Give her time. She'll come around."

Darsh grunted. He didn't want to have to persuade someone to love him.

Christ. His mouth went dry. How could he have been so stupid as to fall in love with Erin Donovan, a sharp-tongued, stubborn, independent, control freak? Who was also sexy, smart, dedicated, and incredibly beautiful? He stared out of the window at the cold snow, and it reminded him of how it had felt to be abandoned by a woman who shouldn't have had to be forced to love him. It had felt cold and desolate and lonely as fuck.

He swore.

Erin felt something for him, he knew she did, she was just skittish after that hellish experience with her asshole ex and from everything happening on the case. She'd almost died yesterday, she was bound to be shaken up and confused. And she was mad because he hadn't told her about visiting Hawke in Riverview. It was a mistake. He should have told her, but he'd known she'd be angry.

He'd see her again in a few minutes. Apologize. Convince her that he meant what he said—that what they had was worth pursuing. They could go slow and easy. He wouldn't mention the "L" word. That would be his secret. It would scare the hell out of the woman.

Ully flicked a glance at him and opened his mouth to say something else.

"I don't want to hear it." Darsh put his hand up in defense.

"I was only gonna say I'm sorry. For being an ass when you arrived."

"I thought you were always an ass?"

"Meh, it varies on whether or not I got laid in the last few days."

"Obviously not for a while, then."

Ully laughed and pulled across two lanes of traffic, making Darsh's heart slam into his throat. "Damn straight."

The officer double-parked at the curb outside the hospital doors. They jogged up the front steps then took the stairs, ignoring the press who held out microphones as they expectantly shouted questions.

"Uh, oh," Ully said checking his cell. "Looks like you have some leg work to do."

"What d'you mean?" Darsh opened the fire door at the top of the stairs.

"Erin just texted me to say my car's in the parking lot here at the hospital, and she's flying down to visit her parents."

"Dammit." Darsh's shoulders sagged.

"You could go after her." Ully checked his watch. "Flight won't leave until five."

But inside, Darsh felt hollow. It wasn't the first time someone had left him behind without saying goodbye. It shouldn't hurt quite so much, but hell if it didn't.

He passed Jason Brady in the hallway, and his footsteps slowed. He paused, then turned on the guy. "What are you doing here?"

The kid shrugged, enormous shoulders filling out a Ravens' T-shirt like it was a size too small. Darsh had no clue how Erin had handled the guy at the sorority house that day.

"I got a message from Drew." The guy wouldn't meet his gaze. "He asked me to do him a favor. To find all the people he'd been an asshole to and apologize to them on his behalf."

"You have the list on you?"

Brady dug into the back pocket of his jeans and pulled out a heavily folded piece of paper. Darsh scanned it. It was the same list Hawke had sent him.

"I'm still waiting to hear your alibi for Monday night. People say there were a couple of hours when you weren't at the party?"

Brady's eyes flashed. "I thought you caught the guy responsible?"

Darsh stared hard at the football player. He kept his voice low. "We have someone in custody, but he hasn't been charged yet."

Brady's eyes went wide. "I didn't kill Cassie or the other girl." He swallowed and Darsh smelled fear. "But I don't have an alibi. I just went for a walk. I've outgrown the party scene. Didn't want to be there, but didn't have any choice. I'm gonna move off campus as soon as I can find a place." All the breath went out of the kid. "I just want college to be over."

Darsh nodded his head toward Rachel's room. "So why are you here? She isn't on the list."

Jason straightened from his slouch against the wall. "She's on *my* list." A look of shame crossed his features. "Look." His shoulders slumped. "I saw her on campus before the trial started and said some things I'm not very proud of. I thought she was lying about being attacked." His lips compressed into a bloodless line. "But she wasn't, was she? Everything she said happened." He swallowed noisily. "I told her she made it up because she was desperate for attention, and that she was too ugly for anyone to want." Tears filled the guy's eyes, and he didn't try to hide them. "I need to tell her how sorry I am."

"You can tell her, but I doubt it'll be today. Whether or not she forgives you is something else entirely."

"That's her prerogative." Brady nodded, expression serious. "I need to apologize to Detective Donovan, too. I've been a prick. I saw her earlier, but she was talking with that TA from criminology—"

"Lachlan or Hall?" He didn't want to think about Erin, but she was always on the periphery of his thoughts.

"Lachlan," Brady told him.

"He's also on the list," Darsh noted. "What did Drew Hawke do to him?"

"We got him drunk and wrote on him at a party. Humiliated him." Brady closed his eyes. "Man, there are a lot of people on that list. I've been a prick, and I need to snap out of it before I cross a line that can't be uncrossed." He gave a harsh laugh. "I'm starting a twelve-step program for douchebags."

When their eyes met, a look of understanding passed

between them—the kid had been an asshole but had decided to face the consequences. It took a certain amount of balls to do that. There was hope for him yet. Assuming he followed through.

"You think there's a chance Drew will be released?" Brady asked the million-dollar question, trying to keep the hope out of his voice.

Darsh handed the piece of paper back to Brady. "Depends on what we find out and how the Department of Justice wants to handle it. Either way a judge has to decide—same way a judge sentenced him in the first place."

He went to turn away, but Brady asked urgently, "Do *you* think Drew raped those girls?"

Darsh hesitated, then gave a slight shake of his head, even though he'd never make an official statement.

Brady pulled in a big breath. "Right. Good." Then he resumed his slouch against the wall and began what was sure to be a long wait.

Ully was frantically motioning Darsh toward the door of Rachel's room, and they edged inside the crowded space. The girl looked so fragile and tiny in that big hospital bed surrounded by tubes and machines. Medical personnel were drawing blood and checking her blood pressure. Her skin was about the same shade as the bleached bedsheets. Had Rachel Knight woken up with damage to her brain function? It didn't look like it, but it didn't mean she remembered anything about what happened yesterday. She was talking to the doctors and holding hands with her mother, her father standing at his wife's shoulder. Between family, medical staff, and her bodyguard, courtesy of Alex Parker's security company, the room was full to bursting.

Rachel's eyes searched the crowd and paused when they found his. He edged closer.

"Where's Erin?" she asked hoarsely.

"She wanted to be here," Darsh told her. So why had she left? To avoid him, he realized. The knowledge sat like a tombstone on his chest. "Do you know who did this to you, Rachel?"

She nodded. Despite her ordeal, her eyes were brighter than they'd been when they'd talked the other day. Her greatest fear had come true, and she'd survived. Maybe she could overcome some of the trauma that haunted her. In a war zone they called it "seeing the elephant."

She gripped his sleeve and pulled him closer. His pulse kicked up a beat. "He tricked me into meeting him at the park by saying a girl needed my help. He forced me to walk into the forest where he intended to hang me from a tree and make it look like I'd committed suicide. He said he was the one who raped me last year, and that he pretended to be Drew Hawke. You have to let Drew out of prison, he didn't do it." Her hand shook, not with fear, but with passion. Her thoughts were with the man she'd helped wrongfully convict.

"Who?" he asked, trying not to sound impatient. "Who tricked you? I need a name or a description."

Her eyes filled with tears, and he leaned close so she could whisper in his ear. "Rick. Rick Lachlan."

The words came out as barely an undertone, but they shook him to his foundation. He searched her face to make sure she hadn't made a mistake or been confused, but her gaze was clear and direct. It wasn't the professor. The professor was another stooge, like the quarterback had been. Darsh had been fooled the same way Erin had been fooled.

Erin.

Erin had been with Lachlan earlier…

Part of him wanted to ask Rachel if she was absolutely sure, but that was a stupid question, and he'd already been stupid enough. The final pieces clicked together. The professor didn't have a personal grudge against the football team, but this Lachlan guy did.

He squeezed her hand, nodded curtly to her parents, and strode into the corridor, calling Erin's cell. She didn't answer, but maybe she was just avoiding him. Next he dialed Agent Chen. "Rachel Knight just named Rick Lachlan as the person who attacked her yesterday and said he'd confessed to raping her last year. Can you tell me everything you've got on him?"

Ully stood at his shoulder, looking confused. The bodyguard followed them out.

Chen began reciting information, "Rick Lachlan lived in the same hall as Rachel's roommate's boyfriend. I'm looking at the data I entered for where the victims took classes, and they all had classes in the building where he was based." Which would cross over with Professor Huxley. Lachlan also had access to the professor's office and probably to his house and car keys. Not to mention Mandy Wochikowski's keys from when she'd worked in their lab last summer.

"He gave the impression he was working at the mission on Monday night. Bickham was supposed to follow that up. Call her and ask her to confirm," he told Ully.

"Lachlan's the killer? The professor's grad student?" Ully asked, surprised.

"Yeah." He wanted to slap himself on the forehead for missing the obvious. "Genius IQ. Fits seamlessly into the student population because he is one." Darsh was talking both to Agent Chen and to Ully. "And someone with his intellect would probably be quite happy to not only make law enforcement look incompetent, but also to screw up his boss's career and turn himself into the resident expert. Put a trace on his and Erin Donovan's phones right now. Can you send me a picture of him, Chen?"

"Why Erin's?" Ully asked urgently.

"Sending right now," said Agent Chen. "There's something else. His mother was murdered by his father right in front of Lachlan when he was nine years old. The father violated a restraining order. Shot her and then himself, leaving little Ricky an orphan. It might give him a reason to attack the criminal justice system."

"Yup," Darsh acknowledged. The photograph downloaded, and Darsh showed it to the bodyguard who was hovering in the doorway. "You seen this guy around here?"

His brows rose. "Sure, he's been hanging around on and off since yesterday. He's the guy?" the bodyguard asked, staring at the photograph as if memorizing every line.

Darsh nodded. "You being here probably saved her life."

"That's my job," the guy said. "The mom said he was a friend of Rachel's."

"Which is how he convinced her to meet him yesterday morning. He must have overheard me and Erin talking at lunch the other day, saying Rachel was remembering things from her rape. Erin told me she'd done some lectures for Huxley." And that was the exact moment Darsh knew he'd just figured out the real motive.

Erin. She was the center of this thing. She made all the pieces fit.

"I'm betting Lachlan met her and started to fixate on her.

He probably found out about her history with her late husband and decided they shared a bond because of the way his father killed his mother. Then the football players humiliated him at some frat party, and he decided to use the campus rape issue and the prominence of varsity athletes in these events to not only take them down, but to stick it to the system and ingratiate himself with Erin. After the trial he no longer had her attention, so he figured out another way to get it."

Some of the images he'd seen of her on the professor's wall that morning were old, speaking of long-term obsession. Her hair had had time to grow from a sleek, chin-length bob to way down past her shoulders.

Darsh tried her cell again. Nothing. Ully did the same. When she didn't pick up Ully's call, Darsh felt the first twinge of real fear.

"Get road blocks up ASAP. Pretty sure he will at least try to grab her." Erin had taken down Jason Brady with ease. She could handle a short-ass like Lachlan. That's what he told himself so he didn't start freaking out. Keep calm, keep cool, Erin was fine. Just avoiding him and her fellow cops. "Where's security around here?"

Ully led the way, and they barged inside and demanded the guard replay all footage of the entrances for the last thirty minutes. It didn't take long to spot Erin leaving the side entrance with Lachlan.

"You take the cruiser, I'll take my car." Ully tossed him the keys. "Erin said she left it here in the lot so I'm guessing Lachlan offered her a ride. I've got a radio on me. We can cover more ground this way."

Erin was in danger, and it was his fault. He'd been the one

to target the professor, and part of his dislike for the man had been personal. It should never be personal. He'd fucked up way more than Erin ever had with Drew Hawke. Darsh swallowed twice before he managed to force out, "Let's get a chopper in the air and start searching the area."

He ran to the cruiser and called Agent Chen. "Put out an ABP for whatever Rick Lachlan drives and then inform the cops that our UNSUB is one Rick Lachlan, and he may have Detective Donovan with him. Location unknown. They left the hospital twenty minutes ago. Get the message out to all the surrounding counties, too."

Darsh got in the cruiser and sat with his heart thudding crazily. His hands shook. He couldn't lose her. He should have told the chief to stuff the case that morning and just gone with Erin when the bastard fired her. If he had, she'd be safe now. But he'd needed to finish the job, to prove he was the best, even though it had cost Erin not only her job, but possibly her life.

He sat there, paralyzed. He had no idea in which direction to drive. Lachlan could head to a cabin in the woods, and it might be weeks before they tracked him down—weeks where he got to hurt Erin the way he'd hurt those other women.

Darsh knew Erin could take care of herself, but she didn't know Lachlan was the enemy. She didn't know he was a monster.

Darsh forced himself to remember his training, not only FBI, but Scout Sniper School too. To calm his racing pulse and use his brain. The hunt was always as much mental as physical. He brought up a map of the area. Lachlan knew he didn't have much time before Rachel Knight told the world he'd tried to kill her. His options—assuming he had Erin—were murder,

murder-suicide, hiding, or making a run for it. The young man felt intellectually superior to law enforcement and was a total narcissist, probably borderline personality disorder. Darsh doubted he'd lower himself to suicide. His obsession with Erin meant he'd want to keep her alive, at least in the short-term. To live out the fantasy he'd created for himself with her at his side.

So where would he go?

Darsh zoomed out on the map and had his answer.

The sun was setting in the west, and it would be dark soon. Rick Lachlan was going to make a break for Canada. And he was planning to take Erin with him.

CHAPTER TWENTY-FIVE

Erin swiveled to look at the turnoff they'd just driven past. "Hey Rick, you mis—*ouch*!"

She swung around as he stabbed a hypodermic needle deep into her thigh and pushed down the plunger.

"What the hell!" She knocked it out of his hand before he could inject it all. "What did you give me?" she demanded, digging for her gun, only to realize she no longer carried a service weapon, and her backup was home in the safe because she hadn't wanted to deal with it while flying. She dug out her phone instead, and he smiled, buzzed down his window, tore it from her grasp, and tossed it. There were no cars around to notice.

The guy had gone crazy.

Her heart started to race, and it wasn't fear. She grabbed the wheel and hauled it toward her, trying to force them off the road. She might not want to get in another crash, but she had a horrible feeling it would be preferable to whatever Rick Lachlan had in mind.

He knocked her away, the car swerving violently onto the hard shoulder. He punched her in the face when she wouldn't let go. Dammit. She jerked back against the seat, blood bursting on her tongue from where he'd split her lip. Her vision blurred. Her hands felt like giant boulders on the ends of stick-like arms, and she couldn't lift them. She swallowed the saliva that was pooling in her mouth.

The car was still on the highway. She hadn't even slowed him down.

The thought of losing control of her body made her panic. She groped for the door handle and grabbed it on the second try. But it didn't open. He'd locked it, and her brain wasn't telling her how to unlock it.

"What did you give me?" She needed to know. Needed to hang onto facts rather than fear.

"I had one shot of ketamine left. I was going to give it to Rachel, but I couldn't get into her room alone. Then she woke up." He reached out and touched her face, his arm seeming impossibly long in her drug-warped brain. "I was pretty mad earlier, but I guess it was meant to be."

"Why?" Her tongue felt dense.

"Because I needed her to keep quiet about what she learned yesterday. Who'd have thought she'd survive, huh? Little whiny bitch like that, beating the odds and ruining my fucking life."

"It was you? The whole time?" Her lips weren't working properly.

The smile on his face twisted, and she didn't know if that was the drugs or not. She wanted to punch him right in the teeth, but she couldn't move.

"Yeah. All me. The things I did to get you to notice me."

What the hell was he talking about?

"Yes, you," he said as if she'd spoken aloud. "Who did you think I was trying to impress?"

He'd committed rape and murder to impress her? What sort of insanity was that?

"Then as soon as the rape trial was over, you started ignoring me again. Refusing to meet me for coffee, not taking my calls."

"You killed someone because I didn't take your call? I'm a busy woman with a career—"

"Not anymore."

God, she didn't need that reminder. "Why frame Drew?" she managed to get out.

"He and his pals humiliated me at a party once, and talk about the perfect revenge."

Her brain whirled. His words made no sense, and yet he had no reason to lie. Kidnapping was a federal crime. Fear crawled around inside her brain alongside the ketamine, and she was helpless to do anything as her body and mind no longer seemed to belong to her. She closed her eyes.

"Go to sleep now, baby. I'll figure it out. I always had a backup plan, but I never expected to actually need it. Fucking Rachel Knight." His fingers gripped Erin's thigh, and she wanted to vomit. Her head flopped uselessly, and she was gone.

———

DARSH OPENED THE trunk of his SUV at the police station and pulled on his vest. Then he remembered Rosie squirreled away in the office they'd initially assigned him. There were roadblocks on all the major highways twenty miles out surrounding the area, but he had a bad feeling about this. Unless they spotted Rick ASAP, he would get away, and there was a chance Darsh would never see Erin alive again. His heart pounded.

It didn't matter if she didn't want Darsh when this was over. He wouldn't blame her. He just needed to find her and make sure she was safe—just as Erin had needed to do the same for Rachel yesterday.

He ran inside and grabbed the gun, shouting instructions and orders as he went, ignoring the chief's bluster.

Ully was coordinating roadblocks. Darsh ran back outside and called him on his cell. "Where's the chopper?" he asked.

"Pilot's refueling at the airfield just north of here. Highway 12. Why?"

Darsh slid his rifle into the back seat of the SUV. "Tell him to wait for me. I'll be there in ten minutes."

He was there in seven, and the pilot eyed his weapon with the look of a man who'd seen and done it all. Together with another officer they removed the rear doors of the bird and got Darsh attached to a safety harness. Every second ticked like an explosive in his mind.

When they took off, the cold almost stole his breath. He pulled on his headphones over his watch cap.

"Which way we heading?" the pilot asked.

"Any news from command?" asked Darsh.

"No one's spotted his vehicle yet." Both officers were watching him now. Awaiting instruction.

Lachlan thought he was so much smarter than the rest of them. Instinct told Darsh he'd run for the border, but if he was wrong, Erin might disappear forever.

"Never ignore your gut" was what his old gunnery sergeant always told him.

"North. Go north. He's heading to Canada."

CHAPTER TWENTY-SIX

RICK WATCHED ERIN sleep. Things had not gone to plan, but as the great Charles Darwin had once said, the key to survival was the ability to adapt, and Rick intended to do just that. After his childhood he'd always liked the idea of being able to disappear. He had a bank account under a false identity and had developed emergency escape scenarios when he'd begun his game last year.

Having Erin with him complicated matters, but she was all he'd ever wanted in a girlfriend. Smart, beautiful, someone who appreciated brains as much as brawn. Sure, she'd made a mistake with that FBI agent, who he didn't want to think about. She was under a lot of stress. He'd eventually forgive her the same way she'd eventually forgive him. Once she realized he was trying to *teach* them something, then she'd get it. Then she'd understand.

The justice system was broken.

He'd argued this with his boss over and over again. And people were so stuck in tradition they thought that what they had was the best America could do, which was *bullshit*.

Planting DNA was easy. Manipulating memory took some effort, but he'd done it, and researchers in Boston had recently managed to introduce a *false* memory into a mouse. It was only a matter of time until someone did it with humans.

He wasn't sure how to fix the flaws in the system. Hundreds of years of lawmakers, both federal and state, had created a mire of legal doctrine that cared little for justice. Truth didn't even matter to lawyers. What mattered was getting a conviction. Everything could be manipulated, and few things were sacrosanct.

Mandatory psychological tests applied at a young age could be used to pinpoint those most likely to commit rape or murder. Those individuals identified could be educated, or monitored.

Rick had proven his point to anyone smart enough to figure it out. Maybe they'd change something, but he doubted it. His genius would be labeled madness and banished to the annals of history.

A car passed him on the left. He jolted back to the moment, keeping his attention on the highway. He needed to make it to the woods where he'd tie Erin up and put her in the trunk of the car. She was gonna fight him when the drug wore off, and he didn't want to hurt her. Eventually she'd come to accept him, but he knew it might take a while. She was stubborn, but so was he. He'd source some sedatives to keep her docile in the meantime.

In the short-term he'd buy an RV—he liked that idea—and they could go tripping around the country until he found the perfect spot for them to build a life together. Maybe he'd buy a boat, and they'd sail down to Brazil.

He and Huxley had driven this back route two summers ago. He grinned when he thought about his boss. Professor Huxley would admire his talent and his methods for manipulating the police, and would probably eventually use him as a case study. Rick grinned. The man had also once said he'd love to experience being locked up for a day, for real, not knowing if he was ever getting out, just so he could see the effect it had on the psyche of an innocent man.

Yep, he'd done the guy a favor.

He'd thought about killing the student the professor had been screwing, but once Rachel turned up alive, there'd been no point. He didn't get off on causing unnecessary suffering. Well, not always. He wasn't a monster.

Erin groaned, and he knew it was time to pull over before she regained her senses. A logging road appeared ahead, and he turned onto it, off the highway, even though few cars traveled these roads in winter. He pocketed the car keys and popped the trunk and got out. In the distance the buzz of a helicopter made him glance at the sky. It was probably nothing.

He dug into a bag for a different license plate and a screwdriver. He began unscrewing the one on the car and tossed it into the snow.

It was possible Rachel had woken up a vegetable, but even if she named him to the cops, it would take them time to realize he'd skipped town, and even longer to figure out he'd taken Erin with him. Their standard operating procedures were so slow and predictable he'd probably already outfoxed most of them by traveling fast along the back roads.

The chopper was getting louder now. He looked up into the sky and saw a faint black speck in the distance. He frowned. Time to find cover until it passed on by, even though it was probably nothing.

He closed the trunk and froze. The front seat was empty. Erin was gone.

———————

ERIN USED THE noise of Rick opening the trunk to cover that of her opening the car door. She didn't allow her shaking limbs to falter. She had one chance at this and one chance only.

She felt woozy and her head hurt, but she'd forced herself to move slowly and silently. The martial arts training she'd done for years helped. Knowing she had to be quiet until she'd put a little distance between her and her psycho abductor meant she walked purposely down the road for about thirty yards. Her body was sore and stiff, resisting her efforts, but getting away from Rick Lachlan was the only thing that mattered. An animal track led into the woods so she took it.

Did anyone know she was missing yet? Hell, they might never know. She'd told them she was going home to visit her parents and wasn't sure when she'd be back.

Why did she do that?

Run away when things got hard?

Darsh was right. She needed to get past what Graham had done to her and take a chance on happiness.

Loving Darsh wasn't that difficult. Sure, it was a risk. But the risk seemed minimal compared to being abducted by a madman.

The going got tougher in the deeper snow, but she didn't stop moving. She wanted to run but knew if she did, she'd end up flat on her face.

The sound of the trunk being shut echoed through the forest, and her heart spasmed.

Shit.

He'd realized she was gone.

"Erin," came a horrible, high-pitched voice.

She stumbled.

"You don't want to make me angry, Erin." The sound of a gunshot had her gasping out loud. Dammit. She hadn't known he had a gun. "I've been very patient. Don't make me hurt you."

She started to run then, lifting her feet awkwardly through the heavy snow. Her sneakers felt as if they had bricks tied to the bottom of them. She heard a throbbing noise, but it didn't register what it might be, because suddenly she was out in a clearing on a sheet of ice. A pond.

Oh God. She froze, terrified. She hated this, hated the idea of falling through the icy crust into the water beneath almost as much as she hated Rick Lachlan. She slid to a halt, but a silhouette rippled through the trees, and she saw him moving toward her. She ran, the sound of the ice creaking beneath her boots driving terror through skin and bone right to her core.

The buzzing noise got louder.

At first she thought it was the sound of her own blood rushing through her ears, but as she glanced back at Rick, he was looking at the sky, and she realized he heard it, too. Then it became deafening as a helicopter swept over the top of them. It whooshed overhead and was gone. Erin was terrified it hadn't spotted them because it was traveling so fast, and she cried out in frustration. Then it banked hard, slowing down and then turning to one side. A figure dressed in black held a rifle steadily trained on Rick's chest.

Darsh.

Did he know how much she loved him? How could he? She'd only just figured it out herself.

A voice came over the loud speaker. "Drop the weapon and put your hands in the air."

She turned back to Rick who stood at the edge of the ice, half-hidden behind a young oak. "He's a former US Marine Corps Scout Sniper, Rick," she shouted. She was getting stronger by the second. "Unless you want to die, I suggest you drop the gun."

His features twisted in rage. "You think he's your hero, don't you? You think he's going to save you?"

Erin swallowed down all the regret she felt for pushing a good man away. "I don't expect anyone to save me. But he is my hero."

Rick raised the gun, finger wrapped tightly around the trigger as he aimed at Erin.

The sound of a shot ringing out was deafening. Blood burst from a wound in Rick's shoulder. He dropped to his knees and looked at her. The chopper shifted position, and Rick took the opportunity to raise the gun and aim it at her again.

She should have reacted. Should have run and dodged, but it was like watching Graham all over again—slow motion horror, capturing her attention and making her unable to do anything but watch events play out.

Rick squeezed off a round, then another. Finally, her brain caught up with the danger, and she forced herself to get the hell out of there. He fired one more shot, and her feet dropped from under her, and she crashed into water so cold her heart stopped. The bastard had shot out the ice, and the weight of her wet clothes made it feel like her bones were made of iron. She tried to move her limbs through the frigid murk. She fought, but she didn't go anywhere. The car accident, the ketamine, the stunning effect of the cold water had her opening her mouth and taking a breath. The sensation of her lungs filling with water was so alien and so wrong and so inescapable she panicked even more. Her chest felt heavy and frozen, and her veins seemed to contract as the world started to dim.

Today was the day, she realized with frightening clarity. Today was the day she was going to die.

"GET OVER THE spot where she went in!" Darsh couldn't believe the little shit had tried to kill Erin with his final act on Earth. The ice had shattered into large pieces that floated on the surface. Where the hell was she? Why wasn't she coming up for air? Was she hit?

He handed his rifle off to the co-pilot. Unbuckled his harness, stripped off his hat, jacket, and boots and dove in after her.

The arctic shock of cold made his heart stutter. He'd done this sort of drill several times in the Marines and was well aware the temperature plunge alone could kill a person. Forcing himself into a calmness he didn't feel, he summoned his training and searched for the zone.

The pond was murky and muddy, and he couldn't see a damn thing. He came up for air and spat out a mouthful of rancid sludge. He took a couple of deep breaths. If he panicked, Erin would die. He swung around three-hundred-and-sixty degrees, looking for telltale bubbles, for anything that showed where Erin was. But the ice was keeping its secrets. He took a big breath and duck-dived again, sweeping out on both sides with his hands, deeper, deeper, deeper. Something pale caught his eye among the gloom, and he lurched toward it, the air in his lungs almost gone now. He desperately held on for just a few more seconds. Something brushed his left hand, and he swung in that direction. His fingers curled around material—a coat. Erin! He kicked toward her until he could wrap his arm around her waist and pushed them both toward the surface. She was deadweight. He spluttered when he came up for air, but Erin didn't make a sound.

"Don't you die on me, Erin Donovan." He dragged her to the edge of the pond, staggered over downed tree branches and hidden rocks. He pulled her out only a few feet from where Rick Lachlan lay bleeding in the snow. Darsh laid Erin on the ground, quickly pocketing the guy's weapon.

"Help me," Lachlan begged.

Darsh ignored him and checked Erin's pulse. Nothing. He blew into her mouth, started CPR.

"She's dead. Under too long. Loved her. Help me." The sonofabitch begged.

Thirty fast compressions. The cold would have slowed down her system. Two deep breaths.

"Only thing I'm going to help you do is die, cocksucker." Darsh straddled Erin's chest to get a better angle on her heart. Her lips were blue. Fuck.

Twenty-seven, twenty-eight, twenty-nine, thirty. He pinched her nose and tipped her chin. Breathed deep enough to watch her chest move. And again.

"Imagine what the BAU could learn from studying me."

One. Two. Three. Four. Five… "We'll find out plenty when we dissect your brain. Come on, Erin!" He slammed his fist hard into her chest.

"Are you even listening to me? We could change the whole

legal system. Find a way to make it foolproof."

Dear God, if she died… Darsh slammed his fist into her heart again. "Breathe, damn you!"

She finally spluttered and rolled onto her side, spitting up water. Relief made him lightheaded. Or maybe that was the cold. He wasn't sure. "Thank God."

He pulled off her heavy coat, which was doing nothing to warm her now.

"I tried to make things better." Lachlan coughed up blood.

"You played games with people's lives like you had the right, and indulged your evil appetites. So your childhood sucked. Welcome to the fucking club, asshole."

"Help me," Lachlan demanded, though his voice was getting weaker and weaker.

"I'm not going to help you, Rick. The only way I would help you is by putting another bullet in you. Frankly, I'm kinda happy I didn't kill you outright. The helicopter was buffeted by the wind as I was taking the shot. But this way at least you get a few minutes to know you're gonna die out here in the snow, and no one will give a damn."

Smoky blue eyes blinked up at him.

"Whereas Erin is going to live a long and happy life married to me, making babies and generally having a fucking great time. Something you will never get to experience and never get to enjoy. And I'm going to make sure you are never part of our thoughts or our lives again, asswipe." He scooped Erin up in his arms and started moving, realizing his clothes were stiff with frost. They needed to get warm ASAP. The co-pilot was running down the path toward them.

"Cuff the bastard. I've got to get Erin to the hospital." The cop nodded, and Darsh ran through the uneven snow. The chopper had landed in a nearby field.

"I requested a medical evac—" the pilot began.

"No time." Darsh hugged Erin to him as he hauled them both into the back seat. He strapped her in and put on the harness designed to let him move around without falling out of the bird. "Blast the heaters, and let's go." He covered her in his jacket and began praying. "Hurry or she's not going to make it." But the pilot was already in the air.

———————

ERIN WOKE TO the feeling of heat suffusing her body when she'd thought she'd never be warm again. Struggling to recall what had happened, she cracked open her eyelids.

Darsh leaned forward in a chair, grinning at her. "Hello, beautiful."

"Now I know you're crazy." She raised her hand to touch her brow, but stopped when she realized she was hooked up to an IV. "What happened? Last thing I remember..." It came back to her in a flash. "Last thing I remember is going into that pond and taking in a lungful of water."

He clasped her fingers. "I told you I'd dive in and save you."

"You did, didn't you?" She bit her lip to stop herself from crying.

Darsh looked up as someone came in the room.

"She awake?"

"Who's 'she'?" Erin croaked. "The cat's mother?" It had been her grandmother's favorite saying.

Ully laughed. "Oh yeah, she's awake." He leaned over her and kissed her on the mouth. Then grimaced and wiped his lips. "Pond water. Yuk. There goes my fantasy."

"Good." She rolled her eyes at him. "Idiot." But the taste in her mouth was scummy. She'd be on antibiotics for months. "What about Lachlan?"

"Dead," Darsh said without inflection.

She held his dark gaze. "Thank you for saving my life."

"Hey," Ully interrupted. "What about me?"

It hurt to laugh. "What did *you* do?"

Ully tilted his head to one side. "I set up roadblocks. Co-ordinated the search." His eyes twinkled. "Anyway, we're all glad you're back. Unhurt." He winced a little looking at all the tubes she was hooked up to. "Or maybe just alive. Strassen's making like he never fired you and it was all a big misunderstanding. Professor Huxley has been let out of jail, although the university isn't very happy he was screwing that student."

"What student?" she asked.

"He lied about being at the soup kitchen Monday night because he was shagging an undergraduate named Monica Ripley." Darsh filled her in. "Another female student who claimed to be Lachlan's girlfriend found Monica tied up in Lachlan's bedroom. He hadn't hurt her beyond scaring the shit out of her, probably because Rachel woke up, and he had to scramble and change his plans."

Erin tried to take it all in.

Ully stole a piece of fruit off her side table. "I just got word Stinky Pete—"

"Peter Zimmerman," Darsh growled.

Ully laughed, unrepentant. "Good ol' Peter was extradited to Texas this morning and seems to have found a judge who's willing to overlook him going AWOL on the DUI warrant as long as he agrees to treatment. Miraculously, the guy agreed."

Darsh nodded. "Good."

"You set that up?" Erin asked him.

"I spoke to my former commander. He did the rest."

"Anyway, I've got paperwork coming out of the wazoo so I better get back to it." Ully turned around to leave. "Harry will be in for your statements soon."

"I don't want to talk to Harry." Erin groaned, but it felt good to be alive.

Darsh held her hand, and she squeezed him tight. "When do you have to leave?" she asked.

"You want me to go?" The joy in those dark eyes dimmed.

"No." She swallowed around her raw throat. "But I'm not going to be good at this."

"This?" A spark of hope returned.

"Us."

One side of his mouth curved into a smug smile. "Us?"

"After three years of being alone even trying for a relationship is a big deal." But she hung onto his hand like it was a lifeline, and maybe it was.

"You think it's easy for me? Loving someone like you?"

She knew it wasn't easy. "Broken?" she asked.

Frustration tightened his features. "Someone so strong she doesn't need me for anything. Not changing a flat, not drywalling, not even shoveling snow."

Her throat was almost swollen shut. "How about needing you for happiness?"

He gave a soft laugh. "I make you happy?"

She could barely see him through her tears. She nodded.

"I can live with that." He kissed her hand. "I thought you were dead, Erin. I thought that bastard had won."

She touched his cheek. "I love you."

His eyes flashed in surprise.

"You didn't know?"

He shook his head.

"I'm sorry I bailed on you."

"You were scared. I get it." One side of his lips twisted. "I'm scared too. I already almost lost you once."

She frowned. "I had this dream where you told someone we were getting married and having babies and lots of great sex." She quirked a brow. "It seemed so real."

"No idea what you're talking about." A hint of red hit his cheeks. "But how would you feel about the idea as a possible long-term option?"

She smiled and tried to move. Ended up coughing like an old hag. When she could speak again, he eased her back against the pillows.

"Considering you've seen me at my worst, then you might actually like the person I am on a normal day. How about we take it slow and see how it goes?"

His fingers grasped her so tight she almost winced. He kissed her lips. They both had pond breath.

"You really did jump in and save me." She touched his lips in wonder.

"Always."

She stretched out her legs. Even though she felt weak she hated being an invalid. "I need to get out of here."

Darsh stood and stretched out his back. "You got your job back."

Erin found herself admiring his body in those doctor's scrubs. "If your father could see you now," she teased.

"Hell, no."

She got serious. "The thing is, when Strassen fired me, I

kind of had this other idea of something I might like to do."

Darsh's brows rose. "FBI?"

She shook her head. "I realized I got most satisfaction from trying to help people. People like Rachel."

"You want to be a counselor?'

"I was thinking more victims' advocate with the police service."

His eyes widened. "You'd be great at that." He leaned down to kiss her again. "You know what else I think?"

"No." She held onto him and kissed him longer and deeper. "What?"

"You'd be great at that in Virginia."

"Maybe," she said tentatively. "But what about Drew Hawke?" Guilt crashed down on her. She'd ruined the guy's life. He'd been locked up; Cassie had been murdered.

"DOJ is calling a special hearing to lodge an appeal based on new evidence. Kid might get out in time to finish the spring offseason."

She closed her eyes. "I feel terrible that I screwed up so badly."

He squeezed her shoulder. "Rick Lachlan did this, not you. The bastard set Drew up because he'd hazed him at a party. Was Hawke guilty of being a jerk? Damn right. But that didn't give Lachlan the right to hurt all those girls, or Hawke or Blackcombe or *you*."

"I don't know if I'll ever be able to forgive myself."

Darsh brushed her hair off her forehead. "It's done. You need to figure out a way to move past it. He fooled me by setting up the professor, which I fell for the same way you fell for him framing Hawke. Holding on to the guilt doesn't help anyone."

Erin smiled, knowing she was on the verge of tears. "You'd make a pretty good victims' advocate yourself."

He nodded. "Damn straight." He leaned closer. "Did I tell you I loved you yet?"

She nodded and laughed at his shocked expression. "When you dove out of that helicopter and rescued me from a frozen pond."

He smiled and kissed her again.

Erin recognized a voice in the hallway outside. A loud voice joined by another loud voice.

Her eyes shot to Darsh. "You called my parents?"

He shook his head. "Strassen did 'cause they're listed as next of kin. He was trying to pretend he was a good boss and knew what he was doing."

She grunted and then the door burst open and there was her mom, dad, sister and two of her four brothers. Darsh introduced himself and shook all their hands, and never once left her side. She didn't miss the pointed looks between her mom and her sister or between Darsh and her brothers as they wondered who the hell he was.

She tensed, but after a few minutes, she found the tension easing.

"I guess we need to finish the drywall now we're up here," her youngest brother complained.

"I'm selling it," she said quietly. "If you could help me get it ready for that, I'd be grateful."

A shocked silence followed, but her brothers looked glee-ful. Her mom touched her free hand. "Are you coming home, love?"

Erin looked into Darsh's deep dark eyes. "Yes. A new home with this man. In Virginia."

"But you guys have only just met…" her dad argued.

Darsh smiled. "Look, I know you guys are worried. I know what she went through with her dickhead ex, and that is never going to happen again. You guys can come and stay with us whenever you want."

"You're going to live together?" Her mother sounded horrified.

"Mom," she complained. "I'm thirty-two!"

"What religion are you?" Her mother prodded Darsh.

"Mom!" Erin didn't even know what religion he was, because it didn't matter.

Darsh raised a brow. "What religion would you like me to be?"

Her mother's lips twitched at that.

Her other brother muttered, "Good answer."

"You know the first wedding didn't count?" her mother continued while Erin wished she could just pretend to fall through a big hole in the floor. "They got married in the courthouse without us."

Erin cut in. "We're not getting married—"

"Yet," Darsh added.

Erin grabbed his hand. "Don't encourage her. She's incorrigible."

"I'm your mother."

"God help me."

"Don't blaspheme, Erin Mairead Donovan," her mother admonished.

Erin rolled her eyes and turned to the man who had saved her life in more ways than one. "So, this is a small part of my crazy family," she said brightly. "Still game?"

"Always." He bent down and kissed her softly on the lips despite her family watching. "And forever."

EPILOGUE

DARSH WALKED INTO the church and searched the aisles for a familiar head of blonde hair. He'd had to go back to work in Quantico earlier in the week, but he'd returned to Forbes Pines for this. Erin was recuperating and had refused to do that in Virginia. Stubborn didn't begin to cover it. Thankfully, her parents had stayed with her so he hadn't worried too much. Her house was already up for sale, and he'd cleaned out most of his walk-in closet and half of the drawers, ready for her belongings.

He spotted her on the far right-hand side of the church. She was sitting alone, away even from the other cops. She'd accepted her reinstatement with the proviso she was transferring just as soon as she could arrange a suitable post. Beat the hell out of getting fired.

He slid in beside her, his hip touching hers. Her eyes shot to his, and he could tell she was barely holding on to her composure. Her hand clamped around his. "You came. Thank you."

He kissed her cheek and squeezed her hand. She'd lost more weight, and he was worried about her.

The minister started the sermon. Her eyes swiveled front and center.

The casket was shiny black and had a large picture of

Mandy Wochikowski placed upon it. The girl was smiling, and the sight of her as a living breathing person hit him in the chest and reminded him why he did what he did. Not for the guts, not for the glory, but for the victims.

His eyes scanned the room. Tanya Whitehouse and Alicia Drummond sat up front near Mandy's and Cassandra Bressinger's parents. Cassie's funeral was scheduled for next Monday. He'd arranged to work from home tomorrow and fly back on Tuesday. He was hoping Erin would come with him.

A tiny figure sat between her parents near the front of the left-hand side of the church.

"Is that Rachel?" Darsh leaned down and whispered in Erin's ear.

"She got out of the hospital two days ago." She nodded. "Look who's sitting behind her." She nudged his arm.

At first Darsh didn't recognize the row of broad-shouldered suits who were stacked up behind the Knight family. Then he caught a profile and realized it was Jason Brady. Staring harder he realized the entire Blackcombe Raven's football team was sitting there in silent mourning.

Erin touched his knee. "See who's in the middle of that huddle?"

At first he didn't. Then he sat up straighter. "Drew Hawke?"

"They transferred him to a minimum security facility and gave him a day release for the funeral." She glanced at him from under her lashes. "The president got involved. There's talk of a hearing next week and possibly a pardon."

"Hague?" His brows shot up. He wondered if ASAC Frazer had had a hand in manipulating things considering he and Jed Brennan had a special "in" with the man in the White House.

She nodded. "I need to apologize to him."

"You did your job, Erin. Lachlan and the system screwed him over. Hopefully defense attorneys will work a little harder to earn their fees in the future."

Erin stayed quiet, and he knew she found it hard to forgive herself for arresting the wrong guy.

The service ended, and the pall bearers lifted the coffin and walked it out of the front door to the waiting hearse. Darsh went to stand, but Erin grabbed his sleeve. "What?" he asked.

"I'm not going to the interment."

"Why not?"

"I don't want to create a scene."

People were following the coffin out the door. Alicia, Tanya, Mandy's and Cassie's parents. They shot hostile glances at Erin, and she just silently watched them. The Knights came next. He assumed Rachel would walk on by, given the occasion, but her footsteps slowed and then stopped.

"Would you like a ride in our car, Erin?" she asked quietly.

The cuts around her mouth were healing, but the skin was still red and discolored.

Erin shook her head, eyes flickering to the hulking shadows gathering behind the petite girl. "I drove, but thank you."

Rachel didn't look bothered by her massive entourage. She looked Darsh in the eye, then back to Erin. "I'd like to talk to you when you get the chance." No more timid mouse.

Erin nodded.

The glances the players were sending her were pissed, though. Darsh braced himself for trouble; he really didn't want to get into it at a funeral service. Ully Mason and some of the other cops were making their way towards them, but there was a large group of mourners separating them from Erin. Darsh angled himself slightly in front of her, ready for anything.

Drew Hawke pushed between the massive suit-clad shoulders of his teammates. His hair was freshly trimmed. Jaw clean-shaven. His gaze went from Erin to Rachel and to his team.

"Can I catch a ride to the cemetery with you, Detective? I was hoping to talk," he asked.

Erin went even paler than before, but nodded. "Sure."

Hawke slid into their pew. Darsh watched him give Jason Brady a nod, and the wide receiver hustled the other players outside. Hawke and Erin sat while the rest of the mourners filed slowly past. Ully raised his brows in question, and Darsh pulled a face back. It was obvious Hawke wanted to talk and, although Erin could look after herself, he wasn't about to let her get hurt by anyone else ever again.

So there they sat. Finally the church was empty except for the three of them.

"I owe you an apology," she began.

Hawke stared at the floor but shook his head. "That's not why I wanted to talk to you."

She stopped, clearly uncertain what to say.

"I've thought about this a lot." His lips quirked into a quick smile. "I certainly had time."

Erin's eyes widened.

"The thing is, you were as much a victim as the rest of us. The guy fixated on you, stalked you, and basically tried to seduce you with a crime wave." He turned and faced her. "He was a sick bastard, and we shouldn't have taunted him." Those massive shoulders shrugged. "You were just doing your job."

Her hands twisted in her lap. "I should have done it better."

"And I shouldn't have been an obnoxious jock." He quirked his brows. "Learn from your mistakes, become a better cop, but don't blame yourself. I mean I get it—I'll always blame myself for Cassie's death even though I wasn't there, but…" Tears crowded his eyes. "Rachel told me—"

"You've been talking to Rachel?" she asked quickly.

He nodded and stuffed his hands in his pockets and pulled out a handkerchief to wipe his eyes. "She told me how much you helped her." He swallowed thickly. "I know I was falsely accused and that that's rare. Very rare. But she's planning on visiting some campuses, talking to people about our story. Talking to victims. She's asked me to come with her."

Darsh blinked.

Hawke looked uncomfortable. "She thinks I'd raise the profile. She thinks that seeing the two of us on stage together, both victims, might be a way of changing the conversation about college rape. I can tell guys what they shouldn't be doing, what's unacceptable, and what it's like in prison. She can tell women what to do if they are raped." He huffed out a breath. "Frankly, the idea scares the shit out of me. But when I think about what she went through, what Cassie went through." He rubbed his thumbs over one another in a nervous gesture. "I was trying to think what she'd want me to do."

"Not talk to me." Erin snorted gently.

Hawke smiled at that. "Probably not. But she was always watching out for her friends. Always lecturing them on guarding their drink. She'd be up for this plan, I think, especially after what happened to her." The sheen of tears glazed his eyes. "Rachel wants to ask you to come with us when we do our talks."

"Me?" Erin's mouth dropped open. "The cop who arrested the wrong guy?"

"The cop who wasn't afraid to go after the star quarterback, even though it made her the most hated woman in town. The cop who was the victim of a stalker."

Erin shifted uncomfortably. Darsh knew she hated being seen as a victim, but it didn't change the facts.

"I know our situation isn't ordinary. I know this isn't normal," he offered. "I just think it's an opportunity, and after where I've spent the last six months of my life, I don't intend to let opportunities pass me by." He climbed to his feet and stuck his hand out to Erin, who stood and shook it. "Call Rachel. Talk to her about it." Hawke turned to Darsh and held his hand out to him, too. "Agent Singh." The quarterback angled his head.

"Mr. Hawke," Darsh acknowledged.

"I hear you shot Rick Lachlan. I'm sorry you have to carry the burden of his death, but I can't say I'm sorry the fucker is dead."

"Trust me." Darsh hadn't lost a wink of sleep over Lachlan. "There's no burden."

"Warden said I had you to thank for keeping me in solitary. I appreciate it."

"No worries." Darsh checked his watch. "We should head to the cemetery."

They followed Hawke outside. The way he stood on the front steps and breathed deeply, said just how much he appreciated his newfound freedom.

"Did you know Mandy had a crush on Lachlan?" Hawke said unexpectedly.

"What?" Erin asked, shocked.

"Yeah. Cassie told me about it in one of her letters. And the bastard killed her." Hawke's shoulders shook. He pulled a pair of sunglasses out of his jacket pocket and slipped them on. Then he started walking away.

"What about that ride?" Darsh called after him.

The guy raised his hand. "I'm gonna walk."

Darsh stared after Drew, and Erin entwined her fingers in his.

"He's a pretty special young man." She looked stricken. "And if it wasn't for Lachlan committing more crimes, he might never have been released. He'd still be in prison."

Darsh knew it was going to take time to get over the guilt. "I think you should do it. Go do a few talks with him and Rachel."

"Really?"

He pushed the hair off her brow and leaned down to kiss her. "Yeah. I think it's a great opportunity."

"More people to throw eggs at me."

He growled. "You're right, don't do it."

She hugged his arm, and they started walking to her rental car. He'd taken a cab from the airport. "I'll think about it, if Rachel wants me to."

"You gonna come home with me next week?" he asked.

She hugged him tighter. "Still want me to move in?"

"More than anything. You won't lack for job opportunities, but I don't think it would be a bad thing if you took some time to really figure out what you want to do."

She stopped walking. "I'm not good at doing nothing."

He wrapped his arms around her and pulled her close. "There's always cleaning the house and getting dinner on the table."

She punched him in the stomach.

"Joking." He laughed.

"Yes." She gripped his shirt and rose up on tiptoes to kiss his mouth. "I love you, Darsh Singh. I want to live with you and see if the sex is still great after a couple of months."

"I guarantee it will be." He swung her off her feet. "How about we go test it out? Make sure we didn't miscalculate? Don't want to rush into anything—"

She snorted. "With my mother in the house?"

Darsh pulled a face. "We could check into a hotel."

She gave him a dirty grin. "Seriously?"

He checked his watch. "How long do we have until she gets suspicious?"

"My mom has six kids. She was born suspicious."

He tugged her arm. "Come on. Two hours max. Let's do it."

"I feel guilty."

"I think you need to convert to my religion. There's a hell of a lot less guilt."

"What *is* your religion?"

"Agnostic with a strong dose of atheist."

"And yet, all joking aside, you'd seriously consider converting for me?" She smiled. She was so damn pretty.

He spun her around to face him. "Sweetheart, I'd walk into the depths of hell for you. *You're* what I believe in. You. Me. Us."

She looked like she was finally starting to believe him. Finally starting to get it. She touched his face, almost as if she was finally seeing him clearly. "I'm glad you walked into that bar all those years ago, Marine."

"*Semper fi*, baby." He folded her fingers over his heart. "*Semper fi.*"

USEFUL ACRONYM DEFINITIONS FOR TONI'S BOOKS

ADA: Assistant District Attorney
AG: Attorney General
ASAC: Assistant Special Agent in Charge
ASC: Assistant Section Chief
ATF: Alcohol, Tobacco, and Firearms
BAU: Behavioral Analysis Unit
BOLO: Be on the Lookout
BORTAC: US Border Patrol Tactical Unit
BUCAR: Bureau Car
CBP: US Customs and Border Patrol
CBT: Cognitive Behavioral Therapy
CIRG: Critical Incident Response Group
CMU: Crisis Management Unit
CN: Crisis Negotiator
CNU: Crisis Negotiation Unit
CO: Commanding Officer
CODIS: Combined DNA Index System
CP: Command Post
CQB: Close-Quarters Battle
DA: District Attorney
DEA: Drug Enforcement Administration
DEVGRU: Naval Special Warfare Development Group
DIA: Defense Intelligence Agency

DHS: Department of Homeland Security
DOB: Date of Birth
DOD: Department of Defense
DOJ: Department of Justice
DS: Diplomatic Security
DSS: US Diplomatic Security Service
DVI: Disaster Victim Identification
EMDR: Eye Movement Desensitization & Reprocessing
EMT: Emergency Medical Technician
ERT: Evidence Response Team
FOA: First-Office Assignment
FBI: Federal Bureau of Investigation
FNG: Fucking New Guy
FO: Field Office
FWO: Federal Wildlife Officer
IC: Incident Commander
IC: Intelligence Community
ICE: US Immigration and Customs Enforcement
HAHO: High Altitude High Opening (parachute jump)
HRT: Hostage Rescue Team
HT: Hostage-Taker
JEH: J. Edgar Hoover Building (FBI Headquarters)
K&R: Kidnap and Ransom
LAPD: Los Angeles Police Department
LEO: Law Enforcement Officer
LZ: Landing Zone
ME: Medical Examiner
MO: Modus Operandi
NAT: New Agent Trainee
NCAVC: National Center for Analysis of Violent Crime
NCIC: National Crime Information Center
NFT: Non-Fungible Token
NOTS: New Operator Training School

NPS: National Park Service
NYFO: New York Field Office
OC: Organized Crime
OCU: Organized Crime Unit
OPR: Office of Professional Responsibility
POTUS: President of the United States
PT: Physiology Technician
PTSD: Post-Traumatic Stress Disorder
RA: Resident Agency
RCMP: Royal Canadian Mounted Police
RSO: Senior Regional Security Officer from the US
     Diplomatic Service
SA: Special Agent
SAC: Special Agent-in-Charge
SANE: Sexual Assault Nurse Examiners
SAS: Special Air Squadron (British Special Forces unit)
SD: Secure Digital
SIOC: Strategic Information & Operations
SF: Special Forces
SSA: Supervisory Special Agent
SWAT: Special Weapons and Tactics
TC: Tactical Commander
TDY: Temporary Duty Yonder
TEDAC: Terrorist Explosive Device Analytical Center
TOD: Time of Death
UAF: University of Alaska, Fairbanks
UBC: Undocumented Border Crosser
UNSUB: Unknown Subject
USSS: United States Secret Service
ViCAP: Violent Criminal Apprehension Program
VIN: Vehicle Identification Number
WFO: Washington Field Office

COLD JUSTICE WORLD OVERVIEW

All books can be read as standalones

COLD JUSTICE® SERIES
A Cold Dark Place (Book #1)
Cold Pursuit (Book #2)
Cold Light of Day (Book #3)
Cold Fear (Book #4)
Cold in The Shadows (Book #5)
Cold Hearted (Book #6)
Cold Secrets (Book #7)
Cold Malice (Book #8)
A Cold Dark Promise (Book #9~A Wedding Novella)
Cold Blooded (Book #10)

COLD JUSTICE® – THE NEGOTIATORS
Cold & Deadly (Book #1)
Colder Than Sin (Book #2)
Cold Wicked Lies (Book #3)
Cold Cruel Kiss (Book #4)
Cold as Ice (Book #5)

COLD JUSTICE® – MOST WANTED
Cold Silence (Book #1)
Cold Deceit (Book #2)
Cold Snap (Book #3) – Coming soon
Cold Fury (Book #4) – Coming soon

The Cold Justice® series books are also available as **audiobooks** narrated by Eric Dove, and in various box set compilations.

Check out all Toni's books on her website
(www.toniandersonauthor.com/books-2)

ACKNOWLEDGMENTS

Huge bunches of awesomeness go to my amazing critique partner Kathy Altman—she stops me making a total fool of myself on a regular basis. Also, thanks to my editors, Alicia Dean, and Joan Turner at JRT Editing. Syd Gill—cover artist extraordinaire and so very talented at creating the covers of the *Cold Justice Series*. Paul Salvette (BB eBooks) does a great job of formatting my ebooks—thanks! And to all the other people working behind the scenes to get these books on the shelves, I appreciate your help and support.

Thanks to my good friends, Rachel Grant, Carolyn Crane, and Sunny Lee-Goodman for lively discussions on the subject of diversity. I'm envious of their upcoming adventures in San Diego! Big smackers also go to Rachel for doing a speed-read at the end when I had a mini-panic. Thanks to Eric Dove for his brilliant narration of the CJS audiobooks. I love working with him.

I want to thank my husband and kids for putting up with the craziness of having a writer in the family. Their under-standing when I attend "parties" online. The fact that I research "hot guys" on a regular basis, and require their detailed feedback my covers. Here's to us having a kitchen and an office back sometime in the near future! I love you guys!

AUTHOR'S NOTE

This was a difficult book to write. Any book that deals with rape or sexual assault often is, but this one seemed to come at a time when the issue is front and center in people's minds (as it should be). Unfortunately, rape occurs with horrific frequency all over the world. I tried to treat the subject matter with the respect it deserved while still writing the kind of Romantic Suspense novel that my readers expect. I hope I succeeded.

ABOUT THE AUTHOR

Toni Anderson writes gritty, sexy, FBI Romantic Thrillers, and is a *New York Times* and a *USA Today* bestselling author. Her books have won the Daphne du Maurier Award for Excellence in Mystery and Suspense, Readers' Choice, Aspen Gold, Book Buyers' Best, Golden Quill, National Excellence in Story Telling Contest, and National Excellence in Romance Fiction awards. She's been a finalist in both the Vivian Contest and the RITA Award from the Romance Writers of America. Toni's books have been translated into five different languages and over three million copies of her books have been downloaded.

Best known for her Cold Justice® books perhaps it's not surprising to discover Toni lives in one of the most extreme climates on earth—Manitoba, Canada. Formerly a Marine Biologist, Toni still misses the ocean, but is lucky enough to travel for research purposes. In late 2015, she visited FBI Headquarters in Washington DC, including a tour of the Strategic Information and Operations Center. She hopes not to get arrested for her Google searches.

Sign up for Toni Anderson's newsletter:
www.toniandersonauthor.com/newsletter-signup

Like Toni Anderson on Facebook:
facebook.com/toniandersonauthor

Follow on Instagram:
instagram.com/toni_anderson_author